THE D]

Stories of the adventures, frustrations, tribulations, laughs and life experiences of a baby commercial diver on Scotland's Clyde coast in the early 1990's.

PAUL (SCURVY) OBERNAY

Published by Paul Obernay

First printed in July 2023

Copyright ©2005 Paul Obernay

Twitter: @ObernayPau28712

thedivers520@gmail.com

www.facebook.com/paulobernay/thedivers

All rights reserved. No part of this publication may be reproduced, stored in a retrieval system, or transmitted in any form or by any means, electronic, mechanical, photocopying, recording or otherwise, without the prior permission of the copyright owner.

Cover designed and prepared by the author.

Images on Pages 4, 5, 56, 149, 307, 329 & 340 supplied by the author.

Kissing Dolphins on page 5 by Mandy Sinclair.

All other Artwork including front cover by Nick Gott bookanartist.co : Nick Gott Artistry

The characters, events, establishments and entities depicted in this book are fictitious. Any similarity to actual persons, either living or dead or other real life establishments or entities, past or present is purely coincidental.

I neither confirm nor deny if there is any truth in what you are about to read. Mainly so as to protect the guilty.

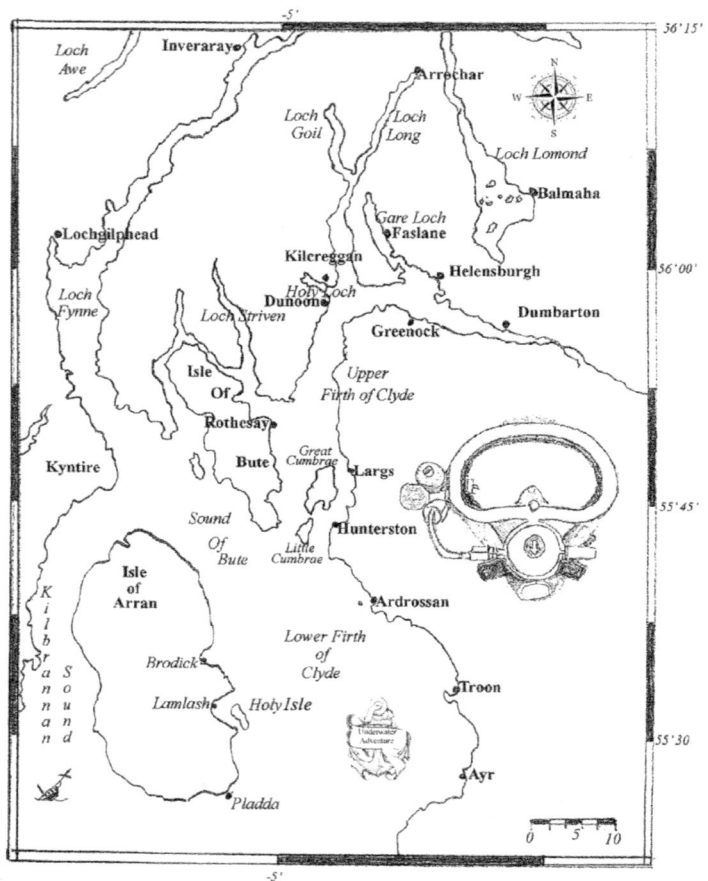

The waters, island's and sea lochs of the Clyde coast

Trivia question for mariners:

What is the brightest light on the Clyde?
Answer on page 356.

To my loving wife Yui,

I was once a ocean wave, wondering aimlessly, sweeping the oceans and seas of our world seeking a tranquil shore.

Yui, you became the safe harbour of my soul.

FOREWORD

The phrase 'Baby Diver' is not derogatory term by any stretch of the imagination. It is more of a kind-hearted, benevolent expression. It is used to identify someone new, who is just starting out in the diving industry. It is also used by a dive team to identify the youngest and usually but not always, the most inexperienced diver on a diving team.

Thus, when being introduced for the first time to highly experienced members of a dive team or even to clients, they know they have to keep an eye on the new member of the crew. They have to be tolerant of the inexperience and lack of acquired knowledge of the new team member, in order to guide them and keep them safe.

For at the end of the day, the underwater world and maritime environment can be a very cruel and dangerous place. Their lives ultimately depend on being there for one another. Even the most experienced diver may find themselves in a situation where they need the help of the most inexperienced member of their team to save their life.

My time as the baby diver with Glasgow based inshore commercial diving companies on the Clyde, provided me with a phenomenal education. I spent my days illuminated by real life characters, 'legends in their own lunchtimes' who brought colour to my life in such ways that no painter's pallet ever could.

During that time, I learned of, became trained, experienced & competent in many different things and had adventures that few other vocation's could ever provide.

The stories herein are derived around my days on the Clyde Coast.

This Publication as well as being an interesting and entertaining story. Is also of intrinsic technical value in the study of the inshore diving profession of the time. The technical information contained herein also goes as far as to explain how ice forms under the water at depth whilst being surrounded by water.

It also provides interesting information with regards the history behind the magnificent buildings of Glasgow's Mitchell Library and Kelvin Grove Museum and Art Galleries along with the history and charitable acts of the Glasgow sewerage ships.

Additionally, mention is made of the lesser known history of an event from the 1850's in Rothesay on the isle of Bute. Also the importance that Bute, Loch Striven and the surrounding area played during the second world war.

The stories also provide interesting information on Police diving operations, body recovery and the psychology of diving in black water.

There is interesting information on Salmon farming with facts that will give the reader an understanding of the life cycle of a Salmon and an in-site to the husbandry that is involved in farming Salmon.

Also contained herein is accurate technical information of how to test for the purity of gold and the identification of genuine gold coins. As well as an introduction into methodologies used by the rich to hide their wealth from the tax man and the courts.

Paul (Scurvy) Obernay.

IN DEDICATION AND ACKNOWLEDGEMENT

To the Clyde coast divers, dockers, tug boat & ships crews, charter boat skippers, fishermen, Strathclyde Police Underwater Search Unit, shipyard workers, ICC members*(g-317)*, my surrogate uncles Tommy Sutherland, Donald Cameron, and Agnes my favourite pub landlady.

The men and women that I knew, worked with and met during my time on the Clyde were some of the funniest, wittiest, sharpest minded people whom I have ever known. Given that at the time of writing this, I have travelled the world, twice over.

Their language though explicit, licentious, indelicate and often salacious was in many ways poetic. For it has a natural flow when spoken. Their tone lacked the blatant vulgarity, crudity and coarseness that is often heard in the less well travelled parts of Glasgow.

They made TV and theatre comedians look like amateurs. The speed of rapport of their off the cuff flippancy was lightening fast, razor sharp and completely unrehearsed. A flippancy that showed no mercy, granted no quarter in which no subject was taboo or person's out of bounds.

I maintain to this day, that as a result of the time I spent with these colourful and often mischievous characters that came into my life. Alongside everything else, I served an apprenticeship in flippancy. Of this, I am proud to say, I was trained by the world's leading experts in the subject.

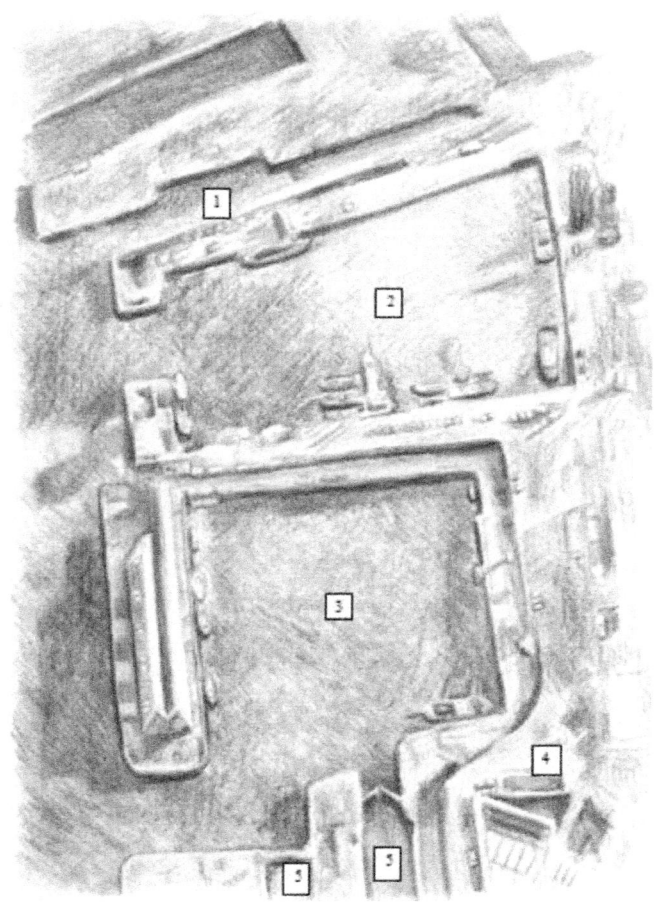

Greenock docks

1. Cartsburn Dry Dock   2. Victoria Harbour

3. East India Harbour   4. The Marine Bar

5. Graving (Dry) Docks

C0NTENTS

Map of the Clyde coast
The safe harbour of my soul
Forward: The Baby Diver
Dedication & Acknowledgment
Greenock Docks

Chapter 1	The dog dives as well
Chapter 2	How Scurvy got his name
Chapter 3	A great leveller amongst men
Chapter 4	What's in a name
Chapter 5	Of pride and prejudice
Chapter 6	Getting busy with the busies
Chapter 7	When the north wind blows
Chapter 8	The cold, the dark, the deep and the downright scary
Chapter 9	All that glitters is not gold or is it?
Lyrics	Song of the Clyde / The Scotsman / I recall a gypsy woman
Glossary	Definition of terminology
Appendix:	Interesting technical information
About the author
Special thank you
Artists biography & contact details
Answer to trivia question from page 4

CHAPTER 1

Throughout the chapters in this book you will come across topics, phrases and information that the reader may be unfamiliar with. You will find definition, clarification and more information about these in the glossary and appendix at the back of the book.

For ease of quick reference, the appendices will be numbered complete with a page number *(1-318)* and the glossary will have letter g and the page number *(g-312)* listed next to the subject.

THE DOG DIVES AS WELL

It was 5.15pm, on a chilly dark Friday evening. The thin veil of a cold damp fog was hanging low in the air. A white Scania tractor unit mired with the spray of filth from a very long day on the road, with a low loader flat bed trailer in tow. Slowly entered through the gates of Drumcavel Quarry, transporting a hired Caterpillar 320 series tracked excavator, which was actually brand new.

The quarry was closing for the weekend with all the workers making a hasty exit, desperately trying to avoid getting caught in the rush hour slow moving traffic, which was sure to be hampered further by the encroaching fog.

Pulling up and with a loud hiss of air activating the trucks air brakes, a broad shouldered, dark haired driver with a course black stubble and thick black moustache, leaned out of the cab window. He called to the scrawny, malnourished weasel looking security guard on the gate.

'Hey Jimmy, where you want me to off load this?'

The driver of the truck who spoke with an strong harsh eastern European accent. He didn't actually know whether or not the security guard's name was Jimmy. But in Glasgow, it didn't really matter as everyone who was a stranger to you was called Jimmy.... even the women.

The security guard retorted somewhat indignantly with the authoritarian tone of a jumped up little gobshite which, appeared to be a prerequisite job requirement for such positions.

'Eh, what time do you call this? We're shutting up shop for the night, you were supposed to be here at hauf ten this morning.'

Taking no prisoners, the driver retorted sharply. 'Hey don't give me hard times or my friends from the KGB will come to visit you while you sleep in your bed at night. I got stuck on some mountain top half arsed single lane road called the A66, halfway between Penrith and some backwater called Sowerby for hours on end this morning. There had been an accident in the early hours this morning causing a tailback for miles. It took them 6 hours to clear it. Road's barely wide enough for horses and carts and this is your main road into Scotland from English land. So no more of your pish Jimmy, or I will unload this in the middle of your gate and fuck off with the keys.'

A somewhat now less than self righteous security guard replied. 'Aye awe 'right nae danger pal, keep your hair on. I was just wondering, that wis awe. Just eh, pull up there about 30m in front of the office block, and then haund in your paperwork to Mr Lamont the Manger in the offices there'.

Then pointing with his finger on his out stretched arm. 'See where these twa rows of blue 20foot containers are. Well there's a tracked road that runs between them, it goes down tae the pond. Can ye aff load and park up the excavator doon there between the containers facing west along the track. Cause they will be heading doon tae the pond to start work with it first thing on Monday morning.'

Trying to make peace with the driver, the security guard asked. 'Eh, dae you need a haund to get it aff? I'll happily gie ye a haund.'

Now smiling the driver replied 'No is okay Jimmy, I do this all the time, I'll be fine, but tanks all the same.'

Out of his office window, Archie Lamont the quarry general manager spotted the articulated low loader pulling into the yard.

Muttering unto himself. 'Oh, chuffin Nora, It'll be after 6 O'clock before I'm out of here. I'm supposed to be taking her to that gaggle o' hens Wi'men's Guild meeting tonight. I've been late home every night this week, if I am late home tonight she'll throw an Annie Rooney. I canny be daein with that.'

There is an old Scottish saying having an Annie Rooney' which means someone is displaying a fit of rage and anger, usually a woman.

As the delivery driver pulled up outside the office block, Archie Lamont dashed out of his office allowing the office block door to slam shut behind him locked on the Yale and took off for home in his car. Fearing being on the receiving end of a tongue lashing from a wife scorned should he be late home again and on this night of all nights.

A somewhat tired and weary delivery driver slowly and carefully unshackled the excavator from the low loader. Then as neat as ninepence, reversed it off the low loader. He parked it up facing west along the track between the two rows of shipping containers as instructed by the security guard. Lethargic and drained from his very long day, he clambered down from the excavator's cab leaving the keys in the ignition.

Before departing the quarry to head for the lorry park at Riggend where he could finally relax and lay up for the night. In absence of the manager, the driver of the low loader got the security guard to sign the paperwork. Leaving the security guard the pink carbon copy page confirming the safe delivery of the excavator to the quarry.

As was becoming common place in the early 1990's, due to cutbacks that were rearing their ugly head again. Factories and worksites that closed for the evening or weekends no longer kept a permanent security guard on site all through the night. Instead the site security or gate guard would finish around 7pm on a Friday. After that, a roving patrol from a private security firm in this case Scamps Security, would normally drive by one or two times during the night and do a site walk. Often accompanied by a fierce looking long haired Alsatian which generally had the resemblance of scraggy bear and often as not a temperament to match.

Being as these security guards were only paid about £2.75 an hour, if they were lucky. The site walk rounds especially on cold, dark, damp, foggy nights were generally done quickly and without much in the way of diligence. They just wanted to tick the box of having done it, let the beast of a dog out to do a jobby and get back in their Ford Escort van where it was warm and dry then drive off to the next site.

A jobby for those reading this story and not so formally acquainted with the colloquialisms of the Scottish language, would be the equivalent of polite society making use of the phrase 'a No.2' or having a poo.

Drumcavel quarry was actually in the process of being decommissioned and would close for good in a few months time. It had quarried stone primarily used in road building.

But over the last few years, due to the dramatic reduction in the construction of new roads, and very few new housing or industrial estate developments being built in the country. With no prospective change in these markets on the foreseeable horizon. Drumcavel quarry was no longer a financially viable operation. It also didn't help that supper quarries like Glensanda on the Morven peninsula, which could accommodate and supply massive bulk carrier ships with stone. Thus reduce road haulage costs up and down the country, were able to produce stone at a much lower price. Hence the winding down and ultimate closure of Drumcavel.

Stone quarries often had large ponds on site which were used for supplying water for washing out the accompanying unwanted sand from the quarried stone. Drumcavel quarry was no exception. Its site pond was manmade and due to the required increases in water capacity on site over the years it had become irregular in shape, being around 95m at its longest and around 50m in width at its widest point.

Apart for the eastern edge of the pond. The rest of the land surrounding it was wild, overgrown with a broad diversity of foliage and was sheltered by trees. For a manmade pond, it was also deep with depths reaching 35 meters in some places.

On Sunday evening, around 10.30pm, the dank foggy miserable weather was now accompanied by a fine drizzle. The Scamps security guard was parked up outside the quarry gates at the south end of the site. Sitting in the dry & warmth of his van looking out through the windscreen at the dank drizzle and fog outside. Contemplating whether or not to once again venture out into the cold, wet, miserable dark of the night to patrol round the site which, would normally take him a good half hour or so.

He turned to look at the wet and now rather smelly, shaggy long haired Alsatian that was curled up on the floor in the caged portion of his van with its chin resting on its paws and said. 'Well Rebel, what will we do, are you up for it? Once more unto the breach.... and the dreach, cold, wet misery of the night? Please tell me you don't need another jobby.'

The Alsatian now very much enjoying the warmth afforded to him by the vans warm air heaters. Without lifting his head from between its paws, just looked up at his colleague with his big brown eyes and breathed out heavily through its nostrils like a human making a sigh. Clearly having no indication of desire for going back out into the rain.

'Or will we just give this one a miss tonight and go and hide out down Dewars Lane for hawf an hour or so before going to Coulthards? That way we can both get our heads down for a bit. At least at Coulthards for most of it we can go inside where its dry. What do you think to that for a plan?'

The pair had clearly done this before for on hearing this the dog lifted his head and gave a single bark in agreement and gently whished his tail which had the effect of seeping the van floor.

'Good lad.' Said the guard. With that he put the van into gear and headed off for the seclusion of Dewars Lane to be hidden from view.

As the security guard pulled away in his van from the entrance gates on the south side of the quarry. A group of teenagers were climbing through a hole in the wire fence at the north end of the quarry.

The clanking of bear cans and chinking sounds of glass bottles banging together that came from the plastic carrier bags that they held in their hands, were the giveaway sounds that these rapscallion teenagers were sneaking into the quarry to look for some shelter for an underage drinking sesh.

Three of the group of four were through the fence, when the last one in the group as he climbed through the twisted mesh of the fence cried out. 'Awe ya bastard, I've ripped ma jaiket.'

'Fuck sake Jody, keep it doon.' Replied Malky sharply in a hushed voice. Malky was the eldest of the group, about 17 years of age and by all accounts the leader of this mischievous troop.

'Och, gies a haun ma jaicket's stuck in the wire.' Pathetically begged Jody.

Malky turned to look at a young girl of about fifteen. 'Jeanine, go an gie him a hand to get through the fence. You know, that boyfriend of yours can be a right mincing fanny sometimes.'

'Och its no his fault he stuck, it's the fence.' Said Jeanine coming swiftly to the defence of her boyfriend.

'Aye right, what-ever.' Retorted Malky with indifference. 'We'll meet yous doon at they containers.' pointing at the containers with his hand that was holding the bag with some tinnies in it. Because his other hand was holding the collar of his jacket over his head to try to keep the rain from running down his neck. 'That first wan on the left there is normally open, the workies have got a wee brazier in there and it's generally full of old pallets and cardboard. We can make a fire in there. It it'll be just dandy.'

Arriving at the open container door, having walked past the excavator sitting inbetween the two rows of containers. Malky turned to his girlfriend who equally could only be fifteen, maybe sixteen at a push and said. 'Janet doll, get the torch oot and gee us some light.'

Janet took a small two C cell torch from her pocket and switched it on sweeping the container with the beam of light. Sure enough, the inside of the container was just as Malky said it would be. All be it grubby, dank and a bit smelly with a small puddle of water in the entrance from the rain.

As Malky set to work getting a fire going in the brazier, a soaked Jeanine and Jody along with his torn jacket, arrived with a carrier bag containing two bottles of Oddbins cheapest wine.

Seats were fashioned from pallets covered with cardboard and upturned plastic 5 gallon drums. The yellow orange glow of the dancing flames of the fire reflecting off the grubby white walls of the container provided their illumination from the dark. The heat from the brazier was now starting to fend off the cold of the night.

'How did you know all this would be here Malky?' Jody asked.

'Ma uncle works here sure. He is always bragging about how all the workies take turns at fucking the dog in here, especially when it's raining. He's had me on site with him few time sure. Wan time he even let me have a go driving one of they big digger machines. It wis pure dead brilliant.'

And so, with the container doors only partially open, enjoying the warmth of the fire and the shelter the container provided from the rain. With the smoke of the fire starting to mask the damp smell within, the four now cosy in their den, sat and got merry on tins of lager and bottles of cheap wine.

After a while, feeling a little light headed and sleepy from the booze, the two teenage couples lay down on beds of pallets layered with cardboard cosy with the heat of the brazier couried up boy with girl like field mice in a nest and crashed out.

At around 1.30am in the morning, Malky woke up feeling a deep chill in the air. The fire in the brazier had gone out with only a dim red layer of dying embers left. The container was in darkness. He gave Janet a shake by her shoulders to wake her. 'Janet, Janet wake up, where's the torch, the fires gone oot.'

A bleary eyed Janet now awake from her slumber and starting to feel the deep chill in the air put her hand in her pocket and gave Malky the torch. 'Chuffin Nora Malky it's cold, get the fire gawn again.' She exclaimed.

Flashing the torch over to where Jody and Jeanine were cuddled together, he shone the torch light in their eyes. Malky called over to them. 'Jodie, Jeanine wake up, the fires oot.' A bleary Jody replied. 'Whit's gawn on, whit's the Hamden roar?'

'Come oan. Get up.' Malky replied. 'It's time to make tracks and get hame.'

'Bloody Nora Malky its gone helluva cold.' Moaned Jody with a deep shiver.

'Aye I know, we'll be aw 'right once we get on the move.' Malky assured him. As often occurs with a cold shiver down one's spine with that bitter cold in the air, Malky developed the sudden need to pee. Being fire savvy, Malky pished on the burning embers in the brazier to extinguish the remnants of the fire, to prevent any accidents that would stop them from returning here on another night in the future.

'Oh you dirty bastard, that's fucking rancid.' Cried out Janet.

Those of us who have experienced the smell of steaming urine on hot coals can relate to Janet's repulsion. For we know only too well the mephitic, pungent, acrid and far from redolent aroma that results from this emanation. For those of you who haven't had the experience, well it's probably best that you just accept my description of it.

Upon making a hasty exit from the container, the gang of four become immediately aware of a change in the weather. The temperature had dropped below zero, there was now a thin veil of ice forming on the ground and over puddles. Frost was gripping every surface it touched. The rain clouds had gone and a full moon was now illuminating the landscape.

They found the freezing temperature of the night brisk and quite sobering. With the bright light of the full moon, Malky now noticed for the first time the excavator parked up between the two rows of containers. 'Wow, look at that, come on we'll climb up and have a look.' He exclaimed boldly. Malky climbed up onto the tracks and looking in through the cab door window with the torch he saw the keys in the ignition. 'Ya dancer.' He cried out. 'The keys are in the ignition, I'm goony try and start it.' Reaching for the cab door handle, he opened the door and sat himself down inside.

'Hey Malky, ye better no man, we should just go and get hame.' Said a nervous Jody, who was now starting to get a bad feeling in the pit of his stomach.

For Jody, his ripped jacket aside, up until now had actually quite enjoyed his little adventure in the dark of night. However, he was now developing a deep dread that things were about to go very badly wrong.

'Stop being a fanny, it will alright, we'll have a laugh with this.' Shouted down Malky now bold with the drink. Turning the ignition key, the excavator's diesel engine fired up and roared into life as Malky pressed his foot down on the accelerator pedal.

Using the torch to look at the symbols on the levers Malky worked out how to lift the shovel. Excited and euphoric grinning to himself, he placed the torch in his mouth so that he could now use both hands. He started fiddling with knobs and switches pushing and pulling other levers. Then all of a sudden the excavator jolted and started moving forward. The sudden jolt caused the torch to fall from Malky's mouth. It landed on the floor and stopped working.

At first Malky didn't seem bothered about the loss of light, for he was quite high on the fact that the excavator was now trundling along the track on its own. Instead of watching where the machine was going, he was leaning out of the cab door facing back towards his friends, giving a thumbs up shouting at them. 'Woay this is magic.' Whilst completely oblivious to the danger ahead of him. However, his joy didn't last for long. His friends following along behind started to shout and wave their arms and point at Malky. But their shouts of warning were being drowned out by the sound of the excavator's diesel engine.

Malky turned to face forward and what he saw in the moonlight put the fear of God in him. The excavators tracks were just starting to touch the foreshore of the pond. Not knowing how to stop the machine and in a blind panic, Malky jumped from the machine onto the ground. Just in time to watch the brand new excavator trundle out until the tracks were fully submerged and then suddenly it just disappeared below the surface of the pond, then silence. Gone, it was if it had never existed.

They all stared wide eyed, gobsmacked in disbelief. For a moment nothing was said, then the reality of what had just happened began to take effect on them. Especially Malky, for the gravity of what would happen to him if he was ever found out, had caused him to physically shit his pants.

8am, Archie Lamont the quarry manager was just getting his feet under his desk with a coffee in hand when Alec the site excavator driver barged into his office and exclaimed. 'Hey Archie, your never gonny believe this.'

Looking over the rim of his glasses Archie lethargically replied. 'Aye maybe not but try me anyway.'

'Some fuckin Houdini has done a disappearing
.h our excavator.'

'Whit are you havering aboot ya dafty?'
ed Archie.

'I'm no a dafty! I'm telling you man. It's gone,
aewhere to be seen. Look for yoursel.'

o uniformed Policemen were standing at the edge
the pond at the end of the track. There was now a
eet of ice over the pond. Except for a rainbow
)loured slush patch caused by leaked diesel fuel
here the excavator had sank in the wee hours of the
.ight.

The two Policemen were looking at the mini
oil slick. Turning to face one another, the Sergeant
said to the young constable. 'I'll give Mr Lamont the
good news and let him know that his excavator wasn't
stolen and has been found.' Then grinning. 'You can
tell him where we believe we have found it. But it
clearly didn't end up in there by itself, so we'll need to
get the underwater search unit down. At the very least
so they can check for cadavers.'*(g-314)*

Unclipping his radio from the loop above his
breast pocket, the Sergeant called Juliet Control to
request the attendance of the Police underwater search
unit. 'Kilo356 to Juliet Control, request the
underwater unit to attend Drumcavel Quarry. The
excavator that has been reported stolen isn't actually
stolen. It looks as though someone has parked it in the
big wet garage.'

The female dispatcher at Juliet Control
sounded somewhat perplexed. 'Kilo356, didn't quite
understand that. Could you please repeat, did you just
say a wet garage?'

'Affirmative.' Replied the Sergeant.

The Dispatcher was still perplexed. 'Kilo356 sorry, we don't understand what is a wet garage, could you please explain further?'

The Sergeant rolled his eyes and in a condescending tone replied. 'Here's a clue, were at Drumcavel quarry, part of it is flooded, have a guess what the wet garage is?' There was a pregnant pause on the radio. 'Oh would ye just send the underwater search unit?'

The dispatcher who was still none the wiser replied. 'Rodger Kilo356, underwater unit en route.'

The sergeant asked his constable. 'Who's that dippy whoer on the dispatch desk?'

Smiling the constable replied .'Oh that will be the Michelin Mother fat Alice. She's next to fucking useless. You know the wan, she's got a heid on her like a snipers dream.' Exaggerating with his hands either side of his head.

'Is that her that use to be in the dog branch?' Asked the sergeant.

The Constable nodded his head. 'Aye she got kicked out the dog branch for feeding the dog with pie chips every lunchtime. Mind, she had an Alsatian bitch called Cindy. But it should have been called Candy wi the amount of sweets and snacks she was aye ways feeding it. You know that auld saying that dogs look like their owners?

'Aye.' Acknowledged the Sergeant raising an eyebrow.

'Well her Alsatian looked more like wan o' they Saint Bernard's with the amount of shite she was feeding it.' Explained the constable.

'Och, that's the wan, aye... I remember her now, she's actually been kicked out of almost every department in the force.' Recalled the Sergeant. 'Aye, she only got the dispatchers job because she's no auld enough to be a lollipop woman. Aye... that says it all doesn't it.'

The water was freezing cold, dark, murky and eerie with a yellow brown hue to it. Visibility was less than a meter. His breathing controlled, slow and deep, the Police diver carefully worked his way from the back of the excavator down to the front, following the track along the quarry bed. Then returning to the back, before traversing down the other side, making sure not to get his umbilical caught up in anything.

His umbilical acted as a safety line and provide voice communication back to his team on the surface. Edging his way with gentle fin kicks, so as not to disturb the silt covered bottom and lose what little visibility he currently had. He then moved up to the cab. Finding the door open he looked inside, half expecting to find the operator still inside.

Much to his relief, the cab was empty. Speaking through the microphone in his Aga full facemask*(4-327)*. 'Diver 1 to surface'

'Aye, go ahead Diver 1' Replied his Sergeant sitting in a mobile command station which was parked up at the edge of the pond.

'All clear here.' Then heaving a breath. 'No cadavers*(g-314)* found.' Taking another breath, 'By the way, the keys are in the ignition.'

'Copied that Diver 1, very good. Diver clear to return to surface.' Replied his Sergeant.

In the Managers office, Archie Lamont was talking with the Police Inspector. 'Will your divers recover the excavator for us?'

'Sorry Archie, no can do.' Replied Frank Hill who was the Inspector in charge of the Police Underwater Search Unit. 'Unless it's classed as crown evidence, it's not our remit.'

'Fair enough Frank. Can you recommend a diving company that can?'

'Aye.' Replied Frank with a smile. 'GDMC, here's their number. They're based in St Vincent Street in Glasgow. Ask for Pat Jamieson. He'll sort you out.'

Meanwhile, in the GDMC office, an athletic, handsome young man in his early twenties was filling out some paperwork. Agnes a fit looking, dark haired woman in her late fifties with glasses, sporting a classy half up bouffant walked into the office. She was actually the landlady from the Syxtie's Bar, two doors down. 'Good morning Scurvy lad.' She said with a smile to the young man.

'Hi Aggie, it's a bonnie day eh, I love cold, sharp, frosty, sunny mornings like this.' Acknowledged Scurvy.

'Smiling Agnes replied. 'It is that Scurvy lad, I just thought you might want to let Pirate know, Misty's been lifted again. I've just seen her been hauled into Cranston Street nick.'

Scurvy, was totally unsympathetic. 'Well that's what she gets for being a total slut. Here Agnes, would you do me a favour, You couldn't sit in and mind the phone for me, while I get her out the nick?'

'Aye okay.' Agreed Agnes 'But don't be long mind because I've got the Brewery coming in with a delivery.'

'Thanks Agnes, you're a pal.' Said Scurvy appreciatively. 'I'll be as quick as I can. Patsy will be in shortly. Make yourself a cup o tea and have a Paris bun. I got them in fresh from Hughie's this morning. They're just dandy for having wi tea.'

With the kettle boiling, Agnes noticed three little leather pouches sitting on a shelf in a triangle. Standing next to them was a quartz crystal statue about 8 inches tall of a hard hat diver.

She looked through one of the pouches and turned to Scurvy just as he was about to leave and enquired. 'Scurvy. What are the leather pouches for?'

'Oh these, they're a commercial divers tool kit. I put them up there so as to have a constant reminder of the intellect of the typical diver I have found in this industry.'

'A divers tool kit?' Agnes questioned.

For inside the little pouches was a toy hammer from an Action Man, a condom and a little doll's house scrubbing brush.

'I don't follow.' Said Agnes, frowning pulling her eyebrows together whilst cocking her head slightly to one side.

'Well, it's like this.' Scurvy explained. 'If they don't understand how something works, they'll hit it with a hammer. More often than not, they won't know how to fix it but they'll totally fuck it in the process of trying. But if they can't, fix it, fuck it or get at it to hit it with a hammer, they'll just scrub round it.'

Agnes now smiling asked. 'But why three of them?'

'Again Agnes, you have to understand the attributes and mindset of the typical commercial diver. More often than not, he'll break or lose the first one, the second one he will stash in his kit bag for taking home and the third one will get used on the job.'

Laughing she said. 'Aye, you're a card Scurvy, definitely the joker in the pack.'

'Well you have to have a laugh when you work here eh. Cause if you didn't laugh here; I can assure you Agnes you'd cry. Anyway, kettles boiled, I'll no be long see ya.'

Cranston Street Police station was built in the 1960's. A typical pebble dashed drab government building with no soul and a heavy wooden glass panelled outer door. Once inside, you were met with a high solid oak, all encompassing front desk.

A straight faced Sergeant behind the desk looked at Scurvy with contemptuous eyes.

'I believe you lifted Misty again.' Enquired Scurvy.

'Aye. Becoming a bit of a habit this. You tell Pirate, that if we lift her again, we'll lift him also. He needs to keep a tighter control over her.' Informed the Sergeant.

'I will and you're right, he does. Mind you, maybe banging him up for a while wouldn'y be such a bad thing eh?' Agreed Scurvy with a wink.

'I take it you've come to get her.' Assumed the Sergeant.

'Aye, can I?' Asked Scurvy hopefully.

The sergeant gave Scurvy an exasperated nod of approval. 'Through here then.'

Opening a side a door, the Sergeant led Scurvy through the back, down along a corridor of windowed offices. This took them to a back door which led them outside. Crossing the station car park to enter a another building through a heavy locked steel door. Once inside there was a jangling of keys.

The Sergeant opened a steel barred door complete with wire mesh.

'You've been putting it about again haven't you, ya dirty stop out!' Said Scurvy in disapproval.

With her head down and her big brown soppy sad eyes looking up at Scurvy was a lovely Alsatian bitch called Misty. Her ears were down and her tail was inbetween her legs.

'No use in keeping your tail down between your legs now is there? That's where it should have been last night and was it? No, you were being quite the slut weren't you.' Scolded Scurvy.

Misty with her big sad brown eyes was now all forlorn and sheepish from Scurvy's Scolding.

Scurvy, now pointing at her with his finger, totally straight faced. 'And don't think for a minute you can get round me looking at me like that.'

He put his hand down and sighed 'Oh who am I kidding, how can I be stern with you when you look at me with those big sad, soppy brown eyes. Come on Misty, I'll take you home.'

Instantly, Misty's ears picked up, she wagged her tail and jumped all over him trying to lick him to death. Scurvy snapped on a lead and headed back to the office with a happy, tail wagging, energetic Misty in tow.

Back in the GDMC office Pat Jamieson walked through the door, upon seeing Agnes he asked. 'Where's Scurvy?'

'He's just nipped down to Cranston Street nick. Misty's been lifted again. Explained Agnes. 'Oh, can you give an Archie Lamont a phone at Drumcavel Quarry, here's his number. Something about a job, he says it's quite urgent. I need to dash, see ya later.'

'Thanks Aggie.' Pat Jamieson known to everyone as Patsy, was a fit, broad shouldered man of about 5'10" in his early thirties, with short messy light brown hair, sporting a bushy moustache and numerous tattoos. A genuine and good natured man with a sharp, witty sense of humour. He was actually one of the Directors of GDMC and the Chief diver.

While Patsy was on the phone, Smithy, Pirate, Philip and Belinda walked in. Shortly followed by Scurvy with Misty in tow who was all happy to see Pirate, her master again.

Finishing his call, Patsy immediately put everyone to work. 'Right lads, listen up, hot to trot this morning. That was the manager of Drumcavel quarry on the phone. We've got a Caterpillar excavator to recover from their flushing pond. So let's get geared up. You all know what's needed. The quarry's got a 100 tonne crane from Motherwell Bridge Plant hire on its way down.' Then Patsy pointing firmly with his finger at Pirate 'Oh and Pirate... I want YOU on your best behaviour!'

An offended Pirate replied. 'What do you mean!'

The guys started loading up the necessary equipment into a Transit van, P100 Pick Up and an old Series iii

Land Rover. The kit included 12litre bailout cylinders with backpacks*(g-314)*, two high pressure J bottles*(g-316)*, a two Diver surface demand control panel and coms box. Diver umbilical hoses, low pressure compressor and receiver. Kit bags with dry suits & harnesses. Mk10 Kirby Morgan band masks *(1-321)*, an Aquadyne AH3 diving helmet*(2-323)* and lead weights etc.

As this load out was taking place. The banter started into Pirates romantic exploits from the Saturday night before. Scurvy sparked up. 'Hey Patsy, you and Beverley should have stayed and hung about with us on Saturday night, you missed an absolute picture!'

'Oh aye, what was that then?' Said Patsy intrigued.

Sporting a mischievous grin, Scurvy started to lay the foundation of what had been quite an entertaining event. 'Well, we all ended up in the Savoy and Pirate was going for a name change. He was trying his hand at being Casanova.'

Now chuckling he continued. 'Patsy you want to have seen this thing. Man! Brutal or what.'

'Fuck off'!' Snapped Pirate annoyed. 'Don't listen to him Patsy, he's a gobshite.'

Smithy seeing an opportunity chirped in. 'Oh come on now, be fare. Hey Patsy, you know these big fat Italian opera singer lassies.'

Patsy was now beginning to smirk but was trying to hold it back. 'Aye.'

'Well she was like one of them, only she had a face like a hauf chewed caramel. I mean it wisny just plooks.' Starting to laugh Smithy illustrated further.

'She had mair craters on her face than the bright side of the moon.'

Pirate now scowling and procrastinating in his own defence. 'Fuck off, don't listen to them Patsy. They're talking shite.' Pirate changed his glance towards Smithy. 'How would you know what she looked like, it was dark in the Savoy and I didn't see you anywhere near her.'

Patsy pretending to be unbiased and just, turned to Philip. 'You were there Philip, is there any justice to be had here?'

Philip who with years of practice, had kept a straight face throughout this exchange. 'Well....I don't know if I would describe her as an Italian opera singer.' Pausing then chuckling 'A fucking Greek tragedy mair like it*(g-316)*. Maan you should have seen her! She was a heifer, she looked as though her doctor was a vet. If she disn'y pull carts in this life, she certainly did in a previous one.'

Pirate was now agitated with embarrassment. 'Fuck off!! She wisny a fat lass.'

Scurvy was grinning and unable to contain himself. 'Away man, she had thighs that could kick start a jumbo jet. Hey, it gets better, she was wearing this baggy long Daz white, blouse and trouser suit number. She stood out like a blizzard in the dim lights of the Savoy.'

Everyone was now laughing except for Pirate, who was now scowling. Patsy, trying to retain some assemblance of a straight face asked. 'So Pirate....tell me eh...(Chuckling) did you shag her?'

Pirate went quiet, he averted his eyes to the floor and didn't answer. Just the giveaway that Patsy was looking for. 'Oh! You clarty old weasel, you did shag her. The pock ridden heifer turned out to be a fat rabbit eh. So your efforts weren't wasted after all.'

'Mind you, she must have been gagging for a shag for her to slope off with a clarty git like you.'

'Aye and like you're a fucking Paris painting!' Snapped Pirate biting back.

Patsy, not letting go asked. 'So I take it you went back to her place cause I'm assuming Delilah wouldn't have been too please if you had went back to yours.'

Pirate sarcastically replied 'What do you think?'

Patsy sensed there was still some mileage left in this. 'So, eh where does she bide?'

Pirate reluctantly replied 'Muirhead.'

Smithy splurted out. 'Fuck me Pirate, it's no a lumber she needs, it's a pen pal. That's fucking miles away. You'd need a second mortgage to pay the taxi fare for that one. You would have been cheaper nipping up the street to Blythswood Square and getting a prozi.'

Philip indicating his agreement. 'Aye and any one of they prozi's would not only have been cheaper but they would have been much better looking and fitter as well.'

Pirate tried hard to take the moral high ground. 'Oh fuck off, what would you lot know, it takes more than looks for me to find a woman attractive.'

Scurvy then landed another one in. 'I bet you didn't say that to Delilah when you proposed to her.'

Patsy wanting to get things back on track. 'Aye fair enough, I'm sure her hand writing's lovely. But as much as I want to hear more about Pirates spotty totty. I also want this kit loaded and to be on our way to Drumcavel ASAP.'

'Drumcavel!' Exclaimed Scurvy, who suddenly realised the relevance of the location. 'I forgot that's where were going. Hey lads Muirhead's just before the Gartcosh turn off. We could drop in on Pirates new bird on the way back.' Laughing, looking towards Pirate he said with a smile 'You could introduce her to us all.'

Pirate grimacing faced the group. 'Don't even fucking think about going there.' Then turning to face Scurvy he said. 'You know Scurvy lad, you have your moments, I'll grant you that. But there are times when I could easily smack you right in the mouth.'

Scurvy grinned as he and Smithy were carrying another J bottle out to the van. 'Ach Pirate, I know you don't really mean that. We all know I'm your favourite. Anyway. It's hard to be humble when your perfect in every way. But I'm doing the best I can.'

Pirate drew him a contemptuous look.

Upon arrival at Drumcavel quarry, they were directed where to go and proceeded to set up their equipment. On an upper embankment about 20m to the left of them sat the huge 100tonne lifting capacity road crane from Motherwell Bridge Plant hire. Its thick steel spreader plates laid out on the ground and the stabilizer legs were all ready down. The crane driver was sitting in the warmth of his cab patiently waiting for the divers.

Once their equipment was set up and tested, with two divers umbilicals coiled neatly in separate figure of 8's on the ground close to the water's edge.

Everyone, except for Pirate went up to the site managers office for a toolbox talk and operations briefing.

Meanwhile, Pirate was meddling with the low pressure compressor air receiver.

At the end of the briefing Patsy asked. 'Right, that's it then. Are there any questions?'

Scurvy cheekily with a grin asked. 'Just one, why is orange jam called marmalade and not orange jam?'

Patsy sardonically replied. 'I meant about the job, ya git.'

Scurvy smiled.' Eh, no, it's as clear as a bell.'

Upon returning to the dive site, they discovered that Pirate had the compressor relief valve in bits and had lost some of the pieces.

Patsy in disbelief exclaimed. 'Pirate, what on earth have you been doing man?'

Pirate replied defensively. 'It kept blowing off, so I thought I'd fix it.'

Scurvy who had a healthy contempt for Pirate replied. 'You can't fix what's not broken. It's meant to blow off. It's to stop the receiver from over pressurising.'

Pirate demonstrating an innocent air of stupidity replied. 'Aye I know, but is was doing it all the time.'

Scurvy struggled with Pirates ineptitude. 'It will do, if the compressors running and the airs not being used. It will blow off every minute or so.' Turning away and rolling his eyes Scurvy muttered to himself. 'Ya Fuckin Muppet.'

Smithy exasperated announced. 'You've lost half the bits man. Were scuppered because we don't have another one.'

Archie the quarry manager stepped in to save the day. 'We use a lot of pneumatic equipment on site. We should be able to give you something that will do out of our maintenance department.'

A grateful Patsy replied. 'Thanks very much, that would be appreciated.' Then angrily, he turned to Pirate. 'Pirate, don't touch anything else.'

Pirate in a conceited tone retorted. 'Now Patsy, just you remember who I am.'

Patsy caste Pirate a sarcastic look and bit his tongue. He looked over at Scurvy and Philip. 'Right you two, get into your Liberty Bodices and get your Bondage gear on. Scurvy, you're in first.'

'Smithy, you help them on with their gear, then acts a tender to Scurvy & Philip. I'll man the panel and help you with the umbilicals as required.'

Pirate piped up 'And eh, what about me?'

To which Patsy swiftly replied. 'Pirate. You stay out of the way and don't touch anything.' Then Patsy, aggressively pointed with his finger and then his thumb. 'AND YOU JUST REMEMBER WHO I AM!'

The air receiver now fixed, Philip and Scurvy were suited and booted. Philip as stand by diver was sitting down on the back step of the transit van with his KMB10 *(1-321)* band mask resting on his thighs.

Scurvy was now fully rigged for diving with air being supplied to him from the surface. This is commonly known as surface demand or surface supplied diving.

Out of the water his body had to support a tremendous weight of equipment. The Aquadyne AH3*(2-323)* diving helmet on his head is around 13kg. (Diving helmets were often referred to as hats.) 14kg of lead weight belt around his waist.

On his back he carried a 15kg steel diving bottle as an emergency air supply. Add another 4kg for the bulky 7mm neoprene dry suit that will keep him warm in the ice covered water of the pond. There is also the full body recovery harness that he was strapped into, that his life line and umbilical is connected into. Plus around another 4 kg of ancillary items comprising of a large bowie knife, adjustable spanner, a hammer, short pry bar/podger and a pair of black rubber jet fins gave him an overall burden of around 50kg.

Then he has to drag his surface demand umbilical behind him. This consist of a 10mm bore reinforced air hose for his breathing supply, a 6mm bore air pneumo tube (this gives the divers depth reading back to the surface attendant). A combined coms, & power cable and a safety line all entwined together.

With the large rubber jet fins on his feet which are much bigger than clowns feet, he carefully started to wade into the water backwards along the shallow shelf. Smithy, standing at the water's edge, acted as surface tender to the diver, feeding out his umbilical as required.

Once the water was up to his waist, Scurvy dropped down to his knees and stretched himself out to a horizontal position. The weight of all his equipment was now displaced by the water and he was positively buoyant from the trapped air in his dry suit. His equipment was no longer a burden on him. Looking over the edge of the shelf into the abyss below and ready to descend Scurvy asked Patsy for permission to dive.

Patsy replied 'Diver 1 clear to dive.'

With that, Scurvy passed over the edge of the ledge, pulling his umbilical with him. Lowering his legs, then leaning slightly to his right whilst lifting his left arm above his head. This allowed the air inside his dry suit to vent from the dump valve on the wrist of his suit and he began to sink. The bright light of the day was rapidly blotted out as he descended below the surface into the depths and darkness of the tea coloured murky water.

Slowly and carefully feet first Scurvy made his descent down a cliff face in the eyrie dim light of the cold dark water. On the inside front of the helmet was a small neoprene pad. He pressed his nostrils against it so he could equalise the air pressure in his ears. He injected short puffs of air into his dry suit as he went so as to control his rate of descent. This also prevented his dry suit from squeezing his body as it compressed with the water pressure which increased with depth.

At a depth of around 7m the cliff face changed to a slope. Scurvy changed his body position from being vertical back to being horizontal. Then began to carefully fin down along the slope head first whilst keeping off the bottom, dragging his umbilical behind him. At around 14m depth he bumped into a large solid object, giving himself a bit of a start, which caused a sudden sharp intake of breath. Scurvy had found the excavator.

It was sitting upright on its tracks. It had come to a stop here as a result of the excavators boom jamming into the pond bed out in front where the pond bed had raised up again. Exactly as the Police diver had described it. The turbid water dulled the illumination of his helmet mounted light, reducing it to not much more than a dim glow instead of a bright white beam. He could just make out the word CAT in big white letters on the counterbalance weight on the back of the excavator.

'Diver 1 to surface, over.' Survey called.

Patsy was listening carefully over the coms to Scurvy's breathing. 'Surface from diver 1 go ahead, over.'

'Diver on Bottom, I've found it and have located to the two pad eyes on the back.' Confirmed Scurvy. His voice sounding tinny & fuzzy over the coms. This was caused by his helmet microphone picking up the sound of his every inhaled and exhaled breath which also picks up the harsh pitch from the sound of his exhaust bubbles in the water.

'Surface from Diver 1, Good Lad. I thought you had. Your breathing gave you away. What's the viz like?' Enquired Patsy.

'Diver 1 to Surface. 'It's like smoked glass, I am about a meter from the back of the counterbalance weight and I can just make out the CAT sign and no more. Over.'

'Surface copied. Okay, just caw canny when moving about the thing. Now attach the surface marker buoy to the right hand side of the crane cab and send it to the surface. This will mark the drop spot for the crane hook. It should give us a near perfect balanced lifting position for the crane wire. Over.' Instructed Patsy.

'Rodger will do, over.' Replied Scurvy.

Scurvy made his way hand over hand to the back of the cab, being careful to make sure his umbilical didn't snag on anything. Here he removed a rolled up orange tube attached to a small hand reel with white cord which was clipped to his harness. He clipped the reel by its carabineer to a handle on the side of the cab. He placed the open end of his umbilical pneumo tube into the open end of the now unravelled orange roll.

'Diver 1 to surface over.'

' Surface from diver 1 go ahead over.'

'Flush through the pneumo so that I can fill the surface marker buoy. Over.' He instructed Patsy.

'Understood Diver 1, Flushing now, over.' Confirmed Patsy. With that Patsy briefly opened the air valve to the pneumo tube and a burst of bubbles came out the end filling the long orange roll. It's now the shape of a large orange sausage of around 1.75m long.

'Okay stop there. Over.' Instructed Scurvy.

'Surface from diver 1. Copied all stop on pneumo.' Confirmed Patsy.

Scurvy let the inflated tube go, where it instantly shot to the surface like a Polaris missile. On bursting through the surface it stood tall and erect with the cord line pulled taught below.

'Surface to diver1.' Called Patsy. We've got it. A big orange hard on marks the spot over.'

'Diver 1 to Surface. Nice one, over.' Replied Scurvy.

'Surface to Diver 1, take your umbilical to the left side, stand on the track and wait there for the crane hook. We will lower it down slightly towards the right of the buoy, over'

'Diver 1 to Surface. Understood, over.' Replied Scurvy.

He had already been making his way to the left track as this had been discussed at the operations meeting earlier. By waiting on the left track, the excavators cab would provide Scurvy some protection should the crane hook drop suddenly for any reason.

'Surface to Diver1. Booming the crane over now. We will stop the hook as soon when the longest sling touches the surface of the water to reset the line out counter. There is a strobe attached to the hook and light sticks attached to the slings Over.'

'Diver 1 Copied, over.'

By zeroing the line out count of his crane wire at this point. It allowed the crane driver to inform Patsy exactly how much line has being paid out. Patsy could then position and stop the wire at an exact depth in relation to the depth the diver was at, which is indicated by the divers pneumo tube.

'Surface to Diver 1, crane hook coming down slow, over.'

'Diver 1 to Surface Copied that.' Confirmed Scurvy.

The crane wire was lowered at a rate of a quarter a meter a second. About 40 second later, Patsy over his hand held UHF radio called an all stop on the crane. Then he spoke to Scurvy.

'Surface to diver1, cranes all stopped, The bottom of the slings should be about 1 meter in front of you and about one meter above you, over.'

'Diver 1 to Surface, copied that. I can just see the light sticks and the strobe light. Slowly slew the crane boom about 2 m to the left so that I have the hook right above the forward fixing points, over.'

'Surface from Diver1 understood, on the move.' Gently the crane hook began to creep to the through the water.

'All stop on the crane and stand by.' Called Scurvy once the hook was parallel to the forward lifting points.

'Crane all stopped. Standing by, over.' Acknowledged Patsy.

'Diver 1to Surface. Retract Jib 0.5m and stop.' Instructed Scurvy.

The jib was retracted exactly as Scurvy had asked. 'Surface to Diver 1' Now all stopped on the crane, over.' Confirmed Patsy.

The crane hook was now directly above the knuckles from two powerful hydraulic rams connected onto either side of the boom of the excavator. On each side Scurvy had to feed the eye from one end of a steel wire sling between the ram and the side of the boom. Under and around this very strong load bearing point and hook the eye of the sling back into the crane hook.

Sitting atop of, straddled with his legs on either side of the boom, Scurvy instructed Patsy to come down on the crane wire until the hook was about half a meter above the boom. Taking a 2m length of 13mm diameter rope which he had stowed tucked into his harness. Using a clove hitch he tied it off onto an end of the wire sling just below the eye. He then lowered this down under and around the mounting point. He then tied of this rope to one of the steel hydraulic feed pipes on top of the boom. Pushing the sprung loaded safety gate of the crane hook forward to open it. He then lifted the eye of the wire off the hook and let it hang on the rope.

Taking another 2m section of rope which was in a cargo pocket on his thigh he did the same thing again on the other side of the Boom. Only this time he pulled the eye of the sling all the way through and hooked it back onto the crane hook. The safety gate snapping shut as he did it.

Unfastening the rope holding the first wire sling, he started to pull it through. Just as he got the eye of the sling over the tip of the hook he felt this powerful thump on the side of his helmet and a large dark mass pushed past him at tremendous speed. It attacked the strobe light taped to the crane wire just above the hook and was trying to bite into the 40mm thick steel lifting wire of the crane.

Reeling back in fright he exclaimed. 'Fucking Nora what the hell was that!' As he almost fell off the crane boom.

His heart was now beating twenty to the dozen and his breathing became rapid. In the combined illumination of his hat light and the glow sticks on the slings. Scurvy could make out that a huge Pike, easily a meter in length if not longer, its jaw stacked with razor sharp spiked teeth had attacked the strobe light.

Patsy & Philip both realised something was wrong. Patsy called out over the comes with a tone of concern as Philip was getting ready to pull on his band mask. 'Surface to Diver, what's wrong, are you okay?'

Scurvy taking a moment to compose himself. and trying to control his breathing replied. 'Surface from Diver 1. Aye I'm okay, I just a got a hell of a fright. A fuck off massive Pike has just attacked the strobe on the crane wire.' Getting his breath back and composing himself. 'The fucking thing came from nowhere, went shooting right past my head like a torpedo, I near shat myself... Over'

Patsy & Philip were trying hard not to laugh. 'Are you all right, where is it now?' Patsy enquired pretending to sound paternal and caring.

'I'm alright. it's gone, it just gave me quite a start.' Replied Scurvy. I think it will need a dentist after snapping its gums over the crane wire though. Over.'

'Good, can we continue?' Asked Patsy still trying not to laugh.

'Diver1 to Surface, aye, aye were good to go.'

It was quite common for large man made ponds and flooded quarries to be well stocked with fish. And for predator species such as Pike to grow to considerable size. The fish got there by two means. Firstly, from fish eggs that would have been on the legs of birds that had become attached to them from other water courses, such as rivers, streams, lochs and other ponds. Secondly, was by man. It was common enough for people who enjoyed fishing to catch fish elsewhere and transfer them to manmade ponds to populate them for their own angling pleasure.

Scurvy now kneeling on top of the boom arm instructed Patsy to move the crane wire up slightly and slew to the right to take the crane hook to the back of the Excavator, setting the first two slings into place.

The two lifting slings on the rear were much easier to install. These just shackled into easily accessible pad eyes on the back of the Excavator. Once they were in position, Scurvy returned to his safe zone on the left side of the cab. Standing on the track, he instructed Patsy to move the crane hook back to the midpoint and set the lifting slings just short of taught.

'Diver1 to surface. All good here, am I clear to return to Surface?' Asked Scurvy.

'Surface to Diver1, yes clear to surface.' Confirmed Patsy.

As Scurvy began his assent back to the bright light of the day, Smithy pulled in and carefully coiled his umbilical. Once back on the surface, with his helmet removed, Scurvy sat next to Philip and they waited fully kitted for the lift to begin. They would not de kit and disrobe until the crane had the excavator suspended just below the surface, just in case any problems were to arise under the water during the lift.

Now came the moment of truth. Everyone from the quarry was now gathered around the shore of the pond, to include two of the quarry's company Directors.

Patsy now handed over this stage of the recovery operation to the crane driver and his banksman. With a throaty roar from the cranes big diesel engine and a puff of black smoke bursting out of its exhaust pipe. This mighty crane began to take the strain. The crane driver was expecting to see around 18-20 tonnes on his load cell before it should start to move. The weight on land for this machine is around 23tonnes. However, due to Archimedes principle of buoyancy in water this is approximately one fifth less.

Creeping the crane wire, after only about two inches of movement the wire went bar tight, this was expected. The tone changed on the powerful hydraulic motor of the cranes winch drum as the crane started to pull against the weight of the excavator, 18 tonnes, 19, 20, 21 tonnes then the load cell dropped back to 19 tonnes and the wire started to move upwards. The excavator was now off the bottom. Once the excavator was 2m of the bottom, the crane driver stopped lifting and very slowly slewed the excavator 15m over to the left away from the cliff wall of the pond. Thus performing the recovery of the excavator to surface in clear unobstructed water.

Very slowly continuing to raise the wire, the driver stopped the lift once the crane hook had just cleared the surface. The load was kept suspended there whilst they stopped for lunch and to allow the divers to remove their equipment and vehicles away from the edge of the pond. This was because that space was needed so that a low loader could reverse down track for the Excavator to be loaded onto.

With most of the equipment loaded back in the vehicles, Scurvy was standing over at the crane talking with the crane driver whilst having a sandwich and a hot coffee. His dry suit unzipped and half off around his waist.

Archie Lamont came over to chat with him and to thank him for a job well done. Archie brought the conversation around to asking about Pirate.

'Tell me, whose the scrawny weasily guy, the one you call Pirate?' Enquired Archie.

'Believe or not, but he is one of the Director's of the company.' Replied Scurvy. 'He's a Fuckin menace, a complete eejit and a total embarrassment.'

'He told me he had been a SAT diver out in the Persian Gulf.' Said Archie with a tone of doubt in his voice.

SAT is an abbreviation for Saturation Diving. This is highly specialised commercial diving methodology for deep diving or long term submersion where the diver breaths Oxy Helium mixed gas instead of air. The divers stay under pressure in specialised habits for up to twenty eight days at a time. It is lucrative, very highly paid and prestigious but not without its risks and dangers. It is most commonly used for deep diving in water depths beyond fifty meters.

It was not uncommon for divers who were bluff and bullshit merchants to make this claim. By saying they worked in the Persian Gulf it meant that in most cases, their claim was unverifiable, therefore was difficult to challenge.

Chuckling sarcastically and rolling his eyes Scurvy replied. 'Well, he might have sat next one and the closest that cunt ever got to the Persian Gulf would have been fingering a travel brochure in Thomas Cook's.'

'So eh, why do you call him Pirate?' Enquired Archie.

'Well, there are two reasons for this.' Explained Scurvy. 'Firstly, to refer to him by anything else would only result in a mouthful of profanity and obscenities. And secondly, he's a total scam merchant. He'd steal the sugar out your tea and sell his Granny for a packet of fags if he thought he could get away with it. You need to watch him like a fucking hawk.'

'Aye, I know what you mean. He's certainly got that shifty, furtive look and demeanour about him.' Acknowledged Archie. So tell me, what does GDMC actually stand for?'

'It depends on who you ask.' Replied Scurvy.

'Well I'm asking you.' Said Archie.

'Garbage Drivel, Muck & Crap.' Replied Scurvy sarcastically.

'And If I am writing the cheque out for your boss?'Asked Archie.

In his best Sunday accent Scurvy replied. 'Glasgow Diving & Marine Contractors Ltd.'

Looking over towards the foreshore where there was a bit of a commotion going on. Archie start to laugh to himself and said to Scurvy. 'Well, I'll tell you this, that's some outfit you work for here son.'

'Oh really and why is that then?' Scurvy asked.

Archie pointing towards the commotion taking place in the water at the shallow shelf and exclaimed laughing.

'The Dog Dives As Well!'

Scurvy looked round to see Pirate who for reasons known only to himself is now in the water, bobbing about in a flurry of bubbles. He has an old band mask*(1-321)* that he has attached to a Scuba cylinder. It isn't secure on his head because the retaining spider is burst. Misty who has managed to get out of the Land Rover, has got a snorkel out of one of the kit bags and was now doggy paddling around pirates flurry of bubbles, with the tube of the snorkel gripped between her teeth.

Scurvy looked on in disbelief and despair. With a deep sigh and his head falling forward showing his frustration said. 'Semper im excretia Solemn propondum variat.'

Archie was quite impressed by Scurvy's statement. 'That sounds most profound and has all the hallmarks of an expensive education. 'I'm impressed and from a diver too. What does it mean?'

Scurvy with a look contempt for Pirate sighed 'We are always in the shit, it is only the depth that varies. And it wasn't from an expensive education, I went to Renfrew High, the local comprehensive. But I liked hanging about with catholic school girls.' And winked.

'Brilliant, I like it.' Laughed Archie.

Philip who was still zipped into his drysuit, waded into the water, grabbed Pirate by the hood of the band mask and dragged him ashore, followed by an energetic and excitable Misty.

Patsy went ballistic and shouted at Pirate. 'Ya fucking idiot! What the fuck do you think you are doing! Get that kit off and back in the van. Get that drysuit off and get that loopy dog of yours out of the water and back in the Land Rover. And stay out of the fucking way!'

'Right let's get this show on the road and complete the final stage of this before we lose the daylight.' Barked Patsy.

The diving site now cleared, with all the vehicles relocated up to the quarry car park, the low loader was able to reverse down into position ready to receive the excavator.

Once again, the cranes mighty diesel engine roared into life and the crane driver commenced the lift. As the excavator cab and boom broke through the ice and made an appearance the crane driver slightly increased the speed of the lift until the tracks were clear of the surface of the partially frozen pond.

There was a big hooray and wolf whistles of approval from the gathered ensemble of quarrymen, and the crane driver who blasted his horn. He held the excavator suspended about 2metres above the surface of the pond, to allow the water to spill out of the cab and drain off from the superstructure. After a couple of minutes, he continued the lift, and then gently swung the excavator over and lowered it onto the low loader road transporter.

Feeling very pleased with themselves and rightly so, for a job well done. After unloading the equipment back at the office, the motley crew sauntered along to the Syxtie's bar just two doors up on the corner of St Vincent Street and Pembroke street, for a celebratory drink or three. Well four or more would be more like it.

They walked through the Pub door to the sound of a Karaoke singer murdering Tammy Wynette's 'stand by your man'. But to be greeted as always by the warm, friendly smile of Agnes, the pub's landlady.

Patsy got the first round in as the merry troop begin reciting for anyone who would listen or was within listening distance the exploits of their days adventure. Where Scurvy's brush with the giant Pike began to grow arms and legs and now turned into a scene from the 1970's movie Barracuda.

As the evening went on, the bars punters started to argue over who was getting to sing next. So, to settle this Agnes suggested they use spin the bottle for the next and subsequent singers. Upon clearing a table a bottle was spun. When the bottle stopped, by some fluke it was pointing at Scurvy who wasn't even involved in the Karaoke. All the people in the pub pointed at Scurvy chanting. 'Ge us a song, ge us a song, ge us a song.'

Scurvy turned around to look behind him only to realise he had been standing with his back to the wall.

Patsy, Smithy, Philip and Pirate were also chanting in unison. ' Ge us a song, ge us a song.'

Realising there was no escape, Scurvy somewhat reluctantly turned to the DJ. 'Oh all right then. What am I singing anyway?'

Grinning the DJ replied. 'The Road to Dundee.'

'What! You must be Joking.' Exclaimed Scurvy in disbelief.

As the music started up and the words came on the screen Scurvy started to sing. 'Cold winter was howling oer moor and oer mountain. Wild was the surge on the dark rolling sea. When I met upon daybreak a bonnie young lassie, who asked me the road and the miles tae Dundee........'

Whilst all attention was focused on Scurvy. Pirate believing he had been unseen by the rest of the divers, quietly sloped off, out of the pub.

Patsy addressing Philip & Smithy as he spied Pirate sloping off nodding towards the door of the pub. 'Where's that slimy old weasel sloping of too?'

Philip replied 'I don't know, but by the furtive look about him. I am willing to bet he's off to Muirhead to try and get his hole with that Big Mac with cheese that he picked up in the Savoy on Saturday night.'

'Big Mac with cheese?' Questioned Patsy.

'Aye well. What we forgot to tell was that we were talking to the fat birds mate on Saturday night. She let it slip that the Big Mac's got a raging yeast infection and she canny get rid of it.' Divulged Smithy.

Grinning Patsy asked. 'Did you tell Pirate that?'

'Na, of course not.' Retorted Philip shrugging his shoulders. 'Fuck him, he's an arsehole.'

Patsy chuckled. 'Ha, I'd love to be a fly on the wall when Delilah cops for that.'

Sniggering Smithy and Philip nodded their heads in agreement.

As Scurvy got to the instrumental before the last verse of the song. He looked down to see a fit, attractive young woman whose hair was long dark and enveloped with soft curls, holding her head in her hands. Kneeling down in front of her, with the microphone in hand he asked. 'Bless you lass, why do you look so sad, do you come from Dundee?'

'To which the young woman looked up at him and replied sarcastically into the microphone for all the pub to hear. 'No son, I can sing.'

For a brief instant, Scurvy was dealt a wounding blow, and simulated this with his fist being stabbed in the heart. The whole pub including the divers, erupted into a roar of laughter.

'Right, you're getting it now.' Turning to the DJ he said. 'Some real music maestro, you know the one.' Scurvy placed the microphone back on the stand. Holding this young woman's gaze he sang an smouldering rendition of Don Williams I recall a gypsy woman.

At the end of the song Scurvy received a round of applause, cheers and wolf whistles of approval. The young woman who had humiliated him earlier came up to him to apologise. 'I think I owe you an apology, that was brilliant.'

Scurvy having now redeemed himself said. 'Thank you but there is no need. The road to Dundee sucks. Can I buy you a drink?'

'Yeh sure.' Replied the young woman. 'A cider and Baby Cham.'

Scurvy & the young woman walked over to the bar where Scurvy gave Agnes the drinks order. 'Agnes, cider and Baby Cham please.'

Agnes never one for missing an opportunity. 'One cider and Baby Cham and what will the lady be drinking?'

'Aye , you never miss a trick do you Agnes.'

Smiling she said 'Well you know how it is Scurvy lad, when you see the target, you just have to fire.'

Enjoying the banter Scurvy replied. 'Southern Comfort and Irn-Bru for me.'

As the night went on, Patsy, Smithy & Philip started drinking games with a couple of the pubs regulars. Smithy had done a hand stand with his back against a wall. Patsy holding a pint of heavy to Smithy's lips was trying somewhat successfully to drink it whilst upside down. Much to the hilarity and chanting from others in the pub.

Scurvy smoothly whispered to the young woman. 'Things are starting to get silly. This might be a good time to thin out and fuck off whilst their attentions are focused on Smithy. Cause if we don't, I'll end up getting dragged into this.'

The young woman looked deeply and sultry into Scurvy's eyes and said. 'Your place or mine? I live just around the corner in Berkeley street.'

'Yours then it's nearer.' Said Scurvy in agreement.

With that, the two left the pub. Scurvy turned to look back at the circus as he walked through the door. He smiled and gave Philip a nod and a wink who reciprocated the same in return.

CHAPTER 2

The DSV Loch Ranza

HOW SCURVY GOT HIS NAME

Patsy, Smithy, Philip and Scurvy were onboard the good ship Loch Ranza heading doon the Clyde for Port Bannatyne, on the shores of Kames Bay on the Isle of Bute. The job, to demolish a derelict, old wooden pier which had been condemned.

The DSV Loch Ranza was the company's dive support vessel. Originally built by the Lighthouse Authority for performing crew transfers and resupply to Scotland's inshore lighthouses. She was about 45ft in length, had a dark blue painted hull with fine lines, heavy built of a carvel planking design. Her superstructure consisted of a two tone painted steel wheel house. There was a raised coach roof behind over the engine room, which housed the legendary Gardener 6LXB marine diesel engine.

Mounted onto the coach roof aft was an orange painted steel box section framework. This provided a mounting frame for a winch wire pulley system that led over the stern. This would raise and lower a steel cage that the diver would stand in to transport him to and from the seabed or act as a work platform for him in mid water. However today, the cage would be lowering and raising a special piece of equipment for the diver. On the port and starboard side of the wheelhouse was a set of bull horns on which two divers umbilical were wound in figure of 8 fashion.

Patsy was at the helm, with Philip chilling out on a bench in the back. Scurvy and Smithy were hanging out by the port and starboard doorways taking in the fresh air. It was a bonny day, clear skies, bright sunshine, a flat calm sea and stunning scenery. It was quite sublime.

'So whose is this mob that we are going to bail out then?' enquired Smithy.

'BBDS and were not bailing them out.' Replied Patsy. 'We've been sub contracted by them because they are busy on the Skye bridge project.'

'What does BBDS stand for?' Enquired Smithy'.

'Bluff, bullshit & downright shoddy.' Replied Scurvy cheekily.

Patsy, looked at Scurvy as if he was looking over an imaginary pair of spectacles, correcting him reproachfully.

'Brian Bullock Diving Services.'

Scurvy with a grin. 'Aye, that's what I said.'

Then casting a stern look over at Smithy, Patsy warned. 'And I want you on your best behaviour. Brian's going to be there himself to oversee the operation.'

'Smithy replied pretending to be offended. 'What are you looking at me like that for?'

'I mean it. Brian's a hard bastard, he's been around. For by, if this goes well we'll get more work from him.' Said Patsy trying to be serious for a minute.

Philip chirped in. 'Aye, he's some man for one man is Brian. A legend in his own lunchtime, or so he have you believe anyway.'

'Dinna you start Philip.' Said Patsy trying to remain serious. 'I don't want you stirring it and I don't care what you think of him. Brian's got a lot of work on now, but he's not got the divers or the kit to meet the demand. We could do well out of this providing you lot don't go noising him up.'

Philip wanted to return the conversation to a more jovial tone and to quench the thirst of a curiosity. Changing the subject of the conversation to Smithy, who was sporting a beauty of a black eye. A question which had been on everyone's lips and had just been waiting for the right moment to be asked.

'So Smithy, are you going to enlighten us as to how you got that magnificent black eye?'

Smithy answered whilst trying to be coy and nonchalant about his second prize. 'Eh, oh it was nothing really, I eh walked into a eh, cupboard door.'

Patsy wasn't accepting this for a minute. 'Aye, cupboard door was it.... bit of an old chestnut that one. Do you really think we came doon the Clyde in the proverbial tinny? Go on, try again. What really happened?'

Smithy knowing that the game was up from the start spilled the beans. 'Oh fuck, all right. I suppose you will find out soon enough. Well you know how Brenda from the grocers next door was saying about her washing machine leaking water. Well I stopped in after work on Saturday to have a look at it for her. I dragged the machine out and whilst I was bending down to take the back cover off, she made a comment about me having a big arse. So I stood up, turned around and dropped my breeks and my skants and said to her with my hands on my hips. It takes a heavy hammer to drive in a long nail.'

The guys started laughing then Philip asked. 'So what was her response to that?'

'Well initially she was like a rabbit caught in a cars headlights. You know, frozen with the wide eyed stare and her mouth open. Then I might add, I saw a cheeky little grin starting to form at the corners of her mouth.' Replied Smithy.

Scurvy interjected. 'Oh man. That's class and they say romance is dead.'

Smithy continued with his tale. 'Aye well, it was somewhat short lived, because what I didn't know was that Shuggie was had been upstairs having a cat nap. And it was just at that moment that he appeared at the kitchen door. Next thing I knew, I was flat on my arse and my face was throbbing.'

'So what happened then?' Asked Scurvy sniggering.

'Fuck all.' Replied Smithy. 'I went scurrying for the door like a bat out of hell, with ma troosers and skants at ma ankles before he could get the boot in.'

Patsy shaking his head, 'Your fucking mad ya big dafty. It is just as well you're out here with us. It'll keep you clear from Shuggie's for a few days till he calms doon and forgets about it.'

Smithy asked. 'Do you think he will?'

'Fuck aye.' Replied Patsy. 'Anyway, with Shuggie it's a bit like the pot calling the kettle black. He's in no position to get steamed up about it. He's always on the shag when he's out delivering groceries and Brenda knows it too. Aye, you will probably still end up getting your hole off her yet!'

Smithy wondering with a bit of hope. 'Do you think?'

'Is the Pope Catholic?' Replied Patsy. 'Anyway, I saw her up the Savoy on Saturday night and she told me all about it. Aye, you're still in there big man. For by, it's no Shuggie I'd be worried about. It's your Francis I'd be more concerned about. If she ever finds out what you did, it will be curtains for you ma lad.'

'You wanker, you mean you knew all the time.' Said Smithy in surprise.

Patsy grinning giving Smithy a wink. 'You'll need to get up very early in the morning to get one past me Smithy. Speaking of Francis, what story did you give her?'

Smithy thinking he had been clever. 'I told her Scurvy was taking the valve off a cylinder, but it was still slightly pressurised and it fired out on the last thread, shot across the room and hit me in the eye.'

On hearing this, Scurvy was not impressed. 'You said what! Thanks a bunch, not only am I now implicated in this menagerie but Francis is going to think I am a complete fucking nugget as well. Could you not have come up with a story that didn't involve me. Like; you walked into a fucking cupboard door. Ya prick. Oh sweet Jesus mother of God. Semper im excretia solemn propondum variat.'

'Smithy I'll give you some advice.' Continued Scurvy. 'See in future, if you're going to implicate someone in your alibi, one, don't make it me and two be sure to fucking tell them about it first!'

'Scurvy's right.' Said Patsy in agreement 'You would have been better off telling Francis that you walked into a cupboard door. Now, if you had said it was Pirate who was taking the valve off under pressure.... well that would have been believable.'

As the Loch Ranza motored into Kames Bay on the Isle of Bute, Brian Bullock came out to meet them in a RIB. He acted as Pilot and guided them over to the old wooden pier that was to be demolished.

Corralling the pier and acting as an exclusion zone, was a containment boom similar to that used for containing oil spills at sea. On the adjoining stone built quay sat a road crane with a 30m extendable boom. The Loch Ranza dropped her fore and aft anchors so as to lie off parallel to the end of pier.

Brian Bullock came alongside the Loch Ranza and shouted to Scurvy. 'Take a haud of this line laddie!'

Scurvy grabbed the RIB's painter line and made it fast to a cleat amidships on the Loch Ranza's gunnels.

Brian Bullock was a broad shouldered, foreboding, giant of a man. Six foot four inches in his stocking soles. Built like a brick shit house, bald as a billiard ball, a head like a farmers bull. With a loud, deep, hard sounding voice to match.

Climbing aboard the Loch Ranza, he was met by Patsy and they shook hands. Brian had a handshake with a grip of death. Patsy introduced Smithy and Scurvy. Philip he already knew.

'How was your trip here, you had fine weather for it?' Brian asked.

'Aye. It's been bonny Brian, just sublime. Acknowledged Patsy, 'It's been plain sailing all the way.'

'That's grand.' Replied Brian.' Well, we'll no waste ony time. Basically, as you can see the top side work is already done. All you've got to do is dredge doon a foot or so below the seabed for each pile.'

'Then starting with the piles on the outer reaches of the pier working your way in towards the middle. You will place the special shaped explosive charges down into the excavated area at the bottom of the piles. They have their own built in sandbag moulded over the top of the charge to keep them weighted down into the hole, and so as reduce the vertical speed of the shockwave. We don't want locals complaining about the noise.'

'For the divers and everyone else's safety, the blast initiation of the explosives will be fired with a non electric detonator connected with Shocktube. Four piles will be connected in parallel, fed from one surface initiator. There will be a quarter second delay between each detonation. Each explosive charge consists of 800grams NEQ*(g-317)* of PETN*(g-318)*. It's safe enough to handle, just don't go banging it about unnecessarily. We will blow the piles at high tide so as to maximize the force of the shock wave and reduce the sound from the blast.'

'Oh and wan other thing, when handling this stuff, if you see me running, try to keep up.'

'You will need to, sling and buoy the piles before cutting them, for this is Greenheart timber. It's so dense that it sinks. We've slung the first 6 for you. Once the piles are cut, you will hook them up to the crane. It will lift them out the water for transport to the mainland for recycling into fire place mantles, garden furniture and such like.'

'Och aye man. It's child's play. A walk in the park for Scurvy and Philip here. Patsy Assured him. Then taking charge Patsy set his team to work. 'Well lads, don't hang about, you heard the man. You're not out here on a stipend from the tourist board to take in the scenery.'

'I don't want to hear you down that back deck babbling. The only thing I want to hear next is Splash.'

It was common practice for this type of excavation operation to be done with an airlift*(8-333)*. However, it is difficult to control where the exhaust spoil from an airlift would end up and in this case, it could end up backfilling the areas that you had previously dredged. So, for this operation, Brian Bullock had provided the divers with a hydraulically driven underwater dredge pump which meant that the spoil could be exhausted away from the pier. It was also easier on the diver to manipulate the suction hose especially around the piles, than what it was to try to manoeuvre a 3m long, 15cm diameter aluminium dredge pipe of an airlift.

The dredge pump and its 20m length of 100mm diameter reinforced plastic suction hose was secured in the divers basket. It was lowered over the stern of the Loch Ranza about 2meters below the surface. The boat was about 4 meters out from the middle of the pier with the spoil exhaust hose pointing out into the bay away from the pier.

Suited and booted, with pre-dive checks completed. Scurvy strode of the side of the Loch Ranza hitting the water with a splash. Dropping below the surface with a flurry of bubbles rising up from around him. He inflated his drysuit slightly to give him some buoyancy. Smithy held him tight on his umbilical as Patsy passed down the end of the dredge hose.

Venting the air from his drysuit Scurvy descended to the seabed and made his way over to the pier. For the dredging works he would start with the furthest away pile in the middle of the pier and work his way backwards. Then do the same again dredging all the piles to his left and then all come back to the middle and do all the piles to his right.

With the water being shallow on the cusp of a high tide and about to turn, the visibility was really good. He could see from the seabed to the surface and for about seven meters or so ahead of him. The seabed around the base of the piles was mostly course sand, with some pebbles, assorted small shellfish and patches of seaweed.

As with all piers, it had become a haven for small fish and associated sea creatures. Various species of crabs, winkles and welk's. Tompot Blenny's, Ballan and the colourful Rainbow Wrasse, small shrimps, anemones, assorted starfish, squat lobsters, limpets and sea urchins were in plentiful supply. Quite a hive of life all going about their daily affairs, completely oblivious to the fact that with a bang they were going to lose this artificial reef that had provided a sanctuary for little sea creatures since 1857.

Once in position at his start point, Scurvy called to Patsy. 'Diver 1 to Surface over.'

Patsy at the ready replied. 'Surface from Diver 1 go ahead.'

'Diver in Position switch on the pump.' Informed Scurvy. 'Let's see what this Hoover can do.'

Smithy opened the hydraulic supply to the underwater dredge pump.

'Surface to Diver 1. Your live.' Confirmed Patsy.

After a couple of seconds, the sand and everything else in the nozzles path started to be sucked up rapidly into the mouth of the hose. For it then to be ejected out of the back of the eductor pump, relocating the little sea creatures it sucked up in the process some 20 meters or so away, from what had been their home into the open plain of the bay.

'Diver 1 to surface, it's working well. If it all continues like this we'll be finished dredging today ready for blasting to tomorrow.' Scurvy said confidently.

Meanwhile, back at the GDMC office in Glasgow. Pirate was doing a dodgy deal with an equally dodgy character called Kenny (or Kenny the Con as he was referred to by anyone who knew him) for a second hand Mercedes car that Kenny had acquired for sale.

During the conversation, Pirate kept rubbing his crotch and wincing.

Kenny knew exactly how to push Pirates buttons. 'She's a fuckin beauty Pirate. It's only once in a blue moon that an opportunity like this comes along. A Merc 190E, in Gold too. Just your favourite colour if my memory serves me correctly. It's less than 4 years old and a bargain price to match.'

Pirate who himself was forever on the scam and as such was wary of Kenny, thinks he has seen this car before.

'Aye it is that. This car looks overly familiar? But I smell a rat. What's the catch and how did you come by it?'

Kenny who had an answer for everything replied. 'Aye its true what everyone says. There's no flies on you Pirate and you're right to recognise it, because it's usually parked a couple of streets down outside Caddona's Café. It belonged to old man Caddona. Well you know he died a couple of weeks ago.

'Fuck so it is.' Said Pirate recognising it now. 'So how come you've got and why are you no keeping it for yourself?'

The astute Kenny was ready for his question. 'Well the Caddona's and I go back a long way and old Caddona's widow, well she disn'y drive. So she asked me if I could sell it for her. She is jist wantin a quick sale hence the bargain price. As for me, ah couldn'y afford to run a car like this. Whereas a wealthy diving company Director like yourself could.'

Pirate gave Kenny a distrusting look.

'Why do you keep rubbing your crotch when you're talking to me, gony stop it, that's worrying man.' Said Kenny somewhat disturbed by this inescapable observation. Kenny continued with his sales pitch, which was that of a self assured seasoned con man.

'Look if you don't believe me you can ask the widow herself. Logbook and everything's there. And old man Caddona kept it fully serviced at Henderson's. Anyway, it's yours for seven & half grand.'

'Just think, It won't just be Philip with a Merc now. And it's only fittin with you being a Director of a Diving Company that you should be seen drivin aboot in a classy car like this. As opposed to that battered old Volkswagen estate.'

'I mean, it's no right that one of your employees has a better car than you. Is it now? Of course its no.'

A look of deluded glee come across Pirates face. 'Aye your right it's no.' Said Pirate in agreement. 'I'll gee ye three & a half for it.'

Kenny with a twinkle in his eye, knowing he had Pirate hooked, entered into the negotiation process. 'No chance a belter of car like this six seven fifty. You're pushing your luck at that. Think of the poor widow.' He said throwing in the sympathy card.

'Poor widow my arse. It's your commission you're crying over, four five.' Retorted Pirate not entertaining the sympathy plea for a second.

'I'll tell you what Pirate seeing as how we go back quite a bit, just for you six two fifty. I canny go any lower than that.' Returned Kenny, now playing the old friend's card.

Pirate thinking he had the upper hand
'Five Five that's my final offer, take or leave it.'

Kenny the sly, wily fox that he was, sensed closure was near. 'Fuck sake Pirate. That disny leave anything in the deal for me. It's no gony be worth ma while trying to sell it at that. I've got expenses too ye know. Tell you what seeing as how were old pals, for auld time's sake Five six fifty cash on the nail and you throw in that Avon dry suit that you've got through the back and you can have the car today.'

'But that's it. If you don't want it at that I'll take it elsewhere. And you'll jist have to watch in envy as Philip drives about in his Mercedes while you drive about in that battered auld Volkswagen estate.' Said Kenny knowing that he had landed his fish.

Thinking he's got a bargain and with a smug look on his face Pirate closed the deal. 'Aye okay done.' And shook hands on the deal with Kenny. 'Wait here, I'll get the cash.'

'Would ye stop rubbing your crotch and wash your hands before you get the cash.' Demanded Kenny.

As Kenny watched Pirate go downstairs into the basement to where the safe was to get his cash. He turned away and said quietly to himself with a grin. 'Done.... Aye ye huv been.'

Back onboard the Loch Ranza, it was approaching 4.30pm, Brian Bullock decided to call a halt to the days operations. 'Patsy, it'll be dark in a about an hour, so get your diver on deck and we'll call it a day'

'Perfect timing. 'Patsy replied. 'Scurvy has just finished dredging the last Pile.'

'I've booked you all into the Royal Hotel, it's just at the end of the Pier there. Brian informed him. 'I'm off; I'll see you all in the bar for around seven thirty with drinks at the ready. The first two rounds are on me.'

'Aye right you are Brian, we'll be there washed and polished.' Acknowledged a happy Patsy with a smile.

With that, Brian took off in his RIB for the shore.

'Smithy.' Shouted Patsy. Switch of the power pack and get ready to bring up Scurvy. It's playtime and Brian's buying!'

'Surface to Diver 1 over.' Patsy called over the coms.

'Diver 1 to Surface, go ahead over.' Replied Scurvy.

'Diver, return to surface, games over for the day. Brian's getting the drinks in.' Patsy informed him.

No sooner had Patsy finished his sentence, Scurvy had popped up on the Surface and said over the coms. 'Don't hang about man, get us out.'

Philip had already started de-kitting. As Smithy hauled in Scurvy's umbilical, Patsy was hauling up the dredge pump and it's hoses. Scurvy climbed back aboard the Loch Ranza via a steel open framed boarding ladder that had been lowered over the side for him. As Smithy removed his band mask*(1-321)* Scurvy looked at him smiling and said 'Party time.'

The lads trooped into the bar of the hotel at 7.30pm on the dot to be greeted by a loud and obnoxious Brian Bullock who was full of the drink. On seeing the divers he shouted across to them. 'Over here lads.' Then turning to the bar maid he said. 'Get them all a drink, these lads did a fine job today especially this one.' Clapping Scurvy on the back.

Brian pushed a young local man out of the way who had been standing at the bar next to him, then without fear Brian loudly announced. 'Make space for some real men. They're no like you sheep shaggers, choochters and porridge wogs.'

Then addressing an elderly but distinguished man, who appeared fit, of a lean, and wiry build, who had been standing to the right of Brian and who hadn't moved. Brian demanded. 'Here you ya old Porridge Wog slide oot the way and let these real men into the bar!'

The old man, totally unphased by the roar from this obnoxious giant calmly turned to face Brian and said. 'I have been more than tolerant of your rude, obnoxious, behaviour and foul, offensive language. But I consider it an insult and take great offence at being referred to as a Porridge Wog.'

To which the very drunk and bold Brian Bullock replied whilst making a circular movement with his finger pointing at his own face. 'Eh, is this the face of concern and what the fuck are you gony dae aboot it?'

Politely but with an air of self assured confidence the old man said. 'Well, if you would care to step outside, I'll show you. There we can resolve this matter in a more gentlemanly fashion.'

Scurvy sensing a opportunity to make some easy money turned to the guys and said. 'Here lads, do you want to make this interesting?'

Philip replied. 'Aye, what have you got in mind?'

Scurvy touted. 'A tenner says the old fella will floor the big man.'

Philip laughed and said. 'Are you wise? I'll take them odds. I've seen the big man in action.'

Patsy and Smithy decided to ride the bus with Philip on the bet.

'Right then Choochter.' Said the bold Brian. 'lead the way.'

As the old man turned to walk to the door, Brian with all his size and might, cowardly hit the old man with a rabbit punch to the back of the neck.

The old man, stopped dead in his tracks. Yet unfaltered and unphased he turned around to face the dishonourable back stabbing Brian.

Cooley, calmly, and firmly he said. 'That was extremely underhand and not what I would consider gentlemanly fashion.'

Brian stood there in shock and surprise, his legs starting to tremble with the colour draining from his face. The old man punched Brian square on the chin with a body twisting upper cut, which had the effect of Brian taking flight doing the flying angel backwards. To then come crashing down on the pub floor, leaving Brian sparkled.

Patsy, Philip and Smithy looked on in awe. Scurvy impressed by the old man, was also very pleased with himself, for he was now £30 up. Philip asked Scurvy. 'What made you so sure about the old fella?'

Scurvy took his winnings from the guys. With a smile and a wink he replied. 'I have done more than being a diver.'

Patsy, Smithy and Philip picked up the now blabbering and dazed Brian Bullock and sat him down on a bench seat in a corner of the bar.

Scurvy approached the old man and said to him smiling. 'Excuse me sir, I have just had a bit of a wager with my friends here over your affray. As result, I am now thirty quid up. I would like to use some of my winnings to stand you a drink or three in good favour, to show you that not all divers are Fuckwits.'

The old man welcomed the friendly gesture and asked. 'What's your name young man?'

'Scurvy.' Replied Scurvy.

'Scurvy eh? Well Scurvy, how could I refuse such a polite and honest gesture? A Macallan if you please.'

With a pleasant ambiance now restored to the Pub. They all sat down together, settled around a table with their drinks. With an air of genuine curiosity, the old man asked. 'Scurvy, I presume isn't the name you were given at birth.'

Scurvy shaking his head replied with a smile. 'No.'

'So how did you end up being called Scurvy?' Enquired the old man.

'Well, there's a story to that.' Replied Scurvy. 'But it's not what you're thinking.'

'Oh and what I am thinking?' Challenged the old man.'

'Your thinking I'm called Scurvy because I got the Clap from shagging some dirty slapper. You couldn't be more wrong if you tried. I've never had a sexually transmitted disease in my life.' Said Scurvy with some pride.

'Well that did cross my mind.' Admitted the old man. 'Go on then, I'm intrigued. You have my full and undivided attention.'

As Scurvy started to narrate his story, the whole pub had gone quite and everyone listened in. 'It all started on a cold September's morning in 1991. We got a call out by 3C's Ltd. A Glasgow based Construction Company, which, by their letterhead reads Campbell's Construction Company Ltd.'

'Or Cunts, Cowboys and Chancers by anyone else that knows them.' Chimed up Patsy, Smithy & Philip in unison.

Scurvy smiling and nodding his head in agreement continued on with his story. 'Anyway, Strathclyde Waterways were privatising certain aspects of their operation. Part of which were the motorway storm drains, which capture the run off rainwater from the roads and allow it to flow down to the Clyde. Well, one of them failed a flow test. We were called into to investigate and rectify the problem. It turned out it was under an embankment for the M8 motorway just before the road joins the Dean Park at the Hillington flyover.'

'3C's had excavated the embankment to expose a concrete storm drain pipe about a meter in diameter. Using a Stihl saw, they cut an access opening out the top so as to allow us to get in with our gear.'

'Smithy here was Supervising and Philip and I entered into the storm drain wearing Aga sets*(4-327)* with life lines. You know the same gear that the Police divers use. We made our way along it. About 12m in we came up inside a huge rectangular concrete manifold section, that three other concrete pipes of the same size connected into. It was 1.5meters high inside the manifold. We were now actually under the motorway. The manifold wasn't actually fully flooded and the water was only about 1meter deep. The water was near freezing and was as black as molasses due to the amount of sediment that was suspended in it. We had 150watt underwater lights but the sediment was so dense that the light stopped at the lens. As you can imagine, it wasn't a pleasant place to be in.'

'Apparently, when the manifold had been built they had used timber shoring for the framework, which they hadn't removed. Over the years, this timber had decayed and had now collapsed creating a dam. As a result, all the dust and dirt washed off from the motorway and was no longer able to flow away to the Clyde. So for around 23 years, it had been building up into huge mounds, which was now restricting the flow of water.'

'So the remedy was fairly straightforward. Remove the rotted timber, bucket and bag the silt and dump it outside the culvert. Where the guys from 3C's would then dump it into the skip that they had onsite.'

'So there we were filling sacks with silt and dragging them out. It was just before we stopped for lunch when it happened.'

'I felt something tugging at my dry suit boot and then the near freezing water started to seep in. I reached down to try to feel what it was when I then felt something tugging at my hand. Because my hands were numb with the cold I couldn't feel any sensation. Just this tugging.'

'I brought my hand to the surface and here was there not a Rat*(13-344)* hanging off the end of my fingers gripped on with its teeth.'

'Fuck, you should have heard me, I screamed like a girl. For I hate rats, I means ooh.' And Scurvy shivered. 'I hate rats.'

'Wow.' Said the old man in surprise, 'What did you do?' He asked curiously.

'I shook this thing for dear life but the bugger just wouldn't let go. It just looked at me with its black beady eyes. So I smacked it off the manifold wall. It let go then. Dropped into the water, came to the surface, shook its head, drew me a dirty look and then swam off.'

'At first Smithy and Philip here were quite concerned when they heard me scream. But soon found it highly entertaining when they realised the cause of my distress had been a rat.'

Smithy and Philip were now sniggering like cheeky children.

Scurvy continued with his story. 'Well when we stopped for lunch, I striped off my dry suit to the waist. It was then I realised I had been sweating like an Alabama cotton picker on a white rape charge. But all the time I thought it was just because I was working so hard in the culvert.'

'Well, we finished the job around four o'clock. Smithy had received a message from Patsy asking if we would go down to the docks as the "Loup de Mere" which was berthed in the East India harbour, had taken a rope round her prop. The skipper had left fifty quid behind the bar for us if we would take it off for him that night.'

In the hotel bar everyone was intrigued with Scurvy's story and were listening intently.

'So we did the job. Well, fifty quid goes a long way in the Marine Bar. It was while we were in the bar that I felt this tingling sensation in my hand, which had now turned all blotchy and pink. Also I became aware of a thin red track leading off from my hand up onto my forearm.'

'But now having had a few sherbets in me, I just laughed it off. The story of my encounter with the rat being was told around the bar and my pink blotchy hand became the cause of much hilarity and amusement. This ended up with Angela the barmaid ringing the bar bell shouting unclean, unclean bring out your dead every time I went to the bar for a drink.'

'Well, when I woke up the next morning I felt really ill. The tracking in my arm was spreading. But now, I also had this tracking going up my leg from my foot. The Lymph gland at the top of my thigh had swollen into a big pain full lump. It was like having a third ball only the size of a table tennis ball. It was quite discerning. So I phoned work to say that I would be late in and went to see the doctor.'

To say that there was now an air of trepidation amongst the bar's ensemble would not be an exaggeration.

'When the doctor examined me after hearing my story she insisted on getting a second opinion from her colleague. It transpired that what I had was lymphadenitis and Cellulitis basically blood poisoning. However, because it had progressed so far and so quickly, she put me on a massive dose of penicillin to try and halt the spread. She told me to come back first thing the next morning for a check up.'

Later that evening I started to develop a goose bump type rash all over my arms. When I went back to the doctors the following day she told me that my body had rejected the penicillin because I was so weak. So she put me on Erythromycin antibiotic tablets. She told me if it got any worse I would need to go to hospital to get intravenous antibiotic treatment. But the first sign of it getting any worse-straight to casualty.'

'So I went home straight to bed. Well later that evening I was in some considerable pain. I was struggling to breath and was feeling incredibly weak. Bearing in mind that this was a Saturday night, I thought to myself casualty will be heaving with the walking wounded from the pub fights, well I was living in Paisley at the time. So I thought I would just wait till the morning and go then.'

'But by 10pm I was in so much pain that I could barely see straight. So I got a taxi and booked myself into casualty.'

After waiting in casualty for almost an hour I was eventually seen by a casualty nurse. A cocky gob shite bastard I should point out. Whom when I told him that the GP said I should come here, his response was" "Fucking GP's they think we've got nothing better to do with our time than to treat their patients." Bearing in mind that I was near dead on my feet at this point and in and out of consciousness.'

'However, when the duty doctor saw me and heard my story, he had me put on a stretcher straight away and sent me for a full set of chest X-rays and then sent up to quarantine. I had a room all to myself; it had a big plain glass window with curtains and a vase with plastic flowers in it. The room door had a coded lock on it.'

'It had just gone midnight when the nurses were taking my personal details and getting me hooked up to an antibiotic drip. One of them said happy birthday. For it had just turned thirteenth of September, my birthday. I stayed in quarantine for a few days until they were satisfied that what I had was not contagious. They then moved me into a ward for a week or so until I was well enough to be discharged.

'While I was in the ward Philip, Smithy and Patsy came to visit. It was then that Patsy nicknamed me Scurvy. I kept the name because I had become very complacent with life. Typical diver, thick as fuck. You see, I wasn't going to go to the hospital that night. I only went because I thought my GP would be very annoyed with me if I hadn't gone. The toxicologist assigned to my case told me that had I not received intravenous treatment when I did. I would have passed out and died in my sleep shortly afterwards that night. I wouldn't have seen my birthday. So Scurvy, I became. I kept the name as a constant reminder to guard against complacency. For no matter what I experience in life now, if I am unsure I am no longer complacent. I check and double check. I don't leave room for complacency anymore.'

Everyone in the bar was now in awe of this young man. The old man sitting with them said. 'Well Scurvy young man, that was most illuminating. I'm pleased to hear that you've learned from your experience. And your right in what you said earlier this evening, not all divers are Fuckwits. But I think your man here, (pointing to Brian who was only now just gaining full consciousness) is.'

    Scurvy, turning around to look at Brian replied. 'I couldn't agree with you more.' Scurvy pointing to the old man's empty glass asked. 'Another Macallan?'

    'If you please.' The old man replied.

    At the bar the Scurvy eyed up the barmaid. 'Another round please and whatever you fancy yourself.' The barmaid looked Scurvy up and down with a smouldering sultry eye.

    After a few more drinks, Smithy and Patsy picked up Brian with his arms around each of their shoulders. He was still a bit dazed as they carried him off to his room. All the while Brian kept mumbling and slavering. 'I'm alright, I'm all right.'

'Of course you are.' Said Patsy 'Here we go now, off to the land of nod. with you.'

Back inside the bar Scurvy took his leave. 'Well if you'll excuse gentlemen, I must take my leave for I have an early start in the morning.'

The old man, smiled. 'It's been a pleasure talking to you Scurvy. I'll not tell you to take care for I know that you will, and thanks for the Macallan.'

Scurvy replied. 'Likewise, it's been a pleasure and you're more than welcome. It was the least I could do to make up for our man there. I'll not tell you to take care because I know that you can. That's a fair right uppercut you've got. Good luck to you.'

'Aye and you Scurvy lad.'

The two men shook hands and went their separate ways. Scurvy went off with the barmaid, who has now just finished her shift.

The next morning, Smithy was in the RIB lowering a plastic crate containing four of the explosive charges down to Philip who was on the seabed at the end of the pier.

Gently Philip placed the four explosive charges neatly into place around each of the piles. Ensuring they were sitting low down in the excavations that Scurvy had created the day before. At the same time being careful not to damage the Shocktube and its connections.

Originally, the task that Smithy was now performing was to have been done by Brian Bullock. However, Brian was curled up on the back deck of the Loch Ranza with his head in his hands. Still quite the worse for wear. Nursing a colourful, very badly bruised and painful swollen jaw as well enduring the mother of all hangovers. Therefore, was of little use to anyone including himself.

Once all the explosive charges were securely in place Philip returned to the Loch Ranza. Today, Scurvy was wearing an Aga set*(4-327)* acting as standby diver. Once Philip was onboard, Scurvy removed his Aga Set and Patsy fired up the boats engine. Scurvy raised the anchors and then Patsy took the Loch Ranza 75m away from the pier, out into the bay. They dropped the bow anchor again.

Smithy who was in the RIB now motored slowly out to meet them. The Shocktube that was connected to the explosive charges was on a drum reel. Smithy carefully fed it off the drum laying it out in the water as he made his way out to where the Loch Ranza was anchored and tied up alongside.

Patsy contacted the security team ashore on the radio to let them know that they were ready for blasting.

After closing the barriers to the road, they called back to gave Patsy the green light to continue.

Patsy passed over the initiator and primer cartridge for the Shocktube to Smithy who loaded the cartridge into the initiator and connected it up to the Shocktube. He then called Scurvy over and said to him. 'In recognition of you saving our name and good relations with the locals last night. You can have the honour of firing the first set of explosive charges.'

Smithy then handed the initiator to Scurvy who was sporting a huge smile.

Patsy sounded one long blast on the boats fog horn, which was the standard warning agreed with the local authorities and the shore team that they were going to detonate the explosive.

Scurvy removed the safety pin from the initiator and upon releasing the firing pin there was a loud bang and a bright flash of light as the Shocktube was initiated and shot out the end of the initator. Followed virtually immediately by four dull bangs in rapid succession. Four flumes of water and mass flurries of bubbles appeared on the surface followed by four piles starting to topple over and sink to the seabed below.

Patsy then gave 3 short blast on the Loch Ranza's fog horn to single the all clear. He then shouted over to Scurvy. 'Hey Scurvy, you don't get to do that in an office job eh.'

'Indeed you do not.' Replied Scurvy still sporting a massive grin that near took over his whole face.

Brian Bullock was unable to take any joy at all out of the event. In actual fact, he would probably had welcomed death at this point if it were to take away the misery from his current pain and suffering. Unfortunately for him, another ten sets of these explosions would take place before the day would be done.

That evening in his hotel room Patsy was on the phone to Belinda who was the company secretary. 'Yeh, okay, I've got that Belinda. I will head back tomorrow morning. I'll be on the 8am ferry to Wemyss Bay. I'll get the train connection to Port Glasgow and pick up my car from the dock. Make an appointment with him for 11am tomorrow. Tell him I'll meet him at his office.' Instructed Patsy.

'What about the boat and the job?' asked Belinda. 'The jobs almost done, they'll be finished by tomorrow afternoon, It's just clearing up operations now. The guys will manage that on their own.' Replied Patsy.

After the call, Patsy went down stairs to meet the guys in the bar. 'Slight change in plan lads.' Patsy announced. 'I'm heading back to Glasgow first thing in the morning.'

'Oh, so what the rush to get back to Glasgow?' Enquired Smithy.

'I've got to go and price up another job tomorrow. It's at the sewerage treatment plant at Dalmuire Quay.'

'What's the job?' Enquired Scurvy, not relishing the thought of working inside the big jobby tanks.

'Don't actually know, they weren't too keen to tell Belinda very much about it over the phone. But I'll find out soon enough though.' Replied Patsy, who didn't really care as he would be sending in Philip or Scurvy to do any shitty work pardon the pun.

'So Philip, you're in charge' Announced Patsy. 'And if anyone asks, Brian was Supervising whilst you were setting the explosive charges, okay doke.'

'Yeh, okay doke, it's fine by me. Sure it's not the first time we've worked with a man or two short.' Philip agreed smiling.

'You should be finished tomorrow by about 2pm, then steam back at your leisure to Port Glasgow. 'I'll see you all back in the office on Thursday morning, bright eyed and bushy tailed.' Said Patsy.

Early the following morning, on Rothesay pier. Patsy walked up the gangplank to board the Caledonian McBrayne ferry MV Saturn, bound for Wemyss Bay.

The MV Saturn was the youngest of three car passenger ferries of that time which operated successfully on the Clyde. The other two were named Jupiter and Juno.

The MV Saturn

Saturn had been Clyde built by the Ailsa Ship building company of Troon in 1977. These sister ships had earned a nickname of the 'Clyde Streakers'. Instead of conventional propellers, all three of these ships had two fore and aft Voith Schnieder units *(g-319)*.

This propulsion system made these ships fast and highly manoeuvrable compared to other vessels of the day. This greatly reduced sailing and turnaround times. So begs the question; Now in 2023, given the current Scottish ferry building fiasco, what did they know about building ships on the Clyde back in the 1970's that they have forgotten about today?

CHAPTER 3

A Great Leveller Amongst Men

Patsy called round to Scurvy's flat to pick him up on the way to the office. 'Scurvy ma lad, it's a cold one this morning.' Said Patsy greeting him with a smile.

'Aye, but it's a crisp fresh kind of cold. I like that. It means it'll be a good day on the water.' Acknowledged Scurvy.

'Were going to be pretty busy for the next few weeks Scurv, so we'll be taking on some extra divers to help us out.' Patsy informed him. 'So eh... Billy and Burt will be joining us for a short while.' Replied Patsy.

'Who Bodged It & Scarper, You've got to be fucking joking. Ones an idiot head case the others a fechan eejit.' Retorted Scurvy in disapproval.

'Aye, you're awfully harsh on them Scurvy. You want to cut them some slack man. We know that eh they're not eh .....how shall we say, overly perfect.' Said Patsy in their defence.

Scurvy with a look of despair and disbelief rolled his eyes and sighed 'God Almighty.'

'You just want to be a little more tolerant with them. A bit more understanding and forgiving for the areas where they're eh ...lacking. For by, they're the only divers we could get at short notice.' Said Patsy trying to make his decision acceptable to Scurvy.

'You mean they're the only ones that'll dive for the poultry remittance that your prepared to pay them.' Replied Scurvy without stopping to think.

'Hey! Just remember who it is that pays your wages. And another thing, they've got the one thing that you've not got. And as there is a good chance that we will get a visit from an HSE inspector. So I am going require to have some genuine certificates on hand.' Quickly responded Patsy, bringing Scurvy into check.

'Oh aye, fair play.' Said Scurvy somewhat sheepishly with his eyes cast downward.

'Good that's settled then cause you're going to meet them at the office. And I want you all to be pals. So to bring us all together, I've booked a table at the Jade Palace for tonight. Think of it as being a team building exercise.' Announced Patsy bringing the conversation back to an amiable tone.

'What about the old adage, never mix business with pleasure?' Questioned Scurvy.

'Total bollocks. Diving is our business and do you not get pleasure out of diving.' Replied Patsy.

Scurvy nodded his head in agreement.

'Well, there you are.' Confirmed Patsy.

As Patsy pulled up to park the car outside the office, Pirate and Smithy had just arrived in front of them in Pirates recently acquired Mercedes.

They greeted each other as they got out their cars. Curiously, Patsy asked Pirate. 'What are you doing driving that?'

Pirate Proudly replied 'Do you like it? It's a beauty isn't it? It's my new car.'

'Aye right, who's it and what are you doing with?' Replied Patsy in disbelief.

'No seriously!' Pirate said defensively. 'It's mine I bought it from Kenny the other day. I talked him into giving it to me at a knock down price.'

'Kenny! What, not Kenny the Con?' Said Scurvy incredulously. 'You talked him into a knock down price?'

'Now, now young man. Don't be taking that tone. You're not a bad diver Scurvy, I'll give you that. But you just don't know how to go about doing business.' Instructed Pirate.

'Aye well fair enough, maybe not. But I know enough about business to know not to have any dealings with Kenny the Con.' Clarified Scurvy.

'Ignore, him Pirate.' Said Smithy interjecting. 'He's just winding you up. I think it's a smashing car.'

In the GDMC office, Philip, Burt and Billy were there already, the usual pleasantries were exchanged. Smithy put on the kettle and made the coffees. With everyone settled, Patsy divided up the group into two separate squads.

'Smithy, Philip, Billy & Scurvy you go to the East India dry dock. The dock flooded the other night when the gates leaked with the gales. The Arctic Penguin floated of her supports as such they want to get her out of the dock. So you'll need to clear the ways and then inspect her Hull for damage.'

'Then you'll need to clear the entrance to the dock gates. She's been in there for years. There's an old fishing smack sunk in front of the gates, you may need to drag it out the way.'

'The Port Authority has organised a crane and a low loader to take it away if we can get lifting strops under her. You'll be using the Loch Ranza, so everything will be on board that you'll need.'

'Pirate, Burt & I will be at Dalmuire Quay. Apparently the Skipper of the Garroch Head was three sheets to the wind when he brought her alongside and well, miss judged his approached and smashed up some of the Greenheart piles.'

'What again. That man's a liability. But then again he is keeping us in work.' Remarked Smithy.

'That's what I like about you Smithy, you always find the good in all things bad.' Acknowledged Patsy.

'Poofs! You're a bunch of faggot's man. It's no like it's real diving work, no compared to the stuff we used tae do oot in the Persian Gulf.' Ejected an arrogant and offensive Burt Murchison.

Burt was a short wiry man in his mid forties with cropped short brown hair, who didn't have a courteous or descent bone in his body. He was typical of the phrase 'short man syndrome.' Though well balanced, for Burt had a chip against life on both his shoulders.

He was always acting like he was some sort of hard man, gangster come superstar of the diving world. When in actual fact he was just a wee fanny. A last resort hire, detested by everyone who ever had the unfortunate displeasure of him crossing their path. Furthermore, Scurvy was right, he was cheap.

Billy who was known amongst the lads as Silly Billy threw in his two pence worth aiming it at Scurvy. For Billy was Burt's side kick or dog to kick would be a more accurate description. 'Aye, you don't know what real diving work is until you've been out in the Persian Gulf.'

'My, you're ma hero's, your pure dead hard. Can I run about with you? Can I be in your gang?' Scurvy instantly fired back, totally unphased by their big man talk.

'Watch it son, remember I've been in the Gulf.' Responded Burt trying to play up a losing position.

'It's true what they say about "divers memory" because you were just saying that.' Said Scurvy holding his ground.

Patsy cut in quickly so as to stop this from completely unravelling, drawing Scurvy a warning look. 'Hey! Knock it off Scurvy. I think you're the one suffering from divers memory.'

Scurvy backed down without a word.

At the East India dock, Smithy met up with the owner of the Motor Sailing Ship Arctic Penguin and looked her over.

The dry dock was indeed now fully flooded and the ship was now floating. Many of the 200mm diameter timber pit props that had supported and held the ship in position when the dock was empty of water, could now be seen floating about inside the dock.

A large percentage of these pit props were still trapped under the ship's hull. It was the diver's job to clear these out from under the hull. So that they could be removed from the dock and allow the diver to inspect the ship's undersides for damage.

The guys also needed to get the dock gates fully open, so that the ship could be taken out and so as to ensure that the dock remained fully flooded with enough water at all times to prevent the ship from keeling over. Should the now flooded dock start to lose the water from within.

The Arctic Penguin was a thirty meter long, four hundred tonne iron hulled, triple masted, schooner sailing ship. Now modernised, converted to diesel. Originally built in Dublin in 1910 for the Irish Navigation Authority as a lightship. She had a few owners over the years, had seen service as a youth adventure training vessel, then converted to a 20 passenger cruise ship which accidentally sank after hitting a submerged object in the late 1980's.

Salvaged, re-sold and now restored, she was to become a museum piece to be berthed at the pier at Inveraray as a tourist attraction.

Philip, Scurvy and Billy brought the Loch Ranza over and berthed her up alongside the quay next to the dock gates.

Meanwhile, over at Dalmuire Quay, Burt Murchison was being lowered over the side of the quay in a personnel basket. Suited and booted, sporting a bright orange AH3*(2-323)* divers helmet and carrying a hydraulic chainsaw.

On this job they had two cranes. One for the diver's basket, the other for lifting out the damaged section of the large Greenheart pier piles which were about 60cm square.

Here Burt had to cut away the damaged section of pile in preparation for a new section to be installed with a steel case that would join the two sections together and reinforce the joint.

Out of a needs must situation, due to still being one diver shorthanded, Pirate was acting as standby diver. The marine Superintendent for the quay had lent Patsy the services of two stevedores *(g-319)*. They were to assist with rigging, slinging and handling the diver's umbilical and chain saw hydraulic hoses. Patsy Supervising was wearing a Dave Clarke headset so that he could talk to the diver.

'Diver 1 to surface, all stop over.' Growled Burt over the coms.

Patsy signalled to the crane driver who was controlling lowering and lifting of the basket to stop and lock of the crane in that position.

'Surface to diver. All stopped.' Confirmed Patsy.

'Diver to surface starting the cut.' Informed Burt.

So began the arduous task of cutting a large Greenheart pile to square it off after being hit by the MV Garroch Head sewage ship. This had split the pile below the surface when it came into berth a few days previously.

The MV Garroch Head was just one of a fleet of vessels, which for decades took Glasgow's sewage out past Garroch Head Point on the southern tip of the Isle of Bute in the firth of Clyde. Here they would dump the sewage on the outgoing tide.

This operation was performed by coastal cities all around Britain. Originating and first used as a result of an incident on London's River Thames.

These were fair sized ships, almost 100metres in length with a gross weight in excess of 2200 tonnes. The ship's crews often referred to them as the 'Bovril Boats' in relation to the colour of their cargo. However, the people of the Clyde coast affectionally nicknamed them the 'Banana Boats'.

A name created by parents who didn't want to tell their kids that the boats carried the city's sewage, so they told them they carried bananas. Which was actually quite believable as the ships sported a similar livery to the cargo ships that carried Fyffe's Bananas up the Clyde from around the world.

Despite the unpleasant cargo these sludge ships carried, they were spotlessly clean and were well respected in the maritime industry, being without doubt ships to be proud of.

What few people actually knew, was that there was an extremely kindly tradition performed by the Glasgow City Corporation, the Captains and crews of these vessels. A tradition that had being carried out since before the time of the first world war. This was the charitable act of organised day trips of non paying passengers.

These passengers were generally societies elderly who were very poor and would not normally have been able to afford a day trip cruise down the river.

During the later years of world war one, the Banana Boat Shieldhall carried soldiers, sailors and airmen convalescing from their war injuries. The kindly act of the free day trip became extended to other disadvantaged groups in society.

This tradition of providing free daytrips to the disadvantaged in society, injured and disabled soldiers etc continued right up until 1994. When the European Union said that you could not dump sewage at sea anymore.

MV Garroch Head

The result of this was that all of these ships were disbanded and took up new lives performing other tasks all around the world.

Back at the East India dock, Scurvy & Billy were suited up for clearing the pit props from underneath the hull of Arctic Penguin.

Scurvy turned to Billy and asked. 'Billy do you want to clear the ways and do the hull inspection.'

Billy looking at how dark and murky the water was replied. 'Eh no, no it's okay, I don't mind if you do it.'

Scurvy sensing Billy's trepidation replied. 'What's wrong Billy your looking a bit worried? I thought you'd be wanting to show us how it was done. You know demonstrate some of that Persian Gulf oilfield diving.'

Billy tried to bluff his way out of his fear of black water. 'It's like you say Scurvy, I've done all that, whereas you need the experience. This is nothing compared to the Persian Gulf.'

Scurvy, wasn't willing to let go. 'Aye I know what you mean. It's black and murky in there. No like the crystal clear waters of the Gulf eh.'

Billy, now finding himself in a corner, tried to come over all hard. 'Whit are you insinuating? Whit's he saying Philip? You trying to say I'm feart.' Billy then reached for the knife strapped to his thigh. 'Ya goby bastard I'll fuckin show you who's feart!'

Philip quickly intervened to defuse the situation. 'Now now Billy. I'm quite sure Scurvy meant nothing by it. Calm down man. Isn't that right Scurvy?'

Scurvy, totally unfazed and quite amused by Billy's theatricals replied. 'Aye aye, fuck sake man. There's nothing in it. And your right enough, I do need the experience. You just eh, relax man. Sit back and take the money.'

'Fucking right I will.' Grunted a huffy Billy.

Billy who was about as much use as a one legged man in an arse kicking contest acted as standby diver on the surface. Scurvy then descended into the flooded dock. He was wearing an Aga set*(4-327)* SCUBA set*(g-318)* complete with coms link lifeline and an open faced yellow helmet on his head.

The water in the dock was murky but there was about a meter of visibility. However, under the ship it was pitch black with the hull of the ship blocking out all daylight from above. This operation was done largely by touch and the dim glow of an underwater torch.

Starting at the stern of the vessel feeling around the starboard propeller and the rudder he checked for damage and trapped timber. Scurvy made his way very slowly, with his hands outstretched in front feeling his way hand over hand.

For the last thing he wanted to do was to hit his head or face on one of the many submerged pit props that were trapped under the ship's hull. Buoyed up under the water between the centre keel and the bilge keels that ran along the hull on either side of the ship.

This was quite an awkward task to do. For the diver has to swim at a vertical angle and sweep the hull with his hands, feeling between the edge of the bilge keel and the central keel for trapped pit props. Upon finding one, he has to try jam his body against the hull and push the pit prop down and away from the bilge keel so that it can float up to the surface to be recovered by the Philip and Smithy.

Breathing slow and deep, Scurvy made his way along the keel, half an arm's length at time releasing pit props as he found them. Whilst skimming the ship's hull with his gloved hands feeling for damage. Down one side then repeating the process along the other. With a final swim feeling along the central keel of the Hull.

At Dalmuire Quay Patsy recalled Burt to the surface to stop for lunch. The crane fired up its engine and recovered the personnel basket back to the surface.

Slowly hauling it up, swinging it round then gently lowering down onto the quayside. Burt with one hand holding onto the cage and the other holding the hydraulic chainsaw, emulated a picture postcard pose of a surface demand diver.

Patsy removed the Aquadyne helmet(2-323) from Burt and started to unbuckle him from his ARVest. This was a bright orange divers waist coat with built in harness which also supports his bail out cylinder, lead weights and to which his umbilical is attached.

Burt said to him. 'That Greenheart timber is hard stuff.'

Patsy replied. 'Oh aye. It's so dense that it's the only wood that I know that sinks. Watch this.' Patsy cut some slivers from the timber pile and threw them over the side. Sure enough, they sank.

Pirate watching this said 'I would never have believed that wood could sink if I hadn't seen it with my own eyes.'

To which the condescending Burt retorted. 'Aye I've seen that before in the Persian Gulf.'

Patsy and Pirate looked at one another as if to telepathically say. 'What a wanker.'

With the ways cleared for the Arctic Penguin, this task completed. Philip and the crew had also stopped for lunch.

'Here Philip, I'm just going to nip out the dock and across to the shops to get a few things for home.' said Scurvy.

'Aye right you are Scurv.' Acknowledged Philip.

Scurvy was making his way back to the dock when he passed a pharmacy with an advert for Immac in the widow. This was a popular brand of cream at the time used by women for removing unwanted body hair. This gave Scurvy an idea.

Sitting on the dock side, Smithy was griping to Philip about still being hungry after having had his lunch. 'I'm still hungry.' Moaned Smithy.

'You canny be. I've just watched you trough a doner kebab wi' chips, downed with a whole bottle of Irn Bru.' Remarked Philip incredulously. 'Aye I know, I would have been alright if my kebab had been as thick as the girl that served me.' Replied Smithy ruefully.

With lunch over, back on board the Loch Ranza they were getting prepared to dive again to remove the sunken fishing smack away from the front of the dock gates. This time Billy was going to have to go in as it was a two diver job to place the lifting strops under the keel.

Scurvy prepared Billy's Kirby Morgan band mask*(1-321)* for him with a liberal coating of Immac inside the neoprene hood. Smithy ensured that it was strapped down tight onto Billy's head.

Scurvy and Billy descended into the murky water of the harbour and swam along to the stern of the fishing smack. Here they fed in one of the strops under the hull, through the gap between the rudder post and the propeller and took the ends up and laid them over the gunnels at the stern.

They then swam towards the bow where they fed in another strop under the keel about two meters back from the bow. They had to dig into the seabed here to make a gap so as to get the strop through to the other side under the keel.

As they were doing so, a large Conger eel darted out of a hole in the hull where Billy was working and gave him the fright of his life. Billy panicked and shot to the surface making for the diver's ladder.

Philip pulled him on board. 'What's wrong with you man?' Asked Philip with a note of concern.

'A fuckin giant Conger attacked me!' Shouted Billy through his band mask.

'Away and behave. More likely you scared it and it darted out of its lair to get away from you.' Replied an unsympathetic Philip.

'I scared it!' Exclaimed Billy in disbelief at Philips lack of sympathy.

Smithy called Scurvy over the coms to let him know what had happened. 'Surface to Diver 1 over.' Called Smithy.

'Diver 1 from surface, go ahead over.' Replied Scurvy.

Billy got a fright by the resident Conger. Can you finish the job on your own or will I need to send Philip in? Over.' Informed Smithy.

'No It's okay. The strops through on the other side, I just need to pull a bit more through then bring both ends to the gunnels ready to hook up to the crane.' Replied Scurvy.

With Scurvy still in the water but now on the surface, the crane manoeuvred a spreader bar with the wire attachment slings over the area of the fishing smack, the middle of which had been marked with a buoy.

As the lifting wires touched the surface of the water, Scurvy held onto one of them as it descended down to the sunken wreck.

Controlling the cranes movements over the coms. Scurvy stopped the descent and hooked up the wires to the four ends of the lifting strops. Instructing the crane to come up on his wire just until the strops and began to take the weight. He stopped the lift there, then existed the water. Repositioning the Loch Ranza out into the dock away from the lifting path. The lads watched as the crane lifted the old fishing boat out of the water and lowered it onto a low loader on the quayside. For it to be taken away to be scrapped, well ultimately burnt.

Billy's hair was starting to fall out in clumps from the Immac that scurvy had coated the inside of his band mask hood with. Scurvy who took great delight in this, laughed at Billy and said. 'You must have got one hell of a fright Billy, your hairs falling out all over the place. Did they not have Conger eels in the Persian Gulf?'

A somewhat ego battered Billy holding clumps of hair in his hands blurted. 'Bastards, bastards, your all just bastards.'

Billy received no sympathy or support from either Smithy or Philip. For Philip had worked in the Persian Gulf and he had a great distain for blowhards like Billy and Burt.

That evening the divers were all together in the Jade Palace Chinese Restaurant in Greenock. This was Patsy's team building night out, which he was hoping would bring all the guys together as one happy family so to speak.

Billy was also there, but was wearing a baseball cap which he refused to take of his head. The waiter was taking their orders. Burt ordered first. 'So what shite do they cook up in here then. It'll be fuck all compared to what the Chinky cooks use to make for us out in the Persian Gulf. Man they were brilliant. They use to make some fantastic curries. Too hot for the likes of you soft soaps to handle.'

Scurvy seeing an easy target took aim. 'Obviously I don't know about that, but these guys here do a pretty mean special curry. It's too hot for me but somebody like you might, be able to handle it.'

'Might! Fucking bring it on.' Boasted Burt. As the waiter took the order, with Burt having had a few drinks in him before arriving at the restaurant, he continued with his bravado. 'Hey China, just as hot as you can, I'll show these guys a thing or two.'

At this Scurvy winked to the waiter who he knew well. As the waiter took Scurvy's order he asked. 'Scurvy, Mr Lee was asking if you could get him some more Clabby doos?'

'Yes sure.' Scurvy replied. 'Tell him I will drop in with a sack at the end of the week.'

'He will be very grateful.' Appreciated the waiter.

'No problem, he's more than welcome.' Acknowledged Scurvy with a smile.

The Clabby Doo is the Scottish common name for the Modiolus Modiolus, the black northern horse mussel. The Scottish name is derived for the Gaelic *clab* enormous mouth and *dubh(doo)* black. They can grow to 150mm in length and be the size of a closed fist. They are commonly found on the seabed of the Clyde coast down to about 10 meters water depth.

By the end of the meal Burt had a shade of red about his gills and was feeling extremely hot under the collar. In actual fact he was sweating like a fat lass shagging in a sauna. He just managed to choke out trying to keep up his bravado 'Aye well, I've got to hand it to them that was not a bad curry, Still no a patch on what we use tae get out in the Gulf.'

The following morning on board the Loch Ranza. Scurvy was kitted up as standby diver.

Burt had just descended below the surface to carry out some underwater welding work. A few minutes later he shouted over the coms. 'Diver returning to surface, get me up quick!' Burt called over the coms, sounding extremely distressed. Smithy who was operating the diver's air panel asked 'What's wrong, what is it?'

'Just get me up fast, oh Jesus help me.' Came back Burt. Sounding even more distressed but now somewhat feeble.

Smithy called to Patsy and Philip. 'Patsy, pull him up fast something's wrong.'

With Burt now unceremoniously pulled on board, Patsy and Philip removed his band mask*(1-321)* and AR Vest.

Smithy asked him. 'What's wrong man, you're in a hell of a distress.'

'Unzip my dry suit quickly I desperately need to get to a lavvy.' Blurted out Burt in extreme distress.

Patsy with no sympathy refused Burt's request. 'Fuck off. You will have been farting like a poor boys

Jacuzzi. The inside of your dry suit will be stinking. And am not wanting the first whiff of it.'

To which a desperate Burt who was in some considerable despair, near begging cried 'I've no been farting. The state my arse is in I canny trust a fart. Christ I'm about tae shit ma self. Unzip me, for Christ sake, unzip me.'

Scurvy now coming for his second strike at the target said 'I'll unzip you Burt. I'm decent that way, ask anybody. Isn't that right Smithy?'

'Aye Scurvy you are that.' Agreed Smithy laughing.

Donning his band mask*(1-321)*, Scurvy stepped up behind Burt and unzipped Burt's Drysuit. Everyone laughed as they watched Burt struggling to get out of his drysuit, scurrying to get to the toilet below decks with his drysuit and his joggy bottoms around his knees.

He shouted back at the guys who were in tears laughing at him and in a combination of rage and extreme distress he shouted. 'What are yous looking at? Ya bunch of bastards.'

To which Philip shouted at him with great delight. 'Aye, it's a great leveller of men when your seen scurrying for a bog with your troosers at your ankles. It's a right dignity stripper. Not so fucking hard now are you?'

Then in unison they all started singing.

'Oh, it's just not funny when yer bums all runny

Do Da, Do Da

Sitting on the pot

> With the Shanghai trots
>
> All the Do Da Day.
>
> All the Do Da day
>
> All the Do Da day
>
> Oh, It's just not funny when your bums all runny
>
> All the Do Da day.'

The guys had no sooner finished singing their delightful parody when they heard Burt screaming in excruciating paid from below decks. Smithy asked with a smallest touch of concern. 'Christ, do you think he's all right?'

Scurvy being somewhat coy replied. 'Ach he'll be fine. Burt's just found out what was special about the special curry that he had last night.'

'Oh, what was that then?' Enquired Smithy.

'It burns five times as hot on the way out as it did on the way in.' Answered Scurvy with delight and a wicked grin.

Later that day, back at the GDMC office, Pirate was sitting with a dry suit on his lap replacing a neck seal while watching a porn tape that was being played on the CCTV video recorder.

Patsy, Scurvy, Smithy and Philip arrived, still laughing about Burt Murchison. Scurvy put on the kettle and the rest of the lads took their equipment down to the cellar.

Two doors down, Agnes the Landlady from the Syxtie's bar was throwing a drunk out of her pub when she saw a recovery wagon starting to load up a gold Mercedes that was parked outside at the front of the GDMC office.

She walked into the office and asked the lads. 'Do any of you guys know who it is that owns the Gold Mercedes, that's parked outside the front of your office?'

At which Pirate replied. 'Yes my darling Agnes, it's mine, why do you fancy going for a spin in it with me?'

Agnes smiling informed him. 'You got two hopes of that happening Pirate, no hope and Bob Hope and Bob Hope's dead.'

'What's more, you've no hope of driving home tonight in it either. For it's in the process of being loaded onto the back of a car transporter.'

'What! What! What do you mean?' Cried Pirate in disbelief.

'Looks to me like it's being repossessed.' Agnes informed him smiling.

Pirate in a scrabbling panic, scurried out of the office into the street. Swiftly followed by the lads, who were sensing a scene of entertainment.

Parked in front of Pirates Mercedes, which he had only recently acquired from Kenny the Con, was a recovery wagon. A repo man who stood about five foot four was in the process of inching Pirates Mercedes up the ramps onto the back of the recovery wagon.

Pirate in a panic shouted at the man. 'Stop! Stop! What do you think you're doing man. That's my car.'

The repo man still with his finger on the button for the winch control. 'Mr Caddona?' He enquired.

'No, Mr Shawlands.' Pirate informed him. 'Mr Caddona's dead. He died two weeks ago. I've bought that car from his wife.'

'Well Mr Shawlands, I have a court order here that says the car is to be repossessed and returned to The Consolidated Finance Company. It's not been paid for.' The repo man informed him.

'Now, now you listen here my good man.' Stuttered out Pirate. 'I have paid for that car. I paid for it in cash. And would you stop what you're doing!'

The repo continued to winde the car up the ramp not entertaining Pirates request replied. 'Well apparently, his wife hasn't paid your cash to the finance company. So the cars to be repossessed until the finance company's been paid.'

'Now listen here my man. But do you know who I am!' Announced Pirate as though he was someone of authority and importance. 'I'm warning you. Stop what you're doing.' Pirate demanded.

'Look Mr Shawlands your business dealings are fuck all do with me. Whatever your disputes are with this car, you'll have to take it up with the finance company or Mrs Caddona. My job is just to recover car.' The repo man informed him.

Pirate was now extremely irate, frustrated and desperate. 'No! No! Now stop what you're doing!'

The repo man continued unfaltered.

'Now I'm warning you for the last time. If you don't stop what you're doing I'll get Smithy here to kick you in the balls.' Pirate informed him.

While everyone else's attention has been focused on the comical scene which was unfolding in front of them. Scurvy has spied that the repo man was not alone. Sitting in the passenger side of the crew cab was his colleague. Scurvy, gave Patsy and Philip a nudge and quietly pointed him out to them.

Still working the winch, The repo man trying to calm the situation said to Pirate. 'Now look here Mr Shawlands, don't go doing anything stupid. I just trying to earn an honest living so I can feed my wife and wains and buy new school shoes for their feet.'

Pirate was having none of it, he turned to Smithy and said in a tone reminiscent of a Laird taking to his manservant. 'Right that's it you've had your chance. Smithy! Kick him in the balls!'

Smithy who stood six foot two inches in his stocking soles and was broad across the shoulders and back, towered over this little man. At one time, Smithy had actually been the south of Scotland Shotokan Karate champion.

Without thought, Smithy obediently at a great rate of knots and with tremendous force, kicked the little man square in the balls. The poor little guy didn't stand a chance and fell to the ground in wailing agony. He dropped like a sack of spuds. All be it like a small sack of spuds.

At this point Scurvy, Philip, Patsy and Agnes who has stayed around to watch the show, burst into fits of laughter.

Pirate looked down at the little man, who now with both hands was clutching his crotch, had a tear running down from the corner of one eye.

In a self righteous tone Pirate said to him. 'Now, you can't say I didn't warn you.'

It was at this point that the repo man's colleague silently climbed out of the crew cab. While the repo man who had been operating the winch was a little man, the same could never have been said of his colleague. For the person rapidly approaching Smithy was a giant of a man, who made no sound. A man who stood a good head above Smithy and who's formidable frame cast such a shadow over Smithy that it blocked out the sun.

Upon turning around then looking up and seeing this mountain of a man coming towards him, Smithy's jaw dropped. For a brief instant Smithy froze with fear. His survival instincts kicked in at lightning speed and Smithy took to his heals and ran like the clappers up St Vincent Street.

Pirate looking towards and up at the giant, in a combination of total disbelief and awe which quickly turned to intense fear. Swung his head around to look at Smithy for protection. Only to see Smithy legging it up St Vincent Street like an Olympian sprinter. He then looked down at the poor little winch man who was lying on the ground, then back to the giant, then back to Smithy. Swiftly taking to his heals after Smithy shouting. 'Smithy what are doing! Where are you going! Wait for me!'

By now everyone else was near on their knees with laughter. And as much as they wanted to, they couldn't do anything to help the poor repo man who was still in some considerable pain and suffering.

The repo man's giant colleague helped him to his feet. Scurvy who was trying very hard to stop laughing so as to be sympathetic and sincere said to him. 'Here come on inside man and sit down and I'll get you and your mate a cup of tea.'

Agnes, the lovely woman that she was said. 'Aye lad, you away in there and sit down. I'll get you something stronger than tea and a bag of ice to cool down your bits.'

Scurvy, despite laughing at the little man did genuinely have sympathy and compassion for him. 'I'm really sorry for laughing', Scurvy said to him. 'But you had to have seen this from where we were standing. Man, you couldn't have made that up for a script.'

The little repo man who despite his own pain had managed to choke out a smile, recognising Scurvy's kindness. 'What's your name lad?'

'Most people call me Scurvy!'

"Scurvy?' The repo man said incredulously. 'Well Scurvy, I think you're worse off than me.'

'How do you mean?' Wondered Scurvy.

'Well, my pain will go away in a little bit. But you'll have that name for the rest of your life.' Smiled the repo man.

CHAPTER 4

Of Pride and Prejudice

It was a lovely sunny summer's Saturday morning in East India dock. It was the Greenock Seaman's charity fete & dock open day. The dock was full of families enjoying the sun & amusements. Scurvy was walking along the quayside on his way to the harbour masters office.

Upon entering the office he saw the harbour master sitting behind his desk. 'Morning. You've got a fine day for the fete.' Scurvy announced.

'Aye it is that Scurvy' replied the harbour master smiling.

'You don't by any chance have the five day weather forecast in yet?' Enquired Scurvy.

'I have, I'll print you off a copy.' Offered the Harbour Master. 'So what are Patsy's plans for this week?' He enquired handing Scurvy the five day forecast.

'Well, Patsy wants to bring the Loch Ranza round to berth seventeen for refuelling tomorrow morning. Then the plan is to head down to Ayr. Where on Monday morning we'll begin the salvage a fishing boat that has sunk in the harbour there. And then off to Troon harbour to repair Ailsa's dry dock gates.' Scurvy informed him.

'That'll be the Golden Harvest that's sunk in Ayr .' Replied the harbour master.

'Aye, how did you know?' Asked Scurvy in surprise.

'Seagulls tell all.' Replied the harbour master.
'With regards to berth seventeen, Andrew Dickinson will be arriving today with a new motor yacht, which he's just taken ownership of from Prossers. He's

booked berth seventeen for a few days as a temporary measure until Inverkip Marina can clear a berth for him there.'

'But he is supposed to be going on a day cruise to Rothesay later on tomorrow morning, eager to impress his socialite friends I suppose. So depending on what time Patsy wants to refuel he may have to berth alongside him or wait till Andrew has departed for Rothesay.'

'Aye thanks for that, I let Patsy know.' Confirmed Scurvy.

'Oh Scurvy I nearly forgot'. Remembered the harbour master. 'Auld Faither Tain was looking for you he's having a wee problem with his engine. Would you stop by and have a look at for him.'

'Aye of course I will, anything for the auld yin. I'll nip along and see him now.' Acknowledged Scurvy.

Further along the quay, Auld Faither Tain was standing in the well deck of his fishing boat Flash. He was wearing a pair of turned down thigh length sea boots. An old dark blue boiler suit with the sleeves pushed up to his elbows, a fine chequered collarless shirt aptly known as Gran Pa shirts to the younger generation and a flat cap bonnet on his head to keep of the sun of his bald patch.

He would have been in his late sixties, though no longer commercially fishing. He still took his boat out onto the Clyde, doon the water for trips away.

He was a kindly old man who Scurvy had known his entire life. So much so, that Scurvy referred to him as his uncle Jimmy.

The heavy steel framed, wooden panelled engine box had been lifted off and was sitting on its side. Now exposed was a very old but generally very reliable Perkins P6 72 horse power diesel engine. Which had a Parsons cone clutch marine gearbox attached to it. Auld Faither was standing above the engine looking down over it scratching his forehead.

'Jimmy, how's it going auld yin?' Asked Scurvy greeting him with a smile.

'Ach good and bad. I'm all right, but I'm having a few problems with ma engine here.' Replied Jimmy. 'How's the diving?'

'Aye Good Jimmy, works steady.' Replied Scurvy.

'Can I no persuade you to come to the fishing with me. I mind when you were a boy, you were going to be my Chief Engineer.' Said Jimmy jovially.

'But Jimmy, I am your Chief Engineer. What's wrong with your Perkins?' Enquired Scurvy.

'Ach she's a bit lumpy and I'm getting a wheen o black smoke out the exhaust.' Replied Jimmy.

'Flash her up and let's get look and listen and we'll see what we can do.' Suggested Scurvy.

Scurvy checked over the engine and had a listen to the cylinders using a screwdriver pressed to his ear as a bone conductor. 'Aye she's misfiring on cylinders 2 & 4 and judging by the black smoke out the exhaust, I reckon the injectors are dripping. Pull all the injectors Jimmy. I still ken one of the lecturers at the James Watt College. He'll let me service and reset them in their test bay. By the time I'm finished, I'll have your engine running like a Singer sewing machine. These old P6's will run forever. A fine example of British Engineering.' Scurvy assured him.

Just at that moment, Andrew Dickinson came motoring into the harbour with his flash, shiny new Trader 47 motor yacht. Scurvy and Auld Faither climbed up onto the quayside as Andrew tied up with the aid of the harbour master.

People arriving for the harbour fete gathered round to look at and admire this lovely new motor yacht that has just berthed along the quay. Many of them were families of men who worked on the Clyde in one form or another.

Andrew switched of his engines and began to strut about his yacht with a G&T in one hand and cigar in the other. He was dressed like a complete ponce. White slacks, leather boaters, blue blazer, white shirt, Paisley pattern cravat and a Breton cap.

He strutted up and down on his yacht telling everyone within hearing distance what a wonderful vessel she was, being a complete bore.

Upon seeing Auld Faither Tain up on the quayside, who was dressed like the old man of the sea that he was. Andrew sparked up in a rather loud, pompous condescending droll. 'You there my good man!'

At this Auld Faither turned around to face him.

'Yes you there.' Continued Andrew. 'You look like a man who is no stranger to the sea. You strike me as being a mariner who has traversed an ocean or two in your day. You'll recognise a fine ship when you see one. What do you think of my boat?'

The old man peered down at Andrew contemptuously over the rim of his spectacles. Taking the roll up cigarette from between his lips shaking his head, being frank and honest replied. 'Man, she's no worth a Fuck for the creels.'

On hearing this, Andrew dropped his glass, his cigar slipped from his mouth as his jaw dropped in complete astonishment and surprise at Auld Faither Tain's answer.

The gathered ensemble who were standing on the quayside, many of them knew and respected Auld Faither burst into fits of laughter pointing at Andrew upon hearing his answer.

As Scurvy made his way back to the Loch Ranza, he was met by the harbour master who informed him that a tug boat in the Victoria Harbour had sucked something up into its Kort Nozzle and asked if they would go to assist.

On arriving at the Loch Ranza, Scurvy told Patsy and Philip what has happened. Casting off, they headed round to the adjacent harbour. They tied up alongside the tugboat MV Thunderer, which was now at anchor. Its big propeller powered by the immensely powerful 2400BHP Humboldt Deutz diesel engine, now immobilised by whatever it was that had become jammed up in its Kort nozzle.

Scurvy, suited and booted, with a Kirby Morgan band mask*(1-321)* strapped to his head, strode off the side of the Loch Ranza to investigate.

What most people do not appreciate is the size of a tug boat below the waterline and how big a tug boat's propeller actually is. This tug boat had a draft of around 3meters. The diameter of the 4 bladed propeller's Kort nozzle was that big that Scurvy could stand up inside it with headroom to spare.

Tugboat Thunderer

What he saw before him needed to be seen to be believed. 'Diver 1 to surface, you're never going to believe this over.'

'Surface from Diver. Maybe not but give it a go.' Replied Patsy.

'There is an industrial washing machine jammed up between the propeller blades and the nozzle. You will need to send in Philip with the Broco*(7-332)* to burn it out. Over.' Exclaimed an astounded Scurvy.

'Surface from Diver 1.Well that's something you don't see every day. No problem Philip's on his way in. I will also send down the tugger wire with a hook so we can pull it out after he's made the cuts.'

Philip went in with the Broco torch*(7-332)* to carefully cut into the washing machine without burning the propeller of the Kort nozzle. Then they would use the tugger wire to pull out the discarded washing machine in two pieces.

Broco is an underwater cutting torch that uses short consumable hollow metal alloy exothermic burning rods in which pure oxygen passes down through the middle of the rod. The rod burns at a temperature of around $5500^{\circ}C$. In many respects, it looks like an arc welding torch the main difference being is that it also has an oxygen supply as well as a DC electricity supply. Broco will cut through virtually all metals and concrete. As such the diver has to take great care where he places the rod.

It was not uncommon for vessel crews to dump things like this overboard under the cover of darkness so that the vessel owners could avoid Stevedore*(g-318)* handling fees and harbour disposal fees.

Philip swam down towards the Kort nozzle, following but staying clear of Scurvy's umbilical, ensuring that neither of them got tangled up. To find the unbelievable sight of a large washing machine crushed and jammed up inside the Kort Nozzle.

Philip had a look around before making the cut, so as not to burn into the propeller or the nozzle. 'Diver 2 to Surface, in position. Make it hot. Over.'

'Surface from Diver 2, copied.... You're hot to trot.' Replied Patsy.

Upon striking the tip of the rod against the washing machine it burst into a ferocious bright yellow and orange illumination around the area of the burn. There was a continuous bursting and popping of explosive hydrogen gas bubbles. These were being generated as a result of the high temperature burning process and dancing of orange and yellow flame from around the tip of the rod. The water started to become smokey as a result of the burning process.

With the washing machine material being quite thin, Philip was able to burn through it in no time at all.

'Diver 2 to Surface make cold and secure Over.'

'Surface from Diver 2 Copied.... All cold' Informed Patsy.

Philip returned to the surface with the Broco Torch and came back down with the winch wire which they fed through one section of the now split mangled washing machine.

The two pieces now had some free movement inside the nozzle. Philip instructed Patsy to take up some tension on the winch wire. With a bit of wrangling from Philip and Scurvy, the first section came clear and fell away nicely.

Upon getting it to the surface, Patsy picked it up high on the winch frame. Then he and Smithy landed it out onto the deck of the Loch Ranza.

The second part of the washing machine then came away fairly easily and was also recovered to deck. After checking that there was no damage to the propeller or the Kort nozzle, Scurvy and Philip returned to the Loch Ranza.

The obstruction now cleared, the huge engine of the tug boat Thunderer growled back into life. Weighing it's anchor, it headed out of the harbour up the Clyde to assist a container ship which was getting ready to leave the King George V docks in Glasgow.

Back at the East India Harbour the guys unloaded the wrecked pieces of the washing onto the quayside for the Port Authority to collect for disposal.

A short while later, Andrew Dickinson, who had now recomposed himself, was standing on the quay shouting down to the Loch Ranza. 'Ahoy there, I say ahoy. Is there anyone aboard?'

Philip looked up from the wheel house window and said to Scurvy. 'It's that pompous prick Angie Dick in hand, will you talk to him. I canny be arsed with the likes of him.'

'Fuck, alright then. Said Scurvy dejected. Sticking his head out through the door he replied. 'Hello there squire, can I help you?'

'Is your boss Mr Jamieson onboard? Enquired Andrew.

'No sir, can I help you at all.' Replied Scurvy trying to be amiable and polite.

'If you would be so kind as to pass a message.' Replied Andrew. 'Could you tell him that Andrew Dickinson has requested that he not berth alongside my motor yacht when he comes to refuel tomorrow. But rather to wait until I depart for Rothesay yacht club later in the morning.'

'I don't want that scabby old bathtub of a boat making my lovely, new motor yacht all dirty. God knows I may even get rats of it.' Announced the impertinent Andrew.

Most people will never appreciate the restraint that Scurvy so quickly had to apply to that invisible little devil that sat on his shoulder when he answered Andrew.' I'll be sure to pass on your request verbatim, post haste.' Scurvy replied.

'That's one conceited, arrogant, pompous bastard.' Said Philip as Scurvy tucked his head back inside. 'But I have to say scurvy I'm impressed by your restraint. You were very polite and reticent. That's not like you. I was expecting you to give him a verbal shellacking.'

'Well I was tempted.' Acknowledged Scurvy. 'But I thought the less said the sooner we'd be rid of him.'

'Aye your right enough.' Agreed Philip. 'Well played Scurv.'

'For by, when I tell Patsy what he just said. It'll be tears before bedtime for Angie Dick In Hand.' Said Scurvy with a smile.

Later that day Scurvy passed Andrews's message onto Patsy, who was absolutely livid. 'What!! The fucking arrogant, pompous bastard. Right I'm going sort that cunt out. It's time to bring him down a peg or three.'

Later that night, in the wee small hours. Patsy wearing a Scuba set*(g-318)*, slipped over the side of the Loch Ranza and swam over to Andrews boat. Where he proceeded to remove the lock nuts from Andrew's propellers.

Upon returning to the Loch Ranza Patsy started to paint his large black Yokohama fenders with black graphite grease.

The following morning Andrew was preparing to head off for a cruise down the Clyde to Rothesay

Yacht club. His invited guests, all dressed head to toe in their finery were now aboard.

Casting off, throwing the wheel over to starboard and engaging both engines into gear to move slow ahead away from the quay, he lost all thrust from his propellers. After a little commotion, he managed to tie the boat back up to the quay.

With a lot of embarrassment, Andrew walked over to the Loch Ranza. Where with some difficulty trying not to appear as though he was there cap in hand, asked Patsy for his help. 'Excuse me Mr Jamieson, I was wondering if one of your divers would be able to check my propellers. It's just that they seem to have come off.'

'Oh really.' Replied Patsy. Trying to sound surprised. 'You'll not go far without them.'

'Yes, well, so it would appear. So eh are they eh, available? It's just that I have a boat full of guests and I was intending to take them "doon the waater" to Rothesay for the day. It would be very much appreciated if you would.' Said Andrew sounding almost but not quite humble and near chocking on his words.

'Well it's our intention to head out shortly ourselves. But in the best of maritime relations as a fellow seafarer to another. We won't see you stuck. I'll send in Scurvy to see what can be done.' Replied Patsy, now securing the moral high ground.

'But I'll have to come alongside mind. Diving at Work regulations you see. But don't worry, I'll keep out my Yokohama fenders so that this scabby old bathtub of a boat doesn't make your shiny new motor yacht all dirty.'

With much embarrassment and shame Andrew managed to choke out a thank you and quietly voiced his appreciation. Then made his way back to his guests.

'Right Scurvy ma lad. Get suited and booted your going in.' Patsy informed him. 'Smithy, flash her up and take her alongside Angie's, Port side to. Instructed Patsy enthusiastically.

Once alongside and tied up hard against Andrew's Motor Yacht. Scurvy donned his band mask*(1-321)* and jumped in straight away.

Scurvy saw that the props were missing and reported back. Patsy told him to look around for the props as they couldn't have gone far. Patsy relayed the information back to Andrew.

After about five minutes of searching Scurvy found the propellers and returned to the surface with them.

Patsy informed Andrew that if he went to the dock chandler, he could get the necessary nuts and pins and that Scurvy would refit his propellers.

About fifteen minutes later, Andrew returned from the chandlers with two stainless steel castellated nuts, washers and split pins.

Scurvy, re entered the water and one at a time refitted Andrews propellers.

Once Scurvy was back on board the Loch Ranza, with his Kirby band mask*(1-321)* removed. Andrew somewhat humbly and quite grateful though having difficulty showing it said to Scurvy. 'Thank you Scurvy, Are you sure they won't come off again?'

'You may rest assured Andrew.' Scurvy confidently replied. 'These props are secure, they won't come off accidentally. You have my word of honour on that. For this I am known.'

'I can only imagine that there were no split pins in the shafts and when you kicked your engines astern yesterday as you berthed up, the nuts shook loose. Then when you engaged gear today they spun off along with your props.' Explained Scurvy.

'Well I suppose that would explain it right enough.' Accepted Andrew. 'Prossers will be getting the sharp edge of my tongue on Monday morning.'

'Well Andrew, you'll not want to be hanging about wasting time with idle chitchat. Best be making up for lost time and head for Rothesay with your refined guests'. Said Patsy eager for Andrew to be on his way. 'If you give it full steam you'll still make it in time for lunch at the Yacht club.'

'Smithy, cast her off so that Andrew can clear his berth. Just eh, move ahead of her and tie up alongside the pier piles there.' Instructed Patsy.

As Andrew and his hoity toity party of friends pulled away, motoring out towards the harbour entrance. Scurvy somewhat perplexed, turned to Patsy and asked. 'That's no like you Patsy. What are you up too?'

'Just smile and wave Scurvy lad, Just smile and wave.' Replied Patsy with a big cheesy grin.

With Andrew now on his way. Smithy and Philip begin their journey down to Ayr in the Transit van. Once the Loch Ranza was fuelled up, Scurvy and Patsy headed out down the Clyde bound for Ayr harbour.

It was a warm, calm, sunny day on the Clyde. Perfect for a day trip cruise 'doon the waater'. As Andrew motored down the Clyde for Rothesay, he received cheers, smiles, waves and tooting horns a plenty from all the other people out cruising on the water that day.

Andrew was feeling rather pleased with himself and incredibly proud of his shiny new motor yacht. Once again taking on the roll of a pompous arse. A role that came naturally to him.

As he berthed alongside the pontoons in Rothesay, Andrew and his party made a hasty disembarkment in order to make it in time for lunch at the Yacht club.

The Loch Ranza was now making passage for Ayr. It was a very pleasant enjoyable voyage passing the Cloch Point Lighthouse, taking in the islands of Bute, Cumbrae, Arran and Lady Isle with its colony of permanent resident Grey seals. Passing the shores of the coastal towns of Largs, Ardrossan, Prestwick and Troon. Finally arriving at their destination, Ayr Harbour.

At the Yacht club Andrew boasted profusely about his shiny new yacht & invited the yacht club Commodore back to his yacht for a G&T prior to them heading back to Greenock.

However it was only upon their return to the yacht did they see what it was that everyone including the divers were really cheering at him for.

All the way along the starboard side of the Yacht in big black greasy letters was written.

I'M A WANKER

The result of the impression of Patsy's handiwork left behind by the Loch Ranza's big Yokohama Fenders*(g-319)*.

Andrew's party including his wife, were absolutely mortified, they were completely black affronted (Pardon the pun). So much so they refused to sail back to Greenock with him. Instead they took the last ferry to Wemyss Bay and got the connecting train home.

Andrew embarrassed and fuming tried to wipe off the grease. Only to end up smearing it all over the shiny white hull of his pride and joy. Leaving him even more outraged and unsure as to which was worse, the before or after he tried to clean it.

To add insult to injury, despite Andrew's protestations, explanation and grovelling apologies. The pompous Commodore from Rothesay Yacht Club administered Andrew a magnanimous helping of his own medicine. Declaring Andrew banned sine die from returning due to him brining the yacht club into disrepute with this vulgarity.

With the Loch Ranza berthed safely in Ayr harbour. Scurvy and Patsy met up with Smithy & Philip at their B&B. After a shower and a change of clothes they headed out to a nearby hostelry to toast Patsy's act of genius.

'I wish I could see Angies face now.' Remarked a happy Patsy very pleased with his one upmanship over Andrew.

Andrew motored back to Greenock alone. His face was a picture, but not one for a photograph that he would want for his mantle place.

CHAPTER 5

WHATS IN A NAME

In the GDMC office, Patsy was on the telephone. Smithy was talking to Belinda and Pirate was making a cup of tea.

'Yep, not a problem. We've been working in Ayr and Troon harbour all this week. 'I'll have the Loch Ranza in Ardrossan harbour for around 11AM. We can start work on the cable straight away.'

'Yes certainly, we'll meet the SSEB rep at the harbour masters office Fax us through the proforma and I'll get things moving. Yes, right you are. Okay, bye now.'

'That was CTC on the phone.' Patsy informed them. 'They're sub contracting us to bury an electricity cable for the SSEB at Ardrossan Harbour.'

'Who, **C**olin's **T**renching **C**owboys.' Remarked Smithy sarcastically.

'Why do you call them that?' Belinda asked.

'Ignore him.' Interjected Patsy. 'It's **C**olin **T**elford **C**ables Ltd. And we get quite a bit of work from them.'

'That's because They **C**an't **T**rench **C**able.' Said Pirate chipping in his two pence worth.

'Enough of that.' Warned Patsy. 'The SSEB rep is going to be there. So I don't want any snide remarks like that flying about, because he'll go straight back with it CTC. Then that'll be the end of these nice little earners that we get from them.' Patsy warned them.'

'Whose the SSEB rep?' 'Enquired Pirate.'

'Dicky Paddle Arse' Announced Smithy with a grin.

'Dicky Paddle Arse? No way you've made that up.' Said Belinda in disbelief.

'His real name is Richard Rowbottom.' Patsy informed her.

'Rowbottom, hmm, I don't believe that either.' Replied Belinda unconvinced.

'Row- paddle, bottom - arse , paddle arse.' Explained Smithy.

Wanting to get things back on track, Patsy gave Belinda some instructions. 'Belinda, give Scurvy and Philip a phone at their B&B in Troon. Philip was going to be taking the good ship Loch Ranza back to Greenock this morning. Tell him to stop in at Ardrossan Harbour on his way. And tell Scurvy that once he is finished with the paperwork with Ailsa's site manager, to take the RIB and meet us all in Ardrossan Harbour.'

'Smithy, do you want to go and give silly Billy a knock. See if he wants to come out & play? We can use him until Scurvy arrives with the RIB. Then just head straight down to Ardrossan.'

'Aye sure. This'll be entertaining.' Replied Smithy with a smile.

'Pirate, you and me will go and meet the SSEB rep. I'll drive Philips car down for him. That way he can go straight home from Ardrossan tonight. 'I'll meet you in the harbour car park. You can take the Land Rover.' Instructed Patsy.

Pirate was a bit miffed. 'Why can't I drive Philips car and you take the Land Rover?'

'For the simple fact that Philip would have a hairy fit if he ever found out you drove his car.' Replied Patsy. 'That aside, I'm much more suited to driving a Mercedes. For by you dress like a tinker, you'd get pulled by the polis if they saw you driving a Mercedes, they'd think you'd stolen it.'

'Whereas, you wouldn't look out of place driving a battered old Land Rover. I would. Also, let us not forget what happened the last time you drove someone's else's Mercedes. That's settled then good lets go.' Said Patsy leading the way.

Pirate scowled and looked down at the floor. Shaking his head, he mumbled to himself about how he's been hard done to. He was like a little boy who couldn't get his own way. 'I'm Director of this company too, who's he to pull rank over me. I'm no having this. It's not on, I'll sort him out later.'

Pirate climbed into the Land Rover with a big sigh. Started the engine which clattered, knocked and rumbled into life and he began the noisy, rattley and draughty drive down to Ardrossan.

Patsy settled himself comfortably into the driving seat of Philips Mercedes. Casually opened the electric sunroof and switched on the CD player upon which the Bellamy Brothers' let your love flow' came to life.

'Oh yes, this is definitely me.' Said Patsy speaking to himself whilst glancing in the sun visor vanity mirror as he slipped on Philips driving sunglasses. Engaging the automatic gearbox into drive, Patsy effortlessly accelerated off for a drive down to the coast.

Philip and Scurvy are about to check out of their B&B when Scurvy received the phone call from Belinda. 'CTC really, Colin's Travelling Circus.' He replied to Belinda's news as she relayed Patsy's instructions.

'Why do you call them that?' Asked Belinda.

'Because most of the guys that work for them are clowns.' Laughed Scurvy.

Do any of you guys have a good word to say about any other companies in the industry.' Asked Belinda, rolling her eyes.

'Eh… No.' Replied Scurvy.

Belinda continued. 'Anyway, if Philip could take the Loch Ranza straight round to Ardrossan Harbour and as soon as you are finished at Troon you are to follow on in the RIB.'

'Aye will do Belinda. Many thanks, bye now.' Acknowledged Scurvy. He informed Philip of the change in plan and the two set the plan in motion.
At the harbour, Scurvy gave Philip a hand to cast off and waved cheerio as the Loch Ranza motored out of Troon harbour for Ardrossan. Scurvy then walked up to see the manager at Ailsa' shipyard's offices.

Pirate was still travelling along the road in his bone shaking Land Rover. He was not a happy camper and hadn't stopped mumbling to himself since leaving Glasgow.

Patsy on the other hand had just arrived at Ardrossan Harbour. Patsy got out of the car, closed the door and almost forgot to close the sunroof. As Patsy casually closed the sun roof with a touch of a button on the remote control. A Rolls Royce pulled into the car park and parked up close by.

The driver got out of the Rolls Royce looking like an impersonation of Charles Endell Esquire. He was wearing a camel Crombie coat, stripped Oxford shirt with tie, black stay press slacks, paisley pattern silk scarf, black wool felt trilby hat, black spats on his feet and was smoking a large Cohiba cigar.

Two little boys of about 11 years old came running up to him. 'Hey mister, watch your motor?' Asked the red headed, freckled little boy.

In a snobby contrite, condescending south side tone, looking down at the boys, the owner of the Roll's took the cigar from his mouth and said. 'Watch my motor, I don't need you to watch my motor.' Turning to point at the back seat of the car and said 'I've got a Rottweiler.'

The two little boys looked through the partially opened window of the rear door to see a large menacing Rottweiler growling, baring its teeth and slavering.

Lightning quick and totally unphased by the dog, the dark haired boy of the two turned to the owner and said in a cock sure galas manner. 'Rottweiler eh, can it put oot fires?'

Quite taken aback, but impressed with the young boys shrewd & clever response the owner of the Rolls said. 'Here's a pound each, if there's no harm done to my motor when I come back there'll be another pound each in it for you.'

The two boys grinned and hi fived each other as they took the money. Then sat on the wall next to the car, quite content & delighted with their negotiation and subsequent deal. The Rolls owner headed off to the club house.

Shrewd, thought Patsy to himself. Though pleased that they never tried that with him. Meeting up with the SSEB client rep, Patsy took him for a liquid brunch at the marina restaurant.

'Good morning Richard, good to see you again, it's been a while when was it I saw you last, it must have been on the Rhu to Rosneath job.' Said Patsy convivially.

'Pat, how are you keeping?' Enquired Richard. 'That job, that was about a year ago, though from what I remember we had a cracking time of it in the Ardencaple Hotel.' Richard reminisced.

'Has it been that long? Well if you were to give us the work direct instead of going through Colin Telford we could have good times like that more often. You'll eh, have a spot of brunch while you're waiting for the lads to arrive?' Said Patsy taking on the roll of the consummate sales man.

'Thanks very much, I don't mind if I do, a large malt if you please.' Said Richard taking full advantage of the freebie.

Patsy and Richard returned to the harbour after brunch, where Patsy had timed it perfectly. Pirate was just arriving in the Land Rover as was Smithy with Silly Billy in tow. The good ship Loch Ranza motored through the harbour entrance.

The guys climbed aboard the Loch Ranza. Richard as a result of the three free double malts that he had unreservedly availed himself of via Patsy's generosity, was now somewhat unsteady on his feet.

With everyone on board, Patsy instructed Philip to take the Loch Ranza to the cable end point at the detached breakwater. This was a new electric power cable from the harbour Lighthouse out to the detached breakwater that had been laid. As they motored out of the harbour, Patsy plied Richard with more whisky.

'Here you go Richard, have a little splash of the good stuff here, it'll help you get your sea legs.' Offered Patsy, assisting Richard to become three sheets to the wind.

'Good man just the dab for an old salty sea dog like me. For a minute there Patsy, I was feart you were going to offer me a cup of tea.' Slurred a half cut Richard.

'Not at all Richard, what sort of a man do you take me for? Us ruffty tuffty divers and salty sea dogs must stick together.' Encouraged Patsy as sly as an old fox who knew Richard to be an old soak.

'Aye, (hic) you're right there Patsy.' Slavered Richard in mutual agreement.

Once on location and with the anchor down, Patsy gave an enthusiastic Billy his orders. 'Billy, get suited up, you can go in and make a start while were waiting on Scurvy coming from Troon.'

With the Air Lift*(8-333)* set up. Silly Billy who was mad keen to get in the water and prove himself, jumped over the side in SCUBA*(g-318)* with a life line attached. Philip handed him down the 15cm diameter Air lift*(8-333)*. Billy finned over to the start point, which was marked with a buoy attached to a shot line. Descending down the shot line to the seabed, he started sucking a trench for the new power cable that has already been laid which the cable would sink into. The power cable was being used to supply electricity to the navigation light at the end of the breakwater.

Although the water was shallow being only 4.5 meters deep, the visibility was not very good here.

It was only about 1.5 to 2 meters due to it being a sand mud mix seabed. But this made trenching with the air lift quite easy.

Meanwhile in Ailsa's Offices, Scurvy got the final documents signed off by the yard manager.

'Your lot did a fine job of the dock gates and the pier.' Praised the ship yard manager. 'Tell me what does GDMC stand for again?

'Well it depends on who you ask and why you want to know?' Replied Scurvy.

'Well I'm asking you.' Said the manager

'**G**arbage **D**rivel **M**uck & **C**rap.' Which was Scurvy's standard humorous response. 'But if you are writing out Patsy's cheque it's Glasgow Diving & Marine Contractors Ltd.' Said Scurvy changing the tone to his Glasgow Spam belt finest.

Laughing the manager said. 'Aye, it's certainly been entertaining having you lot round for the last week. Where are you off to next?'

'Up to Ardrossan, cable burials job.' Replied Scurvy.

The manager handed Scurvy the completed and signed paperwork along with the cheque and they shook hands. Scurvy then departed for the Marina where the company's centre consoled, 5.4 meter Avon Searider RIB was berthed.

Loading his kit bag onto the RIB, and slipping into a life jacket he flashed up the 75 HP, 2 stroke ELPTO Mercury outboard engine. Untying his single amidships painter line, he gently pulled away from the pontoon and slowly motored out of the marina, past the inner harbour entrance, passing the dry dock gates of Ailsa's shipyard that he had been working on.

Then once in the mouth of the outer harbour, he steadily opened up the throttle and started crashing through the swell that was a permanent feature at the entrance to Troon harbour. A bounce that would send constant shock waves through your spine if you didn't stand up and bend your knees to absorb the shock.

White sea spray burst and spread either side of his bow with the wind blowing it back into his face, the salt from the sea stinging his eyes as RIB bounced through the swell.

Upon getting into open water, he opened up the throttle fully, the engine changed its tone to a higher pitch. The RIB came up on the plane and started skipping at speed over the surface of the sea heading for Ardrossan. It is a fantastic feeling that has the uncanny ability to bring joy to a man's heart and a smile to your face. The breaking bow waves showering all around him with salt spray.

Ardrossan was only 7.5 nautical miles from Troon by sea. With the RIB travelling at around 25 Knots. Scurvy's high speed thrill on the sea was short lived. Twenty minutes later he arrived at Ardrossan Harbour entrance.

Scurvy, spotted the harbour Pilot's launch which was acting as a guard vessel. He also noticed that the Loch Ranza was flying the flags Alpha Romeo Yankee and had a ball, a diamond and ball shaped signs in a vertical line hanging from the signal mast above the wheel house roof. This indicated that there was a diver in the water, slow your speed and the boat was at anchor. There were also two diamond shapes mounted vertical in a line on the Port side to indicate that this was the safe side to approach on.

Scurvy called up the Loch Ranza on the VHF radio for permission to approach. 'Lochranza, Lochranza this is Searider over.'

'Scurvy, your here.' Replied Patsy.

'I am indeed, permission to come along side.' Requested Scurvy.

'Permission granted, come round wide to our port side.' Instructed Patsy.

'Roger, Port side too, understood.' Scurvy confirmed.

Scurvy climbed aboard the Loch Ranza. Philip was kitted up as stand by diver. Pirate was tendering the hose for the airlift and Smithy was tending the lifeline for Silly Billy. Patsy had continued to ply the client rep with more whisky, who seems to have the same ability to absorb whiskey as a sponge absorbs water. Richard was now three sheets to the wind, paralytic with the drink.

'Well, hello there lads, how's it going?' Greeted Scurvy.

'Did you collect payment from Ailsa's before you left?' Patsy Asked.

'Sure did another satisfied customer.' Confirmed Scurvy as he handed Patsy Ailsa's cheque. 'Who's in the water?' Enquired Scurvy.

'Billy.' Replied Smithy casually.

'Billy? Not...Silly Billy?' said Scurvy taken aback.

'Eh, Aye.' Confirmed Smithy with a grin.

'Oh, you've got to be fucking joking. You've let him loose with an airlift. Listen, we don't call him Silly Billy because it rhymes. He's called Silly Billy because he's a Fechan Eejit!' Exclaimed Scurvy in annoyance.

No sooner had Scurvy finished his exclamation did a diver's half mask come shooting out of the water into the air. Swiftly followed by a huge flurry of bubbles on the surface and shortly followed by Billy's head bobbing up in the middle of it coughing and spluttering.

Scurvy shouted to Pirate, 'Shut of the receiver!'

Smithy hauled in on Billy's lifeline and pulled him into the side of the boat. Pirate hauled in the airlift.

Scurvy turned to Patsy in disbelief and asked. 'What's he doing in there on Scuba?'*(g-318)*

Patsy replied, 'He was keen to just get in and get on with it. For by, he's been a bit wary of band masks*(1-321)* every since his hair strangely fell out in clumps after the last time he wore one.' Drawing Scurvy a questioning look of suspicion.

Scurvy looked away with a knowing and mischievous grin and acknowledged. 'Oh aye, I remember that.'

Smithy hauled Billy aboard and once he was seated having got his breath back Smithy asked him. 'What happened?'

Billy with an air of innocent stupidity explained. 'Well I was just working away creating the trench. Well, I was kind of curious as to how fast the sand went up the air lift.'

'So I stuck my head down to have a look and before I knew it. It had sucked the regulator out my mouth and the half mask clean off my face. Pretty powerful things these aren't they.'

'Aye, you don't say.' Replied an exasperated Smithy.

Scurvy turned to Philip with his palms turned upwards & sighed. 'Somewhere there's a village missing an idiot. And I have found him onboard the Loch Ranza masquerading as a commercial diver.' said Scurvy sarcastically.

'Scurvy!' Shouted Patsy. 'Get suited and booted, you're in next.'

As Scurvy was being strapped into his harness on the back deck of the boat, Philip said to him. 'You shouldn't let Billy get to you.'

'I know.' Scurvy sighed. 'But I find him so frustrating, the man's a Fechan Eejit.'

'I know he is.' Agreed Philip sympathetically. 'You know he is, Patsy, Smithy & Pirate knows he is and the big man upstairs (pointing skywards) knows he's an eejit, everyone does.'

'In fact the only person who doesn't know he's an eejit...... is Billy. But he's not a bad person. He's just an eejit.' And with that peril of wisdom Philip smiled.

Scurvy smiled back, now having an understanding on how to rationalise Silly Billy's antics. 'I know, I know.' Scurvy agreed. 'I do try not to get frustrated with him but I really do struggle. How do you manage so well?' Asked Scurvy seeking further guidance.

'Well, being worldly travelled helps.' Replied Philip. 'As you know, I spent quite a bit of time working in the Middle East and Asia. I travelled round Thailand quite a bit. The people there are mostly Buddhist in their beliefs. Buddhism though classed as a religion is actually more of an attitude towards life and the world we find ourselves in. As such, I found the people of Asia, especially the Thai's to be much more reticent, tolerant and forgiving of other peoples how should we say......inadequacies. Also there's a little prayer that I picked up on my travels, that I find often helps. I'll give you a copy of it when the jobs done. I think you'll like. In the mean time, let's get your hat on and get you in the water. The sooner you finish, the sooner we can go home. Alice is cooking a roast for tea tonight and I'm not wanting to miss out on it.'

'No worries Philip, I'll make sure were finished in time.' Scurvy assured him.

'I've every faith in you Scurvy lad.' Replied Philip in confidence.

Now suited and booted, with a Kirby 10 band mask *(1-321)* strapped to his head, Scurvy disappeared below the surface to the seabed. With the air lift in hand, he continued creating the trench that would provide a safe haven for the new power cable. As the day went on then just after 4pm, Patsy decided to call a halt to the proceedings. 'Surface to Diver 1. Okay Scurvy, back on deck mate. We'll call it a day at that, over.'

'Diver 1 copied, But what about the sand bagging and the video survey.' Asked Scurvy.

'We'll come back tomorrow to finish it off. Anyway Paddle Arse is to pished to lift a pen to sign off the Job.' Replied Patsy.

Richard Rowbottom the SSEB rep was lying in a heap on a coil of 50mm mooring rope up in the bow, slavering clutching a near empty bottle of Oban malt whisky.

Once Scurvy was back on deck, both him and Philip striped out of their gear. Pirate had the arduous task of raising the anchor with the hand operated winch gear. As Patsy swung the helm over to turn the boat around, Smithy spied someone at the lighthouse waving to them and rather animatedly pointing towards the car park. 'Who's that? He asked Patsy.'

'I don't know, I can't make him out clearly from here.' Patsy replied. 'Describe him.'

Smithy who was blessed with the eyesight of an eagle began to describe the waving figure of a man. 'Well, he's wearing baggy jeans that seem to be hanging of his arse like a teenager, though he's no teenager. I reckon he's in his fifties, an orange hi viz fleece top. I think he's a ging-er, he looks as though he hasn't shaved for a week or two. Short and stocky, got a bit of a Hobbit look about him. Wouldn't look out of place in a Tolkien novel. Apparently, according to the God botherer that was bashing his Bible gein it laldy in Buchannan street the other week, God made man in his own image. Well, he must have been pished when he made this cunt.'

'Fuck, that'll be Cock In Hand. I could do without him just now.' Exclaimed Patsy.

'Who?' Replied a surprised Smithy.

'Steven Cockerham.' Replied Patsy. 'He's the Harbour Authority Civil Engineering Manager. A born Wanker. Hence why everyone that has ever had the displeasure of knowing him refers to him as Cock In Hand. As for being a manager, he's fucking useless. He couldn't manage sex in a brothel.'

'Do us a favour, when we get along side, You jump off and go and meet him up on the harbour. Just deflect him away from us. Tell him anything he wants hear. Just make up any story that keeps him away from us. Whatever happens he mustn't see Paddle Arse pished, because the nasty little shit will grass him up to the SSEB and that will be Dickies boat sunk. I'll take Paddle Arse home in his car and then get a taxi back to the office to get my car.'

As they headed up to the car park, Philip sensed Scurvy would prefer not have to travel in the van with Billy and knew he definitely would not want to suffer the journey with Pirate in the Land Rover. So he offered Scurvy a lift back to Glasgow with him.

Philip was a kind, good natured man, softly spoken and worldly wise, who generally played his cards close to his chest. Standing about 5ft 8" stocky build but fit and sporting a bushy blonde moustache. He wouldn't look out of place on an old black and white photo of 1950's standard dress commercial diver*(6-330)* seated holding a large spun Copper Siebe Gorman or Morse Mk V helmet*(6-329)* on his lap.

Philip was a highly experienced commercial air diver, who had worked not only in the UK but had spent many years working offshore in the Persian Gulf for well known company's such as McDermott Diving & Salvage, ADAMS (Al Gosaibi Diving and Marine Services) and Consolidated Construction who incidentally also owned Coca Cola Qatar, etc.

'Scurv, you can travel back with me if you like. It'll be much more comfortable for you after a full day's graft in the water.' Offered Philip.

'Cheers Philip, that would be grand.' Said Scurvy appreciatively.' On the road, Scurvy sparked up the conversation. 'Here Philip, why did Patsy stop the job early, I could have still have got some of the sand bagging done.'

Philip replied. 'Do you notice how he kept feeding the SSEB rep with drink?'

'Aye I did, I was wondering about that, especially pouring a £20 bottle of Oban Malt down Dickies neck.'

'Well Think of it as being a very shrewd investment.' Philip explained. 'It means that Patsy can charge SSEB for two full hire days instead of one and a half, plus mobilisation and demob fees. The Client rep is too drunk to dispute otherwise.'

'This way, he'll sign off any invoice that Patsy puts before him now without questioning it, cause he would never want his employer to know he was pished on the Job. That and the fact that Dickie, the old soak is now paralytic with the drink. So Patsy gets to drive his seven series BMW up the road instead of going back with Pirate in the Land Rover.'

'Very clever.' Admired Scurvy. 'I take it Patsy knew he was an old soak.'

'Och aye.' Confirmed Philip. 'Patsy knows him from old. Here Scurvy, you know I told you Alice was cooking a roast joint for tea, why don't you join us? There'll be plenty to go around.'

'Oh I wouldn't want to be a bother to you.' Declined Scurvy politely. Yet secretly hoping his refusal would be denied.

'Bother my arse. For by, Alice would be pleased to see you. After all it's been a while.' Insisted Philip.

'Aye all right then I love too.' Agreed a happy Scurvy. 'Stop off at an offy and I'll get a bottle of wine.'

As they arrived into Castlemilk on the southern edge of Glasgow. Philip pulled over to stop outside a little row of shops on Glenacre Drive that included a Victoria Wines off licence. Scurvy got out and leaning over the car door he said to Philip. 'Alice's tipple will be a bottle of the Buckfast then eh?'

'Only if you want to end up wearing the roast instead of eating it.' Replied Philip with a smile.

'Cabernet Sauvignon then?' Replied Scurvy smiling.

'Cabernet Sauvignon will do fine.' Acknowledged Philip. 'If you should pick up a bottle of Wolf Blass, you may even end up with better than Viennetta for dessert. For Alice is quite partial to an Australian Red.'

Upon entering Philips house. Philip shouted down the hallway to Alice who was in the kitchen. 'Hi darling. That smells delicious. You want to set another place at the table. It's just that I went to buy a copy of the Big Issue but I had no money so I offered the lad a free meal instead.'

A shocked Alice darted out of the kitchen. 'Eh what? Philip, you're terrible. Scurvy how you doing son? Come away in, it's good to see you. It's been a while.'

'Thanks Alice. Have you been keeping well? I've brought you a wee something to go with the meal.' Replied Scurvy handing her the bottle of wine.'

Alice was forever the consummate host. 'Make yourself at home Scurvy lad. You'll have a drink?'
Scurvy smiling replied. 'Well, I'll not say no, for I wouldn't want to offend you by refusing your hospitality.'

'Aye that's the Scurvy I know.' Replied Alice Having Scurvy for dinner was actually quite a comfort to Alice, for she knew that Scurvy lived alone and had no ties to his family. So this would mean a lot to him.

'Could I possibly have a quick dance in your rain locker before I sit down to tea?' Asked Scurvy.

'Of course you can. There's clean towels in the airing cupboard upstairs.' Replied Alice.

Patsy who had enjoyed his drive up from the coast in the Seven series BMW, was just pulling into the driveway of Richards home on Elphinstone Road in Whitecraigs on Glasgow's posh part of the south side.

Dragging a paralytic Richard out from the back seat of the car and struggling to keep him on his feet. Patsy rang the door bell.

A 34D cup, fit, attractive, sexy brunette woman in her late thirties, wearing red skin tight hot pants and a low cut white cheese cloth top answered the door.

With a coy smile and a drunk Richard draped over his shoulder. 'Hello Bella' Greeted Patsy.

'That bastard drunk again.' Responded an unimpressed Bella.

'It's just the fresh sea air Bella, it knocks him for six' Replied Patsy.

Bella wincing at the smell of her husband's breath said 'Fresh sea air my arse, his breath could light the eternal flame. He promised me he would only have three drinks and be home by ten.'

'Oh dear, It looks like he's got them mixed up again, eh Bella.' Smiled Patsy trying to defuse the situation.

'You're to blame for this Jaimison.' Bella Scolded

'Aye now, not so fast Bella. I was just being convivial.' Said Patsy in his defence with a smile. 'Anyway you know how it is. It's better doing business with a drunk professional than a sober idiot.' Patsy chuckled.

Bella with a sly, sexy smile on her lips replied. 'Better for you, you mean; not him. Give me a hand to get him upstairs. He can sleep in the spare room, I'm not have that minging git reeking of whisky & piss lying beside me tonight.'

Bella closed the door to the spare bedroom with her drunken husband fully clothed lying on the bed inside. Patsy with a sly smile of a cunning fox, holding his palms upward asked. 'Bella what can I do to make it up to you?'

Bella slipping her hand down onto Patsy's crotch with a sultry look in her eye Suggested. 'Why don't we go downstairs, have a drink and see what we can do with the first thing that pops up?'

After dinner, Philip, Scurvy and Alice were sitting in the lounge chatting over a drink.

'Alice that was terrific. It's not every day I get fed like that.' Acknowledged Scurvy appreciatively.

'Now that you've brought the subject up Scurvy, when are you going to get yourself a new woman. You know the old saying, all work and no play makes Jack a dull boy.' Asked Alice.

'Alice, what self-respecting woman would be interested in a man as ugly as I am.' Said Scurvy trying to fend off being single for so long.'

'You do yourself a great injustice Scurvy.' Said Alice, giving a boost to Scurvy's self esteem, which had taken a severe knock a while back.

'Well, if you don't think you can get a self respecting one at least get yourself a right dirty one.' Suggested Philip.

'PHILIP!! Your Terrible.' Replied Alice shocked. She paused for a moment then in agreement said. 'But you do have a point.'

On seeing the time and trying to avoid Alice playing at matchmaker, Scurvy saw this as his que to stage exit left. 'And on that note, Philip could you please phone me a Taxi. It will be another early start in the morning with us going back down to Ardrossan.'

In the night rain, Pirate was just arriving home, after a slow rickety journey from Ardrossan in the Land Rover and having to change a tyre as a result of a puncture. He was looking pretty dejected and forlorn.

Scurvy's taxi arrived. In Philips hallway Scurvy bid his goodnight. 'Thanks for having me round. The meal was lovely. It's been a great evening, it was good to see you again Alice.'

'Your welcome Scurvy, anytime. Don't leave it so long till the next time.' Alice told him.

'I won't Alice, I promise.' Said Scurvy sincerely.

Just as Scurvy was about to go out the door, Philip remembered his parting gift. 'Here Scurvy, I nearly forgot.' In the doorway Philip handed Scurvy a folded piece of paper, which Scurvy slipped into the inside pocket of his jacket. 'Thanks Philip, I'll see you in the morning.'

'Aye, you will that Scurvy lad.' Philip assured him. As the door closed, Alice turned to Philip with the concern of a kind aunty. 'You know Philip. I can't help but worry about Scurvy. He's been on his own a long time now and all he does is work. He's a kindly soul. It makes me quite sad to know that he goes home alone to an empty house every night.'

'I know Alice. His last woman burned him badly. She took his house from him. He left Stranraer with virtually nothing, penniless and homeless. It'll be a while yet before he's ready to trust again. Wounds like that don't heal easily.' Philip informed her.

'You do look after him when he's in the water don't you Philip?' Asked Alice concerned. 'It's just that I don't trust that parcel o' rogues that you work for. They'll take every advantage of him at the first opportunity.'

'Now don't you go fretting yourself lass. Of course I look after Scurvy.' Philip assured her. 'Eh, but wait a minute. While I'm looking after Scurvy, who's looking after me?'

'You don't need anyone, your far too long in the tooth for the likes of them to get one over on you.' Replied Alice. Philip gave her a loving kiss and a cuddle.

Arriving home to his flat in darkness. Scurvy switched on some lamps and the telly then flumped down into an armchair. Reaching into his inner jacket pocket, he took out the piece of paper that Philip gave him, unfolded it and reads.

<u>A Prayer For The Stressed</u>

Dear Lord
Grant me the sincerity to accept
the things I cannot change.
The courage & fortitude to change
the things I cannot accept.
And the wisdom to hide the packet of laxatives that I
used when making the coffee for those people who
pissed me off today.
Also Lord, help me to be careful of the toes I step on
today, for they may be connected to the arse that I
may have to kiss tomorrow.
Help me always to give 100% at work.
12% on Monday
23% on Tuesday
40% on Wednesday
20% on Thursday
5% on Friday
And Lord..... Help me to remember.......
That when I am having a really bad day
And people are trying their hardest
to really piss me off.
That it takes 42 muscles to frown
and only 4 to extend my middle finger
and tell them all to
Fuck off!
Amen.

    Seated in his armchair, Scurvy smiled to himself. Then sighed deeply. His eyelids feeling heavy gently closed, falling asleep in his chair, all on his own.

CHAPTER 6

Getting Busy with the Bizzes

It was nearing the end of the day. Scurvy was carrying out the last stretch of a grout inspection of the large keystones that were used to build the quay walls of the Victoria harbour.

It was common place with harbours of this construction for the grout between the large blocks of sandstones to become washed out by the powerful propellers and thrusters of the tug boats. This often resulted in the sandstone being washed out and large holes to appear in the quay wall which would need to be repaired.

The harbours were known and disliked by many a diver for their black water. Working in the gloomy, extremely low visibility, where the majority of the work is carried out by touch. When suddenly Scurvy's hand touched something that scared him so badly he felt his blood run cold and his heart missed a beat.

'Oh Jesus!' Exclaimed Scurvy with his breathing becoming shallow and rapid.

'Are you alright Scurvy?' Asked Smithy who had been listening intently over the coms. Sensing something was amiss.

Scurvy didn't answer. Not speaking he was still trying to get control over his breathing. 'Talk to me lad. Are you alright?' Asked Smithy now concerned. Smithy shouted over to Patsy to get Philip ready to go in the water.

'Scurvy, talk to me lad. Whatever it is you must speak to me. Are you alright?' Said Smithy trying to give Scurvy some comfort from hearing his voice.

Breathing heavily Scurvy managed to find his voice again. 'Diver 1 to surface. I'm okay Smithy, I just got a hell of a fright. I've........ I've found a body. By the mess of long blonde hair, I reckon it's a woman.'

'Now just relax Scurvy. just breath, deep and slow, deep and slow. Now are you sure?' Asked Smithy trying to keep Scurvy calm.

'Aye, as sure as eggs is eggs.' Scurvy confirmed.

'It's okay Scurvy, it's alright. Just stay where you are till we work out what to do.'

The body was still intact. It was also lying face up which was unusual for a submerged cadaver. How long it had been in there for wasn't possible to know at this stage.

With the water temperature of the dock being cold, at only around 11°C, it would have played key part in the reduction in speed of putrefaction and state of decomposition.

'What's wrong?' Patsy asked Smithy.

'Scurvy's found a deed body at the bottom of the quay wall. What to do?' Replied Smithy.

'Fuck, your shitting me. Is he sure?' Asked Patsy in surprise.

'As sure as death and taxes. No pun intended.' Replied Smithy.

'I'll phone Frank Hill at the Police Underwater Search Unit. Just tell Scurvy to hang on where he is.' Instructed Patsy.

'Scurvy lad. Patsy's going to phone Frank Hill. You've to stand by there.' Smithy informed him over the coms.

'Aye Okay. Just don't take too long about it. I no like this.' Scurvy replied.

'What way, you no like.' Asked Smithy.

'This is unsettling man.' Replied Scurvy.

'Relax Scurvy, just think of happy times. You've nothing to be afraid of here. It's dead man, it canny harm you.' Said Smithy trying to reassure him.

The dark murky water with the cadaver at Scurvy's finger tips now became an eerie, creepy place for Scurvy to be. Scurvy had to focus hard to remain calm, rational and controlled.

Few people could ever appreciate the psychological stresses placed upon divers who work in black water. Nor could they appreciate the nerves of steel, restraint and control that they have to apply to their imagination. For it is not uncommon, for the diver to touch something that they were not expecting, that feels unpleasant or even to touch something that is alive. Equally, for something alive to touch them in the darkness without their seeing.

For although the Clyde, unlike the tropics provided very few dangerous creatures and shark sightings underwater were as a rule uncommon. There were still many creatures that had poisonous sharp spines or could and would bite in a defensive reaction when startled. Such as crabs, especially large brown backed crabs, Lobsters, Conger eels, Angler fish, Scorpion fish, Weaver fish, spiny sea urchins and even on the very rare occasion, the shark. Most of which as a rule were common enough in harbours especially in cavities on quay walls.

In a dark, murky, environment like this, it is all too easy to spook oneself by allowing your imagination to run wild thus terrify yourself.

Patsy was now off the phone after talking to Frank Hill of the Police underwater search unit. He spoke to Scurvy over the coms. 'Surface to Diver 1. Scurvy I am going to send Philip down with a shot line and a buoy to mark the spot. Then you and him will recover to surface. Understood over.'

'Understood.' Scurvy replied. 'I'll watch for him coming. Over'

'Good man.' Acknowledged Patsy.

Philip followed Scurvy's umbilical. Once he was a few meters away, Scurvy could just make out the dim illumination from Philips hat light. Scurvy took great comfort from having someone else in the water with him at this point, especially knowing it was Philip.

Once back on board the Loch Ranza, Scurvy started to undo his harness to de kit.

Patsy called to him. 'Don't de kit Scurvy, you'll be going back in shortly.'

'What do you mean?' Said Scurvy in surprise.

'Frank Hill said we're to recovery the cadaver$_{(g-314)}$. He doesn't have a team available until tomorrow. One team is up in Oban looking for a lost diver on the Breda and second team are at Garvel Dock doing depth conditioning chamber dives. So, as we're on contract to them and we are working here already, he wants us to do it.' Patsy informed him. 'He's going to organise the local plod with a Forensic Pathologist to come and collect it. So you will be going back in to do the recovery. It's for the best. Trust me.' Said Patsy being serious and sincere.

'The Pathologist will advise you Scurvy on how to handle and bag the body and how to search the site before removing the body.' Explained Patsy.

A deflated, speechless Scurvy sat down fully kitted next to Philip on the edge of the coach house roof. Dreading the thought of not only going back to the cadaver*(g-314)*, but having to get up close and personal with it.

Especially knowing what state any exposed flesh of the cadaver would be in. Partly from normal decomposition and putrefaction. But also from the crabs and other sea creatures that would have been making free with this feast that had been lying on the seabed before them.

Philip who had been watching his young friend closely, thoroughly understood the turmoil that was going through Scurvy's head. He knew only too well the stomach churning dread that was taking place in his guts. He also recognised that Scurvy did not want to go back in the water.

'Scurvy lad, I know what you're thinking, I understand what's going through your head right now. But I am with Patsy on this.' Philip confirmed. 'You have to be the one who does the recovery. You also have to do it on your own. Because if you don't do this now. Believe me, you will never go back in the water again.'

'You will want to be the stand by diver, you'll make up all sorts of stories and excuses for not going in the water. The stories and excuses will become to sound ridiculous and pathetic. For those who don't know you as we do, they will ridicule and demean you for it. You will end up not only afraid of the water but also afraid of the dark. But there's no need to be.'

'Focus on the fact that a cadaver can't harm you. Sure it's not a pretty sight, especially when you see it on the surface. To describe the experience as unpleasant doesn't even begin to do it justice. So, whilst you're doing this, don't think of it as a dead body. Think of it as just another asset, an object that was once topside and is now on seabed needing to be recovered. Just as you have done many times before. I know this sounds cold and callous. But you need to think like this to keep you mentally detached.'

'Also, the Police divers do this on a regular basis and one or two of them are wankers. So if they can do it, we all here have every faith and confidence that you can. Oh wait, don't take that the wrong way, I'm not saying you're a wanker. No, none of us think you're a wanker. Ach, you know what I mean.'

'Anyway once your back in the water, after five maybe ten minutes and it will be all over and done with, no drama. You must know we all have a lot of respect for you Scurvy. And if you do this now, I can assure you will have earned your fins. In our eyes and in those of the Police underwater unit you'll no longer be seen as a baby diver.'

Scurvy knew that Philip was completely correct in what he had said about not wanting to go back in the water. Scurvy also knew that the reality was that he was the one who had to go back in.

To an extent, it can be compared to falling off your bike as a child, only this was a more extreme, adult version of the same thing. Scurvy found Philips approach and advice on this whole event actually quite comforting and reassuring. It helped him to rationalise what it was that he was about to do. He was very glad to have Philip as a colleague and a friend.

When the Police and Forensic Pathologist arrived on site, it was time for Scurvy to face up to his challenge. The coroner explained to Scurvy about carefully searching the seabed around the body for anything that could have been used as a weapon, or for jewellery, personal belongings, other items of clothing or any other items that could potentially be associated with the Cadaver.

The Pathologist then handed scurvy a zip lock bag which strangely contained two pairs of women's knee length pantyhose. These were for putting over the hands and feet of the cadaver so as to protect any evidence that may be contained under fingernail etc should it turn out that foul play was afoot. The Pathologist took out one of the stockings and showed Scurvy how to apply it to the hands and feet of the Cadaver.

The reason for this was that until known otherwise, it should be treated as a crime scene. As such an attempt must be made to inspect for, preserve and gather evidence just as the CID would had done if the body been found on land.

The coroner also explained how best to handle the cadaver for placing it into the body bag. Again this was to try to preserve the body as intact as possible for the Post Mortem examination.

Gloomily and perturbed, Scurvy returned to the water. On the surface he finned over to where the orange buoy marked the spot.

He descended down the shot line into the eerie gloom to the grey decaying corpse which was lying face up in the silt below. The only sounds to be heard were the rush of air from his Band Mask demand valve*(1-321)* as he breathed in, the sound of his exhaust bubbles as he breathed out and the basic but brief communications with the Smithy on the surface.

In some ways the poor visibility of the turbid, stout coloured harbour water on this occasion was actually a benefit to Scurvy. For it meant that he couldn't get any clear definition of the face or exposed flesh areas where the sea creatures would have been feeding on the corpse.

Remembering what Philip had said to him and now thinking about his task more as an underwater detective instead of the gruesome task of a dead body recovery. Doing exactly as the Pathologist instructed. Scurvy began a very slow fingertip search of the thin silt layer that covered a reasonably firm seabed. performing this where possible over a distance of approximately two meters from the outer edges of the cadaver. All the time trying to stay focused and rational not allowing himself to become spooked.

After completing the search and finding nothing. Scurvy's next task was the preservation of evidence over the hands and feet of the cadaver.

In the murky water, slowly feeling his way hand over hand he touched the side of the cadaver furthest away from the quay wall. He could feel his heart starting to pound in his chest, a shiver ran down his spine. Upon locating the hand, feeling squeamish, he laid it over her stomach.

The fact that Scurvy could move the arm in such a way demonstrated that rigor mortis had passed. This was important information for the Pathologist.

Green and velvet crabs were crawling over her body and her face. For reasons unknown to him, deep from within, Scurvy suddenly found the psychological strength to just pick the crabs off her.

Some of the exposed skin and some of the flesh from her hand and face had been eaten. The remaining skin was appeared blanched and wrinkled. Her body, face and limbs had a partially swollen look to them, her skin had a greyish tinge to it.

Taking out the zip lock bag from his drysuit thigh pocket he removed one of the rolled up nylon pantyhose. He pushed his fingertips into the toe of the panty hose and partially rolled it back over his own fingers. Then very carefully, he picked up the left hand of the cadaver by its finger tips and began to roll the pantyhose over her hand and up her arm.

He repeated the process for her right arm and then with both her feet.

He returned to the shot line and then to the surface to find the Police officers and the Pathologist standing on the quayside above. They lowered down a rolled up body bag to Scurvy.

Descending the shot line once more, once on bottom Scurvy unrolled and unfolded the body bag just below her feet but parallel to the cadaver. Due to the fact that more than half of the human body is made up of liquid and fat, the average adult only actually weights around 6kg when fully submerged in water. Thus making a cadaver an easily manageable weight to swim with under the water.

Scrunching her skirt hem up in his hand just above her knees and doing the same with her denim jacket just below her chest. Scurvy floated her up about 150mm off the seabed and swam with her to lay her gently down on the body bag. He laid her long blonde hair over her shoulder on one side so that it came down over her chest.

Folding the body bag over the top of her he zipped the two half's of the bag together. He then paused for a moment. Sitting on the seabed with the cadaver sealed in the bag, his breathing & heartbeat had now returned to normal.

Scurvy was not in any way a religious man. He did not believe in the Church, or the bible or any other form of prescribed religious teaching or any such like. However, he did believe that the world was far to structured, aesthetically pleasing, creative, methodical and logical for it to have been created as a result of two giant boulders colliding in space making a big bang. Scurvy did believe that there were powers far greater than mortal man. What shape or form they came in well, that was something else altogether.

Sitting on the seabed in the murky, dark water of the harbour, with the bagged cadaver in front of him, Scurvy felt a sense of calm, a satisfaction. He felt that he was no longer alone, instead had a companion in the water next to him. In his own thoughts, he told himself that what he had just done was good thing, an act of kindness.

It now seemed all okay to him. He was no longer perturbed by the situation that he found himself in. Speaking calmly over the coms he called. 'Diver 1 to Surface. Over.'

'Go ahead Scurvy.' Smith replied

'Bringing the Cadaver to surface.' Scurvy informed him.

On reaching the surface the Police officers threw down to Scurvy, a rope with a Karabiner attached. He clipped it into the looped handle at head end of the body bag . Then watched as two uniformed Police officers unceremoniously dragged the dead body of the woman up the quay wall.

As they were tying up the Loch Ranza back in her berth in the East India Harbour, Pirate came motoring into the harbour on the RIB after having been diving for clabbydoos. Shortly after, they walked through the door of their second favourite, yet most often visited watering hole, the Marine Bar. Which was all too conveniently located on the quay, only 40 yards from where the Loch Ranza was berthed.

'There you are Scurvy, get this down you. There's nothing like the Hebrides finest for stiffening the sinews after the day that you have just had.' Said Patsy, handing Scurvy a large Bunnahabhain (Pronounced bu na ha venn) single malt whisky.

'You know Patsy, what really struck me was how undignified and unceremoniously the two coppers dragged her up the quay wall. I mean, at the end of the day, she is still someone's daughter and I think she deserved better than that.' Said Scurvy thoughtfully.

'I know Scurvy and you're probably right. Best not to dwell on though eh. You really don't want to know anything about her. It's done now, forget about it. Move forward, it's best, trust me. Here you want a laugh, watch this.' Said Patsy aiming to take Scurvy's mind off it.

Patsy picked up one of the Clabbydoos from the sack that Pirate has brought in for the pub regulars. He split it open at the bar and shouted to the barmaid who was collecting glasses from the tables. 'Hey Angela.'

'Aye what is it?' The bar maid asked

'See this.' Said Patsy holding up the opened Clabbydoo. 'This looks like your fanny.' And laughed.

Angela, not impressed put down the glass tumblers she had been collecting, then belted Patsy with a hefty right hook which knocked him clear off his barstool. Wow, talk about taking one for the team.

The whole Pub, including Scurvy erupted into uncontrollable fits of laughter. Not sure which got the greater roar of laughter, Patsy's wise crack or Patsy being sent flying.

By the end of the night, Scurvy was three sheets to the wind with the sadness and unpleasantness of the day behind him.

Early the following morning, in the living room of Patsy's house, Scurvy woke up on the sofa with a blanket around him to Patsy giving him a kick. 'Hands of cock, pull on socks, stand by your bed. Time to get up, come on now, let's not dilly dally.' Roared a surprisingly sprite Patsy.

'Eh, what time is it?' Groaned Scurvy.

'6.30am. Come on we need to get going. The Loch Ranza needs to be at Rothesay dock for 10am, remember?' Patsy reminded him.

'Oh aye. Christ ma heid. What was I drinking last night?' Moaned Scurvy trying rather unsuccessfully to come alive.

'Everything and anything. At one point you were minesweeping off the tables.' Patsy informed him.

'Oh man, this hurts. Don't let me do that again.' Moaned Scurvy regretting his over indulgence.

Patsy with some sympathy and understanding handed Scurvy a glass of Resolve. 'Here Swallow this and you'll be fine. There's a bottle of Irn Bru in the car.'

Resolve and Irn Bru two little gifts from God for hangovers.

Arriving at the East India harbour, Scurvy was still a little worse for wear. Smithy and Philip were waiting for them with the Loch Ranza's engine warming up, ready to depart.

'Oh here comes a drunken sailor.' Observed Philip with a companionate smile.

'Well, we huvn'y a long boat to throw him into, so what's your plan for getting him sober?' Asked Smithy.

'Not a problem, we have just the very thing for medical emergencies such as this.' Replied Philip.

Philip broke out the emergency oxygen resuscitation kit and passed the oral nasal mask to scurvy who was now sitting on the coach house roof with his head in his hands.

'A couple of whiffs of this Scurvy and you'll be right as rain in no time.' Philip said confidently.
Heading out of the entrance of the East India harbour, the Loch Ranza made her way for Rothesay Dock further up the Clyde towards Glasgow.

'Are the Bizzes going to meet us along there?' Asked Smithy.

'Aye they checked for bodies last week and didn't find any. There's five stolen vehicles to recover, so quite a bit of rigging involved. Rothesay Dock is quite a nasty spot. with a lot of debris So they want additional diving support for the job.' Replied Patsy.

'Five vehicles to recover, wow. A popular spot is Rothesay dock.' Remarked Smithy.

Rothesay dock finally ceased to be a working dock a couple of years prior. The result of which was it had sadly succumbed to vandals and had became a popular spot for joy riders and villains to dispose of stolen cars. Ultimately, these cars became crown evidence in criminal investigations and trials. As such had to be recovered.

Up on the quayside at Rothesay dock were three flatbed trucks and a crane. The mobile surface support unit for the Police Underwater Search Unit was there also. The Police divers had marked the locations of the five cars with surface marker buoys.

With the Loch Ranza tied up alongside the quay, the divers got kitted up. Inspector Frank Hill of the underwater unit took overall charge of the recovery operation.

So as to keep separation of umbilicals between the two sets of divers. The Police divers prepared the lifting rigging on the vehicles nearest and furthest away from the Loch Ranza. Thus allowing two cars to be rigged up at the same time, so as to reduce the length of time the Police Underwater Unit was tied up with such operations.

The Erskine road suspension bridge spanned across the River Clyde connecting Renfrewshire to West Dunbartonshire at Erskine and Old Kilpatrick accordingly.

A car stopped half way across the bridge. The driver, a young dark haired man in his late twenties, got out of the car. His car now blocked the road.

Calmly he walked to the side of the bridge and climbed over the barrier to the outside. He stood on the outside edge of the bridge, with his hands behind his back holding onto the barrier. He looked east across the horizon towards Glasgow city, then cast his eyes down at the river Clyde 48 metres below.

The second car had just been lifted out of the water when Frank Hill called a halt to the diving operations. He had just received a call to inform him that there was a potential suicide standing on the edge of the Erskine bridge threatening to jump. The Police divers along with the Loch Ranza had been summoned to the scene.

They made their way three miles upriver to stand by upstream of the Erskine Bridge. They were slightly upstream of the bridge because they were on a flood tide. About thirty minutes after arriving on location, a RIB came out to meet them from Bowling harbour with a Police Forensic Medical Examiner. He climbed onboard the Loch Ranza.

'Hello there.' Said Scurvy taking the RIB painter line and helping the M.E. aboard. 'Kind of pre empting the end result are you not. You've obviously not got a lot of faith in your psychologist. Who do you have up there the apprentice? Do you not think you're being a wee bit quick to be on the negative side. I mean the guys not dead yet.' Said Scurvy trying to be a bit positive about the outcome.

'Sadly, it's become standard procedure in situations like this.' Replied the M.E quite matter of fact. 'If he does jump, he'll go from travelling at 70mph to zero instantly. Depending on his body weight, the force of him hitting the water at that speed will be around 350,000 pounds per square inch maybe more. This will result in a broken neck, a broken back, a ruptured spleen, lacerated aortas, other ruptured organs and massive internal injuries and bleeding. His chances of survival are none and fuck all. I'm just here to certify him dead if he does jump. It means that we don't have to call an emergency paramedic crew off of the front line.' Explained the M.E making the picture a bit clearer for Scurvy. 'Besides, it's a fine day and it gets me out of the office.' Smiled the M.E.

Up on the bridge, this sad dejected, pitiful soul of a young man was still on the outside of the barrier. The Police had moved the young man's car so as to reinstate the flow of traffic and had cordoned off one lane. There was a cordon of Police Officers trying to hold back the mangy dogs of the gutter press and media vultures who were clamouring for a photo and a story. In the air, a helicopter had been chartered by one of the gutter press or media vultures. So as to be guaranteed the perfect video or photo opportunity should the young man jump off the bridge.

    The Police psychologist was trying his best to convince the poor soul into climbing back over the barrier to a place of safety.

Onboard the Loch Ranza, it was a long wait. The Police divers were waiting patiently, playing cards, ready, fully kitted should they need to go in to recover the body. For sadly, all too often they have been here before.

Frank Hill and the M.E. were listening closely to the radio, waiting for the worse to happen whilst hoping for the best. Patsy was at the helm, holding the Loch Ranza in position against the stem of the incoming tide. Philip was standing in the wheelhouse doorway just taking in the air.

Scurvy was up on the bow, sitting in the sun thumbing through a copy of Diver magazine and Smithy was beside him singing little parody's to himself.

'Aye, aye, aye aye
Se se senora
My sister Belinda she pished out the window
All over my brand new Sombrero
Aye, aye, aye, aye
Se se senora

Small boys are cheap today
Cheaper than yesterday
Standing up or lying down,

They're only half a crown
Older boys cost three n six
Cause they've got bigger dicks

Bigger dicks they aim to please
A tighter hole they have to squeeze'

'Stop it Smithy, you're scaring me.' Said Philip quite abruptly. Smithy shrugged of Philip without any concern. 'Whaat? You know the M.E. is as bent as a nine bob note. I'm just trying to make him feel at home with us.'

'Pish, you're stirring it. Just because he's gay doesn't make him a pedo. But we've got a boat full of coppers here and if they hear you singing that, it will be you that will be banged up under suspicion of being a pedo, no him.' Replied Philip.

Smithy grinning continued with his parodies.

'Roll, roll, roll your joint,
twist it at the end
take a puff, that's enough
now pass it to a friend.'

'Jack and Jill went up the hill to smoke a little leaf.
Jack got high and dropped his fly
and Jill said 'Where's the beef?'

'Jack and Jill went up the hill
so Jack could lick her candy
But Jack got a shock
and a mouth full of cock
Cause Jill's real name is Randy.'

'Jack and Jill went up the hill so Jack could lick Jill's fanny.
But all Jack got was a mouthful of cock,
cause Jill's a fucking tranny.'

'Jack and Jill went up the hill to smoke some marijuana
Jack got high and opened his fly and Jill said I awanna.'

'Little Miss Muffet sat on a tuffet
Her clothes all tattered and torn

It wasn't a spider who crept up behind her
But Little Boy Blue with his horn.'

'Old mother Hubbard went to the cupboard
to fetch her poor dog a bone.
But when she bent over
Rover took over
and the bitch got a bone of her own.'

Philip smiling then frowning asked Smithy. 'Where did you pick this pish up from?'

'I can't help myself.' Smithy replied. 'It's ever since Tricky Dickie has been coming into the office, he's full of them and now they're stuck in my head.'

'I'm somewhat deeply suspicious about Dicky. There's something highly questionable about him I can assure you.' Said Philip with a distrusting tone. 'He said to me the other day, I am a member of a very exclusive club, it's a club that you'd never be able to hold membership of. Going by what you've just said, that's just confirmed for me what he meant.'

No sooner had Philip finished speaking did Frank Hill get a warning message over the radio.

'It's not looking good Frank, have your diver ready.' Came a voice over the VHF radio.

'Patsy bring her starboard side too. Okay lads get ready it looks like he's going for it.' Instructed Frank to Patsy and the divers.

'Oh Fuck! He's gone off the bridge.' Came the voice over the radio.

They all looked up to see a sad and extremely troubled young man spread his arms and perform the flying angel off of the bridge taking his own life.

The young man's body hit the water of the Clyde at a great rate of knots with a tremendous force creating a loud thud and a large splash. He had covered a vertical distance of approximately forty eight meters in about three seconds. His speed upon impact would have been around 70mph.

He was a tangled mess with a broken neck and spine, bleeding from his orifices, with severe internal injuries. Some of his ribs had broken and had punctured the skin and one of his eyeballs had popped out and was hanging by the optic nerve.

However, just before the Police diver went into the water to retrieve the body.

'Okay judges, marks out of ten?' Asked the Police Sergeant. All the Police officers held up little white placards to score the high dive of the suicide victim. '7.5, 7.5, 8.4, 7.5 & 8........ A very respectable 38.9. Well placed to take the silver this year I think.' Tallied up the Sergeant.

This act by the Police divers should in no way whatsoever be seen as a desecration of the young man's life or as a trivialization of the young man's suicide. For the purpose behind it couldn't be further removed.

What you have to appreciate here is that as a Police diver, a high percentage of their work is looking for and physically handling up close almost cheek to jowl, mutilated and usually severely decomposed dead bodies. More often than not performing this task in some of the most disgusting of aquatic environments and sadly, often with children. This has a phenomenal psychological impact on any human being. I defy, anyone to legitimately claim otherwise.

As such, to prevent the nightmares, the visions, to enable then to continue with this awful, incredibly unpleasant, yet necessary job. They act like this amongst themselves as a coping mechanism. It is their way of keeping themselves emotionally detached and sane.

'Okay lads, you've had your fun now get in and get him before he sinks.' Ordered Frank Hill.

The Loch Ranza motored up closer to the cadaver. The Police diver jumped into the water, collected the cadaver, then swam back towards the boat, with the body in tow. Once again, the cadaver was unceremoniously dragged from the water.

The body was examined by the M.E. who pronounced him dead. The Police then placed the cadaver into a black body bag and zipped it closed.

'Aye Frank, dead as a Dodo. Time of death 16:24hrs. Cause of death, suicide by bridge, resulting in multiple fatal injuries caused by blunt force trauma.' Informed the M.E.

The M.E turned to face Scurvy. 'As you have seen Scurvy, jumping itself isn't fatal, It's the landing that kills you. And it's not always an instant death. Some jumpers take a minute or two to die and they die in extreme pain and mortal agony.'

'It is not uncommon for jumpers to find themselves with their bodies smashed and internal organs ruptured to still be conscious. For them to then endure the pain and trauma of drowning over and above that. Fortunately for this lad, his death was instantaneous.'

'People are quite deluded into thinking that jumping off a bridge is a light airy way to end your life, a bit like going to the Angels. But as you have just seen. It is an urban myth, a myth I'd love to shatter.'

'You hit the water hard, very little difference from hitting concrete. As you've seen it's not a pretty death. But until you have seen the brutality of the effects for yourself, it's ni on impossible to convince someone otherwise.'

As the Loch Ranza motored the short distance up to Bowling harbour to off load the Cadaver, the Police divers, de kitted and packed up. The mood had changed and all were quiet onboard.

It was late in the day now. Once the Police divers had disembarqued, Patsy took the Loch Ranza down river back to her berth in the East India Harbour in Greenock.

'Well Scurvy, what a day. You just never know what will be thrown at you next.' Said Patsy breaking the silence.

'You can say that again, but tell me Patsy, is body recovery always so cold and uncaring. It just doesn't seem right. I mean it seems awfully cheap, inconsiderate, disrespectful and demeaning.' Said Scurvy confused.

'It's not that we're disrespectful or lack any feeling, empathy or emotion for what has happened to these people Scurvy.' Replied Patsy. 'It is just that you have got to detach and harden yourself to their deaths. Otherwise, you end up becoming emotionally involved, having sleepless nights and not wanting to go in the water for fear of it. As a working diver it's part of the job. And you have to do whatever it takes to allow you to continue doing the job. Get use to it Scurvy, because like it or not there will be more.'

With the Loch Ranza tied up securely to her moorings. This little band of brothers climbed up onto the quayside. 'Come on lads. let's celebrate life.' Invited Patsy.

'That's the best thing I've heard all day.' Replied Philip.

Inside the Marine Bar, they met up with their fellow mariners and started to enjoy the crack. Standing at the bar, Patsy has got the first round of drinks in. He raised a toast.

'Here's to Life
There are good ships, there are wooden ships.
There are ships that sail the sea.
But the best ships are friendships
And may they always be.'

In unison they clinked their glasses together and shouted 'To Life. Slàinte Mhath.'*(g-318)*

As the evening wore on, the divers were having a laugh with the crew of one of Cory's tugboats. The skipper and crew got up to leave, they were three sheets to the wind.

'Safely home now lads.' Scurvy bid them.

The skipper waved goodbye and they staggered out of the bar.

Patsy said to Scurvy. 'Safely home. They're not going home Scurvy, they're going out to sea. They're going to meet one of the coal carriers arriving into Hunterston.'

'What you're joking, they canny be. They're three sheets to the wind man.' Said Scurvy in disbelief.

'I'm being serious.' said Patsy. 'Come look and see.'

At that, Patsy, Scurvy, Smithy and Philip spilled out of the pub door. They watched in disbelief and amazement, the tugboat crew with their Skipper in front stagger and meander down along the quayside to where their tugboat was berthed. Then by some miracle, the tugboat's crew walked perfectly straight across the makeshift scaffold board gangplank onto the tug.

A few minutes later, it's powerful British Polar diesel engine growled into life and black smoke puffed out of its exhaust. The lights came on, the gangplank pulled aboard, the mooring warps having been cast off were pulled aboard and coiled neatly on the deck.

Up in the bow of the boat, a seaman crashed out asleep in a coil of thick mooring rope. The sea going tug snaked its way across to the mouth of the harbour, narrowly missing another tug tied to its berth. Then made its way out of the harbour and meandered down the Clyde to meet up with another three tugs. Their role was to assist with the berthing of a giant 240meter long coal carrier. Which was carrying 230,000 tonnes of coal that would be arriving shortly into Hunsterton jetty to be offloaded for Britain's power stations.

The divers turned to look at one another in disbelief and amazement then burst into laughter. Smithy Patsy, Scurvy and Philip, linked arms and then burst into song, dancing on their way back to the Marine Bar for a final drink before closing time. In unison they sang a parody to tune of the Lewis Bridal song.

Oh step we gaily on we go
Singing and dancing heel to toe
Arm in arm, row on row
All for a ride o' Mhairi
(Acting out the next couple of lines)

Skirts up and troosers doon
Willies swinging all around
Shagging up and down the town
Wi the slutty Mhairi, Mhairi, Mhairi

Oh step we gaily on we go
Singing and dancing heel to toe
Arm in arm, row on row
All for a ride o' Mhairi

SMITHY
(Solo)
Sipping whisky & slugging beer
Grinning fae ear tae ear
Awe the blankets fur tae tare
When your shagging Mhairi

SCURVY
(Solo)
Red her cheeks as rowans are
Bright her eye as any star
A sailors friend from near or far
Is oor darling Mhairi

PATSY, SCURVY, PHILIP & SMITHY
(In unison)
Oh step we gaily on we go
Singing and dancing heel to toe
Arm in arm, Row on row
All for a ride oh Mhairi
PATSY
(Solo)
Ample breast for a gentle feel
Plenty meat to fill her creel
Plenty bonnie bairns as weal
That's the toast o' Mhairi

PATSY, SCURVY, PHILIP & SMITHY
(In unison)
Step we gaily on we go
Singing and dancing heel to toe
Arm in arm, row on row
All for a ride oh Mhairi

Step we gaily on we go
Singing and dancing heel to toe
Arm in arm, Row on row
All for a ride oh Mhairi

Whistling the remainder of the tune as they crashed in through the door of the Marine Bar just in time to make last orders.

CHAPTER 7

When the North Wind Blows

The North wind doth blow

and we will have snow

what will the people do then, poor things.

They'll turn up the heating, wear woollen jammies

and big thick house coats

to keep themselves warm in bed, poor things.

The North wind doth blow

and we will have snow

what will the divers do then, poor things.

They'll freeze their fuckin bollocks off that's what they'll do.

Poor things and nobody will give a damn.

Until that is, the people wrapped up warm in bed desperately need their services.

The above poem is a parody of the children's poem
The north wind doth blow

There are few vistas' on the Clyde coast that can beat the snow covered mountains and shore line that envelope Loch Striven on a crisp, sharp, calm winters morning. Especially, when a clear blue sky holding the winter's sun above, is sparkling over the flat surface of the water like a mirrored reflection.

That is exactly how it was on this December's morning when the motley crew from GDMC along with the good ship Loch Ranza were cleaning the fish cages for the Salmon farm on the north west side of Loch Striven. They had a new member on the team with them on this project, Big Nigel or the Big Nig as he was often known for the obvious and not so obvious reasons.

Nigel was a pleasant, easy going big fella who had been a working diver for a few years now. He was in his early thirties, tall and slim, though broad across the shoulders. He had short thick black hair, an olive complexion and a black moustache. In many ways, complexion aside, he and Smithy could easily be mistaken for brothers. In fact it was often said though not in their presence, that their mothers had the same milkman.

There were sixteen circular cages in total to be cleaned. In addition to this, all their associated mooring lines were also to be cleaned and then inspected. Each cage was thirty meters in diameter and the bottom of the cage net was in about eighteen meters water depth.

The cages were set into two separate groups of eight. Each group forming two parallel rows with four cages in each row. They were moored about two hundred and twenty meters from the shoreline where the water depth was about twenty five meters deep.

Each cage had the capacity to hold approximately six thousand live salmon, which just swam around the cage in a circle demented. The fish were bred from eggs in onshore freshwater hatcheries. The fish will have been transferred into the cage once they were twelve to sixteen months old. At this stage they are known as Smolts.

At this age, they go through a change called smoltification. This change enables a Salmon to live in seawater. Each fish will weigh between 100 to 200 grams and will be about 150-200mm in length. After smoltification, they will be reared in the sea cages for around eighteen to twenty four months until they reach market size which is between 2.5 to 5Kg in weight.

It is also not uncommon to find a thousand or so large Lump Fish (Cyclopterus Lumpas) inside Salmon farm cages. They can grow up to 50cm in length and 5Kg in weight. Fish farmers introduced this species into the pen to help keep down the sea lice population that is unfortunately associated and are endemic with farmed fish.

One of the group of 8 cages were empty, these were the ones that were to be cleaned and inspected first. After which the Salmon in the other group of cages would be transferred into the newly cleaned cages so that the other group of cages could then be cleaned.

This was quite a major contract for GDMC as it would take them between six to eight weeks to complete weather depending. So for a winter contract it was quite a prize.

'Isn't it beautiful here Philip.' Admired Scurvy as he was climbing into harness. 'Intensely cold, but beautiful none the less.'

'Aye it is that, enjoy the vista while it lasts Scurvy because according to the forecast were due to get a major blizzard tonight.' Philip informed him.

'Really, it looks so serene and the air is so still here.' Said Scurvy surprised.

'Aye, it's right enough Scurvy, this is the calm before the storm.' Confirmed Philip. 'According to the 24 hour forecast a major low pressure front is on its way. There's a Northerly cyclone coming straight across from Greenland over the Rockall Rise. The west coast is going to get battered with it. A major Arctic storm will be upon us by the wee hours of tomorrow morning.'

'It should mean we'll get a couple of extra days in Rothesay on weather pay to put our feet up in the comfort of the B&B until it blows over.' Said Smithy with a smile who always tried to find the good in all things bad.

'Therefore Scurvy lad we need you to make haste and get in the water so we can report some progress to the client before this blow kicks in.' Instructed Patsy who had been standing at the wheel house door listening to the conversation.

Smithy, lifted up Scurvy's Aquadyne AH3 helmet*(2-323)* and locked it onto the make-up yolk with the neoprene neck seal which was around Scurvy's neck. Then clipped in the securing harness that held the helmet down which stopped it from wanting to float off his head.

After the usual deck and coms checks, Scurvy strode off the side of the Loch Ranza into the near freezing but clear waters of Loch Striven. Rising to the surface surrounded by a flurry of bubbles, Scurvy swam to the side of the boat so that Nigel could hand him down the retro jet net cleaning lance*(9-335)*.

The retro jet was basically a high pressure water jetting lance that had a second jet of water coming out the back of it to stop the diver from being pushed back by the force of the water jets. The lance was balanced with buoyancy attached to it so as to minimise fatigue on the divers arms.

This particular lance instead of it having a single jetting nozzle, had a broad head on the front which was about 25cm across, the head had five fan nozzles on it in a single row. This meant that the diver could clean a quarter meter wide path in a single sweep. Making the operation more efficient especially when working at the deeper section of the net.

Most of the heavy marine fouling was in the first ten meters of water depth. Here there was a lot of weed growth, algae, mussels, anemones, and starfish blocking up the nets.

The mesh size of these nets varied from 1.5cm to 2.5cm squared depending on the age of the fish therefore the size of the fish. As such, the marine growth created several problems for the farmers. It restricted the flow of oxygenated water to the fish. Equally, it reduced the amount of naturally found zooplankton and amphipods in the water column that get to the fish. For these form part of their diet as well as the feed the farmers provided for them.

As well as this, the Lump Fish that the farmers keep in the nets to delouse the Salmon, preferred to feed of the bio fouling on the nets rather than the sea lice on the Salmon because it is a much easier and far more nutritious meal for them.

It also placed additional extreme stress on the cages and their mooring systems by not only increasing the weight of the cage but tidal current and sea swell would now push on the sides of the cages as opposed to being able to pass through the cages. Thus generating tremendous side loading forces.

Scurvy started his dive at a depth of around 11meteres. The bottom of the heavy bio fouling zone. The underwater visibility was really good, over 10 meters in both the vertical towards the surface and horizontal direction. He would sweep around one half of the cage being able to clean a1.5meter tall swath with the lance in one vertical sweep. Once completing one half of the cage he would return to his start point then repeat the process around the other half of the cage.

He would then return to the start point and come up 1.5meters shallower then repeat the process again working his way up towards the surface.

Based on the US Navy diving tables*(11-337)* which were the go to table for commercial divers of the time. At 11meters he had a no decompression time of 3hours. But as he would be constantly working up towards a shallower depth, thus performing a multi level dive. It meant that he could actually have a dive time of over 4 hours before coming to the surface and another diver taking over. Unless the cold and fatigue got to him first.

After which, he would return to the surface and then Philip would go would in and the Big Nig after Philip.

'Diver 1 to Surface ready for jets, make hot over.' Called Scurvy. 'Surface to Diver 1, pressures on, the lance is hot.' Replied Patsy.

Scurvy held the lance carefully over the top of his shoulder so that the retro jet*(9-335)* was pointing clearly behind him. Pulling the trigger, he started blasting the bio fouling off the net in an up and down sweeping motion, which to his pleasant surprise made quick work of cutting through the dense bio fouling that had attached itself to the cage.

The retro jet was actually quite noisy under the water, but Scurvy was grateful to Patsy for letting him use the Aquadyne helmet*(2-323)* instead of a Kirby Morgan Band Mask*(1-321)* that Philip had been given, as it helped to block out some of the noise of the water jet.

With Smithy keeping him on a tight umbilical, it was actually not as physically demanding a task as Scurvy thought it would be.

The temperature of the water at this depth was somewhat colder than normal for this time of year at around 7.7ºC. Normally thanks to the North Atlantic Drift which comes off from the Gulf Stream current from the warm waters of central America and the Gulf of Mexico. The waters of the west coast of Scotland are normally a degree or two warmer than this. However, this December it was on a par with the Northern North Sea which is fed from waters of the colder Norwegian sea.

Due to the constant physical movement, the 200gram Thinsulate under suit, Damart thermal underwear (usually associated with old aunties) and the 8mm neoprene drysuit that Scurvy was wearing he didn't really feel the cold. That was except for his hands. Even though he was wearing 5mm thick neoprene gloves, because his fingers were just gripping the lance and not moving, he lost all feeling in his hands with the cold. Initially they felt extremely cold. this passed until he lost sensation in his hands altogether. But this was something that he had become accustomed to every since he started diving from the age of 15.

As the bio fouling came clear of the nets with the lance cutting through it like a knife through butter, the gentle current of the outgoing tide carried away the detritus, thus maintaining good visibility in the water column.

This plume of highly nutritious food source in the water column had attracted a shoal of Pollock that where now feed ferociously upon it. They were everywhere swimming in and around Scurvy as he continued to add to their banquet. It was quite a sight to behold.

The four hour dive seemed to pass quite quickly for Scurvy. He had become quite focused and was actually thoroughly enjoying the task especially being surrounded by the shoal of Pollack. For from the very start he was able to see instant results which he took enormous satisfaction in.

By the time Patsy recalled him back to the surface, Scurvy had actually cleaned the cage net as a complete circumference from the 11meter starting depth right up to 4.5meters from the surface. Though he was very pleased with the efforts and outcome of his work, Scurvy was extremely glad to get out of the water so as to get something hot to eat and drink and to get direct heat back into his body again.

It was only after passing up the jetting lance to Nigel, did scurvy start to fully appreciate the complete lack of sensation in his hands. For his hands had become so stiff and numb that he could barely grip the rungs of the dive ladder as he climbed out of the water back on board the Loch Ranza. Smithy had to keep him on a very tight umbilical as he climbed over the bulwarks with Nigel giving Scurvy a helping hand up and over. Smithy and Nigel stripped Scurvy of his equipment and Patsy, the good man that he was, had a mug of hot soup ready for him to hand.

Still zipped into his drysuit, with his neoprene gloves removed, his hands dried and a pair of fleece gloves in their place, Scurvy stiff fingered, held the mug gingerly in both hands and relished the hot soup warming his throat and his body.

He began to feel the heat of the mug coming through the fleece gloves as the circulation started to return to his hands. Slowly but surely he started to feel pins and needles in his fingers, then a little pain akin to a burning sensation which came and went. The stiffness began to ease as movement and flexibility returned to his hands once again. With the gloves off, he was now holding the mug of hot soup in one hand and a thick hot roll and bacon with tattle scone and brown sauce in the other. Heaven.

Patsy couldn't get a word out of him until Scurvy had wolfed this lot down and was starting on his second bacon roll and after having finished his mug of soup, now had a mug of hot coffee in his hands.

'So Scurvy, how's it looking down there?' Patsy asked.

'It's looking really good if I do say so myself.' Replied Scurvy, very pleased with what he had achieved. 'That Retro jet*(9-335)* is fantastic, it cuts through that heavy marine growth in no time. with having the broad head you see large results instantly. It's quite an impressive bit of kit. You've just got the last 4.5m to surface to do and this sections complete. The bio fouling below the 11m meter is fairly fine, you can brush a lot of that of by hand. So this lance will skoosh through it when we come to do the deeper section.'

'Good man, that's what I like to hear. You've done us proud Scurvy lad.' Commended a very pleased Patsy. 'Right you change places with Nigel and we'll get Philip in next. Nigel, let's get you into your bondage gear. You will take over from Philip as Stand by diver.'

'Philip, you feeling fit, you're up next. Here's the plan. I want you to go down to the 14 meter mark. Make your way around and up to the 11m mark where Scurvy started. Then we will bring you up to the 4.5 meter mark and you can finish that section as your gassing off. Savvy?' Explained Patsy

'Yep understood, no problem. Scurvy's done the lions share anyway. If I get this done the client will be well pleased with the progress.' Acknowledged Philip.

'By the time you have completed that, it will be too late in the day to start another section. So we will get you back on board and make preparations for heading into Rothesay harbour for the night. I want to get the Loch Ranza tucked up safe and sound inside the inner harbour for this blizzard that's coming in tonight.' Said Patsy.

After Smithy gave the Aquadyne Helmet*(2-323)* that Scurvy had been wearing a clean out and quick disinfect Scurvy and Smithy helped the Big Nig to get suited and booted with the surface demand assembly that Scurvy had been using.

Nigel as stand by diver, was now seated as comfortably as one can possibly get where Philip had been. Philip now with Kirby Morgan*(1-321)* strapped to his head strode off the side of the boat into the cold clear waters of Loch Striven to take over jet blasting the bio fouling from the cage. Three meters below where Scurvy had started.

Smithy was now manning the diver control panel. Patsy was tending Philips umbilical and Scurvy was handling the high pressure water supply hose for the jetting lance. The Big Nig was sitting down fully kitted as comfortable as one can be with the volume of equipment he was strapped into, just enjoying the view.

Turning to Nigel, Scurvy said.' It's beautiful here, so tranquil.'

'Aye, it is that Scurvy lad. But at one time it wasn't you know. At one time, the air around here was filled with the roar of the Merlin engines and whine of the propellers of Mosquito fighter bomber aircraft.' Nigel informed him.

'Really. Why was that?' Enquired Scurvy curiously.

'Well, you will no doubt know of the renowned Vickers engineer Barns Wallis and the famous bouncing bomb that he developed for the Dambuster raid on the Dutch dams during world war two.' Asked Nigel.

'Oh Aye, of course I do. Wing Commander Guy Gibson, 617 Squadron and Operation Chastise in the Ruhr valley. Christ, name a school boy that grew up in the 70's that doesn't.' Replied Scurvy enthusiastically.

'But you said Mosquito Bombers, I thought 617 Squadron were modified Avro Lancaster bombers?' Said Scurvy confused.

'Good man'. Said Nigel with a smile, very pleased with Scurvy's response. 'And you are quite right, 617 Squadron the famous Dam Busters were indeed modified Lancaster bombers.'

'However, what isn't so well known Scurvy, is that Barnes Wallis developed a second bouncing bomb called a Highball bomb. It was a smaller, lighter, slightly more spherical version of the original Dambuster bouncing bomb. That could be carried by faster more agile aircraft. The smaller bomb was originally designed to be used against enemy battleships at their moorings. Whilst they were surrounded by anti submarine nets to protect them against torpedo attacks.'

'Well that smaller bomb was tested here on Loch Striven. The tests were carried out by carried out by De Havilland Mosquito fighter bombers of 618 Squadron which were based further down on the Ayrshire coast at RAF Turnberry. They practiced here on Loch Striven, to use the bombs against the Tirpitz whilst she was berthed in the Norwegian Fjords. I know this because during the war, in 1943, my granddad was based at Turnberry. He was a Mosquito Navigator with 618 Squadron. He took part in these trials. He reckons there must be around 200 of these test bombs lying here on the seabed in the deep waters of Loch Striven.'

'None of the test bombs contained explosives, most were filled with concrete to simulate the weight and mass of a real bomb. They use to fly as low as 20m above the surface of the sea when they let go the bomb. What a buzz that must have been. Unfortunately, due to various reasons, the bomb was never used in anger. The following year the squadron was disbanded and along with my granddad they were relocated to the South Pacific for aircraft carrier operations against the Japs.' Regaled Nigel with a great deal of pride.

'Wow, that was really interesting, thanks for sharing that Nigel.' Said an appreciative Scurvy.

'Aye your welcome Scurvy. It was in the south Pacific where he met my Grandma, she was a nurse from the Philippines. She was working at the US naval hospital there.' Nigel acknowledged.

'Oh, so that explains the touch of the tar brush in you then.' Said Smithy laughing.

'You're a cheeky bastard.' Replied Nigel taking Smithy's remark in good humour.

'Ach, I know, so sue me. You know how it is Nigel, when you see the target you just have to fire.' Said Smithy with a chuckle.

'I'll give you another piece of interesting trivia about Loch Striven and the war.' Continued Nigel completely unphased by Smithy's flippancy.

'The famous X Craft Midget Submarine training exercise were carried out here. In fact, the once luxurious Kyle's Hydro Hotel at Port Bannatyne had been requisitioned by the Admiralty for their headquarters. The Admiralty designated the hotel as

HMS Varbel, which served as the headquarters for the midget submarine attack on the Tirpitz. It's a pity the hotel was demolished in the 70's. I think it should have been kept as a museum to the X-craft.'

'And as a point of note, Ardtaraig House. situated at the north east of the Loch here, was also requisition by the Admiralty and served as the headquarters to the 12th Submarine Flotilla Midget Submarines. It became known as HMS Varbel ll.'

'Aye, the area has quite an interesting history right enough.' Replied Scurvy. 'And that's one of the things I like really enjoy about this job.' Said Scurvy sincerely. 'Every day is a school day and you constantly meet people with an interesting story to tell. Your day's never dull.'

It was approaching 3pm when the sun was dropping and the sky changed from clear blue to a dark grey with the day light starting to fade. An extremely cold, sharp, bitter, cutting north westerly wind was starting to freshen. Carrying with it, fine flakes of snow that had begun to lay and remain on the deck and superstructure. The sea had changed from being a mirror finish to dark, short, tight packets of waves that slapped and bounced of the fish cages. Patsy gave the order for Philip to be recovered to deck and for preparations to be made for to get underway for Rothesay harbour.

Once Philip was back on board and down below in the fo'c'sol re-warming himself, the Loch Ranza slipped her mooring ropes from the Salmon cage and started to make passage south for Rothesay.

The wind continued to freshen and ice was starting to form on the decks, superstructure and on the divers umbilicals that were coiled in figure of eights on the cow horn racks. Patsy instructed the guys to cover the umbilicals with tarpaulins to help protect them from the freezing wind and snow build up. As a result of the driving snow, visibility was now down to half a mile. Fortunately the passage to Rothesay would only take an hour.

At this time of year, except for the most hardened of leisure mariners, most leisure craft had been hauled out of the water at their respective boatyards or marina's for hull cleaning and general maintenance. Also, with it being a week day, it meant that there was plenty of available quayside berthing space in Rothesay's inner harbour for the Loch Ranza to tie up to.

Smithy had originally come down in the transit van on the ferry. He had parked up on the Mid Pier of the harbour conveniently located right next to where the Loch Ranza was now berthed.

By the time they had arrived in Rothesay, the wind had picked up severely and the snow was blowing thick and hard. The temperature had dropped dramatically. Even though they were all wearing Mullion foul weather two piece suits the guys still found it bitterly cold in the wind.

Everything was covered in snow and ice. Everything and anything that had been wet and had become covered in snow, was now crystallising as ice from the wind. The motley crew hurriedly piled into the van with their going ashore bags to get out of the weather. Then gingerly creeping off the Mid Pier, Smithy drove the van following the shoreline out along the freezing snow covered Mount Stuart road to the St Ebba Guest house, which was only three quarters of a mile from the harbour. The guest house had been booked and paid for by Ocean Harvest the owners of the fish farm. They had a long standing commercial relationship with the guest house.

'Who was St Ebba? That's a patron saint that I have never heard of before.' Enquired Smithy.

'St Ebba the younger, the chaste of Berwick also known as the martyr of Coldingham. She was an Abbess in the 9th century.' Replied Scurvy. 'The story goes that her monastery came under siege from Danish Vikings. Whilst apparently, she didn't fear death, she did fear for her chastity. So in front of her nuns, it is claimed that she took a razor and cut off her nose and her upper lip in the belief that the hideous results would protect her virginity. The act was apparently then imitated by the rest of the holy order.'

'By all accounts, this monstrous spectacle which confronted the Viking invaders worked and did protect their virginity. However, the reality of their predicament was that the Vikings were so repulsed by what they saw, that they burned down the monastery with the nuns inside it. Hence the old adage cutting your nose off to spite your face.' Scurvy informed them.

'Wow, interesting. How did you know that Scurvy, I never took you for being a Tim.' Said Smithy who was well impressed.

'I'm not, but I've shagged catholic girls.' Said Scurvy with a grin. 'When you are in that cosy after shag cuddle place, you would be quite surprised at some of the things they then come out with.'

The van pulled into the driveway of the guest house and parked up. The guys piled inside the entrance with their bags. Relieved to now be inside a building that was toasty warm. They were met by Anne the landlady who was a fit, attractive, brunette divorcee in her early fifties. A hostess with the mostest, who welcomed them in.

After stripping off their Mullion suits, Anne showed them into the spacious, comfortable well appointed guest lounge. It had a large bay window which although currently was blocked out by the blizzard outside and the falling darkness, had a fantastic view across Rothesay bay and out towards Loch Striven. The bright orange and yellow flames from a well stacked log stove roared away radiating a welcoming warmth that was appreciated by all.

'Get yourselves seated there lads, there's plenty of hot water in the urn. There's teas, coffee, hot chocolate and snacks on the sideboard. There's also hot broth in the soup kettle there, I made it fresh this afternoon. Help yourself guys, you must be completely foonert*(g-316)*. You get yourselves warmed up and relax a bit first then I'll get you signed in and allocate your rooms.' Said Anne sympathetically.

'Thank you Anne, that's kind of you and very much appreciated.' Acknowledged Patsy knowing that he was speaking for them all.

'And I thought that with the weather being so harsh that you might want to eat in this evening rather trudging through the snow to dine out. You'll also find menus on the side board and if I do say so myself, I do a hearty, warming beef stew. So once you are settled just let me know what you would like and I'll take care of it from there.' Anne informed them.

'That's sound great Anne, thanks very much. Can't beat a home cooked meal on a night like this and a hearty beef stew sounds just sublime.' Replied Patsy.

Just as Patsy had finished speaking a lively and extremely friendly young black Labrador came bouncing into the room to greet his new house guests. He bounced around the guys sniffing and licking their hands with his tail wagging back and forth nineteen to the dozen. He stopped and sat down beside Scurvy who he decided was going to be his new found friend.

'Oh, where did you come from? Jennifer, come and get your dog.' Called out Anne. 'My daughter will be the death of me. Jennifer where are you, come and get your dog?'

An extremely attractive, fit, young woman of around 23years of age came into the lounge. She was wearing red plaid leggings that hugged her thighs so tight they looked as though they were painted on, along with a figure hugging cream cashmere C neck jumper. Which accentuated every curve and appropriate bump on her body.

She had beautiful long, soft curly brown hair all the way down her back. Fine facial features with sultry brown eyes with thick dark brown eyebrows nesting above.

'Oh, I'm sorry, he escaped from out the kitchen. I'm sorry if he's bothering you.' She said apologetically with a silky smooth voice.

'Oh, no need to apologise we've just become friends, haven't we boy. Besides there something very comforting about having a dog in the house. He's fine with us.' Said Scurvy clapping the dog who was enjoying the new found attention.

Scurvy couldn't take his eyes off Jennifer. She was causing him to have a deep stirring in his loins and he couldn't stop wondering if her collar and cuffs matched. Into himself he thought, St. Ebba the Younger ha, there's nothing chaste about this girl.

'What's his name?' Scurvy asked.

'Shark.' Replied Jennifer with a smile.

Scurvy chucked, ' No really what's his name.'

'Straight up, I called him Shark.' Replied Jennifer.

'Shark, seriously, oh that's brilliant, I like it, I like it a lot.' Replied Scurvy laughing.

'Oh don't encourage her.' Said Anne. 'They've been banned from every beach on Bute.'

'She would have him off the lead and he would be running out into the water. Then Jennifer the mischievous minx, would be standing at the water's edge looking out to sea shouting after him at the top of her voice. Shark, Shaark. People would be grabbing their kids and taking them out of the water. Oh you've no idea how much trouble she's caused me over this. We've had the town council and the Mayor at our door.'

'The Council even tried to get the Police involved. Fortunately we have a good man as a Sergeant and he chased the Mayor. He politely pointed out that it wasn't a crime to name your dog Shark, though probably not the smartest thing to do either when living on an island. Fortunately, there wasn't anything on the Statute books about it either.'

'Oh man that's brilliant, that's class.' Said Scurvy laughing. Then pointing his finger at Jennifer whist grinning and said. 'You and I have the same mischievous, wicked sense of humour.' Scurvy could see in Jennifer's eyes that a great deal of fun was going to be had by both during his stay.

Shortly afterwards, Anne allocated the guys their rooms. The St Ebba was a grade 2 listed, grand old Victorian Sandstone built villa. Like most buildings of this period, it was spacious with high ceilings and large windows. It had a lot of character and was quite quirky inside. The guys all had their own rooms, which they were pleased at. For it was not uncommon for them to have to share.

But given the length of time that this job would take, Ocean Harvest wanted the guys to be comfortable and well rested on an evening, so as to be able to maximise their output when in the water working.

Although this was well out of season and the divers were it's only guests. Scurvy's room was actually a small single room up in the attic. This was because three of the double rooms were in the process of being redecorated. With Scurvy being the smallest and ultimately the most junior of the team, well them was the breaks.

Scurvy didn't mind. For although his room was a tiny attic room, it had a compact and bijou en-suit. It also had a small dormer window that had a commanding view out over the harbour and the bay toward Loch Striven and the mountains of the Cowal peninsula, a stunning vista by any measure.

Also, he knew it was the perfect hideaway from everyone else in the house for the fun he was hoping he would have with Jennifer during his stay. Being two flights up, it was ideally situated so as to be unheard or disturbed by anyone else in the house.

After settling in to their rooms and having hot showers which thoroughly reheated and refreshed them. The lads met up downstairs in the lounge for a drink before sitting down to their evening meal.

'I have checked the forecast again and have spoken with Ocean Harvest. The weather is going to be up for the next two days. So it will be Thursday or maybe Friday before we set out to the fish farm again.' Patsy informed them.

'It's official it has been named Blizzard Betty. The wind is a cyclone blowing North, North West. It is virtually coming straight down from the Arctic. The temperature is dropping sharply as I speak. They are expecting the temperature to drop to at least 15 degrees below zero. So it's going to get an awful lot colder. Also, the ferry's off. The winds are Force 9 gusting Force 10, above 60mph, which takes them way out of operational limits. There will be some big seas out there for the next couple of days.'

This was met with a uniformed 'Hooray' from the lads.

'So with that, you can have a long lie in tomorrow morning. But I want two of you to come with me to the harbour tomorrow to check the boat's moorings, sometime mid morning say around 10.30am. So if you are all down here for breakfast at nine, that will be fine.'

'We'll be down for nine bright eyed and bushy tailed.' Confirmed Philip.

With the blizzard howling outside, the big log fired stove burned brightly in the lounge with Shark curled up in front of it. St Ebba was a welcome, cosy, comfortable haven to be in.

Scurvy was very glad he was here and not back at his flat alone. After dinner the lads gathered back in the lounge for a few drinks. That was, all except for Scurvy.

Who with his belly full after stuffing his face with hot broth soup, a copious helping of beef stew with roast potatoes and a large portion of homemade apple pie with hot custard, was now feeling quite tired. His eyelids had become heavy, his belly bloated and all he wanted to do was to curl up and get cosy in bed. The long 4 hour dive of his day had started to take its toll on him. So he made his excuses, then made his way up the two flights of stairs to his small but warm and cosy attic bedroom.

He looked out of the small dormer window of his room across at the lights of the harbour through the blizzard. With the sound of the wind howling around him, violently battering the roof of the house. Scurvy found the scene tumultuous yet magnificent for there was something majestic about a winter storm. Yet at the same time, strangely he also found it comforting and was unconcerned in his warm, cosy attic nook of the solidly built sandstone house, with its heavy slated roof. His designs on Jennifer were going to have to wait another day. For all he wanted to do now was drift into a deep, deep sleep and dream of the land of Tir na nÓg *(g-319)*.

Scurvy woke early the next morning at around seven, feeling quite refreshed. He filled the room kettle, switched it on to boil then had a quick shower. Once dressed he made himself a coffee. Looking out of his window, it was still dark. The wind was still howling but the snowing for the time being had stopped. In the illumination of the street lights he could see the streets and everything therein were covered in a thick blanket of snow which helped to reflect the street lighting making the scene appear much lighter than it would have been without the snow.

He laid back on his bed, relaxing watching TV for a bit. Whilst thinking through a plan for making a move on Jennifer. For now re-energised after his good night's rest, a deep stirring was returning to his loins.

Just before nine, Scurvy made his way down to the dining room to meet up with the rest of the guys for breakfast. Smithy and the Big Nig were talking about having no water in their room this morning.

'Has the water gone off in any of your rooms?' Smithy asked the group.

'Not as far as I am aware.' Patsy replied. Scurvy and Philip answered the same.

'Nig and I had no water this morning I tried to take a shower and brush my teeth about twenty minutes ago and couldn't, not a drop of water to be had. I ended up using bottle water to brush my teeth with.' said Smithy somewhat perplexed.

'Oi stinky. I hope you used what was left of your bottled water to go round the houses with and applied a liberal amount of deodorant this morning.' Replied Philip with a grin.

At that, Anne and Jennifer followed by an excited Shark came into the lounge. 'I am really sorry to inform you guys, but the water has gone off. I have phoned a few of my neighbours and friends around the island and we are all in the same boat. I have tried to phone the water authority but the line is permanently engaged.' Explained Anne. 'I hope you weren't inconvenienced this morning by this.'

'Only smelly and stinky there.' Said Patsy with a grin pointing to Nigel and Smithy.

'Eh, not quite, we were able to go round the houses with a flannel and the bottled water we had in our rooms.' Said Smithy defensively.

'Look guys, I don't want you worry about food and drinks. I had filled the urns both in the lounge and the kitchen last night before I went to bed. I made the stock for the soup last night also.'

'We have plenty of bottled water and I have 5 15litre barrels with a hand pump for just such an occasion.'

'The island had the water cut off for 3 days about 5 years ago due to a fire at the pumping station. So I have been the last Girl Guide every since.'

'Also at the time that it happened, one of my guests was an engineer with CalMac. He kindly rigged up a little electric pump to the two rain water butts at the back of the house for me. This supply's the cistern in the downstairs guest toilet. He tee'd it into the normal supply with a check valve. So you just press and hold the switch after use until you stop hearing the toilet filling, that's the ball valve closed. Other than that you can use the toilet as normal. So we still have a flushing toilet that we can all use. I am sure your stay will still be a comfortable one.' Anne assured them.

'I think I can speak for all of us here Anne, when I say we're impressed. You have no need to worry Anne, we have no intention of moving out. We are all very comfortable here. Besides, it all adds to the adventure. It's not your fault and as you said the whole island appears to be in the same boat. And where would we go anyway?' Replied Patsy smiling reassuring her.

Anne was quite relieved to hear this for it was rare for her to have so many guests for a long term stay out of season, especially in December.

'Here, I have an idea.' Said Scurvy. 'Why don't we gather up snow and fill the baths and the basins etc to create snow melt and we can heat that for washing water.'

'If we compact snow to make small snowmen sized snowballs we could put them into black bin bags and empty them into the baths. Then we would have plenty of washing water allowing us to preserve the bottled stuff for drinking and cooking etc. If we do that this morning after breakfast between the five of us we would fill them in jig time. Then do the same again this afternoon once they have melted.'

'Six of us.' Chimed in Jennifer who thought the plan was quite clever.

'Nice one Scurvy.' Said Philip to him with a knowing wink.

'Wow, that would great if you are willing to do that guys. But let's get you fed first.' Said an appreciative Anne.

The wind though still blowing hard wasn't at fierce as it had been during the night but the air temperature was without doubt Arctic. With the amount of snow outside, Scurvy's plan worked really well on both counts. Within an hour they had filled all the baths and wash basins in the guest house with compacted snow. Shark, much to his upset was kept inside during all of this so as to avoid the issues of the yellow snow.

Scurvy and Jennifer worked together as a team on this, which began to ignite the flame Scurvy was hoping for.

Once they were finished, Patsy, Philip and Scurvy went to the harbour to check on the Loch Ranza. Patsy wanted to make sure the mooring lines were still secure and allowed adequate drop for the tide. He also wanted to check for any potential damage from the night's gales.

Rothesay bay was filled with large white crested waves clouded by a dark grey sky. The un trodden snow that covered harbour looked like a scene from a shortbread tin. In the air the wind howled and there was the out of tune orchestral chinking and twangs coming from the rigging of the few boats and yachts at their berths.

All was okay with the Loch Ranza. Though due to the wind, the drifting snow was a foot thick and more in places on the decks. Fortunately Patsy had the presence of mind to cover the umbilicals with tarpaulins during the steam into harbour the day before. Otherwise they would have been frozen together as a huge block of ice.

Going down below, Scurvy checked over the engine for any signs of a cracked block and pipework. With all appearing to be okay, Patsy fired up the engine and ran it and the Ebersparcher diesel heating system for 30 minutes. While they all helped to clear the decks and superstructure of the bulk of the snow and ice.

The main task of the day now done and Patsy happy that all was well with the Loch Ranza, the trio returned to the comfort of St Ebba. Looking forward to a hearty lunch and a relaxing day.

It was around the back of one when there was a chime of St Ebba's front door bell. Anne opened the door to be met by the local Police, a Sergeant Varney and two non uniformed gentleman who were clad in matching dark blue Helly Hanson high collared sailing jackets.

'Hello Jim, come away inside to the warm.' Said Anne addressing the Sergeant. 'What brings you out on a stormy day like this?' Enquired Anne.

'Aye, it's not the kindest of weather to be out in Anne that's for sure. Anne, would I be right in saying that you have a Pat Jamieson and his divers staying with you?' Asked the Sergeant.

'Yes I have, they're in the lounge. Why is there something wrong?' She enquired.

'Aye well, I suppose there is in a matter of speaking but not in a wicked way, nothing for you or them to worry about. Mr Ian McAskil and Mr Stuart Anderson here are from the Council. They need help with fixing the water supply problem that we now have on the island and they think Mr Jamieson and his crew are the very people for the job.'

'My role is to just give some authority and ease open any doors for the unusual help that will be needed.' Explained the Sergeant.

'Come away in and I'll introduce you.' Said Anne willingly. Anne showed them into the lounge where the guys were sitting chatting over coffee and cream scones.

'Pat, this is Jim, I mean Sergeant Varney. Mr McAskil and Mr Anderson here are from the Council. They'd like a word with you.' Introduced Anne.

'Have a seat, would you like a coffee you look as though you could do with a hot drink, Scurvy get these gentlemen a coffee.' Said an accommodating Patsy. 'Now, what brings you out to me on a day like this?'

It was Mr McAskil who spoke first. 'Well Mr Jamieson we have a major problem and we need your help to put it right. When I say, we have a problem Mr Jamieson, I mean we in the collective sense, as in we, the whole of Rothesay and Port Bannatyne.'

'Well gentlemen. it sounds very serious. You have all our undivided attention.' Replied Patsy keenly, sensing that this was going to be very profitable for the company in more ways than one.

Mr Anderson spoke next ' Mr Jamieson I have been authorised to finance whatever is required in order to get this rectified as quickly and effectively as possible. So you just invoice me direct and any additional equipment or logistic support your require for this, we will organise and put into play immediately.'

'Okay, well eh, I suppose you tell me what the problem is first and I will let know if it is within our ability to fix it.' Replied Patsy with pound signs rolling in his eyes. For on hearing this, no matter how impossible the problem was going to be, Patsy would be setting the team to work on it regardless.

'Well Mr Jamieson the problem is this.' Mr McAskil started to explain but was briefly interrupted.

'Pat, call me Pat, there's no need for formalities with us.' Said Patsy ingratiating himself.

'Very well, Pat. The problem is this. We believe that the intake debris screen of the island's fresh water reservoir pumps on Dhu Loch have become severely iced over. As such we need you guys to go into the reservoir and de-ice it'. Explained Mr McAskil.

'Really?' Replied Patsy in surprise. 'How close to the surface is it?'

'Well that's the problem, it's not. It is sited about 8 meters out from the shore line and is actually 6 meters down below the surface. The intake is box shaped, 1.25 meter square and is basically made up of steel grills about 20mm apart to protect the pumps from sucking in debris. It sits about half a meter off the bottom of the reservoir bed.'

'The water basically passes through this big strainer and then goes into a large ante chamber which has an underground tunnel connecting it to the pumping station.' Replied Mr McAskil.

'You'll need to excuse my ignorance here Mr McAskil but are you suggesting that the entire reservoir is frozen all the way through, all the way down to 6m. I can't believe that.' Said Patsy in complete disbelief. 'I mean I know this is an arctic wind and that its freezing outside well below zero, but it's not that cold.'

'Sorry, my apologies.' Replied Mr McAskil. 'Hear me out, allow me to explain. Yes you are quite right Pat, the reservoir isn't a solid mass of ice. The air temperature outside is down to minus 16°C and the surface water in the reservoir is between minus 3 to minus 4°C depending on the wind. So what we have is a frozen surface layer and a slush layer underneath, laying out from the shore line down to around 1 meter down. This has resulted in extremely fine almost microscopic ice crystals forming in the water column called Frazil ice.'

'Frazil ice build up occurs when super cooled water enters a pump intake. For freshwater reservoirs, the level of super cooling is probably in the region of one to several hundredths of a degree centigrade below the freezing temperature of 0°C. Now, super cooled water promotes the build up of Frazil ice through several processes. Unless heated, every surface of the intake in contact with super cooled water can be cooled to below freezing.'

'Once the temperature of a surface is below freezing, however slight, ice can adhere to that surface. The adhesion force of the ice is dependent on the surface material and the ice & surface material temperature below freezing. The extent of the adhesion force, even at these small levels of super cooling can be substantial.'

'With that, super cooled water carries with it small pieces of ice, Frazil. These are growing in size and are able to adhere to the intake's surfaces, especially the intake debris strainer.'

'The Frazil crystals are disk-shaped with a diameter between 0.1 to 2.0 mm. Frazil crystals are easily transported along by the water flow because of their small size and low buoyancy, in fact they are probably slightly negatively buoyant. Hence why they are drawn down through the water column by the suction of the pumps.'

'Then once attached to a surface, heat convection from the Frazil crystals allows them to adhere to the strainer intake surfaces enabling them to grow. The processes of collision-adhesion, and growth through heat convection, are the two common sources of Frazil build up on fresh water reservoir intakes. Once the strainers have a layer of Frazil ice over them, anchor ice then forms. From that, large thick layers of ice of around 20cm thick form on top of that.'

'With the ice forming on the strainers blocking the strainers, the pumps start to draw high current and then trip out on over current and low water level. As such we can't restart them until the strainers are cleared. That in a nutshell, is how we get ice build up under the water, in the water.' Explained Mr McAskil.

'And that Pat is where you and your divers come in. We need you to go into the reservoir and clear the strainers of ice and keep them clear until we can find a way to prevent the frazil ice build up or until the air temperature rises by about $5°C$ so that the water temperature rises by a degree or two.' Mr Anderson informed them.

'Wow. According to the forecast, that could be another two or three days.' Exclaimed Smithy. 'Oh man, can you imagine all these houses with unflushed toilets for three days. Their bog pans will be crammed full to the brim, overflowing with jobbies and pish. Eagh, their houses will be stinking. You could end up with a Cholera outbreak.'

'Yet, once again Smithy, you are quick to grasp the pragmatics and reality of a problem. Your eloquence in explanation is as consistent as usual. Which has provided us all with a visual graphic that we could have well done without. However, that said it does exemplify the more serious nature of the problem.' Replied Philip.

'There is many a truth in what you have said Mr Smith, eh Smithy. For this island has seen Cholera before, back in the 1850's. We are all very keen to ensure that it is never seen here again.' Exclaimed Mr Anderson.

'So if I have understood you correctly about the Frazil ice growth, we would need to be cleaning this almost constantly for two to three days?' Asked Patsy.

'Potentially, yes that is about the jist of it.' Replied Mr McAskil.

'So tell me do you not have a back flush facility or trace heating system to prevent this from happening?' Asked Patsy.

'We do have a back flush system that we use for removing fine biological growth build up, to keep the strainers clear but it won't shift this. Once you've got the strainer clean, we may be able to use the back flush to help at least slow down the process of Frazil build up but not stop it. We don't have a de-icing or ice preventative system. This is a phenomenon that to the best of my knowledge has never been experienced in this country before. I only know of it and recognised the symptoms because I did a 6 months staff exchange program in Canada through Argyll & Bute Council a few years ago. Where I experienced and learned about it then.' Explained Mr McAskil.

'Well lads, what do you think, are you all up for it?' Asked Patsy.

'We're game.' Said the team collectively.

'This will be a story for you to tell your grandchildren eh Patsy.' Said Scurvy with a smile.

'Okay then, Sergeant Varney, Mr McAskil, Mr Anderson. it's game on.' Confirmed Patsy. 'First though, we are going to have to sort out some logistics, some equipment and technical support.'

'Sergeant Varney we can't be lugging all of our surface demand equipment from off the boat so we are going to have to do this on Scuba*(g-318)* with a coms / safety line for the divers. But we are going to need breathable high pressure compressed air and endless amounts of it. I know that Rothesay sub aqua club have a 5cfm Bauer HP compressor on the island. Could you possibly get in touch with the Diving Officer to organise with him for us to have access to this. Also, could you ask if the club members would be willing donate their the Scuba bottles for the duration. It is just so that we have a constant supply of air on location because at these temperatures my lads will be sucking these bottles dry in no time. 12 & 15litre bottles if possible or twinsets if they have them.' Asked Patsy.

'Consider it done already, for I am the club Diving Officer.' Grinned the Sergeant. 'I'll ensure you have plenty of air and my Constables will organise the bottles to and from site for you. Is there anything else that you need from me?'

'Just one other thing, Can you get in touch with Ocean Harvest on my behalf and bring them up to speed on the events and the fact that we have been requisitioned so to speak?' Asked Patsy.

'Certainly, Mr Anderson and I will smooth over the waters for you there, pardon the pun.' Replied the Sergeant.

'Mr McAskil, I will need quite a bit from you. Now by the time we get set up on site it will be dark.

Can you organise two generators and plenty of portable flood lighting. You know the kit that used when working on the roads on a night shift. Can you organise a low pressure site compressor, the type you use for road works. We have a CP9 Rock Drill *(10-336)* with chisel blades on the boat, it is ideal for this and will make short work of the ice build up surrounding the intake strainer.'

'Also, what are the chances of there being a diesel driven high flow, high pressure water jetting pump on the island, something of around 80 litres per minute, 200bar capacity?' Enquired Patsy.

'I think the one the Works Department uses for tank cleaning is around that capacity. But how will the diver be able to use it under the water, surely the force of the jet will push him backwards? Said Mr McAskil.

'Yes if he uses your lance it will, but not if we connect our retro jet lance up to it. Once we have got the bulk of the ice off with the CP9*(10-336)*, our retro jet*(9-335)* will remove the thin layer of ice below it and clear the strainer itself. Oh, I am also going to need several tonnes of rock salt, Calcium Chloride is preferred if you have got it and a dolav box from the shell fish factory.'

'We will also need a few labourers to shovel salt and for various manual handling tasks. Oh, and a drum of 10mm nylon rope, a dozen wooden handled wire brushes, some strong metal scrapers, a couple of one inch chisels and two 2lb lump hammers and a couple small pry bars.' Explained Patsy.

'Can you also organise a slurry pump and around 40 metres of 50mm hose with a half meter length of 50mm pipe to act as a nozzle?'

'Oh and one last thing can you organise some sort of heated shelter for the guys to get changed in & kitted up in, somewhere they can sit down warm up and re energise inbetween each dive. Oh and hot food, drinks, a box of Mars bars and a box of AA & C cell Duracell batteries.' Asked Patsy.

'We have a crew cabin on site that's heated and we will organise everything that you have asked for. Also, I have a truck and a 4x4 on its way down to pick up you, your men and your equipment from the harbour. Your transit van won't make up the country road in this snow.' Confirmed Mr McAskil.

'You have vehicles on their way down now. How did you know we would agreed to the task?' Asked Patsy.

'Given the importance and seriousness of the problem, what decent human being wouldn't at least attempt the task. Anyway Pat, your reputation preceded you and something about a motto No sea to rough, no... eh, sorry I've forgotten the rest.' Smiled Mr McAskil remembering who was present sitting in their company.

'Don't worry about hot food, Jennifer and I will take care of you guys, on that front.' Said Anne with some pride.

'Oh, Mr McAskil, can you supply us with a few pairs of these fleece lined rubber gloves that I've seen road workers use. I'll put latex cuff seals on them Patsy. It will be warmer on our hands with thin wool liner gloves than the neoprene wetsuit gloves.' Said Smithy.

'Sergeant Varney, is there an aluminium fabrication company on the island that use Mig or Tig Welding plants?' Enquired Nigel.

'Yes Port Bannatyne boatyard has a Fab shop with that capability. Why do you ask?' Enquired the Sergeant.

'Well they often use pure Argon as a shielding gas in Aluminium welding. Do you think we could get some Argon decanted from their J bottles to two of our pony cylinders. We can use this for suit inflation. You see Argon is almost 40% denser than air. This will dramatically improve the insulation and the warmth of the diver.' Explained Nigel.

'I'll organise it.' Confirmed the Sergeant.

And so the mobilization of Operation Jobby Flush as Smithy kept referring to it as began and so became named.

Dhu Loch which was the primary water supply for Rothesay was only a couple of miles away from the town. However, due to the snow covered hill road and track, getting there took around half an hour.

Mr Anderson was true to his word, everything that the team had asked for was there. Along with over a dozen helping hands from the Council and the Police. Once on site, the guys were suited, booted and had all their equipment set up within an hour. It was now close to 6pm, the cloak of darkness had now enveloped them and the wind was freshening again.

The Big Nig was first in the water. The surface of loch was frozen over with a coating of ice of around 75mm thick. Two Council workers with a little midi excavator had created and were keeping clear a large hole in the ice for the divers to enter through.

Suited and booted, Nigel was wearing an Exo26 full face mask*(3-325)* along with a white skateboarders helmet which was covered in 3M Scotchlite tape. There was two Pelican Sabre Light torches mounted either side of the helmet strapped to his head. Nigel made his way along the little foot bridge that accessed the intake valve house, at the bottom of which was where the inlet strainer was located. Nigel climbed down a temporary ladder that had been set up into the freezing slushy waters of the reservoir.

Smithy lowered down the CP9 Pneumatic rock chisel*(10-336)* to him and tended the air hose for it. Nigel, heavily weighted made his descent below the ice into the blackness of Dhu Loch.

Patsy was manning the coms and acting as tender for Nigel's safely line. Philip and Scurvy now suited up remained inside the crew cabin to stay warm as Scurvy would be up next to dive.

Nigel made his way cautiously hand over hand out to the pump intake. Even with the two Sabre lights, the visibility was quite poor only about a meter or so.

When he got there, it was exactly as Mr McAskil had described it, completely covered in ice. An incredible phenomena, at 6m down, there was solid ice under the water surrounded by water. He made his way to the outer end of the filter box.

His plan, which was a good plan, was to start here. He would chisel away the ice to clear the outer edge of the end of the box then he would chisel away at the end face to clear the body of ice from it and then move onto the top of the filter box.

Calling for the air supply to be switched on to the CP9. Nigel began to chisel away at the ice. Just like Patsy had said, the CP9*(10-336)* made short work of it. For the CP9 was actually designed for drilling and chiselling through rock and concrete. Nigel had fitted the 50mm bolster chisel to the tool which cut away large blocks of ice at a time. As the chunks of ice fell away, they would float very slowly up towards the surface. The outer layer of ice down to the bars was around 100mm thick. By the time his thirty minute shift was up Nigel had actual cleared the end face and the greater portion of the top of the filter box.

Patsy was limiting the duration of each dive to thirty minutes maximum. He knew that this was a marathon task and not a sprint. He was also concerned about potential for frost bite of the diver's extremities, fingers and toes. He also understood that as the night went on and turned into day then back into night, the fatigue on the divers could very well result in hypothermia and a diver becoming extremely lethargic even comatose underwater the water. Two things that Patsy would do everything in his power to prevent.

As Nigel broke through the slush on the surface, his full facemask, head, shoulders and top of his cylinder became covered in slush and chunks of ice. Smithy pulled up the CP9 and immediately submerged it into a bucket of heavily salted water to prevent it from freezing over on the surface.

Between his Damart thermal underwear, the thick 200gram Polar Bears Thinsulate under suit and using Argon gas for suit inflation. Nigel was still warm in his drysuit and the dry gloves that Smithy had made up were proving to be very effective. As his fingers were still warm and hadn't gone stiff.

Though to look at him you would never had thought that because as the wet outer surfaces of his drysuit and equipment became exposed to the freezing wind of the night air, everything started to ice over. On seeing this, Patsy quickly disconnected his safety line and unplugged the coms cable from his mask and walked him straight into the warmth of the crew cabin before removing any of his equipment.

The ice on Nigel's equipment quickly started to melt away as the crew cabin was toasty warm. Extra Calor gas heaters had been brought in to ensure it stayed that way for the duration.

As Smithy and Patsy stripped Nigel of his equipment, Nigel explained what he had achieved in such a short space of time and how effective the CP9 was at cutting through the ice.

Next up was Scurvy, who was actually sitting ready suited and booted with his Swedish Aga twin set on his back and full face mask*(4-327 / image page 216)* in his hand ready to be strap to his head and to have his safety line and coms link connected.

'Scurvy, when you get down there, finish the top section first. Then starting on the top, use the CP9 chisel blade to get inbetween the bars. Depending on how you get on you can do the same on the end face also. If you can, chisel gaps inbetween the bars. Then when Philip goes in, he can take the retro jet and blast the gaps clear. Because with that done we can start stage two before clearing the ice from the side faces. It will also buy us more time and help delay the ice building up again.' Suggested Nigel.

'Gotcha, I understand, sounds like a good plan.' Confirmed Scurvy.

Patsy pulled the straps of the mask spider tight to Scurvy's head and over the top of that Scurvy put on the yellow helmet with torches mounted on either side. The same one that he had used when diving under the Arctic Penguin a month or so before. Taking Scurvy outside, Patsy connected up the safely line to Scurvy's harness and the coms cable to the microphone and bone conductor of Scurvy's Aga mask.

Carefully Scurvy climbed onto the ladder and descended into the black, ice laden waters of the loch, taking the CP9*(10-336)* with him.

Doing just as Nigel had told him, he finished the top section first. Then going to the outer end, he found the edges of the grill bars. Holding the CP9 with the chisel blade in a vertical orientation, he started to slice through the grills. Every so often the tone and the vibration of the Chisel action would change as he hit a cross bar, at that point he would reposition and start again.

As with Nigel, Scurvy was quite surprised at how quickly and efficiently the CP9 chiselled through the ice.

Although there was not such a great body of ice to have to clear at this stage, it took Scurvy just as long to clear the slots as it did for Nigel to clear the large body of ice from the top and end face.

This was because Scurvy had to be careful not to cut through the cross bars of the grill and had to keep stopping and find new start points as he came up against crossbars and began a new slot. This was not a quick process in the low visibility of the turbid water of the loch which was almost as black as molasses's.

When Patsy had recalled Scurvy back to the surface things were starting to look promising. The lads had made good headway. The top and end face of the strainer now had gaps in the slots which was allowing water to flow into the ante chamber and the tunnel.

Next in was Philip with the retro jet *(9-335)*. Only now it was fitted with a small single high pressure jet nozzle. A very different nozzle assembly to the one that they had used to clean the Salmon nets with. Cold water under very high pressure, almost 200bar is actually an extremely effective method for removing ice blockages.

Philip knew this from his previous life. For before he was diver, Philip had served his time as a plumber, who was no stranger to frozen pipes and drains in Glasgow's winters.

Many a time Philip had experienced the speed and effectiveness of using a high pressure cold water jet to clear long passages of ice choked drainage and water pipes. So he was quite confident that he would make quick work of this.

Philip blasted away at the grills clearing all the ice from the exposed grill bars which meant there was now a completely unobstructed surface on the top and the end face of the strainer. With this task done, Philip returned to surface so that the next stage of Patsy's cunning plan could be put into place.

As it had actually only taken Philip about fifteen minutes to complete this task, he stayed in the water whilst Patsy got set up with stage two of his plan.

Patsy had organised for the big blue dolav to be half filled with the Calcium Chloride rock salt and lowered into the water and tied off just so the top of the dolav was submerged just below the surface so that it created a thick slurry of brown, highly concentrated salty water. Smithy had now swapped out Philips retro jet for the 50mm diameter hose which was now attached to the output of the slurry pump.

Patsy's cunning plan was to pump the concentrated salt slurry down onto the top of the strainer box, spreading it all over the top so that it would fall through the grill. In doing so, it would create a dense layer of extremely salty water inside the strainer and around the bars of the grill effectively killing off the Frazil ice growth. That is until the pumps were to be started again.

But at least now, the guys would be able to fully clean the sides of the strainer without ice regrouping on the cleaned sections. It would also help to dissolve and loosen the ice around the bottom portion of the strainer that was difficult to get at.

The idea behind how this works is that salt water is much denser than fresh water, especially at the slurry concentrations that Patsy had created. As such, the slurry would sink through the grills and create a layer and a solution of very dense salt water inside the debris filter and around the grill itself. The freezing point of a liquid can be lowered by adding another compound to it. This is known as freezing point depression. Calcium Chloride (Road Salt) is very effective at doing this.

The basic principle is this. All matter is made up of tiny molecules and temperature dictates how much these tiny molecules move. Like everything else, water is made up of molecules which move about, colliding and bouncing off of one another.

However the colder the water gets, the slower the molecules vibrate. Until they get to the point that they move about so slowly, that they start to hold on to one another and begin to crystallise forming a lattice. As more and more slow moving molecules attach, the bigger the growth of the lattice thereby forming ice as we know it.

When we add salt into solution, especially Calcium Chloride, the salt dissolves and separates into three ions, one Calcium ion and two Chloride ions. These three ions now mix with the water molecules and make it much harder for them to stick together to create rigid ice bonds. Thus the ice bonds start to break apart and the ice begins to dissolve.

Once Patsy had pumped the full dolav load of Salt slurry, he recalled Philip back to the surface. Nigel was once again kitted and ready to go back in. This time he cleared the thick ice that was blocking both sides of the strainer using the CP9. The ice broke away in large blocks the size of rugby balls and house bricks.

The divers repeated the same process as before twice over. Nigel handing over to Scurvy then back to Philip. Until the suction strainer was completely cleared of ice and three slurry loads had been pumped into and around the strainer.

Now was the moment of truth. All of the divers were keen to be in the Pump House control room to see the start up of the pumps. As honoured guests of Mr McAskil, they all stood around the pump motor control panel and watched as the control room technician started the pumps, one at a time.

In many ways, the switching on of the pumps itself was a bit of an anti climax. When the Technician pressed the start button for the first pump, its amp meter kicked up as the motor started to turn the pump then dropped back slightly for a second before kicking up again to a higher amperage as the electrical switch gear change its configuration from start mode to run mode.

The process was repeated upon starting pumps #2 & #3. The whine from the electric motors and their cooling fans was extremely loud. But then they were big.

Water was now being pumped into the waterworks huge storage tanks which were located under the shell filters. These filters made from crushed seashells were used in the final stage in the water treatment of Rothesay's water supply. Once the storage tanks were full, water was then pumped to the large underground tanks that were to be found in various location around Rothesay. Then the water supply would be opened up to the various main lines that fed the town and the surrounding area.

The Divers were feeling very pleased with themselves and Mr McAskil and Mr Anderson were now very much relieved.

'So Pat, what we have to do now is to keep a constant watch on the pump motor currents. When we see them starting to rise, we will have to switch them off. For it means that ice is starting to build up and block the intake strainers again.' Explained Mr McAskil.

'In the meantime, once the holding tanks are full and as soon as the demand drops for the night, we will shut down two of the pumps and only run on one. This will reduce the speed of the flow through the filters and should hopefully buy us some time inbetween blockages.'

'When that happens your divers will have to go back in and unblock them again. That said, because our technicians are now on site constantly monitoring the pumps, we can catch the ice build up at an early stage. So it should be easier for your divers to clear them again.' said Mr McAskil confidently.

'We'll be camped out on site here, ready to go back in at short notice.' Patsy assured him. Who was almost tripping over his feet unable to see where he was going for pound signs covering his eyes.

Just as the guys were arriving back at the site hut a maroon coloured Land Rover Discovery pulled up outside. Two very sexy figures got out, wearing matching pale grey and pink one piece ski suits. Followed by a very excited black Labrador.

This was a welcome sight indeed. It was Anne and Jennifer who had brought a veritable feast for the lads of hot cooked food and drinks.

'Here you are lads, steaming hot Stovies, there's plenty of it to go around. I though you would appreciate something comforting on a night like this, especially after diving in the frozen waters of the loch.' Anne announced. 'I've also brought hot apple pie, hot Custard and creamy hot chocolate. And there two air pots of hot water for you to use along with tea, coffee, milk and sugar.'

'And in this tin are some homemade cookies that Jennifer has baked special for you. There from an Italian recipe Baci Di Dama.' (Translates to Lady's Kisses). She said passing the tin to Scurvy with a smile.

'Oh excellent, you girls are heaven sent angels to be sure.' Said Nigel with a welcome smile.

The boys got stuck in for it was only now with the aroma of Anne's home cooking did they realise how hungry they were and how long it had been, apart from a Mars bar since they had eaten last.

When the girls discovered that the water was back on again even though it may only be for a few hours, Jennifer now revered Scurvy not just as her next lay but as her new found hero. Scurvy, of course was lapping up every minute of it. Still he could not stop wondering every time he looked at her if her collar and cuffs matched.

Whilst Jennifer was hanging tight with Scurvy. Patsy, Smithy and the Big Nig were jockeying for position around the very attractive Anne. Who was looking quite fetching in her ski suit. Philip, was just sitting back, coffee in hand relaxing and enjoying the show.

The girls left shortly after the lads had finished eating. With warm food in their bellies and after having the company of two attractive sexy women who had come up specially just to see and feed them. The guys were re energised and in a happy place despite the sparsity of the portacabin surroundings and the ferociousness of the cold outside.

The made themselves as comfortable as they could in the portacabin and cat napped for a bit. Patsy and Philip had a secured a bench each to lie down on whilst Nigel, Smithy and Scurvy pulled up a space on the floor for a lie down.

It was just after 3am when the divers got the call via a messenger from the Pump Station, telling them that pumps were icing over again and had to be shut down. So it began all over again. Only this time because a watchful eye was being kept on the pumps, the ice build up wasn't as severe. As such, they were able to clear the blockage quicker. By encompassing the same method as before, they had the pumps back up and running in the space of two hours.

Back in the site hut, the divers had only got their heads down for a few hours when to their delight, Anne and Jennifer reappeared with cooked breakfast and fresh coffee for them all. This was the nicest awakening Scurvy had received in several years.

He couldn't believe his eyes at first when he awoke from his slumber to see the gorgeous Jennifer kneeling in front of him with a mug of hot coffee in her hand for him. I doubt most people will ever appreciate how much restraint Scurvy had to apply to not take the mug from her hand and pull her down onto the floor next to him. Again although the girls visit was short, it was welcomed, appreciated and thoroughly reviving.

Just before 10am Mr McAskil came into the Portacabin and informed them that now as water demand was at a high, the strainer had frozen over again. Back into the ice bound waters they went.

It continued like this for the next 36 hours until the weather changed for the better. Early on the Thursday afternoon an area of high pressure carrying a warmer south westerly wind came across from the mid Atlantic. Within a few hours, the air temperature changed dramatically from minus 16°C to a balmy minus 4°C and was steadily continuing to rise.

With all my years at sea, it still never ceases to amaze me at how quickly a storm tossed sea with tumultuous violent crashing waves can so quickly change in the space of an hour or two to nothing more than a gentle splash then to a calm sea. Just as it did in Rothesay bay that afternoon.

This change in weather was much more than Mr McAskil and Mr Anderson had hope for. It also brought welcome relief to the divers who were now thoroughly exhausted and wouldn't have been able to have kept this rota up for much longer. Having packed up their equipment and re-stowed it aboard the Loch Ranza. The guys, dirty and very smelly for not having washed for almost 3 days returned to the comfort and warmth of St Ebba. They were welcomed as hero's by Anne, Jennifer, a highly excitable Shark and their very grateful neighbours.

As much as they appreciated this and really wanted to take part in a party to celebrate the success of operation Jobby Flush. They couldn't for they were exhausted, totally spent from the cumulative fatigue and exertion over the last 3 days and 2 nights.

For all the guys wanted to do now was to have a long languishing shower or for those that had one, soak in a hot bath. Then collapse in to bed and drift off into the land of Tir na nÓg *(g-319)*.

Ocean Harvest who, thanks to Sergeant Varney and Mr Anderson were fully aware of the work done by Patsy and his crew. They not only understood the enormity and importance of the task that the divers had performed but were equally grateful for the efforts that they went to in order to secure the town's water supply. For most of their staff that worked on this particular fish farm lived in Rothesay and around Port Bannatyne.

In appreciation of this, Ocean Harvest informed Patsy that the guys could have a couple of days off on weather down time rates to recover from their marathon. As such could start back on the fish cages in earnest on the Sunday morning. What they didn't know was that Patsy had negotiated an extra two day's day rate from Mr Anderson to cover this also.

On the Friday evening, the celebrations for Operation Jobby Flush began. What an eventfully party it was. For if there is one thing that divers are known for, it is how to party. What a party it was, going on well into the wee small hours of Saturday morning. It was just as well that they had the whole of Saturday to recover.

For bright and breezy at 7.30am on Sunday morning the divers were casting off the mooring ropes of the Loch Ranza and were heading back out to the salmon cages for business as usual. Though maybe that's not quite the most apt description of their working day. For there was nothing 'usual' for the divers except for adventure and you never knew what the day was going to bring.

You think I've missed a part of the story. You want to know what became of Scurvy and Jennifer. You want to know if he found out if her collar and cuffs matched?

Well, Scurvy being a gentleman, possessed an attribute in abundance which many people completely lack. For he was the very soul of discretion. Scurvy was a young man of honour, who always made a point to never kiss and tell.

So you're just going have to use your imagination and form your own conclusions on that one.

CHAPTER 8

The Cold, The Dark, The Deep

And The Downright Scary

The Corries singing 'Barrat's Privateers' was blaring away from a stereo in GDMC's workshop located in the basement of their office in St Vincent Street. Scurvy was busy servicing a Kirby Morgan mark 10 band mask*(1-321),* when Patsy and Smithy appeared with a disassembled two diver surface demand control panel with mangled pipework and a box of bits. Which they dumped down onto Scurvy's work bench with a clatter and a bang.

'Here Scurvy leave that mask for just now. I need you to repair and rebuild this Panel for me.' Said Patsy.

Scurvy looking at the mangled panel pipework asked. 'Where did you get this from and what the fuck happened too it?'

'It's Brian Bullock's, he put it in for a full service at Undersea in Partick and they had some problems stripping it down. Apparently most of the pipework and fittings were seized. So they gave up with it and handed it back to Brian Bullock as you see it now.' Explained Patsy.

'Aye, he wisny pleased.' Said Smithy with a grin.

Scurvy taking a closer look at the mangled box of bits. 'I bet he wisny. Jesus man look at the state of it. What did they take it apart with? A grenade!' Replied Scurvy in disbelief.

'Aye, it certainly has that look about it.' Admitted Patsy.

'Who was working on it?' Enquired Scurvy.

'It will have been Rinky Dick. 'Said Smithy. 'You know what he's like. He's got hands on him like Belfast hams and fingers like pig's nipples. Anyway, Brian needs it back for this afternoon.'

'This afternoon! Ha, you've got more chance of nailing jelly to a tree.' Replied Scurvy sincerely.

'Seriously Scurv, he's sending it out to a job up in Peterhead. So it needs to leave later today. Just work your magic and apply your silver touch.' Said Patsy encouragingly.

'Patsy, I'm a mechanic no a magician. I use spare parts, hand tools and logic. Not spells, a cauldron and a magic wand. Even without doing a thorough examination, I can tell you now there is no way this can be repaired and rebuilt without a whole wheen of replacement part parts. Which we don't have here.'

'Just look at the low pressure regulators, they've got elongated threaded ports. How the fuck they managed to do that is just beyond me. They'll need new bodies for a start, they'll have to be ordered in. Brian will just have to hire a panel from SMP or Divex. But with the best will in the world Patsy this panel is going nowhere for at least a week. I can't even Jury rig it. But I'll tell you this, in parts alone this will be an expensive repair.' Said Scurvy emphatically.

'Righty ho, I'll pass on the good news.' Said Patsy with a sigh.

'Probably best done over the phone eh.' Said Smithy with a grin.

'Good of you to volunteer, you can let me know what he says. I'm off down to the boat to meet up with Philip. I'll see you guys later.' Said Patsy sloping off an uncomfortable phone call. Just at that moment, the phone rang as Patsy made a sharp exit out of the workshop.

'Aye, you walked right into that one Smithy.' said Scurvy smiling.

'Fuck. Did I ever.' Acknowledged Smithy somewhat miffed.

Meanwhile, the fifty foot trawler Happy Harvester was out on the Clyde west of the Cloch Lighthouse pulling its trawl net. On board was the Skipper Willie May and his deck hand Andre. The sky was overcast with dark low cloud and there was a chill in the air.

Willie's new to the fishing. He had been a maintenance fitter at the Ravenscraig hot strip steel mill. He had been there since he left school at fifteen. After being made redundant as a result of the closure of the steel mill, Willie had been unable to get another job. This was primarily due to the fact that as man and boy he had worked in the same factory, doing the same job for thirty eight years.

Now as a fifty three year old man, Willie had found it very difficult to get another job. Of the few jobs that were available at the time, other potential employers were reticent to employee him despite his skills and competency. This was because they felt that after thirty eight years he would be institutionalised in his way of thinking and his work ethics.

The result of this was that after six months of trying to get another job and facing unrelenting rejection, Willie decided to try working for himself.

Willies hobby had always been sea angling, so three months previously, Willie signed himself up for a Skippers course at the Glasgow Nautical College. Then using his redundancy money and some of his savings along with a Marine Mortgage, he bought the Happy Harvester to venture into commercial fishing. Unfortunately, commercial fishing wasn't quite as lucrative and straight forward as what Willie thought it would be.

Andre, on the other hand was an seasoned, old salty sea dog who had worked all over the world. Now sixty two, he had been at sea, man and boy from the age of twelve. He started his maritime career during the war. Working with his dad on the coastal puffers that use to carry coals and victuals to the coastal and island communities of the Clyde and west coast of Scotland. He had been at sea ever since.

He had worked as an AB (Able Bodied) seaman on everything that floats. Puffers, tug boats, coastal fishing smacks, Icelandic trawlers, whaling ships, super tankers, bulk carriers, warships, cruise ships, oil rig supply boats, saturation dive boats, cable layers, ferries, luxury yachts, even lifeboats. You name it, Andre will have spent sea time on it. Now in his twilight years he was back on a small fishing boat on the Clyde.

'We need a good haul this time Andre, It's been a bit thin this past month.' Said Willie to his deck hand.

'Di'na worry Willie were aw in the same boat, according the fish merchant nane of the boats have had good catches this month.' Replied Andre trying to console his Skipper.

'Aye I ken but there's a new manager at my bank and she's turned oot tae be a right bitch wi a capitol B. I had to borrow extra money to buy a complete new set of trawl gear for the boat as its original kit was shagged. She's putting the pressure on for me to repay the extra I had to borrow. The unreasonable cunt wouldn't let me add to the boats mortgage.' Willie informed him.

It was clear that Willie was deeply concerned about his debt. For throughout his entire life he had never known financial uncertainty, that was until now. The stress of being in debt and not having the comfort blanket of a steady secure income to repay that debt was beginning to take a heavy toll on him.

Especially coming face to face with the fact that the bank could take it all from him if he didn't. With commercial interest rates at 11.5 %, the monthly loan repayments were extreme in relation to the sum of money that he borrowed.

'You've got a wumin bank manager, you have ma sympathies there Willie. Logic and reasoning's lost on a wumin. It disn'y come intae it when you're dealing with a species that's ruled by their hormones, and are generally unbalanced. Far less wan wi a title and power tae boot.'

'Nae sense in worrying about it. Worrying i'll no make it any better. Here I'll ge ye a laugh, you know that old soak Barry Buick, he wis telling everyone in the Marine bar that he's just joined a wine club.' Said Andre trying to take Willies mind off his problems.

'Aye so I heard, but wit he didny tell you wis that they meet under the old railway bridge at 9 o'clock every morning tae discus the finer characteristics and aromas of Buckfast, Thunderbird, Lanlick and El Dorado.' Replied Willie with a smile and a note of sarcasm.

'Aye that's fucking mair like it.' Said Andre grinning. 'I've a feeling were going to have a big catch this time Skipper, I can feel it in my water.' No sooner had the words left Andre's mouth than the boats engine strained severely. The boat lurched over and the stern of the boat dipped down brining the boat to a sudden stop.

Andre grabbed on as he was flung over. Quickly, Willie disengaged the gearbox drive to the boats propeller. 'Fuckin Jesus!! What was that!' Willie cried out.

'I think we've snagged the trawl.' Shouted Andre.

'Awe Jesus no. If I lose this one I'll be finished, I canny afford another one, and I've only just started out.' Exclaimed Willie in despair cradling his forehead with his hand.

Back at the GDMC office, Smithy was on the telephone to Brian Bullock. 'Aye it's in a really bad way, there's no way you'll get it back before the end of the week. But we checked with Divex in Aberdeen and they've said they have a 2 diver panel available for hire.' Smithy informed him.

'Aye right okay, but is it definitely repairable?' Asked Brian resigning himself to having an unforeseen but unfortunately necessary new expense.

'If it was designed by a man, built by a man and operated by a man then it means its logical therefore it can be repaired by a man. And Scurvy's the man to do it.' Confirmed Smithy.

'Aye and what if it was designed, built and operated by a woman?' Brian asked.

Well, then you'd be totally fucked because that makes it hormonal and there's nothing in man's tool box can fix that.' Came back Smithy's with his usual witty repartee.

'Fair play, thanks for the heads up. Let me know as soon as you can when its ready so I can get the Divex panel off hire.' Replied Brian calmly. Which was not how he would usually have replied news of such nature.

'Aye will do Brian, we'll get it back to you ASAP. Bye now.' Confirmed Smithy, thinking in to himself. 'Hmm, Brian must have got his hole last night for I was expecting to get shot for this. Happy days.'

Back on board the Happy Harvester, the atmosphere was far from happy. Willie and Andre were trying desperately to free the snagged fishing gear but to no avail. Andre was on the winch controls and Willie was at the helm.

'Right pay oot Andre.......Stop there.' Shouted Willie. Willie turned the boat's wheel to bring the vessel's heading around.

'Right see if you can haul in noo.' He instructed.

'Okay, here goes.' Replied Andre. As hauled in on the winch, the stern of boat dipped again and the winch strained and stalled. 'It's nae use Willie she's stuck fast.' He shouted.

'Aye okay.' Willie turned his back on Andre then with his fists clenched and in a fit of frustration and despair he released a ' FUUUCK!!'

Turning back to face Andre holding his head in his hands heaving a sigh of deep resignation. 'Pay out twenty feet of wire Andre and get ready to buoy and cut it.' Willie instructed him. 'What on earth are we caught on, according to the Decca Navigator$_{(g-315)}$ we're ni on three hundred yards from any recorded obstructions.'

Andre asked 'What water depth are you showing here Willie?'

'According tae the sounder 138 feet.' Replied Willie.

Andre cocked his head slightly to one side, pursed his lips together, his eyebrows squeezed into towards one another. 'Here, gi us that hand held compass and a look at the paper chart.' Andre took some transit bearings on the shore and then triangulated them on to the paper chart. 'Willie, I think your Decca$_{(g-315)}$ is out by about 350 yards. I think the trawls are stuck fast on the Greenock.' Said Andre confident in his findings.

'What the fuck's the Greenock?' Exclaimed Willie.

'She's an old 180 foot long bucket dredger, sank at the turn of the century after the Burn's Steamer Ape collided with her. Aye a sad day, a young boy lost his life that day. It was the Greenock's engineer's son, only sixteen he was.' Explained Andre.

'Well that's just great, all very interesting I'm sure. I've barely enough money to put diesel in the boat and pay your wages but I've no a penny fur tae buy a new set o' gear wi and nae way of raisin it either. Am done fir, that cunt at the bank's gonny foreclose on me now, for sure.' Retorted Willie.

'Wait a minute Willie, it's no as black as ye think. You've only snagged the trawl and at worst maybe lost the trawl. But all's no lost yet.' Replied Andre rationalising the situation.

'Ach you dinny understand, you don't appreciate the predicament I'm in.' Responded Willie contemptuously and angrily in self pity.

'Now you listen here Willie May, you better get your heid oot yer arse and gi yersel a shake afore I gee ye a fuckin slap.' Responded Andre firmly and angrily. 'You've only snagged and maybe lost the trawl, you've still got your boat and you huvn'y lost your life. I've been at sea man and boy and in fifty years I've been bombarded by canon fire in Korea, shot at by Pirates in the Malaccan Straights, shipwrecked twice, dragged overboard once, capsized once and witnessed my fellow shipmates lose everything from an eye to their lives. And at the age of twelve, I witnessed the HMS Dasher exploding on the Clyde half a mile in front of me, causing 379 men to lose their lives. Some of the survivors I helped pull out of the water myself.'

'So let me assure you of this; predicament fuck all. You don't appreciate how well off you actually are!'

Willie was quite taken aback and somewhat shell shocked by the sudden loud, stern, angry tirade from Andre. For he was normally a calm, quiet, man. Willie found himself waking to the grounded reality of his situation. 'Sorry Andre, your right. I, I just lost sight of things, it's just all the pressure I've been having wi the bank. Having my own boat making a modest living from the sea was all I wanted. And all I could see was that nasty cunt taking it all away from me. Look man, I'm open to suggestions and any ideas that you have would be very welcome.' Said Willie apologetically.

'Well, we know where the gear is. If we get in a diver we might still be able to recover it, maybe not all of it but certainly the warps and Otter doors etc.' Suggested Andre.

'Fair enough Andre, but how do I pay for divers when I am going to struggle to pay your wages?' Willie asked.

'Don't worry about that, I know a man that will help us.' Replied Andre in his normal calm, confident assuring tone.

Back at the GDMC office, Smithy had a coffee in his hand. Grinning and with great enthusiasm, he was regaling Scurvy with his and Patsy's latest sexual conquest, while Scurvy worked on Brian Bullocks surface demand control panel.

'I'm telling you Scurvy, Bella is one horny dirty bitch, we did her as a threesome. Patsy and I spit roasted her in the back of the van in the car park. She took it all ways, no holes barred. She was game for anything and did everything. Patsy was shagging her arse while she was licking mine. And that was as erotic as Hell. Hey Scurvy, we were at it for two hours, my cock was throbbing, by the time we had finished I had a bell end like a blind cobblers thumb. I'll tell you this though, She's got the hots for you, seriously you should get in there man, she'll make all of your wildest dreams come true. She was definitely up for one more to make it four.'

'I don't doubt you for a minute Smithy, but the question I'm asking myself is, do I really want to shag her after you pair of dirty bastards have been up her. Never mind kiss her after she's been licking your arse. That's a million times worse than kissing a smoker.' Replied Scurvy.

'I never took you for a prude.' Said Smithy surprised.

'There's nothing prudish about it. Well let me put it too you this way. Would you kiss her after she had been licking my arse.' Suggested Scurvy.

'I said shag her, I never mentioned anything about kissing her.' Replied Smithy.

Well that's where you've missed out Smithy, because you'll never know what true eroticism is until you've gone two's up, locked lips and had a tongue sandwich with a woman in the process.' Said Scurvy with a smile.

'My aren't you the dark horse, it's all coming out now and I thought you were of the school of never kiss and tell.' Replied Smithy pleasantly surprised. 'I knew you weren't so innocent and squeaky clean, you're a sly fox Scurvy.'

Scurvy raised his eyebrows, & with an air of confidence and knowing replied. 'Let's just say I possess in abundance the discretion that you and the rest of GDMC's reprobates are severely lacking.'

Smithy started sniggering. The office phone started ringing. Leaving Scurvy working on Brian's surface demand control panel, Smithy went upstairs to answer it. Two minutes later Smithy shouted down to Scurvy from the office. 'Scurvy, leave that we need to go Gourock!'

Scurvy put down his tools. He switched off the ultrasonic parts cleaner that was on the work bench, threw the light switch and went upstairs to the office to find out what the tizzy was all about. 'What's the panic?' Scurvy asked.

'There's a fishing boat lost its trawl gear on the Greenock. We or rather you need to go down and recover it.' Replied Smithy.

'Okay doke.' Answered Scurvy nonchalantly.

'Just so you know Scurvy, this jobs a freebie. Patsy's uncle is the deck hand on the boat. If they don't get their gear back the bank will foreclose on the boat and Andre will be out of a job. And there's no many jobs out there.' Said Smithy giving him the heads up.

'Aye nae bother, whatever it takes. You never know, we might need them to bail us out the shit one day. So one good turn deserves another.' Replied Scurvy, acknowledging a friend in need.

'Good man, grab your dry suit and let's go Patsy's going to meet us at Gourock pier with the boat.' Informed Smithy.

The Lochranza motored to berth alongside Gourock pier without tying up just to allow Scurvy and Smithy to jump on board. Then Patsy swung the helm over to starboard and the Lochranza pulled away from the pier and headed out to the Happy Harvester. Which was still held fast in position by her snagged trawl net, less than a mile south west of the Cloch lighthouse.

Further up the Clyde at the Royal Marine Auxiliary Service recompression chamber*(12-340)* at Garvel Dock. The Police divers are running through a diving accident training scenario with the RMAS Life Support Technician(LST). The Police divers have two of their colleagues inside a two man, twin lock 70 inch Recompression chamber*(12-340)*. One acting as the casualty and the other (the sergeant) was acting as the attendant. Outside of the chamber are 4 other members of the Police diving team and the RMAS Life Support Technician who was operating the chamber and providing the training.

'Okay sergeant, as you know, the scenario we are simulating is a diver with a type two bend. So get the patient onto the BIBS straight away and lie him down. We are going to start to blow you down slowly with compressed air to an equivalent pressure of 18m water depth. Then keep the casualty there for 20 minutes breathing pure oxygen through the BIBS.' Instructed the LST via the chambers internal two way coms link.

BIBS, is a Built In Breathing System. An oral nasal mask that is strapped to the casualties face so that the casualty can breathe a medicinal gas mixture different to that which his body is being pressurised with. In this case it was pure Oxygen.

'It is important at this stage that you closely monitor the casualty for any signs of oxygen toxicity as some people can react badly to pure oxygen at this pressure. If the patient shows any signs of oxygen poisoning you must remove the BIBS straight away and switch of the supply.' The LST informed the Sergeant.

'Roger, understood. In the rare event that you do have a patient that reacts badly to pure O2, what do we give him instead?' Asked the Sergeant.

'Initially, he will breath the same air that you are breathing, ambient chamber air. We will then supply the casualty with an oxygen enriched air supply through the BIBS instead. A diluted oxygen supply but richer in oxygen than just air and proceed with the recompression therapy*(12-340)* on a different therapeutic table.

After the first 20 minutes at 18m we will remove the BIBS and put the casualty onto air for 5 minutes and then refit the BIBS and put the casualty back onto Oxygen for another 20 mins. then we would repeat this procedure once again and then reassess the casualty prior to beginning the ascent to surface. Just remember that when we begin our ascent to the surface that you will also have to be on the BIBS and breath pure O2 as part of your decompression schedule to the surface. On the descent, you must also get your casually to try hard to equalise the pressure through his sinuses otherwise this will become quite painful for him and he may also end up with a burst eardrum as well.' Informed the LST.

'How do we deal with this when you have an unconscious casually.' Enquired the Sergeant.

'You will basically have to move his jaw open and closed to try to work his Eustachian tubes to try to clear his ears. Yet at the same time be aware that he might suffer a ruptured ear drum. If that happens then you don't need to work about pressure equalisation of the sinus, at least for that side of his head anyway. Okay we are starting to blow you down to 18M......... now.' Replied the LST.

As the LST turned the handle on a valve, there was the loud noise of hissing air inside the chamber as it became pressurised with compressed air, bringing the internal chamber pressure up to 2.817Bar. Which another gauge on the outside of the chamber read as equivalent seawater depth of 18m.

The Loch Ranza was now tied up alongside the Happy Harvester. It was late in the afternoon and the sun was starting to drop. With it the daylight was beginning to fade. Scurvy was standing on the back deck, suited and booted almost ready to go in. Philip was also suited and booted as stand by diver. He sat on the edge of engine room coach roof holding his band mask *(1-321)* on his lap.

'Scurvy, be very careful on this one, the net will probably be floating with the bell mouth open, watch for this. For you don't want to find yourself swimming inside the net. It's really important that you always stay on the outside of the net. 'Follow a warp down, pass the trawl door and when you get to the bridle follow it up to the float line on the upper edge of the net wing. Follow this round if you can to the other side and try to suss out how and where the net is snagged up on. And be very alert to where your umbilical is at all times, try to have minimum slack, just enough for you to move freely. We don't know if the net has got caught up on the superstructure of it or if it has caught into the bow or the stern of the wreck. Once we know how and where it is caught, then we'll work out how to free it, okay.' Advised Patsy.

'No worries Patsy, I've got it.' Acknowledged Scurvy taking careful heed of what Patsy had told him.

'Another thing, this is a deep one Scurvy. Its 42 metres to the bottom. That means if you touch bottom You've only got a 10 minute bottom here before you end up running into decompression time*(11-337)*. And stay sharp, keep thinking clearly and talking to us we don't want you getting narked*(g-317)*. The light will be fading soon so it's gonny get dark.'

'I'll be fine Patsy. You know me, Last Boy Scout.' Said Scurvy trying to alleviate Patsy's concerns.

'Good lad and remember, if it doesn't look good abandon it.' Said Patsy giving Scurvy the green light to swim away at any time.

'Will do. Are we good to splash?' Asked Scurvy.

'Smithy, are we good to go, is his bailout open? Asked Patsy.

Smithy was acting as tender. Who, as usual had thoroughly doubled check everything. 'Aye Patsy, all tickety boo, he's fully loaded, all tooled up ready to go.' Confirmed Smithy.

'Let's get him wet then, it will be getting dark in an hour.' Instructed Patsy.

Smithy strapped Scurvy's band mask *(1-321)* to his head giving Scurvy a tap on the head and the two exchanged a thumbs up signal. Scurvy looked over to Philip who gave him a wink and the thumbs up.

Placing his hand on top of his head to hold down his bank mask and holding his umbilical with his other hand, Scurvy stepped off the side of the Loch Ranza. Hitting the cold water of the Clyde with a splash, he was surrounded by a flurry of bubbles before bobbing back up to the surface.

Swimming over the one of the trawl warps he began his descent into the cold, dark, deep waters of the Clyde.

Hand over hand Scurvy made his way down the trawl wire into the deep. The further he descended, the more the ambient light diminished Until the only light available was that from his head mounted light and his hand held Birchley torch. Which had a fantastic white beam of light that penetrated the darkness like a light sabre. The noise of his breathing and the exhaust bubbles were the only sounds to be heard in the cold, eerie darkness.

On reaching the steel trawl Otter door, he checked to make sure his umbilical was still reasonably snug with only a couple of meters of slack. He finned passed the trawl door and made his way along the bridle to get to the edge of the net wing. In his torchlight he could see that the net mouth was floating wide open. It was like the entrance to a floating cave.

'Diver1 to surface.' Called Scurvy.

'Go ahead Scurv.' Came back Patsy's dulcet tones over the coms.

'I'm at the net mouth at the top of the head rope float line. It seems to be clear and floating freely. I am going to make my way down to the foot rope to find where its caught up.' Scurvy informed him.

'Okay Scurv, be careful, your current depth is 35m over.' Replied Patsy

'Rodger, understood over.' Confirmed Scurvy. Following the outside edge of the net, Scurvy carefully descended further down to the ground line. Upon reaching it, he started to follow it along the wing edge to the other side of the net mouth where he discovered where the net had become snagged.

'Diver 1 to surface. Patsy, I found the snag point, it looks as though the ground line is caught, jammed up in the bucket gantry of the dredger.'

'But get this, it looks as though they have almost pulled the old dredger onto its side. Over.' Exclaimed Scury in astonishment.

'Good man, Your now at 38meters, do you think you can free it, you've have got 4 minutes before this turns into a Deco dive*(11-337),* over.' Said Patsy, keeping a very close eye on Scurvy's depth and dive time.

"I'll give it a go, I'll try to cut the ground wire with the hacksaw half a meter either side of the bucket lifter. Then reassess it, see if we can float the net over the top. But I'll probably have to do some in water decompression*(11-337),*. Over.' Replied Scurvy.

'You've got 15minutes tops then I am bringing you back to surface no matter what understood. Over.' Instructed Patsy firmly.

'Rodger, understood.' Confirmed Scurvy.

Underwater in the darkness, Scurvy worked away diligently trying to cut the ground wire free. It was slow work using a hacksaw to cut the steel wire trawl cable under the water as the water acted as a lubricant to the cutting surface. Scurvy also had to be careful not to snap the hacksaw blade as he only had the one.

On the surface on the back deck of the Happy Harvester Willie was feeling much better about himself. Somewhat relieved on hearing Scurvy's news that he believed the trawl could be freed and was recoverable with minimum damage.

However, oblivious to everyone was the fact the tide had turned and was now on the flood. The result of this was that the trawl wires were now taking tension because the incoming tide had increased the water depth. Thus lifting the Loch Ranza and the Happy Harvester together which were now acting as a buoyant lift on the wreck of the Greenock. The trawl wires began to creak under the new increasing load.

Suddenly and violently the two boats spun round 180degrees. Scurvy's umbilical was pulled out of Smithy's hand and disappeared overboard like a runaway train. The guys on board the two boats were thrown off balance.

Underwater the wreck of the Greenock started to screech and groan then violently healed over onto her side. 'Oh Shit she's going over.' Shouted Scurvy over the coms. Less than a minute later, Scurvy was on his back on the seabed. His hat light had gone out and then as he tried to draw breath on his next inhalation.... There was nothing.

Sucking in again, the next thing he knew was that the foam sponge under the neoprene seal of the Kirby Morgan face seal*(1-321)* had collapsed and the freezing cold water of the Clyde came rushing in flooding his band mask. Immediately realising he had lost his surface demand supply. He quickly reached up to the knob sticking out from the right hand side of his band mask and turned it fully anti clockwise to switch on his bail out air supply.

Then just as quick, he grabbed the knob sticking out towards the front of his band mask*(1-321)*. He turned it to the right to open it so that a rush of air came gushing into the band mask. This pushed out the water and re-establishing the face seal so that he could breathe again. Which as you will appreciate came as a great relief to him.

'Wow, that was an adrenaline rush.' He thought to himself. 'Nobody ever warned me about that when you lose surface demand. I wonder if any of the guys even know that happens with a Kirby Morgan band mask.'*(1-321)*

Clearly quite distressed from the event, for a minute or so, Scurvy's heart was pounding like an Orangeman's drum and he was sucking air like a galloping horse.

On board the back deck of the Lochranza, Smithy who had lost his balance and was now flat on his arse, shouted over to Philip. 'Fucking Nora what happened there, Philip grab Scurvy's umbilical!'
'Philip reached down and managed to get a grip Scurvy's umbilical and held it fast. Smithy scrambled back to his feet and took hold of it again and secured a rope to it using a prussic loop which he made fast to a cleat on the gunnels.
In the wheelhouse of the Loch Ranza, Patsy was desperately trying to get voice coms with Scurvy. 'Scurvy, Scurvy are you alright, what happened!'
There was a silence over the coms, no response, Patsy couldn't even hear if Scurvy was breathing. 'Scurvy speak to me lad.' Nothing no sound at all.
Patsy shouted down the deck. 'Smithy give him a tug on his umbilical see if you can get a response.'
'Nothing Patsy, his umbilical just goes bar tight.' Replied Smithy.
Patsy shouted across to the Happy Harvester' 'Andre get some lack on the winch wire then get over here, take hold of Scurvy's umbilical from Smithy.' 'Smithy, hat Philip and get him splashed.'
Philip shouted back as he was pulling on his band mask*(1-321)* by himself. 'I'm way ahead of you, way ahead of you, I'm ready to go.'

247

'Philip, get down to Scurvy as quick as you can, I've got no coms with the lad, I think the wrecks shifted and his umbilical is trapped, so take the cable cutters with you in case you need to cut him free. But listen I've got a pneumo depth showing him at 45 metres, so he's now into decompression.' Instructed Patsy over the coms to Philip.

Patsy's voice was now carrying a tone of apprehension, fear and grave concern for the safety and well being of the young diver. Who was now alone in the cold, deep, dark waters of the Clyde, 45m below him. The darkness of the winters late afternoon was closing in on them all.

'I know the drill Patsy, don't worry, Scurvy's half man, half dolphin. He's Clyde born and bred, he's like Irn Bru, built from girders.' Replied Philip with an assured confidence, so as to try to calm and reassure Patsy..... and himself.

'I know. Just bring him back.' Replied Patsy. Patsy, then whispered into to himself. 'Just bring him back alive.'

Under the water, the wreck of the Greenock had shifted for it had now been dragged further over on its side. Scurvy's umbilical was now trapped under the hull, as a result of him pulled him off of the gantry frame and falling down to the seabed.

He was trapped on the sea floor unable to free himself. Unknown to him, the Marsh Marine communication whip on his band mask has been pulled out of its connector and he had lost power to his Hat Light. Fortunately his Birchley light was clipped into his harness so he still had illumination.

He tried calling Patsy over the coms. 'Diver 1 to Surface.' No response. 'Diver 1 to Surface.' Again no response. 'Diver to surface, Patsy can you hear me? Over.' Again no response. In the desperate hope that he may still have partial communications, Scurvy gave one last message. 'Patsy, I don't know if you can hear me, but I'm trapped, the wrecks shifted and has trapped my umbilical. I have lost surface demand so am now on bail out. I need help, send help.'

All alone in the cold, dark, deep waters of the Clyde, Scurvy was kneeling on the seabed, he only had a couple of meters of free umbilical so was very limited in his ability to move around. His surface supplied airline has become kinked trapped under the structure of the wreck cutting off his surface fed air. As such he was now breathing off of his 10Litre emergency bailout bottle*(g-314)*.

A 10 litre bailout bottle when full will provide around 2320 litres of free air. At 45meters water depth where the ambient pressure is 5.5bar (that is 5.5 times greater than air pressure on the surface). This would provide an air supply of around 15 to 20 minutes of breathable air to a fit, experienced diver under normal circumstances. For the diver would be breathing between 110 to 140 litres of air per minute. However, this wasn't normal circumstances.

Scurvy took some comfort in knowing that as soon as they had lost coms, Patsy would be sending in Philip to come and get him. Kneeling on the seabed, having regained his composure he wasn't worried. He kneeled there quite calm, his breathing now slow and deep with the breath rate of a mediating Buddhist monk.

Taking the Birchley Torch in his hand that was hanging from a lanyard on his harness, he started looking around in the torch light. Just out of his reach he saw something glistening on the disturbed seafloor. He laid down on his stomach and tried to reach for it but it was still about 15cm out of his reach. He pulled out his dive knife and just managed to reach it and scrape it towards him.

He picked it up and looked at it in his torch light. It was a small coin about 2.5cm in diameter. 'Jesus, it's a gold coin.' He thought to himself. Scurvy looked around some more with his torch and saw more golden glistening reflections on the rock and sand seabed. There must be about thirty of them glistening in his torch light.

He tucked the gold coin into his drysuit thigh pocket, lying back down on his stomach, straining and breathing heavily he began reaching for the other coins. He managed to get another three but the rest were just out of his reach. He tucked them into his thigh pocket also.

Just at that moment Philip touched him on the Shoulder. This gave Scurvy a fright and he spun round quickly to face into the light beam from Philips hat light.

'Scurvy are you alright, can you hear me?' Said Philip over the coms but received no reply. 'Philip gave Scurvy the okay hand signal.'

Scurvy returned the okay signal to Philip and then turned to his umbilical to demonstrate to Philip that was trapped.

'Diver 2 to Surface, Patsy, he's okay but his umbilical is trapped under the Greenock, there's no way to free it I'm going to have to cut it.' Philip informed him his voice crackling over the coms.

Patsy and the rest of the guys were very much relieved to hear Philips good news. 'Wait before you do that, what's he got left in his bailout' Patsy asked.

Philip Signalled to Scurvy to show him the pressure gauge from his bail out bottle. 'Patsy he's down to 60bar.' Exclaimed Philip.

'Listen Philip, you're going to have to bring him up fizzing, he's well into decompression*(11-337)* He's got a 23 minute bottom time now. He's over the limiting line*(11-339)* for 45m. That means his first decompression stop would need to be at 15m and he'll not have enough air left to finish his first deco stop, never mind do the rest in water and then get to the surface.'

'I have no option but to bring him straight to the surface. I'll call the coastguard and organise a chamber and Heli-Evac.'

'Rodger.' Acknowledged Philip knowing that his friend was about to endure what could potentially cripple him for life.

Underwater on the seabed, Smithy wrote the plan on a divers slate and showed it to scurvy. Before cutting Scurvy's umbilical he called to Patsy to shut off Scurvy's surface air supply.

He then clipped Scurvy to his harness with a buddy line. Philip then cut Scurvy's umbilical to free Scurvy and then he cut Scurvy's umbilical further up to free it from the wreck.

The two divers then began their careful ascent to the surface at a rate of 15meters a minute. Scurvy barely had enough air to get to the surface. Scurvy was about to experience the one terrifying, traumatic ordeal that every diver dreads... The Bends*(g-315)*.

At the call desk of the MRCC Clyde (Clyde Coastguard Maritime Rescue Co-Ordination Centre) a coastguard officer was talking on the VHF Radio. 'All understood Pat, were scrambling a Sea King from RAF Machrihanish for a Heli-Evac and we have alerted the Base Commander at RMAS Gravel Dock to make ready their chamber*(12-340)* to receive your diver.'

'Machrihanish !' Exclaimed Patsy. 'Can we not get one from HMS Gannet at Prestwick.'

'The Sea King at HMS Gannet is down for maintenance. Machrihanish is the next nearest, they have a visiting Sea King & flight crew. Don't worry, they will only be ten minutes difference in the flight time to get to you. He'll be in good hands. Just get him onto pure O2 as soon as he is on surface and prep the decks for the helicopter winch man.' Replied the Coastguard officer.

'Rodger, will do, he'll be breaking surface in a few minutes. Got to go Loch Ranza out.' Replied Patsy.

On board the Loch Ranza, Patsy cleared the decks whilst Smithy tended Philips umbilical and Andre pulled in Scurvy's severed umbilical and secured it around the bull horns. Willie onboard the Happy Harvester had attached marker buoys to each of the trawl warps with ropes and bulldog clips in preparation for cutting.

Patsy had the emergency oxygen set at the ready in the wheel house. He was filled with dread and sadness for his young friend for he knew Scurvy's bend*(g-315)* was going to be a bad one.

Darkness had now descended on the Clyde. A green night light illuminated the cockpit, of the Sea King search and rescue helicopter that sat on the runway of RAF Machrihanish. The Flight Lieutenant requested clearance for takeoff. 'Flight Control, This is Rescue Zulu Echo 3 6 9 requesting clearance for takeoff.'
'Rescue Zulu Echo 369 you are clear for takeoff.' Conformed flight control.
'Thank you Flight Control, Zulu Echo 369 is airborne and en-route for Cloch Point.' Informed the pilot. The bright yellow paraffin budgie lifted off into the black night sky. Where all that could be seen was the red and green position lights from its underbelly and the white strobe light on its tail rotor.

On the deck of the Lochranza, Scurvy was now onboard. He has just finished being de-kitted when he suddenly collapsed. Patsy caught him as he fell. 'I've got you lad.'
'Oh Jesus, my back, oh fucking Nora Patsy, I can't feel my legs.' Exclaimed Scurvy with fear in his voice.
'Here Andre, give me a hand.' Said Patsy trying to lay Scurvy down as comfortable as he could.
Scurvy was shouting in agonising pain, arching his back and near doubling over. His voice a mix of fear and agony. 'Fuuuck, my back. Patsy, fucking Jesus my back.'
Patsy placed the oral nasal mask of the emergency Oxygen set over Scurvy's mouth and nose. 'I know lad, breathe deeply lad, just breathe deeply.'

Said Patsy sympathetically. 'The oxygen will help. The choppers on its way we are going to get you to a chamber soon. And you'll be fine. I promise you.' Said Patsy doing his best to comfort him.

When the Helicopter arrived, it flooded the deck of the Loch Ranza with its powerful search light. They lowered a Medic with a stretcher basket down onto the back deck of the Loch Ranza. The deafening sound of the helicopter's jet engines and down draft from its rotor blades meant that the guys had to shout at the top of their lungs to be heard.

The Medic performed a quick examination of Scurvy. Then together as gently as they could, they lifted him into the stretcher basket and strapped him in. Then up into the air he went. Once onboard the helicopter, it made haste for Garvel Dock. 'RMAS Garvel this is Rescue Zulu Echo 3 6 9 currently inbound with a diver with a type 2 bend(g-315). Our ETA is 3 minutes.' The Pilot informed the radio operator at Garvel.

Inside the Garvel Dock recompression chamber bay The LST was talking to Frank Hill, the Police Inspector in charge of the Police underwater unit. 'Here Frank bit of fortuitous timing for you and your lads, we have a Seaking inbound with a DCI emergency. By all accounts with a type 2 bend(g-315).'

'Do you know who it is?' Enquired Frank.

'No, not yet limited information at the moment but we will get the necessary details from the flight crew. They've got a Diver Medic on board, he would normally be going into the chamber with the casualty. However, this is a prime opportunity for your

Sergeant, he can act as the attendant in the Chamber*(12-340)*. He's going to have to do it for real at some point in his career so it might as well be now whilst the training is fresh in his head.' Suggested the LST.

'Thanks we appreciate that.' Replied Frank.

'Sorry Willie, I'm going to have to cut you lose.' Said Patsy wanting to make haste to get to Scurvy at Garvel Dock.

'I sure , no worries. Here Patsy, will the lad be alright?' Asked Willie with genuine concern.

'I hope so, we won't know for sure until they get him recompressed*(12-340)* but he'll be in good hands. What with giving him O2 straight away and the minimum delay to treatment, he's got a good chance of recovery. Look we've really got to go I need to get to Garvel Dock. Smithy cast us off. Philip, we'll get her tied up at Gourock Pier, pick up Smithies van there to get our cars on the way to Garvel Dock.' Instructed Patsy.

'Aye fine. Patsy that's a plan. That's a bad hit Scurvy's got you know that.' Said Philip with concern.

'Of course I do. I knew it was going to happen even before he left bottom. I shouldn't have sent him down, I should have done the job.' Said Patsy regretfully.

'My arse, sympathy card pish. Who was to know the wreck was going to shift? The same thing could have happened to any of us.' Replied Philip trying to avoid the cancer of the blame game from setting in.

'Aye, I know. But now there could be an HSE investigation and you know what the deal is with

Scurvy. We could all end up in the Jail.' Patsy reminded him.

'Well, we will just have to make sure that disny happen then, wont we!' Replied Philip ensuring that they all stayed together as a band of brothers.

Sure enough, the helicopter landed on the Garvel dock helipad 3 minutes later. The emergency medical team wheeled Scurvy in on a trolley stretcher who was shouting and writhing in absolute agony.

Inside the chamber bay*(12-340)*, the police divers were waiting for the casualty, they recognised Scurvy on the stretcher. The police diver Colin Baker shouted across to Frank Hill in complete surprise. 'Frank, it's Scurvy!' Colin spoke to Scurvy to try to comfort him. 'Scurvy ma lad, it's me, Colin. You're going to be alright lad you're in good hands here. All the gang from the first team are here, Windy Miller, Buffalo Bill, wee Bobby. Andy Gallagher's going to be in the Chamber*(12-340)* with you. You'll be as right as rain in no time, just hang in there lad.'

Scurvy was still in excruciating pain. Though, on recognising his friends from the Police underwater unit and knowing that Andy Gallagher and not a total stranger was going to be in the chamber with him. Brought a great deal of comfort to Scurvy. Scurvy's stretcher was lifted into the chamber where he was transferred from the stretcher to one of the crude chamber bunks and strapped in. The heavy large round steel inner and outer chamber*(12-340)* doors were swung over from the inside and locked into position.

Andy Gallagher turned on the pure Oxygen supply and placed the BIBS over Scurvy's face. He then placed a blanket over Scurvy to help keep him warm. Then the noise of hissing air filled the chamber as they were both blown down initially to an equivalent pressure of 18m water depth.

'Can we not give him something for the pain, morphine or the likes?' Colin Asked the medic.

'Unfortunately not. Any pain killers we could give him would mask the symptoms of the Decompression injury (DCI). Ultimately, whilst in the chamber, it is the symptoms we are treating. So to treat him accurately, we really need to see the full effects of the DCI. And as painful as it is for the patient and as unpleasant as it is for you to see your friend in pain. I am afraid that's the reality of a bend. Also in hyperbaric air, morphine can increase the risk of respiratory depression due to the narcotic effect of nitrogen under pressure.' Explained the Medic empathically.

Colin turned to look through the small 6 inch diameter window of the chamber with the greatest of sympathy for the young diver inside.

After 15 minutes of being on pure oxygen at 18m, Scurvy's symptoms had not improved much. He still couldn't feel his legs and he still had pain in his back, though not as severe as it had been initially. The LST made the decision to compress him down to 6 bar, the equivalent of 50m water depth. The principle being that they would take Scurvy to a depth deeper than where the nitrogen bubbles started. The rational being that the greater pressure would compress the bubbles to be smaller than what they started at, so the body could start to dissolve them in the blood stream.

'Andy, I am going to press you down to 50m so take off the BIBS you'll both be breathing chamber air from now on. Get ready.' Explained the LST over the coms.

Andy acknowledging the LST removed Scurvy's BIBS. Once again the sound of hissing air filled the chamber(12-340). Once at 50 meters Andy examined Scurvy again performing a simple neurological examination. This was performed every ten minutes. Then after 30 minutes of being at 50m and seeing only slight improvement. The LST broke the news to Andy over the intercom.

'Okay, Andy, here's how it is. Although we are seeing some improvements in Scurvy's condition and he is almost pain free. He is still not in a condition to be returned to surface. 'So this is going to be a long one mate. We are going to have to treat him using therapeutic table 54(12-340). That means the best part of another 39hrs in the chamber. 'Scurvy will have to remain at 50m for the next two hours then we will begin the slow process of returning him to surface. As such we will swap out chamber attendants in shifts and I will organise another two LST's to support us here to operate the chamber. We will be able to get one from Faslane along with Dr Mark Smith.'

    A leading seaman entered into the chamber bay with a paper note which he handed to the LST. Over the coms the LST informed Andy of the contents of the note. 'I have just been informed Andy, that we will be honoured with Dr Ledingham himself. He is coming down from the Western Infirmary to oversee the last stages of the oxygen therapy once we get Scurvy up to 6 meters. Apparently he is over here from Dubai on a lecture program. Your friend in there is very lucky to have him. In the meantime, I need you to open up the medical kit located in the chest under scurvy's bunk. take out the large safety scissors and carefully cut off his dry suit. Once I give you the green light pass it through to the outer chamber and we will take it out the way.

With Scurvy's drysuit removed all be it now shredded and cleared from the chamber. Andy was now in the position to begin the necessary medical interventions that were required as part of Scurvy's treatment.

    'I am going to pass you through a Hartmanns solution*(g-316)* intravenous drip via the medical lock. You'll need to put this into the vein on the back of Scurvy's right hand, so we can keep him hydrated.' The LST informed Andy over the coms. 'To go with that you're going to have to lube up a catheter*(g-314)* with lidocaine jelly*(g-317)*. Connect it to a collection bag which is in the medical kit and push it up his bell end because what goes in has to come out and nobody wants the smell stale of pish all over the chamber floor.'

    'Aye all understood.' Confirmed Andy.

'Andy, once you have done that. Connect up the Oxipulse meter*(g-317)* to his right hand index finger and wrap the sphyg balloon*(g-318)* around his left arm. From this point onwards, you will be taking readings and performing medical & neurological checks every 20 minutes.' Instructed the LST.

'Yeh, I understand. Hey, what's the deal for food and something to drink.' Andy asked.

'Well, we want the patient to sleep as much as possible. We will need to keep him awake though inbetween pressure changes and whenever he is on pure O2. So he won't be wanting to eat much.' Replied the LST.

'Aye, that's fine and dandy for him but what about me?' Questioned Andy.

'Oh Aye, don't worry about that, well get the cook from the RMAS Salmoor to make you up something, she's in port on C berth. We'll pass it in to you via medical lock. Pasta is probably best. Some foods don't react well to hyperbaric environments but you'll be safe enough with pasta.' Confirmed the LST.

Treating Scury on the therapeutic recompression table 54(12-340) created a major complication for the LST operating the chamber. For now, not only did he have to treat Scurvy on a therapeutic schedule in the inner main chamber. He also had to prepare and perform decompression schedules*(11-337)* in the outer transfer air lock of the chamber for attendants as they were changed out. Fortunately, the outer air lock also had a hyperbaric toilet so he did have any concerns for the attendants inside on that score. It also meant that they could empty scurvy's urine collection bag when necessary. Nice. As you now aware, a diver with a major bend*(g-315)* requires considerable logistics to support him during his treatment. And this was an excellent example of such.

Later that evening, Patsy, Smithy and Philip arrived at Garvel Dock. they were escorted into the Chamber room by a Royal Navy guard. Here they were greeted initially by Inspector Frank Hill.

'Frank, how's he doing?' Patsy asked deeply concerned.

'I think it's best to have the LST brings you up to speed.' Replied Frank.

'Oh, right. .... Eh Frank, we might need your help with this. Emm, you know Scurvy hasn't got a Commercial ticket, and there will probably be a HSE inquiry into this and all that may mean.' Said Patsy angling for a big favour from the Police Inspector. Frank Hill looked towards the chamber and then back at Patsy, raising an eyebrow with a look of mixed feelings of disapproval and empathy. 'Let's focus on getting the young man well again first.' Replied Frank.

'Oh Aye, aye absolutely.' Agreed Patsy emphatically whilst lifting both his hands towards the heavens with each arm forming a 90 degree angle and then in a strange motion lowered them again.

Philip put out his hand to offer a hand shake with the Inspector. Which as Frank's hand engaged with his. Philips thumb and pinkie finger interlocked in the spaces between Franks. The nails of each of Philips remaining three fingers spread slightly apart pressed into Franks wrist where it joined his hand which Philip then squeezed very firmly. As this happened, a surprised, yet knowing look came over Frank's face and his gazed was met with an assured look and a slight nod of the head from Philip. Inspector Frank Hill then knew what he had to do.

Smithy who was standing at the chamber looking through a 6 inch round viewing port turned to the LST and asked. 'Oh Lord, my god, is there no help for the widow's son?'

The LST knew exactly what that meant. He replied with a knowing nod of his head. Patsy then walked up to the LST and politely, yet quite worried asked. 'How's Scurvy, doing, he is going to be alright isn't he?'

'Well Pat, at first I wasn't sure, it had been a long time since I've seen a case as bad as this. When he arrived his body was literally fizzing.' Replied the LST. 'I gave him a 15 minute hyperbaric O2 session at 18m and this would normally do the trick to settle a patient out, but this time it didn't. His symptoms didn't improve much, only a minor reduction in pain. So I took him down to 50meters. After 30 minutes at this depth he still had some neurological symptoms and a little pain. So he's now on a table 54 therapeutic schedule.'

Patsy's jaw dropped on hearing this news. He looked through the porthole of the chamber to see Scurvy lying down hooked up to an intravenous drip with Andy Gallagher in attendance to look after him.

The LST continued. 'This meant that I had to keep him at 50meters for a further 2 hours. I will be bringing him up to 42m in twenty minutes, where I will keep him for 30 minutes before bringing him up to 36meters. 'Patsy, this is a long treatment, 39 hours in total. You guys should say hello and then get yourself off for some rest, come back in the morning. He's in good hands here. Over the last hour now he has shown signs of progressive improvement, so as long as this continues I think he'll be alright. It is just a long steady ascent to the surface.'

'After he's done 11hours at 9m we will put him back onto pure O2 for an hour. then at 6m and 3 meters he'll do one hour sessions of pure O2 again interspaced with air sessions. 'We've got your number Patsy. we'll keep you informed. Everything will be fine. We'll take care of everything and I mean, everything.' The LST assured him with a subtle wink and nod of the head.

Patsy was emotionally quite confused, he wasn't sure what pleased and relieved him more. The fact that the LST was confident that Scurvy was going to be okay, or the fact that he didn't have to worry about an HSE enquiry and a jail sentence that could have potentially resulted from one. Looking through the observation port Patsy spoke with Scurvy over the coms. Scurvy too tired and weak to speak, gave him a thumbs up signal in reply.

Scurvy exhausted, his body no longer racked with pain, now just wanted to sleep. Despite what he had just been though, his only thoughts were about the gold coins he had found on the seabed that were now in the pocket of his cut up drysuit.

CHAPTER 9

All that glitters is not gold.

Or is it?

It was 8am in the morning. Pirate had just closed the door on the safe in the basement of GDMC's office, after removing the last of the cash. This was £2750 which he had stuffed into the numerous pockets of his two tone blue Berghaus waterproof jacket. He made his way up the stairs to the office just as Smithy and Philip came walking in from the street.

'Oh eh, alright lads.' Pirate said with the look of a startled rabbit who has just been caught in the beam of a car's headlights.

'You're in early. What were you doing down there?' Asked Smithy distrustingly.

'Oh, eh, I was just having a look a Brian's surface demand panel. I was just looking to see if there was anything I could do to fix it, seeing as how Scurvy is eh still in the chamber.' Replied Pirate thinking quickly on his feet.

'You leave that panel alone, it was bad enough with what Rinky Dick did to it. We don't need you adding complications to it. Anyway Scurvy gets out the chamber this morning at nine. Were meeting Patsy down at Garvel to greet him and bring him home. Are you coming with us? Asked Smithy.

'Eh, oh no I can't. I've got to see a man about a dog this morning.' Replied Pirate furtively. 'But tell him I was asking after him and I'll catch up with you all later.' Excused Pirate as he squeezed past Philip scurrying out the door in a hurry.

'That scrawny weasel's up to no good.' Said Philip looking at Smithy with a serious look in his eye.

'Aye I know. But we don't have time to do anything about it now.' Acknowledged Smithy.

'What's that on the desk?' Philip asked pointing to a stack of papers and opened envelopes. Stacked on the desk were about a dozen or so final demands for payments. Red lettered unpaid electricity bill, phone bill threatening disconnection, unpaid suppliers all threatening court action, overdue unpaid rent demands for the office. Their Marine Insurance policy had also expired and was overdue.

'The old bastard. Fuck the safe!' Exclaimed Smithy and immediately ran downstairs to check the safe. Only to find it was empty. Upon returning upstairs Philip hypothesized. 'I take it, it's empty.'

Smithy totally deflated just nodded his head in acknowledgement.

'Well now we know what the old bastard was up to and why he scurried off in such a hurry.' Remarked Philip.

Just as Philip had finished speaking, a man of about fifty wearing a plain brown suit walked into the office. Looking at Smithy and Philip he asked. 'Are either of you Mr Shawlands?'

Smithy and Philip shook their heads.

'Mr Jaimison or Mr Smith?' Continued the man in the Brown suit.

'I'm Mr Smith.' Replied Smithy. 'Who wants to know?'

The man in the brown suit reached forward and touched Smithy gently on the arm with a wax sealed folded document. 'You have been served.' He said in a quiet and unassuming tone. He then placed the document on the desk, turned around and walked out without saying another word.

Smithy looked on, stunned, open mouthed in disbelief. Smithy Picked up the document. Breaking the seal open to find a court decree(g-314) for the non payment of VAT. He slumped down in the chair letting the summons fall from his up turned hands onto the desk. His head fell forward, his arms dropped by his sides, he closed his eyes and sighed as a man betrayed. Looking up at Philip, Smithy announced 'It's game over Philip we're bust. Pirates robbed us blind. Patsy's going to do his nut.'

'What the fuck did you leave Pirate in charge of the book keeping for!' Exclaimed Philip. 'He's the last person in the world you would do that with. Fuck sake, the man would steal the sugar out of your tea if he could. What the fuck were you and Patsy thinking about?'

'Well we couldn't really not. He is the original founding director of the company and on top of that he's my brother in law. I didn't think he would steal from me.' Replied Smithy regretfully still in disbelief.

'Well there's nothing you can do about it right now. Gather up all those papers and take them with you. You don't want Belinda walking in to find this. Oh and not a word to Scurvy about this, not yet anyway he has enough on his plate. I don't want him stressing, I want him on a full recovery that is the least that we can do for him.' Insisted Philip. 'We'll let Patsy know about it and discuss it with him later. Come on, we better get going.' Said Philip taking control of the situation. Even though from the business perspective, him not being a director of the company, this wasn't his problem. But he could see that the betrayed and deflated Smithy didn't have it in him to deal with it effectively.

Upon arrival at Garvel Dock, Philip and Smithy met up with Patsy at the Naval base gate house. They were greeted by Captain Michael Faraday Drake, a four ringed Captain who was the Queens Harbour Master in Charge of RMAS Garvel Port. 'Good morning gentlemen. I take it you have come to see your young colleague.' He announced in a BBC English accent whilst shaking Patsy's hand.

'Good Morning Captain, yes we have.' Replied Patsy. 'I was informed that he would be out of the chamber and able to return home this morning.'

'Quite correct, it was my adjutant that called you.' Confirmed Faraday Drake. 'I will take you down to see him. He is currently with an acquaintance of yours, Commander Mark Smith, the Medical Officer from Faslane. He is just undergoing a final medical examination before we release him to your care. Scurvy is an incredibly strong and resilient young man. He has survived his ordeal and come through it extremely well, remarkably well in fact. He's back on his feet as though nothing had happened. I suppose having youth on his side has a lot to do with it. That along with the rapid effective emergency response to the event.'

Captain Drake escorted the guys past the Chamber bay*(12-340)* and through into a corridor that had offices either side of it and led them into a board room where they waited for Scurvy.

'You have just missed your associates from the Police Underwater Unit, they have not long departed the site. They took it in turns right up to the end to attend your young friend whilst he was in the chamber.' Remarked Captain Drake. 'Inspector Hill and I have dealt with the administration and subsequent reports with regards the event. We have recorded you as arriving on the scene to assist the young man who ended up in difficulty. As a result of an unfortunate turn of events, whilst he was helping his friends with their trapped fishing net.'

'All is satisfactory and there will be no further investigation into the matter Pat. All's well for the widow's son.' Acknowledged The Captain.

'Thank you, thank you very much. I really appreciate that, we all do. If there is ever something we can do in return just let us know.' Replied Patsy expressing his gratitude with complete sincerity.

'Your welcome, but there's no need. The debt was actually ours to repay.' Remarked Captain Drake. 'It turned out that your young friend was once a bouncer in Bonkers Show Bar in Ayr. The Killick LST who treated him when he first arrived here, recognised your friend. It transpired that about four years ago, the Killick*(g-317)*, who was a junior rating at the time. Along with a fellow ship mate got into a bit of bother with some of the locals one night in Bonkers. Usual thing, the local lads didn't like our lads chatting up the local girls. Ended up in a stramash *(g-318)*. By all accounts the lads weren't fairing too well. Outnumbered three to one, the odds were firmly against them.'

'According to the Killick they were getting seven bells beaten out of them, he reckoned they were destined for long stay in the hospital that night. It turned out that your young friend was the only bouncer who jumped in to save them. Apparently when needs must he's a bit of a demon. Who would have thought. You would never know from speaking with him. Anyway, your young friend managed to get the two young sailors behind the bar and into the staff room. Where upon he administered some serious first aid. To include closing up split lips, cuts around cheek bones as well closing and dressing a knife wound on the young seaman's back. He then organised a taxi for them and snuck them out the back door away from the mob baying for their blood. So we are all square, no more to be said on the matter.' Informed the Captain.

'Oh and one other piece of good news. After you departed the scene. Wullie May knowing that Scurvy had managed to cut one end of the ground wire and part cut the other end before things all went south. Decided to try one more time to free his net. Though nearly overturning his boat in the process. He did manage to pull his net free and so saved his net and trawl gear after all. So the young man's efforts were not wasted. I have been reliably informed that Wullie is looking forward to meeting Scurvy to thank him in person. Ah, here's your young friend now.' Observed Captain Drake.

Incredibly, looking none the worse for wear from his ordeal, Scurvy came walking into the board room grinning so happy to see his friends. 'Here, am I glad to see you guys, where's my drysuit?' He asked.

Where's your drysuit? I was expecting that.' Replied Patsy stunned turning to look at Philip and Smithy somewhat surprised.

'It's in the boot of my car. But it's no use to you now Scury. Colin had to cut it off you in the chamber.' Replied Philip

'Oh that's all right as long as I know where it is.' Replied Scurvy.

'What do you want with it. It's in too much of a mess even for you to repair. You're going to need a new one.' Said Smithy.

'Oh, eh, I just want it for sentimental reasons.' Replied Scurvy.

'Anyway, how are you feeling. For someone who has just endured a type 2 bend and 40 hours of recompression therapy(12-340), you're looking and sounding remarkably well, I'm pleased to say.' Remarked Patsy pleasantly surprised.

'I feel fine Patsy, I slept like a log for most of the last 30 hours. I had the best sleep in my life. I can only imagine that the long spells on Hyperbaric O2 have had something to do with it.' Replied a rather chirpy Scurvy. 'I feel as though I've had a new lease of life. I'm keen to get back in the water.' said Scurvy positively.

'Not so fast young man.' Cut in Dr Smith. 'It will be another month before you will be back in the water. But before that you will need to come and see me at Faslane. I will put you through a thorough physical examination to include amongst other things. A Doppler scan*(g-315)*, an ECG*(g-316)*, a Chester step*(g-314)* and Spirometry test*(g-318)*. Pass that, then I will issue you a medical certifying you fit to dive again.'

'Oh come on Doc, I feel fine.' Protested Scurvy.

'I'm serious.' Said the Doctor empathically. 'I'll see you 28 days from today, 10am at Faslane. Just come to the guardhouse at the main gate and ask for me. You should now have lots of rest. No booze for a month, drink plenty of water to stay hydrated and eat healthily. Once you are back at work, light duties only for at least the next two weeks. When you get home from here straight to bed.' Instructed the Doc.

'Straight to bed are you kidding me. I have just spent the best part of the last forty plus hours flat on my back. If I am going to be on my back now there will need to be a very dirty woman on top of me.' Announced Scury. 'Anyway, I'm starving ma belly's growling. I could eat a scabby horse.'

With that Smithy and Patsy turned to look at one another grinning and silently mouthed Bella to each other.

'Here Scurvy. I hate to say it mate but your stinking.' Patsy informed him. 'Captain Drake, we've brought some clean clothes & toiletries for Scurvy, could he possibly have a shower here before we take him home.' Enquired Patsy.

'Yes of course, you can use the shower in the ratings changing room.' Confirmed the Captain. 'Well Gentlemen, if you'll excuse me, my onerous and numerous duties call. Scurvy, I'm very pleased to see that you survived your ordeal and came through it so remarkable well, remarkably well. Should we meet again, I hope it is under less dramatic circumstances. Commander Smith will see you out. Good Day gentlemen.' Said Captain Drake as he bid his leave.

As Scurvy went off to shower and change, Patsy turned to Smithy and Philip and whispered. 'Let's not disappoint Scurvy, you two take him for a big breakfast at Change at Jamaica and I'll organise the rest. Have Scurvy back at his flat at one o'clock on the dot.'

'Leave it to us, we know the drill.' Replied Smithy grinning.

The restaurant Change at Jamaica was located on the south side of the River Clyde under the Jamaica Street railway bridge. This is the bridge that allows the trains to cross the Clyde into Glasgow Central railway station. As well as being known for opening at 6.30AM to provide a hearty cooked breakfast menu. They would also offer to put a fresh head on your pint every time a train went past overhead.

Due to its sheltered and hidden from view location, combined with the generally poor lighting of the street outside. Its location's reputation also extended to being a hangout for some of the cities less attractive demi-monde filles de joie*(g-315)*. Who could be found there plying their trade, from early morning, afternoon, evening and well into the wee small hours of the night.

No sooner had Philip parked up outside the entrance to the restaurant, did he received a knock on his door window.

Upon lowering the window a haggard looking far from attractive woman heavily layered in bad makeup. With overdone bright red rouge covering her lips, which were struggling to hold back the teeth of a horse. Wearing nothing more than a very narrow sparkly boob tube top, which barely supported her bulging 38DD breasts. Whose nipples were large, hard and erect with the cold, leaned her head into the window and asked. 'Looking for business boys'? 'I'll do a discount for the three of you for an hour.'

Philip somewhat startled by this intrusion. His head and shoulders jolted to the left away from the window, as an automatic defensive reaction from the teeth and tits that were now wedged in through the window.

'Eh, oh good morning hen*(g-316)*.' Replied Philip re-composing himself. 'It's a generous offer I'm sure, but we're just here for the breakfast. But thanks for the offer anyway.'

'Aye no worries son, well if you change your minds when you come out, I'll just be here unless someone else beats you to it.' Answered the woman with an unimaginable self surety as she extracted her teeth and tits from his open window.

The three amigos entered the restaurant, secured a table and all ordered the breakfast of champions.

'Wow, she was rough, you can see that beauty has been chasing her but she has always managed to out run it. She couldn'y get a whistle off a boiling kettle. Did you see the size of her nipples though, you could tune in a radio with them.' Laughed Smithy.

'I couldn'y focus on her nipples for fear of her teeth. I thought she was gonny eat me.' Replied Philip. 'You definitely wouldn't want a kiss under the Mistletoe from her never mind a blow job off her.'

'Forget Mistletoe, I wouldn'y kiss her under a general anaesthetic.' Retorted Smithy.

'True, but I'd bet you a pound she could eat an apple through a letterbox.' Replied Scurvy sniggering.

Meanwhile, Patsy had just pulled into a familiar driveway on Giffnock's Elphinstone Road.

After breakfast and dodging the local wildlife upon leaving the restaurant. Philip and Smithy took Scurvy back to his Flat on Main Street in Bridgeton where Patsy was waiting for them at the close entrance with Scurvy's Flat keys. 'Here's your keys lad, I just nipped up and put the heating on for you, I didn't want you coming home to a cold Flat.' Said Patsy handing Scurvy his keys. 'Oh and I have got you in some groceries and things' Patsy informed him whilst tipping Smithy and Philip a sly wink.

'Here's your drysuit Scurvy.' Said Philip as he took it out of the boot of his car. 'As you can see it wrecked pardon the pun.'

'Take a week off on basic pay Scurvy, chill out for a bit and we'll see you back in the office next Friday lunchtime.' Said Patsy in an act of kindness.

'Thanks Patsy, I appreciate that and eh, thanks for everything you did for me guys, I really appreciate it. I'm in debt to you all.' Acknowledge Scurvy sincerely.

'You're welcome, and there's no debt to pay. Because you managed to cut the ground line on one end of the trawl, Wullie May was able to recovery his trawl. So the debt is one I owe to you.' Replied Patsy. 'See you next Friday.'

Walking through the living room door of his Flat Scurvy was met by a most welcome and totally unexpected surprise. For lying on the sofa in front of him was the fit and attractive Bella. Wearing nothing but a Popeye hat, white pantyhose & suspenders, no knickers and a white see through bra.

'Well hello there sailor.' Remarked a wide eyed Scurvy.

'Well diver boy, are you feeling fit enough to growl at the badger?' Asked Bella in a soft, low sultry voice with a filthy smile on her face. As she spread her legs akimbo to show off a thick dark hairy but neatly trimmed bush between her thighs.

'I'm sure you are well familiar with the Diver's moto Bella.' Replied a self assured and highly aroused Scurvy. 'No sea too rough, no muff too tough, I'll dive till dawn. Patsy, consider your debt repaid, were all square!'

Out in the street, Smithy handed Patsy the Court Decree(g-314) that he had been served with earlier that morning.

'That scamming, conniving, thieving, scrawny old bastard.' Growled an enraged Patsy unable to believe his eyes.

'It gets worse, he also emptied the safe before scurrying off this morning.' Smithy informed him. 'There was £2,750.00 in it. Between that and the court summons for over £17,000 of VAT plus interest were bankrupt.'

'I will make that weasily old bastards life Hell when I get my hands on him.' Announced an enraged Patsy.

'There's more.' Replied a sheepish Smithy as he handed Patsy the envelopes he had bundled together with a large elastic band, that Pirate had left on the office desk that morning.

'Fuckin Nora Smithy, just how much debt do we actually owe?' Asked Patsy.

'I don't honestly know.' Sighed Smithy. 'But I am willing to bet there's more red letters to come. I wonder how long we've got before Gourley, Montgomery & Tindal evict us from the office?'

'Well before we find out, we should maybe empty the office and start to scatter the assets and stock.' Suggested Patsy.

'Jesus Patsy, what about the Loch Ranza? Customs and Excise are sure to seize her as collateral.' Exclaimed Philip.

'Na, there's nae danger of that.' Replied Patsy confidently. 'I made sure of that from day one when I started into this venture. You see, the boats in my daughter's name, set up in a trust fund. We, that is GDMC lease the boat from her trust. Clever, eh. The boat and all of its kit & caboodle ultimately belong to her. The fee that the Trust charges us for the boat becomes part of her trust fund which she can collect tax free in 18 years time when she is 21. As such, the boat can't be touched.' Then with a smile of realisation appearing on Patsy's face he said. 'And neither can anything on it. That was probably the only benefit I've had from my divorce and little Katy living with her mother.'

'Nice one Patsy, now that was a very shrewd and ingenious move.' Acknowledge Philip.

'Right, we'll deal with Pirate later.' Instructed Patsy. 'Right now, we need to get back to the office and empty it. We will store as much as we can on the boat and I'll take her somewhere safe for the next few weeks.' Turning to Smithy and casting him a contemptuous look, Patsy added. 'Away from prying eyes and safe from that weasily, thieving brother in law of yours. Oh, and not a word to Scurvy about this, not just now. I don't want him stressing over this.

We'll tell him next week when he comes back. Agreed?'

'Oh aye, absolutely.' Agreed Smithy & Philip in unison.

Early the following morning whilst Scurvy was sound asleep, tired out from his marathon session of debouched, licentious, libertarianism with the more than willing Bella. A worn out but highly satisfied Bella, slipped out of the bed, quietly got dress and left Scurvy's flat for home.

A few hours later, Scurvy woke to find the obliging and near insatiable Bella gone. With a renewed energy and zest for life welling up inside of him, he got of bed and immediately went to collect his drysuit from the living room. It lay where he had dropped it to the floor the day before. After being distracted by the welcome home present of the alluring, beguiling, irresistible, delectable Bella.

Picking it up he rummaged for the coins in its thigh pocket. Much to his relief and excitement they were still there. Four shiny gold coloured, slightly worn coins. Milled around the edges with some of the markings partially faded. But gold coins none the less. His pulse quickened, his eyes stared wide open at the coins in his hand. Picking them up one at a time turning them over looking at them closely, trying to make out the markings. Thoughts and ideas were flashing through his brain like an express train.

He laid them out on the coffee table before him. Sitting back on the sofa he started to calm himself. 'Right, first things first.' He thought into himself. 'I need to try to identify them. Then I need to get them valued.' Taking paper from a note pad and using a soft pencil, Scurvy carefully began to take rubbings of both sides of each of the coins.

On one side was a figure head and he could make out the words GEORDIUS lll BG BRITANNIAR REX FD and a date 1820. On the other side there was a rider on a horse wearing a cape and headwear of a Spartan. Stamped around the outside of the horse and rider were the words:

'Honi Soit Qui Mal Y Pense'

Then looking through the yellow pages, he started to make notes of addresses of art dealers and auction houses.

Once showered and dressed, with a bite of breakfast inside of him. Scurvy got on the bus for the city centre. His first port of call being the magnificent Mitchell Library, then the Kelvingrove Museum and Art Galleries. The Mitchell Library whose' frontage stands on North Street in Glasgow, is one of Europe's largest public libraries. A magnificent work of architecture. Easily recognised by its large green oxidised copper dome, making it one of Glasgow's most famous and oldest land marks.

The library which now contained in excess of one million books and documents, was the result of the generosity of the 19th century, Ecclesmachan born tobacco manufacturer, railways investor and philanthropist Stephen Mitchell. Who bequeathed the bulk of his fortune to the Corporation of Glasgow.

Scurvy was no stranger to this building, he had spent many days over the years here researching and studying diving history, physiology, technology and underwater submersibles. He knew that there was no better place in Glasgow than the Mitchell Library to begin his research.

Two hours later and after thumbing through a dozen or so books, Scurvy found information on his particular coins. If his research was correct, these coins were George the 3rd Gold Sovereigns. It turned out that the rider on horseback on one side of the coins was not a Spartan but a depiction of Saint George slaying the dragon.

The inscription 'GEORDIUS lll BG BRITANNIAR REX FD' basically translated to George lll by the Grace of God, King of the British territories, Defender of the faith.

The inscription on the reverse side of the coin which read.

'Honi Soit Qui Mal Y Pense'
Translated to 'Evil To Him Who Evil Thinks.'

Once again, his heart started to thump with excitement.

His next port of call was the Kelvingrove Museum and Art Galleries. Another magnificent, nae majestic work of architecture for Glasgow to be extremely proud of. Though, one has to wonder what it was that architects of the 1890's knew about and understood that architects of the 21st century seem to have forgotten about today.

The construction of this majestic building was originally funded from the proceeds of the 1888 International Exhibition of Science, Art and Industry. One of four such international events that were held during the late nineteenth and early twentieth century's in Glasgow. It was here that Scurvy hoped to get an idea of the value of the coins in his possession, as the Huntarian Museum of Glasgow University had a coin collection on loan to the Kelvingrove museum.

Amongst this, was a collection of Gold Sovereigns over the ages. In order to add interest to the exhibit, alongside each coin on display was its estimated value. These evaluations had been performed by the Glasgow office of Christies the world famous antique dealers and auction house, three years earlier in 1990.

As Luck would have it, the collection included Gold sovereigns the same as Scurvy's minted in the same year. There were two of these coins, one in mint condition which was valued at £675, the other which was in a similar condition to scurvy's coins. This had been valued at £475.

His pulse quickening Scurvy began to think as to how he could cash these in. He thought to himself, 'As I haven't stolen them and I did genuinely find them on the seabed 45m below the surface of the Clyde. In a wreck that was uncharted lying underneath another wreck and had clearly been there for the best part of 170 hundred years. As such no one else could genuinely, legitimately claim ownership or right to them. And as the old adage of possession is nine tenths of the law. Which is derived from Roman Law, being that if one person is not taking good care of their property then someone else should be given the opportunity to do so. Then I have nothing to be concerned about. I wonder if Christies would buy them from me?' He thought to himself.

With that he was on the next bus back into the city centre. Walking through the gold gilded glass door of

Christies he was pleasantly greeted by a tall slim bespeckled man in his fifties, wearing a paisley pattern & suede waistcoat with matching cravat. 'Good afternoon young man what can I do for you today?' He politely asked.

'Well, I have recently come into possession of these coins which I believe are George lll gold sovereigns. I was hoping you could give me a valuation on them.' Enquired Scurvy sincerely, as he unfolded his handkerchief and laid them out on the glass countertop.

'Certainly sir.' Replied the antiquary.

Putting on a pair of white cotton gloves, the antiquary initially started to move the coins together over the glass countertop without actually picking them up. He then set them into two pairs.

It was at this point that he picked them up and began to take a closer look at them using a small wooden handled magnifying glass. Taking one coin from each pair, he carefully examined them. Looking at the milled edges of the coins then carefully examining the actually stamp work of the coin contents and features. After he few minutes he put down his magnifying glass. He said. 'You should be aware Mr eh.'

'Smith.' Answered Scurvy quickly.

'You should be aware Mr Smith.' Looking at Scurvy doubtfully over the rim of his glasses with a knowing smile. 'That all that glitters is not gold.'

Something deep within Scurvy fell on its side. 'Are you, are you telling me they're not real gold?' Stuttered Scurvy in disbelief. 'They've got to be gold, these coins have been lying on the seabed for the best part of 170 years. If they weren't gold they would be all corroded and oxidised.'

'Please forgive my choice of phrase Mr Smith. It is a term we in the trade use when all is not quite as it seems. But it's not all bad news.' Replied the antiquary sensing the disappointment in the young man standing before him. 'These two coins on the left here, I am fairly sure are the mutts nuts as you youngsters would say. These two coins on the right aren't. I am fairly certain these two are counterfeit.'

'Really, how can you tell?' Asked Scurvy sincerely.

'Well firstly I will perform the full test procedure that is the industry standard for when we evaluate gold coins. This is referenced in the Spink Standard Catalogue of British Coins, this is the coin dealers bible. This way you will be able to verify for yourself.' Explained the antiquary. 'Initially we perform a visual inspection of the coins. Your coins though slightly worn are in reasonable condition compared to some that I have seen over the years.'

'In counterfeit coins there are some common defects that we look for, the milled outer edge is one place that is not quite consistent as an original coin. Also the counterfeiter never quite managed to get the nose of the King quite right for some reason. Also, look at the squares on the border of the coin, you see in the forgery it is not quite the same as the real coin.'

Laying the two coins back down on the glass countertop the antiquary explained in further detail. 'Now what made it easy for me to spot that two of your coins are definitely counterfeit and that two of them are potential genuine is that I could compare them side by side one another. Having the advantage of a comparator demonstrated that they are slightly different to one another. Gold is one of the most dense, therefore one of the heaviest metals in the world. Weighing in at 19.3grams per cubic centimetre it is almost twice the weight of lead for the same volume. Here feel for yourself.' Handing Scurvy one coin from each pair, Scurvy now noticed a difference in weight between the two coins.

'Good heavens, your right.' Scurvy exclaimed. 'It is quite noticeable.'

'Next we look at the size of each of the coins.' The antiquary went on to explain. Although all four coins were exactly the same diameter, I could see that when lying flat on the glass countertop, two of them were slightly thicker than the other two. The thicker coins are definitely counterfeit. This is done because regardless of whatever metal they are made from, if the coins are the exact same physical size there would be a large noticeable disparity in weight Thus alerting the receiver of the coin that it was counterfeit. Therefore to try to hide this, the coins are made slightly thicker than the genuine gold coins so as to increase their weight.' Explained the antiquary. 'Here, I will show you. Let's take what I believe to be the genuine article first. This should weigh 8 grams if it were in mint condition, I suspect this coin may be a fraction under that due to its wear.'

Taking the coin he placed it on a small set of digital scales. It weighed in at 7.98gramms, he did the same with the other real coin which weighed in 7.97 grams. 'Now let us weigh the other two coins.' The Antiquary placed them on the scale one at a time they both came up as weighing 6.1 grams each. 'Going by their weight, these two coins are probable made from iron or some type of ferrous metal and then Electro gold plated. We can easily check this with this small magnet. Electro gold plating had become popular amongst forgers during the period after it was invented at the turn of the 19th Century.' Explained the antiquary.

Sure enough, the two lighter but slightly larger coins stuck to the magnet but the other two didn't.

'The rather high quality of the electro gold plating is what has stopped the coins from rusting in the water. The ferrous metal was completely sealed by the gold plate. Now just before, I perform the final test of the coins, I will check their diameter and thickness of the coins with this digital micrometer to ensure they are sized correctly'. Continued the antiquary. Sure enough, the two heavier yet thinner coins matched exactly the dimensions as listed in the Spinks guide book.

'Now Mr Smith, I will perform the acid test. You may be familiar with this phrase as it has found its way into common usage. But it is here in the antiques and jewellery trade where acid is actually used, as this is where the test and the phrase originated.' The antiquary informed him with a smile.

Placing the coins onto a porcelain dish with a paper towel underneath them. The antiquary brought out a small plastic bottle which looked like an eye drop bottle. 'In here Mr smith we have an acid known as Aqua Regia. When we apply this to the genuine coins it will have absolutely no effect on the coin it will just sit there like water. For pure gold, 22 Karat gold will not react to it. However, when I apply it to the counterfeit coin, this slight patina that you can see on the coin will dissolve off making the coin shiny and the acid will take on a pale green tinge to it.'

Sure enough two of the sovereigns were pure gold much to Scurvy's delight.

'Well, Mr Smith, there you have it. You have two genuine George lll, 22 Karat gold Sovereigns minted in 1820 and two very good counterfeit coins from the same time period, remarkable.'

'Excellent.' Remarked Scurvy with a smile.

As the antiquary was cleaning the acid from the coins, Scurvy asked him. 'So eh how much are they worth?'

'The genuine coins if they were sent to auction could probably fetch around £475 each. The counterfeit coins given they are from the same period and are gold plated of a high quality may be worth around £50. Providing off course you can provide provenance for the coins.' Answered the antiquary.

'What's provenance?' Asked Scurvy.

'Well, Provenance is from the French word provenir, to come from. It is the chronology of the ownership, custody or location of a historical object. Due to the thriving trade in stolen art and jewellery that takes place around the world. Museums, auction houses and art dealers of repute, such as ourselves have a moral and legal obligation to establish the validity of ownership or custody of such treasures. Therefore, you would have to provide provenance for your coins before we would be able to buy or present them for auction.' Explained the antiquary.

'Oh God all mighty. That means going through the Receiver of Wrecks. I nearly died finding these.' Said Scurvy in despair.

'When it comes to gold found on the seabed. Our government acting in the name of that inbred, self perpetuating, robbing, self entitled oligarchs of a monarchy that sit in Buckingham Palace who rob this nations population blind. Have a long track record of being nasty, greedy bastards wanting it all for themselves.' Blurted out Scurvy. 'I am sure you are all too familiar with what happened to Wharton Williams the Aberdeen Offshore Diving Company and their world famous HMS Edinburgh gold salvage. The British Government in the name of the Queen well and truly fucked them over. So little old me has got no chance against her robbing Majesty's inbred self perpetuating, oligarchy and the sharks of her Customs and Excise Office. Of which the 'Receiver of Wrecks' is sure to inform, seeing as how they work hand in glove with one another.' Ranted Scurvy. Once more sensing the rug was about to be pulled from under his feet.

'Yes, whilst that was not the most flattering description of our monarchy and government that I have heard. It is probably though, the most accurate one. I will admit that what you say, is a contention for all of us, though most dare not voice it.' Replied the antiquary in complete agreement. 'You say, you found these on the seabed and nearly died in the process. Have a seat there, and tell me all about it. You have me genuinely intrigued.' Offered the antiquary.

Scurvy regaled his story. Though having the smarts about him to leave out any information or detail that would give away the identity and location of the wrecks.

'Wow, now that was a narrative I wasn't expecting.' Replied the antiquary in amazement. 'Now that you have told me your story, I do recall something being mentioned on Radio Clyde News recently about a diver being airlifted with the bends*(g-315)*. That would have been you then?'

'Yes.' Replied Scurvy.

'And what did you say the name of the wreck was and how many more of these coins did you say you think there was?' Sneakily enquired the antiquary.

Scurvy immediately sensing the antiquary was fishing for the critical location information which he had deliberately left out replied with a smile and said. 'I didn't and in the infamous worlds of Ronald Reagan during the Iran Contra Senate investigation, all I can say is I have no clear recollection of that.'

The antiquary believed that the young man before him was telling him the truth about how he had come by the coins. He also recognised that Scurvy was genuinely guarding his source. He smiled and pressed the subject of the coins location no further. The antiquary had developed a liking for Scurvy. He had a gut reaction that the young man before him was of genuine good character for he had a very likeable ambiance about him. 'How long have you been diving young man?' The antiquary asked him.

'Since I was fifteen, ten years now. I learned to dive with the AA Lion British Sub Aqua Club which use to meet up in the old Story Street Baths in Paisley. The baths are demolished now. But I had known that I wanted to be a diver ever since I saw my first Cousteau documentary on TV when I was about four years old. I never missed an episode as a kid growing up. That and on Sunday morning Inner Space on STV, with Ron & Valerie Taylor about their adventures on Australia's Great Barrier reef.'

'When I was about ten, me and my mates would watch Marine Boy on Saturday morning's on BBC1 then go to the Victory baths in Renfrew and recreate the episodes for ourselves. In the evening we would watch Man From Atlantis, you know with Patrick Duffy. We even learned to swim like him under the water. You remember the way he use to undulate his body in a wave motion.' Answered Scurvy reminiscing, rekindling fond memories from his childhood. 'And now that I have actually found sunken treasure, the dreams of all divers. All be it only a little bit. It's all about to turn into a depressive nightmare.' Said Scurvy disheartened.

The antiquary had some sympathy for Scurvy after hearing his story. As such he decided he was going to try to help the young man before him. Stacking the coins neatly, wrapping them in Scurvy's handkerchief and handing them back to Scurvy he said. 'All may not necessarily be lost Mr Smith. I may possibly be able to do something to brighten your day.'

'Although I, cannot deal in your coins without provenance, there is someone I know who possible will.'

'Oh Really.' Replied Scurvy with some enthusiasm.

'Yes. However, as you enjoy and are currently benefiting from wearing the cloak of anonymity, as does my client. For we both know that Smith isn't your real name.'

Scurvy smiled. 'Okay, I'm listening.'

'I'll have to speak with him first and it just so happens that he will be in attendance at a charity event at Pollock House this evening for which I have been cordially invited. He will not pay you the price that you would expect to receive at auction. However, neither he nor I are cut from the cloth of Arthur Daley. Neither of us want the attention or ramifications that is often incurred from disgruntled customers who feel they have been cheated. I certainly don't want a brick through the shop front window or a petrol bomb flung through my shop door.' Explained the antiquary. 'I believe he would be willing to pay you £375 a piece for the genuine coins. I think he may also buy the untested counterfeited coin from you for £50. Which is quite reasonable given that if you sold them at auction, you have to pay 15% commission to the auction house on the sale price, regardless of how much or how little they sold for.'

Scurvy sensing that he was onto a good thing here agreed. 'Okay, you have just made me a happy man. But given that I have no provenance for these coins. Does this not create problems for your man further down the line, if he was to try to sell them at a later date?' Asked Scurvy sincerely.

'Sadly, I have to confess, provenance is only a problem for you and I when it comes treasure of this nature.' Replied the antiquary. 'The upper echelon of society of which my client belongs. Are able to, how can I say it; generate provenance.'

'Let me explain. It is common for them to have large collections of coins, antiquities etc. Many of my clients buy these as long term investments. Sometimes they give them as gifts or part payments in exchange for lucrative business contracts. They will also quite often lend these collections and antiques to museums. This has several advantages.'

'The museum takes on the insurance for full market value and has to provide the necessary security to guard against theft of such precious valuable items in their care. This relieves the owner of that liability and cost. Thus the items increases in value year on year without any cost to the owner. As part of the lend agreement, the museum will have to agree to loaning out the collection to other museums from time to time. It is common for such loan agreements to be anything from one year to a five years with the option to renew if the owner and the museum mutually desire. Every time an object is loaned to a museum, a contract is created stating that the museum has borrowed the item from Mr X to place on public display for an agreed time period. As a result of the sphere of influence and station that these kind of people hold in society, they are generally deemed by these institutions as being of beyond reproach.'

'Then on top of that there is one other aspect of the obscenely wealthy that I haven't mentioned. That is the foundation of a Trust. This is quite a complex, devious and slippery mechanism of hiding original ownership that was set up by the City of London financial institutions. They are a law onto themselves and do not come under the jurisdiction of the British courts. The two square miles of land that is the City of London is a country within a country. For it has its own Lord Mayor, its own government, its own courts and its own police force. All of whom are completely independent to the rest of Great Britain and do not fall under the jurisdiction of the British Law Courts.'

'Trust's date back to the time of the crusades when the Knights would go off to fight in foreign lands. They would leave their assets and estates in the care of trusted stewards. What Trusts do, is that they play with the concept of ownership, basically they make it complicated and untraceable. This is done primarily to hide wealth and assets from the tax man and from the compensation law courts.'

'The person wanting to place their assets whether it be possessions or money into Trust is called the Settlor. They would place their assets into the hands of a Trustee. Normally today that would be a lawyer. It would be done alleging it was for the benefit of a third party known as the beneficiary. The beneficiary would only have access to the assets upon the death of the Settlor. As such you become legally separated from those assets, there is now a barrier between them and you.'

'You can't be taxed on them and no one is going to be able to find anything about your connection to these assets. The Trust administration office is usually in a country different to that of your nationally or residency. The Trustee will be based in a different country again and the beneficiary will often but not always be located in a country different to that. Though it is important to understand that the beneficiary need not be a person, it could be named as an institution or a charity etc.'

'Now with a Trust, the Settlor still retains full legal control of the monies or assets and how they will be used. For the Settlor decides what the Trustees can and cannot do. Which basically means that the Settlor has full use of the asset and benefit of the money via the Trustees. But it is not traceable to the Settlor because the City of London and its offshore partners have no legal requirements to keep a register of Trusts or details of assets held in Trusts. There are no bodies to certify that a trust has been set up. There are no legal obligations for either party to register it. There are no financial reporting obligations for Trusts. So the only people who know about the agreement are the Trustee and the Settlor. So to all intensive purposes Trusts are invisible arrangements, ultimately with nobody owning the assets. I should point out that today there are trillions of pounds worth of assets and monies sitting offshore held behind these Trusts. It's all very clever, all completely legal but seriously wrong on all counts.'

'So, unless the object has been listed by the police as being stolen unrecovered or a public legal challenge to ownership is in process, the museum will not pursue provenance from the lender as they have no requirement to, for they are not resetting the object. They are in fact putting the object on public display for the whole world to see, in a secure environment. Secure even from the original lender.'

'Most museums often only own a percentage of the items on display. Many of their displays are on loan, without such loans their grandiose museum buildings would be somewhat sparse inside. This contract between the museum and the lender can act as provenance of ownership for the lender. The museum's name and reputation providing legitimacy to the provenance. Every time the object is loaned to another museum an additional provenance is created, providing a chain of provenance. Thus creating unquestionable credulity.'

'So unless the object in question is of famous notoriety or has a serial number or makers mark stamped on it to act as a unique identifier or has a specific defect that could uniquely identify it. Then it becomes very difficult for someone other than the current holder of the object to stake claim against it.'

'Now these collections can be and often are loaned from a museum in one country to a museum in another country. Thus placing the object outside of the jurisdiction of a police force or Tax Authority of the country of residence of the owner. Making it difficult for any official authority to track or trace back the object to anyone other than the claimed owner. Who, in the extremely highly unlikely event, if pursued can make claim that they bought from a village antique shop which no longer exists and who's owner is long dead or inherited it as part of a family heir loom which cannot be disputed.'

That and the fact that as a general rule, those who hold such collections tend to have influence within the police and courts of their country of residence. So for coins like yours, it is relatively easy for clients such as mine to have them blend into their current collections unnoticed and for them to establish provenance accordingly.' Explained the antiquary.

'Wow, that is so wrong on so many levels. But wait a minute, placing the corruption and obscenity of the Trust's thing to one side. Could I not just claim that I bought them from an old antiques shop that no longer exists or claim that I found them in amongst my grandma's collection of antiques.' Challenged Scurvy.

'Yes potentially you could Mr Smith. But do you really want the attention that would then bring. And if you were able to recover any more of these coins, how would you explain them then. On top of that, you would ultimately lose the cloak of anonymity that you currently have the comfort of wearing.'

'No, I don't know and no I don't. I see what you mean, those are three very good points. Okay I'm in.' Replied Scurvy enthusiastically.

'Can you come back and see me on Monday morning around 11:15am?' Asked the antiquary. If my client is interested he will do the exchange that morning. Like you Mr Smith, my client also enjoys the comfort of wearing the cloak of anonymity. As such, you will be dealing with an associate of his. It will all seem a little bit secret squirrel in nature but this is to protect all of us.' The antiquary assured him.

'Why will you not be dealing with it?' Asked Scurvy.

'As I explained earlier, I cannot get involved in any way with the exchange. I am just providing an introduction service.' Replied the antiquary.

'I am curious about one thing though. As much as I really do appreciate your advice and help with this. But what do you get from this, a finder's fee?' Asked Scurvy.

'No, I don't receive any payment for this at all. Certainly not in the way that you are thinking. No it's much more how can I say, subtle than that. Firstly I do sincerely sympathize with you and wish you the best of British luck. That said, by helping you and by brining this opportunity to the attention of my client. It em, earns me a certain amount of Kudos with my clients allowing me to curry favour in certain social circles. Also, it helps to ensure that I continue to receive invites to lucrative events of polite society. Which I am not ashamed to say, I very much enjoy the privilege of. At these events, I am often introduced to new clients by existing clients and various business deals are also done there.' Explained the antiquary sincerely.

Leaving Christies with his golden treasure securely tucked away in the bottom of the front pocket of his jeans, Scurvy made his way back to his flat in Bridgeton. Once seated on the bus he began to relax. Between his energetic feats of the night and day before, along with the emotional rollercoaster he had been riding today. Scurvy began to feel physically and mentally drained.

Though he was feeling very pleased with himself, it was all beginning to feel surreal to him. Finding the sunken treasure at the bottom of the Clyde from a wreck that was underneath another wreck, the helicopter rescue, being treated for almost two days in a recompression chamber*(12-340)*. The unbridled eroticism of Bella, the conversation with the Christies antiquary. Now being the key player in a secret deal with an unnamed buyer for his sunken treasure.

'This is like something out of an Alistair McLean novel.' He thought to himself. Scurvy slipped his hand into his pocket to feel for the coins just to make sure he hadn't been dreaming.

The weekend came and went, with Scurvy finding himself quite lethargic, sleeping for large parts of it. His body still recovering from a combination of his bend, the recompression therapy and Bella. But on Monday morning, he walked through the front door of Christies showroom bright eyed and bushy tailed at 11:15am on the dot.

Once again he was politely greeted by the antiquary whom he had spoken with on the Friday before. He was wearing the same paisley patterned & sued waistcoat with matching cravat. 'Good morning Mr Smith and how are we today?' Asked the antiquary.

'Oh tickety boo.' Replied a breezy Scurvy. 'How did your swaray go on Friday evening, did things go as you hoped?' Asked Scurvy discreetly.

'Perfectly, it went just as I expected, a lovely evening was had by all.' Replied the antiquary with a wink. 'I was telling my client all about your adventure and rescue by helicopter. He found it a fascinating story and would very much like for his associate Mr Jones to meet with you.'

'Mr Jones is going to be in town today, he asked if you would join him for lunch at Carnegies in West George Street at twelve o'clock. He'll be seated in the booth on the far left, he will be facing the door. You'll recognise him by his 3/4 length Pierre Cardin brown leather jacket and black polo neck. Your opening line will be Mr Jones I presume. He will reply Indeed Mr Smith. You will both order lunch. You will exchange the two real coins one at a time. Mr Jones will discretely perform the acid test as I have done to confirm the quality of the gold. After each confirmation he will hand over payment for that coin to you. He will very briefly visually examine the counterfeit coin, then pay you for it. It is done this way so as to provide security for each of you. This gives Mr Jones time to confirm they are real and it gives you time to verify the payment is correct. The booth is very discreet, so no one will see what is taking place. You will both finish your lunch, making small talk about your adventure. It should be played out just like two friends meeting up for lunch and a catch up. You will order coffee, then Mr Jones will pay the bill and leave. You will stay for a while longer, finish your coffee before leaving. Making it look all very natural.' The antiquary informed him.

'Okay I understand.' Acknowledged Scurvy. 'Jesus, this is quite exciting. How many people do this on a Monday morning. Secret squirrel by fuck! That was a bit of an understatement. Well, I suppose I should make haste for Carnegies.' Said Scurvy looking at his watch.

The antiquary smiled and gave Scurvy a nod of the head. The two men shook hands and Scurvy made his way to West George Street.

Carnegies was a chain of bar restaurants in Glasgow. They were very popular. This particular restaurant was down stairs in the cellar under an old Edwardian sandstone building. It was cosy and dimly lit which suited both parties purposes as they were less exposed to unwanted prying eyes. It wasn't far from the antique dealers premises in Bath street to Carnegies, about half a mile. Less than a 10 minute walk. Scurvy arrived in plenty of time. He decided to wait across the street on the corner. For like a midget at a urinal,

Scurvy knew he was going to have to be on his toes here. He wanted to see his Mr Jones arriving.

Sure enough, at five to twelve, a black Range Rover pulled up outside the entrance. Scurvy noted the car's registration number. Two men got out, one wearing a brown leather three quarter length jacket. The other man broad across the back, wearing a black suit with a grey polo neck, they entered the restaurant together. Scurvy waited a few more minutes. Then, taking a deep breath and mentally reverting back to his days as bouncer. Standing straight, shoulders back, confident and composed at the stroke of twelve noon he walked through the restaurant door.

The two men were not sitting together, which was as Scurvy had expected them to be. Mr Jones was sitting in the booth on the far left facing the door just as the antiquary said he would be. The other man was sitting near the door but within sight of the booth. Scurvy made the introduction as instructed.

Everything took place exactly as the antiquary said it would. It was all very calm, civil and strangely felt very natural. The two men just chatted away just as though they were two friends meeting for lunch and a catch up.

After they had finished their transaction and the meal whilst waiting on the coffee being served. Mr Jones said to Scurvy. 'I am impressed with you Mr Smith, for someone so young, you handled this like a seasoned pro. From the conversation I had with our mutual friend, he was convinced you had never done anything like this before.'

'Thank you.' Said Scurvy. 'Praise from Cesar indeed. Our friend is not wrong, I have never done anything like this before and my story is 100% the truth. Whilst I may not have shown it, my fear and apprehension of the unknown here is suppressed by the adrenaline that is currently coursing through my veins. Although I don't have the advantage of time on this earth as you and your colleague in the black suit other there.' Said Scurvy pointing discretely with his finger. 'I am no stranger to having to face the unknown. I was only fifteen years old when I made my first Scuba dive in the sea. I jumped off the side of my uncles boat into 30 feet of water in Loch Goil, on my own. I have performed many more solo dives since.'

'I spent around two years working at night as a bouncer in various discotheque's and bars, believe me that can be frightening. Often I found myself in situation's only to find out that my colleagues had bottled it and ran off. Leaving me on my own with people who had become hell bent on kicking the shit of me, just because I was the bouncer. So far in my life, I have been shot at twice by head cases wielding a 12 bore shotgun. I have performed numerous solo passages at sea and skippered small boats in force 9 gales, two of them were at night.'

'But all that pales into insignificance compared to the unknown and apprehension you face when working as a dock diver in the waters of the upper Clyde. Where the water can be as black as molasses and your only sense... is touch. There is no warning, there is no acclimatisation between seeing something and then being close to it, touching it or being able to react to it. When you touch something underwater that you can't see and you're not expecting, especially if it moves suddenly or if it carries that perturbation of death. You get a fright like an electric shock going through your heart. You have to control that fright and stop it from becoming a fear.' Explained Scurvy. 'Anyway, a week ago I was in a recompression chamber not knowing if I was ever going to walk again or end up spending my life pissing and shitting into a bag. So what's the worst you could have done to me? Rob me of something that I found that didn't cost me any money to get in the first place.' Said Scurvy shrugging his shoulders with a smile.

'Well, if I was wearing one I'd take my hat off too you Mr Smith. You certainly are a remarkable young man.' Said Mr Jones sincerely.

The waiter arrived with a coffee for Scurvy and at that Mr Jones asked for and paid the bill. 'It's been a pleasure doing business with you Mr Smith. Should you find yourself in a similar situation again then by all means visit our mutual friend. Now if you'll excuse me, my colleague and I will take our leave. Enjoy your coffee.' With that Mr Jones and the man in black left the restaurant.

Scurvy sat there alone in the booth. Smiling to himself drinking his coffee amazed at what had just taken place. And that he was sitting there with £800 in his pocket which he had earned by spending nothing more than bus fares.

That Friday lunchtime, Scurvy walked through the doors of GDMC's premises in St Vincent Street. Instantly, something stuck him as being extremely odd. The premises were as bare as old mother Hubbard's cupboard. There was literally nothing there. All the stock and equipment was gone. He walked towards to the main office which had its door closed again this was most unusual. Through the plate glass window of the door Scurvy could see Patsy, Smithy and Philip sitting together. Pirate was sitting across from them with two suits sitting aside of him. One of the suits was a very attractive blonde woman in her late twenties.

Patsy spotted Scurvy walking towards the door on the CCTV and sent Philip out to meet him who closed the office door behind him. 'Hello there Scurvy lad, how are you feeling?' Philip greeted him warmly shaking Scurvy's hand.

'Oh I'm grand Philip, I'm all tickety boo. What's going on in there Philip? And who is the fit, blonde bint in the body hugging pin stripped skirt suit, sitting next to Pirate?' Asked Scurvy with a rising curiosity.

'Well the blonde is a Ms Helena Field, and the man sitting to the right of Pirate is Andrew Wilson. They're from Gambol Wilson & Co, they're Pirates lawyer's. Don't be taken in by her looks. She is a black hearted Whore of Babylon, who is despised by everyone that knows her. And despite her snooty, sanctimonious, condescending attitude. I know that she's been cocked by the senior partners of the firm more times than John Wayne's rifle. Especially by that Andrew Wilson. He and I are in the same Lodge.' Explained Philip. 'Come wi' me, well go to Cottiers for a pint and something to eat and I'll tell you exactly what's going on.'

'Lawyers! Wait a minute Philip, is this to do with me ending up in the chamber?' Asked Scurvy in alarm.

'Naw naw Scurvy, nothing for you to worry about there. That's all cool. Naw, this is business.

We'll get ourselves settled in Cottiers and I'll explain all.' Philip assured him.

The phrase Whore of Babylon is of an apocalyptic figure of evil whose origins can be found in the Bible. One of several incarnations of evil that the bible claims will plague the world till the end of days. She is depicted as the mother of all harlots (prostitutes) and of all abominations of the world. Who is actively engaged in the deception and destruction of the worlds' people.

This encapsulates lawyers perfectly. You pay them money only to end up being fucked by them and for them to fuck other people in the process. They cause devastation and bring destruction to all people's lives wherever they are to be found.

'Oh that's better, I really needed that.' said Philip after taking a large swallow of his ice cold lager and wiping the froth of its head from his bushy moustache.

'So Philip, what's going on. The place is empty, meetings with lawyers behind closed doors. What's that all about, what gives?' Asked Scurvy sensing the worst.

'Well there's no easy way of saying this so 'I'll just tell you straight.' Replied Philip. 'The Company's gone bust and Pirate has been robbing the company blind. The guys have received a court summons for over £17000 of unpaid VAT. There are over a dozen red letters and none of them are gift experiences from Virgin. Virtually every supplier is threatening to serve a court decree*(g-314)* if they are not paid what they are owed within the next 7 days. Not only that, but Pirate plundered the £2750 that was in the safe that was to be used to pay the wages, including yours. Their marine insurance has been expired for the last two months. On top of that Gourley, Montgomery & Tindal are threatening to evict them from the premises for non payment of rent. Then Pirate turned up this morning with his Babylonian Whores to try to get himself off the hook. The devious, sleekit bastard that he is.' Explained Philip cutting straight to the bone.

'Oh well, It was only a matter of time. It was fun whilst it lasted.' Replied Scurvy calmly. Completely unphased by what he had just been told.

'You seem remarkably calm about this Scurvy, did you actually hear what I just said?' Asked Philip surprised at Scurvy's blasé response.

'The truth be told Philip, is that I have known that this has been coming for months now. I was often on the receiving end of telephone calls from the suppliers accounts department chasing up payment on overdue unpaid invoices. I even saw Pirate tipex out the date on the insurance certificate, put it through the typewriter with a new date then photocopy the certificate. That's what's hanging on the office wall now. On top of that I have seen equipment disappear and nobody questioning where it has gone. The reality of it is that all three of the have been stealing from the company. They have been stealing that much that they have lost track of what they stole. Hence why none of them would raise issue with what was missing with one another as they couldn't be sure if it wasn't one of the things that they had stolen. They're a parcel o' rogues. Though I must admit, Pirate is the biggest, most unscrupulous and nastiest one of them all. The one I do have some sympathy for though is Smithy. He and his wife took out a £20,000.00 bank loan to buy into the company. They secured it against their house. A large part of that was supposed to have been used to pay off the outstanding debts at the time. But I know Pirate had been kyyfing off large chunks of that on the pretence that he was paying bills with it. Did you know the old weasel has two cheque books for the company. He was showing Smithy one book with cheque stubs for cheques that had never been written for sums of money to different suppliers and Smithy believed him instead of checking the bank account himself.' Confessed Scurvy.

'As it's a limited company they will just fold and go into receivership being liable for no more than a £1. Unfortunately for Smithy though he still has to pay back the twenty grand he borrowed because they took that out as a personal loan and secured it against their house. I would have slit Pirates throat if he had done that to me. As for Patsy, I wouldn't worry about him. He'll be alright. The Loch Ranza is secure, I know he made sure of that. He'll probably go back diving offshore overseas. But what about you Philip, what will you do. Go back overseas or stay local, You'd get work with Brian Bullocks squad.' Suggested Scurvy.

'Ach no, it's maybe time I was hanging up my fins. I'll probably go back to my trade as a plumber.' Replied Philip. 'Besides, Alice would be pleased if I stopped diving, she aye worries when I'm in the water. Anyway, never mind me. Let's talk about what you're going to do. My advice Scurvy lad is to get yourself offshore. It doesn't matter what you get a job as offshore, just get yourself offshore. Once you have got a start in the offshore industry other doors will open for you. When you see Mark Smith at the end of the month, you'll get the all clear from him. Of this I am certain. You're the fittest man I know. Bella confirmed that.' Remarked Philip

'Eh she what?' Said Scurvy surprised.

'Oh relax All she said was you were like a gypsies' dog with two cocks on steroids. I'd take it as quite a compliment. She said it with a smile. But seriously though, once you've got your medical, get yourself booked into the RGIT *(14-346)* in Aberdeen for your offshore survival *(14-346)*. And whilst you are up there, go knocking on doors. You will do well offshore. I promise you this Scurvy, the opportunities are there for you to see the world. And believe me when I tell you, it's well worth seeing. Get yourself offshore lad. That is the best advice I can give you, I promise, you won't regret it.' Said Philip in all sincerity.

Scurvy was actually quite relieved to have been able to unload the heavy burden of the weighted secret that he had been carrying for the last few months. Especially given that he was now shouldering the weight of a major new secret. Despite the fact that he was about to join the ranks of the unemployed, it felt as though a dark rain cloud had blown away and the sun was shining brightly over him again. With blue skies above him and the sun rising on a new horizon ahead of him. Scurvy set his sights on new adventures in the offshore industry.

Little did he know at the time that these adventures were take him to the four corners of the earth and a myriad of countries inbetween, as well as to the Antarctic at the bottom of the world and back.......... But that is for another story.

Scurvy on board the DSV Lochran 1992.

Song Of The Clyde
by R.Y. Bell and Ian Gourley.

Verse 1
I sing of a river I'm happy beside.
The song that I sing is a song of the Clyde.
Of all Scottish rivers it's dearest to me.

It flows from Leadhills all the way to the sea.
It borders the orchards of Lanark so fair,
Meanders through meadows with sheep grazing there,
And from Glasgow to Greenock,
in towns on each side,
The hammers' ding-dong is the song of the Clyde.

[Chorus]
Oh the river Clyde, the wonderful Clyde!
The name of it thrills me and fills me with pride,
And I'm satisfied, whate'er may betide,
The sweetest of song is the song of the Clyde.

Verse 2
Imagine we've left Craigendoran behind,
And wind-happy yachts by Kilcreggan we find.
At Kirn and Dunoon and Innellan we stay,

Then Scotland's Madeira—that's Rothesay, they say—
Or maybe by Fairlie and Largs we will go,
Or over to Millport that thrills people so,
Maybe journey to Arran it can't be denied,
Those scenes all belong to the song of the Clyde.

[Chorus]
Oh the river Clyde, the wonderful Clyde!
The name of it thrills me and fills me with pride,
And I'm satisfied, whate'er may betide,
The sweetest of song is the song of the Clyde.

When sun sets on dockland, there's beauty to see
The cry of a seabird is music to me
The blast of a horn loudly echoes, and then
A stillness descends on the water again.

Tis' here that the sea-going liners are born
But, unlike the salmon, they seldom return
Can you wonder the Scots o'er the ocean so wide
Should constantly long for the song of the Clyde

[Chorus]
Oh the river Clyde, the wonderful Clyde!
The name of it thrills me and fills me with pride,
And I'm satisfied, whate'er may betide,
The sweetest of song is the song of the Clyde.

Verse 3
(Guitar stays at same rhythm, vocals speed up!)

There's Paw an' Maw doon at the Broomielaw.
They're goin' doon the waater for The Fair.
There's Bob an' Mary, on the Govan Ferry,
Wishin' jet propulsion could be there.

There's steamers cruisin', and there's buddies snoozin',
And there's laddies fishin' frae the pier;

An' Paw's perspirin', very near expirin',
As he rows a boat frae there to here.

With eyes a-flashin', it is voted smashin,
To be walkin' daily on the prom:
And May and Evelyn are in seventh heaven
As they stroll along with Dick and Tom;

And Dumbarton Rock to ev'ry Jean and Jock,
Extends a welcome that is high and wide:
Seems to know that they are on their homeward way
To hear the song of the Clyde.

[Chorus]
Oh the river Clyde, the wonderful Clyde!
The name of it thrills me and fills me with pride,
And I'm satisfied, whate'er may betide,
The sweetest of song is the song of the Clyde.

The Scotsman
Lyrics by Mike Cross

A Scotsman clad in kilt left a bar one evening fair
One could tell by how he walked
That he'd drunk more than his share
He fumbled round until he
could no longer keep his feet
And stumbled off into the grass
To sleep beside the street
Ring ding didle-idle -i-dee-o
Ring dye-didley I-oh
He stumbled off into the grass
to sleep beside the street
About that time two young
and lovely girls just happed by
One says to the other with a twinkle in her eye
'See yon sleeping Scotsman
So strong and handsome built
I wonder if it's true
What they don't wear beneath the kilt'
Ring ding didle-idle -i-dee-o
Ring dye-didley I-oh
'I wonder if it's true
What they don't wear beneath the kilt'
They crept up on that sleeping Scotsman
Quiet as could be
Lifted up his kilt about an inch so they could see
And there, behold, for them to view
Beneath his Scottish skirt
Was nothing more than God
Had graced him with upon his birth

Ring ding didle-idle -i-dee-o
Ring dye-didley I-oh
Was nothing more than God
had graced him with upon his birth
They marvelled for a moment
Then one said 'We'd must be gone
But let's leave a present for our friend
Before we move along.'
As a gift they left a blue silk ribbon
Tied into a bow
Around the bonny star
The Scot's kilt did lift and show
Ring ding didle-idle -i-dee-o
Ring dye-didley I-oh
Around the bonny star
The Scot's kilt did lift and show
Now the Scotsman woke to nature's call
And stumbled toward the trees
Behind a bush he lifts his kilt
And gawks at what he sees
And in a startled voice he says
To what's before his eyes
'Oh, Lad, I don't know where ya been
But I see you won first prize!'
Ring ding didle-idle -i-dee-o
Ring dye-didley I-oh
'Oh, Lad, I don't know where ya been
But I see you won first prize!'

I Recall A Gypsy Woman
Written by Bob McDill & Allen Reynolds
Originally recorded by Don Williams in 1973

Silver coins that jingle jangle
Fancy shoes that dance in time
Oh, the secrets of her dark eyes
They did sing a gypsy rhyme
Yellow clover in tangled blossoms
In a meadow silky green
Where she held me to her bosom
Just a boy of seventeen

I recall a gypsy woman
Silver spangles in her eyes
Ivory skin against the moonlight
And the taste of life's sweet wine

Soft breezes blow from fragrant meadows
And stir the darkness in my mind
Oh, gentle woman you sleep beside me
Little know who haunts my mind
Gypsy lady, I hear your laughter
And it dances in my head
While my tender wife and babies
Slumber softly in their beds

I recall a gypsy woman
Silver spangles in her eyes
Ivory skin against the moonlight
And the taste of life's sweet wine...

Glossary

Antiquary
A person who studies or collects antiques

Bail Out Cylinder
This is the high pressure emergency air tank carried on a divers back when using surface supplied air. These cylinders come in various different sizes from 10litre to 15litre capacity.

Cadaver
Dead Body, from the Latin word 'cadere'- to fall.

Catheter
A catheter is a flexible tube used to empty the bladder and collect urine in a drainage bag. Also known as a Urethral Catheter. In the story, the police sergeant has to insert the tube up inside Scurvy's penis to carry the urine from his bladder to a collection bag.

Chester Step Test
This is an aerobic test using a 30cm high step, at a rate set to a metronome to elicit a heart rate of around 80% maximum heart rate, at a moderate level of exertion.

Court Decree
This is the Scottish equivalent of England's County Court Judgement (CCJ). This is a type of court order which is served against you if you have failed to repay money that you owe. It means that the pursuer can recover the money owed to them with the full authority of the court. In Scotland, the process is called enforcing debt by diligence.

Decca Navigator

This was a hyperbolic radio navigation system which allowed ships and aircraft to determine their position by using radio signals from a dedicated system of static radio transmitters. It's accuracy could be from 1meter to 1000meters depending on the weather and your position in relation to the shore based radio beacons.

Decompression Sickness- The Bends

Decompression sickness (abbreviated DCS) aka the bends or caisson disease is a medical condition caused by dissolved gases emerging from solution as bubbles inside the body tissues, as a diver or tunnel worker ascends from depth (decompression) when the bubbles have not had time to dissolve in the blood. These bubbles expand to several times their original size. They can form and migrate to any part of the body and can cause everything from skin rashes to joint pain, paralysis and in extreme cases death.

Gas bubbles that settle in major joints like knees, elbows or the spine, causes individuals to bend over in excruciating pain, hence its common name.

Demi monde filles des joie (French language)

A woman who provides sexual joy for money.

Doppler Scan

This is an ultrasound scan that is used to detect the presence of micro bubbles in the blood stream.

ECG- Electro cardiogram
A machine that can measure and record the heart's electrical activity.

Foonert
Scottish slang for extremely tired, exhausted.

Greek Tragedy
In general, Greek tragedies feature a character of ordinary moral virtue. This means that the character, though not villainous, exhibits a realistic, inherent defect, or curse known as hamartia that leads to their downfall.

Hat the diver
Meaning to put the divers band mask or helmet on. It goes back to days of old when it took two men to place the heavy copper diving helmet over the head onto the neck collar.

Hartmanns Intravenous Solution
This is used to replace body fluid and mineral salts that may be lost for a variety of medical reasons. It is especially suitable when the losses result in too much acid being present in the blood.

Hen
Scottish colloquialism for woman or girl.

HP J Bottle
High Pressure gas cylinders are given a letter of the alphabet to identify their size. A 'J' bottle stands 152cm tall, 23cm in diameter with a water capacity of 47litres will weigh around 80kg when filled of compressed air to a pressure of 230bar.

ICC-Inchinnan Cruising Club
An amateur boat building & cruising club near Renfrew where Scurvy grew up learning about boats.

Killick
A Royal navy sailor with the rank of Leading Seaman. The equivalent rank in the army or air force would be that of a Corporal.

Lidocaine Jelly
(Pronounced Lye doe kane). It is a topical jelly or ointment that is used on different parts of the body to cause numbness or loss of feeling for patients having certain medical procedures.

Narked- Nitrogen Narcosis
Also known as raptures of the deep. At certain depths, the Nitrogen content in the air that we breath can become a narcotic to the human mind. This is caused by the increased pressure that the air is breathed at. It is similar to alcohol intoxication, being drunk. In so much that it clouds your reasoning and judgement. It can also cause hallucinations, idea fixations and stupor.

NEQ
Net Explosive Quantity is the total mass of the contained explosive substances, found in a charge without the packaging.

Oxipulse meter
This is a clip like devise which is attached to a finger that uses an infrared beam to accurately monitor blood oxygen saturation levels. It also measures your heart pulse rate.

PETN
Pentaerythritol Tetranitrate is a very powerful plastic explosive that is used in industry. It is similar in some ways to Nitro Glycerine only far more stable and safer to handle.

Port & Starboard
Nautical terms for left and right.

SCUBA
Self Contained Underwater Breathing Apparatus (The Aqualung).

Slàinte Mhaith
(Pronounced Slange je vah) Gaelic for good health.

Sphyg Balloon
This is an inflatable cuff that is wrapped around the upper arm which is then attached to a blood pressure monitor called a sphygmomanometer.

Spirometry
This is a simple test using a device called a spirometer to diagnose and monitor certain lung conditions. It measures the amount of air that you can breathe out in one second and the total volume of air you can exhale in one forced breath.

Stevedore
A person employed at a dock to load/unload ships.

Stramash
Scottish term for uproar, fight, brawl or crash.

The Bizzies
Slang term for the Police.

The Land of Tir na nÓg
The Land of the Young, In Celtic mythology this was a beautiful enchanted island off the west coast of Ireland. Here the trees were always green, the flowers were always in bloom, no one every grew old, everyone was young and beautiful with no illness or unhappiness.

Voith Schnieder units
This is a specialized marine propulsion system that provides propulsion and steering in one unit. A circular array of vertical blades in the shape of hydrofoils protrude out of the bottom of the ship.

Each blade can rotate itself around a vertical axis so that each blade can provide thrust in any direction. It is highly manoeuvrable, being able to change the direction of its thrust almost instantaneously.

Yokohama Fenders
Yokohama fenders are large cylindrical, air filled, heavy duty, black rubber fenders. They come in various diameters from 30cm to 450cm and are 0.5m to 9.5m in length. The Yokohama fenders on the Lochranza were 0.75m in diameter and 1.5m in length. The larger of these fenders are wrapped with a chain and tyre mesh.

In 1958, Yokohama was the first company to design such a fender hence the name.

Appendix

1. Kirby Morgan Mk10 band mask
2. Aquadyne Air Hat AH3
3. EXO 26 (BR) Balanced Regulator Band Mask
4. Aga Interspiro Divator Mkll
5. US Divers Conshelf 14 Regulator
6. Spun Copper Diving Helmets of old
7. Broco
8. Air Lift
9. Retro Jet cleaning lance
10. CP9 Rock drill / Chisel
11. Decompression Tables
12. Recompression chamber
13. The Brown Rat
14. RGIT Offshore survival training certificate

About the author

Special thank you

Artists bio & contact details

Answer to Trivia question from page 4

Appendix 1. Kirby Morgan Band Mask KMB10

The KMB mask came on the market in the late 1960's. It quickly became adopted as the industry standard and the most common band mask used worldwide, for both commercial and military diving operations.

Since the original mask was made available several modifications were made, but the basic features remain the same. It has a demand regulator, an oral-nasal mask over the diver's nose and mouth and a side valve assembly.

The mask is held pressed against the face with a smooth neoprene seal which has a soft foam rubber cushion bonded to it and is kept in place by a zippered neoprene hood and five rubber straps (called the spider).

The main valve at the side of the mask is connected to an umbilical which allows air to be supplied from the surface. There is a second inlet for a bail-out cylinder which the diver carries on his back. The mask can be used in the demand mode or in the free-flow mode with compressed air or mixed gas. It features a built in communications system. The mask can also be worn with a protective head shell.

Over the years there have been 6 variants of this band mask, KMB 8, KMB 9, KMB 10, KMB 18 the most recent is the KMB 28. You can recognize newer models by the number: the original was the KMB 8. At this moment KMB 18 and KMB 28 are on the market. They remain the band mask of choice for commercial divers today.

Appendix 2. Aquadyne Air Hat AH3

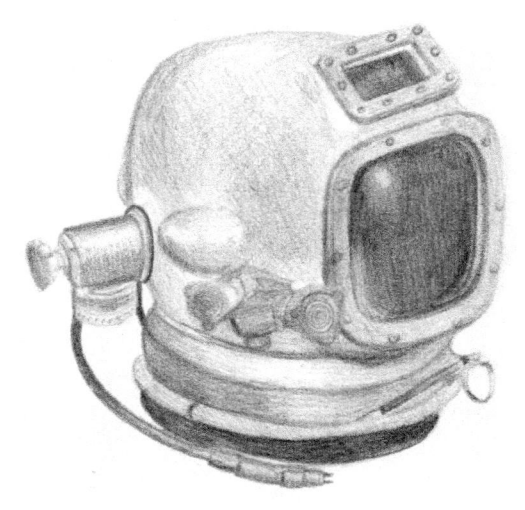

The AH3 helmet was a free flow air hat. This meant that air was constantly flowing at a controlled rate into the helmet. As opposed to being on demand when the diver drew a breath. On the side of the helmet was a sprung loaded exhaust valve that the diver could manually open by pushing it with the side of his head to flush out any CO_2 build up within the helmet.

It was manufactured in bright orange. It was an improved version from the General Aquadyne AH2 black coloured helmet as it was fitted with a Side block and EGS valve (Emergency Gas System).

The helmet could be worn with a neck dam seal or as part of a constant volume drysuit which is a modern day version of the old standard dress, copper hard hat diver. This was commonly used in polluted water as the diver was totally sealed from the environment.

Diver wearing a Viking constant volume suit with the AH3 Helmet.

This is a modern day and superior version of the old rubberised canvas standard diving suit &, copper helmet equipment..This equipment is far more flexible and lighter than the equipment of old as shown in appendix 6.

The Divex AH5 is the current modern day model of this helmet. It is a lighter version of the AH3.

Appendix 3. Kirby Morgan EXO 26 Band Mask

The Kirby Morgan EXO 26 Full Face Mask was designed for both surface supplied as well as scuba diving. By enclosing the diver's eyes, nose and mouth, it allowed nearly normal speech when used in conjunction with an underwater communication system.

The mask's light weight design allowed divers to work long dives without jaw or neck fatigue. The oral nasal mask inside helped to keep the CO_2 levels to a minimum.

It utilized a trademarked Exothermic Exhaust System.

The regulator assembly isolated the intake and exhaust chambers from one another. The diver's own breath assisted in warming certain areas of the regulator. This helped to eliminate freeze up when diving in cold water. It was popular with commercial, police, scientific and sports divers alike.

Appendix 4. Aga Interspiro Divator MkII

This slimline, lightweight full face mask is very popular, not only with professional divers but also with recreational divers who often dive in cold water. It is an excellent scuba mask which is often used with surface supplied air supply.

The mask is available with two types of regulator, an ordinary demand regulator, or a 'positive pressure' regulator which keeps a positive pressure inside the mask. Thus was ideal while diving in contaminated or dirty water for if the mask leaked, it let air out instead of the contaminated water in. The mask is also available with communications equipment to be used by professional divers. The microphone is placed just over the regulator in the front of the mask. The speaker was of a bone conductor design located in the harness just next to the divers ear. The mask was often used with the Interspiro lightweight 300bar twin 4 litre cylinder set, especially by Police divers.

Appendix 5. US Divers Conshelf XIV Regulator

At one time, the Conshelf XlV was the world's most popular scuba diving regulator, especially within the military and commercial diving industry. Due to its reputation and proven capabilities in these sectors it became a highly sought after regulator in the sports diving sector also.

It was made from chrome plated marine brass. A very reliable, durable regulator which performed well in both tropical and cold water conditions. It was one of the easiest breathing regulators on the market regardless of water depth.

Appendix 6. Spun Copper Diving Helmets of old

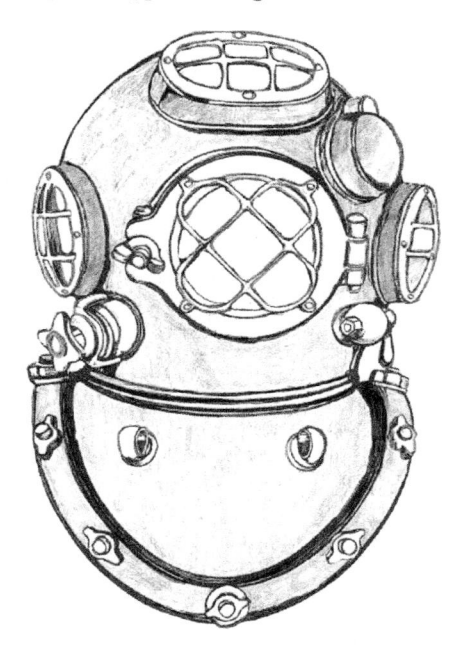

Morse US Navy mark 5 spun copper helmet

Augustus Siebe was the first to design the standard dress diving suit in 1837. This was a waterproof airtight full canvas suit that attached to the helmet. This allowed divers to work horizontally. It was very buoyant, hence why the divers had to wear lead boots and weights around their waist and shoulders to keep them down on the seabed

Siebe and his son-in-law Gorman, formed Siebe Gorman which became the leading manufacturer of diving helmets for nearly a century. Their helmets were copied and emulated by others all over the world.

The original standard diving equipment was a spun copper helmet or "bonnet" (British English) screwed onto a copper breastplate or "corselet" with an 1/8th of a turn, which transferred the weight to the diver's shoulders.

This assembly was clamped to a rubber gasket on the dry suit to make a watertight seal.

Breathing air was pumped from the surface through a hose to a non-return inlet valve on the helmet or breastplate, and released to the surroundings through an exhaust valve.

This equipment was commonly referred as standard diving dress or heavy gear.

The Morse Mk5 Copper helmet pictured on page 329 is the most recognisable of the Spun Copper helmets. It was designed in 1905 and was based on the Siebe-Gorman Davis 6 bolt Admiralty pattern helmet which was used by the British Royal Navy. The Morse Mk5 remained in commercial use right up until the 1980's.

It was not uncommon for divers to lose consciousness while working at 120 feet in standard helmets.

The Scottish physiologist J.S. Haldane found by experiment that this was partly due to a build up of carbon dioxide in the helmet caused by insufficient ventilation and a large dead space. To overcome this he established a minimum flow rate of 1.5 cubic feet (42 L) per minute at ambient pressure to be fed to the helmet from the surface supplied air.

Appendix 7. Broco thermal lance cutting torch

The Broco underwater exothermic cutting system provided the fastest, most efficient and cost effective means of underwater cutting, piercing and gouging tasks. These rods liquefy almost any material in their path. They are fed with oxygen at a pressure of 6 bar above ambient water pressure and use 150amps of DC electrical current.

The exothermic rod burns at 5,530°C. They commonly come in two diameters, 6mm & 10 mm.

Broco rods can quickly cut or melt cast iron, steel, stainless steel, concrete, granite, nickel, titanium, aluminium and exotic metals. These rods cut through marine growth, rust, and mill scale, eliminating the need for pre-cleaning and helping to lower operating costs and reducing bottom time.

Appendix 8. The Airlift

An airlift is constructed from a long length of pipe around 150mm in diameter, it is between 3-to 4meters in length. It is used to suck small objects, sand and mud from the sea bed transporting the resulting debris upwards and ejecting it out of the top of the pipe away from the source.

There is a 1/4 turn air valve fitted about 30cm from the bottom of the pipe. It is connected into an air plenum chamber. Just above the plenum chamber is a venturi (narrowing of the internal diameter).

When the diver opens the air supply, the air rushes upwards towards the surface causing it to increase in speed as it passes through the venturi pulling a vacuum behind it.

It is this vacuum that sucks the sand, silt, mud and debris up the pipe like a vacuum cleaner.

The air lift has the disadvantage of discharging the lifted material relatively close to the suction point. This may result in some of the material settling back into the excavated area. The discharge should be positioned down current to allow the prevailing currents to carry the material away.

Appendix 9. Retro Jet Cleaning Lance

The lance features a second jet that exits the rear of the lance, counterbalancing the thrust that comes from the front nozzle. This allows the diver to stay balanced in position while working underwater, especially when working mid water.

The rear facing jet provides a balancing force in the opposite direction to the cleaning jet.

The retro balance jet protection tube is constructed so as to prevent the operator directing a retro balance jet at himself. They are sometimes known as zero thrust guns for they prevent the diver from being pushed backwards.

The jetting lances operate at a pressure of between 1000 to 1400 bar (14,700 to 20,580 psi.).

Water jetting underwater can be a dangerous task.

Appendix 10. CP9

The CP9, Chicago Pneumatic rock drill and breaker is perfect for drilling into concrete and masonry and can also achieve light duty breaking. The CP9 is considered to be one of the best contenders on the market.

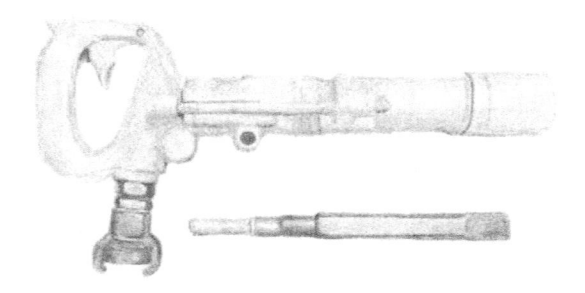

It is powered by a surface fed air supply. The CP9, weighed only 4.5kg and being only 37.5cm in length yet delivered 3420 blows per minute which gives it the ability to drill a 32mm hole through 450mm of concrete.

The CP9 really was a powerful tool.

Nowadays, underwater pneumatic tools have been largely replaced with hydraulic equivalents. This has the advantage of being able to be used at any depth, with no disturbance of the divers vision by the tools exhaust bubbles and they are quieter to use.

Appendix 11. Decompression Tables

When a diver descends below the surface of the water, he breathes air at the same pressure as the surrounding water pressure. The deeper you go the greater the pressure. At 45m water depth the surrounding water pressure is 5.5 times greater than it is on the surface.

This basically causes the tissue in the divers' body to absorb more nitrogen from the air that they are breathing than it would at the surface.

Depending on the time you have remained at a specific depth for will depend on how much more nitrogen the body will absorb than it would at the surface. This nitrogen forms in your tissue and blood vessels as tiny bubbles.

Air diving decompression tables that were developed for the British Sub Aqua Club (BSAC) for recreational diving in 1972 by the Royal Navy Physiological Laboratory (RNPL).

As you ascend from depth these nitrogen bubbles expand. Your body will normally dissolve these bubbles in your bloodstream and safely remove the nitrogen out through your alveoli of your lungs as you breath out. (These are tiny air sacks at the end of the tiny branches of your lungs).

However, it takes time for your body to dissolve the excess nitrogen. Depending on how deep you have been and the duration at that depth depends on how long it takes to dissolve these nitrogen bubbles and safely expel the excess nitrogen as you breath out.

If you do not give your body enough time to dissolve these bubbles of nitrogen, then as you ascend to the surface, they will expand to several times their original size. This can cause extreme pain, serious injury and disability. To include permanent damage to your central nervous system and in some cases it can be fatal.

So to prevent this, divers use decompression or dive tables as they are also known to establish how long they can safely remain at specific depths. This is known as bottom time. If they go beyond their bottom time, they have to perform stops at different depths on the way up for specific times to allow their body to safely dissolve and release the accumulated nitrogen bubbles.

It is widely recognised that in 1908, the Scottish physiologist, Professor John Scott Haldane was the man who developed the world's first safe diving decompression tables. It is as a result of his work and understanding of gaseous exchange in the body that all modern day dive tables are now based.

Various countries and other institutions eventually produced their own diving tables. Commercial, military and sport diving tables may have different dive times and decompression schedules to those shown above. BSAC dive tables have also evolved other the years However, I still believe the RNPL72 table as detailed on page 337 was one of the safest and simplest of dive tables to be have been produced.

Decompression Limiting Line.

The Limiting Line that is found in commercial air diving decompression tables, is where the diver's bottom time will result in the diver being required to perform more than 30 minutes of in water decompression.

When this happens, the decompression schedule would normally require the use of pure oxygen to be breathed at certain depths for specified durations, as well as air to be breathed at other specified depths for specified durations. Thus making the in water decompression schedule logistically more complex.

When divers breath different gasses such as the oxy helium mixes used in very deep diving, different dive tables are required.

Appendix 12. The Recompression chamber

A recompression chamber is used to treat divers suffering from decompression sickness (the bends) or an air embolism. The chambers should be viewed as a medical device and are only as good as the team operating them.

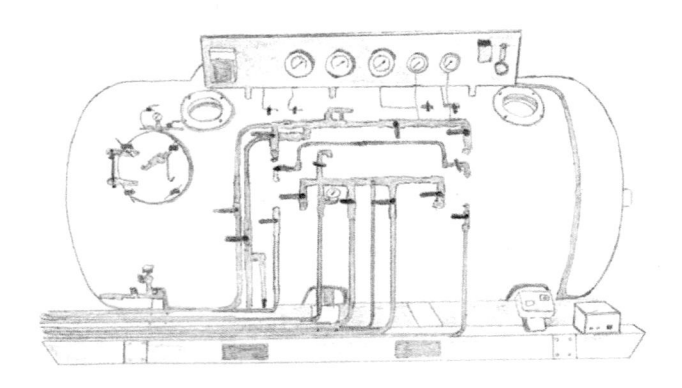

This chamber basically allows the affected diver to be placed back under pressure in a safe, controlled, dry, air environment. To be recompressed so that the expanded nitrogen bubbles can be effectively reduced in size and therapeutic treatment be given to the diver.

Inside a recompression chamber, the diver can be cared for by an attendant who can administer medical aid and assist the injured diver.

The diver is then treated using special dive tables called Therapeutic Tables which are based on different calculation compared to normal dive decompression tables.

If a diver rises to the surface (decompresses) at the right rate, the nitrogen can slowly and safely leave the body through the lungs. But if a diver rises too quickly, **the nitrogen forms bubbles in the body**. This can cause tissue and nerve damage. For an analogy, take a fizzy drinks bottle, give it a shake, then open the lid (decompressing) and watch the gas in the liquid come out of solution to form bubbles and fizz. This is in principle what happens to the gas in a diver's blood stream when he ascends from depth too quickly.

When this happens we put the diver under pressure in a safe environment to achieve a healing process to get rid of the bubbles. There is much more to the treatment process than just putting the diver back under pressure and then controlling the rate of ascent to the surface.

There are basically three pillars of recompression treatment:

Hydration, Oxygen and Pressure (recompression).

Hydration is very important because the more fluid you have, the less bubbles you have. Therefore, good hydration significantly reduces the amount of circulating bubbles.

In simple terms, dehydration will reduce the volume of blood plasma and the passage of blood through blood vessels and tissues (it thickens the blood and reduces blood flow). The blood is responsible for the transportation of nutrients and for the exchange of gases. If the reduction in blood plasma becomes too great, it could lead to the decreased efficiency of gaseous exchange, thus also affecting the off-gassing of Nitrogen and increasing the risk and severity of injury.

Off gassing is where the nitrogen moves from the body's tissues, into the bloodstream, then into the lungs where it is exhaled as you breath out.

It is important for the reader to understand that it is not the bubble that kills you, the bubble is transient, it is only temporary, it will eventually leave the body. It is the damaged that is caused by the bubble to your body that is of greater concern. As such, we need to manage, modulate and moderate the inflammatory process caused by the bubble.

Whilst pressure will reduce the size of the bubble, it won't dissolve them. We don't just squeeze bubbles, there are other complicated processes taking place in the recompression chamber. Dissolving bubbles takes much more than barometric pressure.

Breathing oxygen (O2) helps you to off gas. Breathing O2 effectively washes out nitrogen bubbles, by dissolving them so we can effective get rid of nitrogen in our system. This is sometimes referred to as off gassing.

But we still have the injury and we need to treat this also.

Oxygen is a drug, however, hyperbaric oxygen, that is Oxygen under a pressure of 1.8 or 2.8bar absolute is a very different drug. One which provides other benefits that you cannot get by any other means.

Hyperbaric Oxygen reverts tissue hypoxia (low oxygen levels) thus maximising survival of tissue. It also reduces oedema or swelling and it modulates (has a controlling influence and varies the strength) the inflammatory response of the reperfusion injury (restoration of blood flow) and endothelial damage to the inside of your blood vessels (arteries that are narrowing when they should be opening). It also helps with wound healing and tissue remodelation (repair response). It also promotes blood vessel regeneration.

The therapeutic table used will depend on the severity of the decompression sickness. However, they all use a combination of air breathing at different pressures for set times and breathing pure oxygen at different pressures for set times as well as keeping the patient hydrated and relaxed.

So now you have an appreciation that recompression therapy is quite an involved treatment process.

It was as a result of the experiences in treating divers with hyperbaric oxygen that this developed into a therapy for treating numerous other illnesses and injuries It is now used all over the world for such, not just for treating divers.

Appendix 13. The Brown Rat

(*Rattus norvegicus*)

The brown rat, also known as the common rat, street rat, sewer rat, wharf rat and Norwegian rat is the most common species of rat found in the UK.

Brown rats live in any situation that provides food, water and shelter. They are usually found in farms and open fields. However, the brown rat will often find its way into our homes and gardens in search of food and shelter.

They are also commonly found in docks, factories, sewers and culverts. They are excellent swimmers both on the surface and under the water and have been known to be able to swim distances of up to 4Km at a stretch.

The brown rat is up to 40 cm in length, with a tail shorter than its body, weighing up to 750grams. It has a blunt nose, small hair covered ears and a thick body. Its colour varies from brown to black but this species is distinguished from the true Black Rat which is a smaller rat with a tail longer than it's body length.

Brown Rats carry many nasty diseases which they can spread to humans, normally through their urine. These include; Leptospirosis or Weil's disease, Salmonella, Listeria, Toxoplasma gondii and Hantavirus.

Brown Rats have well-developed senses of smell, taste and touch. They have an acute sense of hearing, frequently using ultrasound to communicate, and are particularly sensitive to any sudden noise. They are dangerous when cornered.

Rats need to gnaw to keep their constantly growing incisor teeth worn down. They damage woodwork, plastic, bricks and lead pipes, and will strip insulation from electrical cables.

The insurance sector have estimated that rodent damage to wiring is responsible for 25% of all electrical fires in buildings.

The brown rat can live up to three years but few survive more than 12 months in the wild. During that time, the female can breed five to seven times, producing litters of between and six and twelve. That's over 80 pups a year and rats can become sexually mature by the age of six weeks.

Some estimations put the UK's brown rat population to be over 80 million! Hence why property owners have a legal obligation under the Prevention of Damage by Pests Act 1949 to keep premises rat and mice free, or, if Brown Rats pose a threat to health or property to report infestations to the local authority.

The story in Chapter 2 in the book of how I got the nickname Scurvy is a true story.

Appendix 14. RGIT Offshore survival training certificate

Robert Gordon's Institute of Technology (RGIT) survival centre was located in King Street Aberdeen (Now Robert Gordon's University) pioneered the offshore safety standards in the oil and gas industry.

It was here the now world famous offshore survival training course was originally developed for the men and women who go to work on the Rigs and ships around the world. The RGIT set the standard for the world to follow.

This certificate of training was a pre requisite for anyone wanting to go offshore. It was valid for four years after which you had to do a two and a half day refresher providing you were not overdue on the expiry date of your original certificate. If you were overdue, you had to do the full five day course again.

In 1978, it was the RGIT's School of Mechanical and Offshore Engineering who designed and built the pioneering Helicopter Underwater Escape Training (HUET) simulator. So as to give realistic survival training for a helicopter that had crashed in the sea. A device that I have trained in many times over the last 30 years.

I have seen the training course content change several times over the years and in my opinion, the survival training offshore workers receive today on these courses isn't anywhere near as good as it was when I first did the course in 1993.

Back then it was an intensive five day course. You covered life onboard an oil rig, helicopter rotor failure with simulated crash landing and evacuation on land As well as underwater escape from a capsisized helicopter module in the environmental tank.

We did ship / platform evacuation exercises into a coldwater pool. Where you had to right a capsized liferaft with wave and wind machines, blacked out lighting and flashing lights to simulate bad weather conditions at sea. You performed fire escape drills over 2 stories high in sealed metal containers with real fires inside wearing full BA equipment. You learned how to use, handle and take control of fire hoses, you put out real fires. If you drew the short straw you had to rescue the full size dummy which weighed in at around 30kgs utilising a fireman's lift from inside the burning containers. You launched and did exercises at sea with ships lifeboats, you also recovered a survivor floating in the water and you actually fired off real flares. You learned about first aid to include dressing wounds and applying bandages. It was an excellent course which became emulated around the world.

Now the course is only three days in duration and nowhere near as realistic or effective as the course I did back in the day. It is no longer called the RGIT survival course, it was renamed a number of years ago to BOSIET (Basic Offshore Safety Induction Emergency Training.

Believe me, it is basic compared to what it was in '93. Much of the course now is watching DVD's. I sense now a' days that everything is about making as much profit for providing as little as possible in return.

About The Author

Paul Obernay was born in the late 60's, he grew up in Renfrew on the banks of the River Clyde. His playground was the Inchinnan Cruising Club located on Black Cart water, a tidal tributary of the Clyde. It was here that his maritime education began.

After seeing his first Cousteau documentary at the age of four Paul knew that he was going to be a diver. As a teenager, Paul learned to dive with the AA Lion British Sub Aqua Club in Paisley.

In 1983 at the age of 15, Paul made his first Scuba dive in the sea. He strode off the side of his uncles boat the Sponel, wearing a homemade wetsuit into 10meters of water at Swine's Hole Loch Goil on his own. Breathing from a Luxfer 55 CuFt cylinder using a US Divers Deepstar demand valve. He stayed down under the water on his own for an hour engrossed in this magical other world.

By the time he was 18. Paul had dived all over the Clyde coast, its numerous shipwrecks, sea lochs and islands and had explored the wrecks and reefs of Argyll. Since then Paul has dived in some of the most exotic locations in the world such as the Maldives, the Canaries, the Galapagos Islands, the Bahamas and the Caribbean.

Upon leaving school at sixteen, Paul served an engineering apprenticeship in the motor trade. In his spare time, he dived and crewed boats for other people. He also spent many days in Glasgow's Mitchell library studying the physiology & medicine of diving, diving & underwater technology.

In his early twenties he went to work for Aquatron Marine in Glasgow where he worked in their PADI dive school as maintenance technician, equipment salesman and was the skipper mechanic of the company's 32ft Aquastar dive boat. Here he performed dive charters around the Clyde coast. His time with Aquatron took him on nautical adventures as far north as Scotland's outer Hebrides.

Paul pursued his underwater career further and went to work with the GMT Commercial Diving Company. It was here that Paul's adventures escalated to a whole new level. Where through GMT, he found himself on secondment with Strathclyde Police underwater search unit.

When GMT ceased trading, Paul went into the offshore industry. Initially as a Rope Access Technician, climbing and abseiling on oilrigs to perform maintenance and inspection work. He then went on to become a Rig Mechanic. After number of years offshore, Paul took a year out and worked with the British Antarctic Survey as the base station Facilities Engineer. Here he was solely responsible for the maintenance and operation of all life support facilities, science lab, field operations equipment and remote field shelters for the Signy scientific base station in the South Orkney Island's Antarctica.

On returning from the Antarctic, Paul secured a position with Oceaneering International. This was the world's biggest underwater contractor. He started as a trainee underwater Remotely Operated Vehicle (ROV) Pilot Technician. He went on to become a Senior Submersible Engineer and ROV system Supervisor. Leaving Oceaneering Paul formed his own underwater services company where he provided services to underwater construction, cable lay / pipe lay, survey and drilling projects all over the world.

Through his company, Paul followed in the footsteps of Cousteau to make a trilogy of professional under water natural history films. The first was shot entirely on location in the Galapagos called 'Il Faut Aller Voir' (We must go see for ourselves). It was glass master pressed, produced as a double disk boxed set complete with an educational cdrom and full colour four page booklet.

The second film was called 'Dreaming of Dolphins' it was shot entirely on location in the Bahamas ridges and banks. A beautiful underwater film of being up close and personal with wild dolphins in the open sea. This film was actual produced as the primary therapeutic media for the Dolphin Dome.

The third film was called 'The Serenity of Whales'. Filmed on location in the abyssal waters of the Commonwealth of Dominica under special licence from the Dominican Government. Paul created a beautiful emotional thirty minute underwater film of being up close and personal with mighty, majestic, magnificent Sperm whales.

This film was on display for many years at the Hull Maritime Museum, which formed part of the museum's world famous historic whaling collection. It was also encompassed in the museum's prestigious 'Turner and the whale' Exhibition. The collection on display were the famous artworks from 1845, depiction the whaling industry by Britain's greatest painter JMW Turner. Which were on loan from the Tate National Gallery of London.

Both Dreaming of Dolphins and The Serenity of Whales can be seen on You Tube: Alcedonia Maris:

Dreaming of Dolphins:
https://www.youtube.com/watch?v=iVbFmaqs-m0

The Serenity of Whales:
https://www.youtube.com/watch?v=TuHVtUeF6Dc

Also through his company, Paul performed the first research and development into Artificial Dolphin Assisted Therapy using the Dolphin Dome. Which he financed, designed and built himself. It had an additional interactive feature that allowed the user to escape into the world of a scuba*(g-318)* diver in tropical lagoons and seas.

The Dolphin Dome provided dolphin assisted therapy in a dry safe environment for people with special needs and depressive disorders. Thus allowing them the benefits of such therapy on a regular basis over the long term, ultimately for free. In recognition for his works Paul was presented with the prestigious PROGGY Award from PETA.

The Proggy Award was for progress in creating a more Humane world. PETA saw the Dolphin Dome as being a technology that allowed people with disability and clinical needs to enjoy the benefit of animals' therapeutic capacities without restricting any animal's freedom. PETA saw the Dolphin Dome as making a wonderful contribution to this end. Visit The Dolphin Dome on Facebook to learn more.

In October 2018, in an act of philanthropic altruism, Paul gifted the Dolphin Dome to Frederick Holmes Special Needs School in Hull.

Through his company, Paul also designed and built the world's first, fully self contained road mobile command station for an underwater robotic vehicle built to a modern offshore standard.

In addition to these, Paul designed and developed the Dolphin Den, an interactive creative educational play den for children made from reinforced layered cardboard. It was based on the underwater world. This had the clever design of being able to fold down into a large educational colouring book.

He also designed LifePod. This was a flat packed emergency disaster zone accommodation module. It was made from a waterproof thermal reflective lined structural engineered cardboard. Paul saw LifePod as being a land based, yet superior version of a ships liferaft and equipped it accordingly. In partnership with DS Smith Packaging, they performed an extremely successful trial of a prototype module which survived gales, rain, snow and shine over a six month period. Thus proving its effectiveness and durability in the field. The modules were designed such that they could be attached together so as to create family units with separate living and sleeping quarters.

As a result of his life in the marine and offshore industry. Paul has travelled the world twice over, lived in Asia and has been to the Antarctic at the bottom of the world and back. He has had amazing adventures and been able to have had experiences in life that most people could only ever dream of or watch on TV documentaries.

Special Thank You

To my friend and published author John 'JT' Roberts. Without who's help, publishing technical knowhow, guidance and motivation this book may not have been written today.

My sincerest thanks and appreciation.
Paul (Scurvy) Obernay.

Artist's Biography

Nick Gott is an established illustrator and portrait artist. Having trained in Theatre Design at Wimbledon College of Art, he has since enjoyed over a decade of bringing life to portraits for clients as well as providing visuals for musicians and authors in order to tell their stories.

He most enjoys using pencil to create expressive and emotive pieces. Illustrating this book has been a great joy to him and has enabled him to dive deep into a story from his new home of Scotland where he is currently based in his creative pursuits as an illustrator and full time artist.

Nick has dipped his toes into writing and illustrating his own stories and hopes to be able to pursue these projects further. He is also skilled in inks, as well as watercolours, acrylic and oil paints and thrives on being a practising artist of many skills and disciplines. He lives in Dunfermline with his fiancé, two young daughters and cat Momo.

You can find Nick's work on 'Book An Artist' where he is available for commission.

Book An Artist: Nick Gott Artistry

Email: nick-gott-sketches@hotmail.com

Trivia question for mariners from page 4:

What is the brightest light on the Clyde?

Answer: Daylight.

Printed in Great Britain
by Amazon